Rachel Cosyns was born in St Ives ⟨...⟩ from home at seventeen to be with ⟨...⟩ went to art school but discovered ⟨...⟩ her, although she still draws and ⟨...⟩ boyfriend and they live together in North London. They have three children and three grandchildren. Rachel has written stories all her life and used to do an online parenting blog for a national newspaper called Two and a Half Teens. *Gone to Pieces* is her debut novel.

...Cornwall. She ran away
...her boyfriend Egan. she
...that line art wasn't for
...ing and paints. She married the

GONE

TO

PIECES

RACHEL COSYNS

ONE PLACE. MANY STORIES

HQ
An imprint of HarperCollins*Publishers* Ltd
1 London Bridge Street
London SE1 9GF

www.harpercollins.co.uk

HarperCollins*Publishers*
Macken House, 39/40 Mayor Street Upper,
Dublin 1, D01 C9W8, Ireland

This edition 2024

1
First published in Great Britain by
HQ, an imprint of HarperCollins*Publishers* Ltd 2024

ISBN: 9780008550912

MIX
Paper | Supporting
responsible forestry
FSC™ C007454

This book contains FSC™ certified paper and other controlled sources to ensure responsible forest management.

For more information visit: www.harpercollins.co.uk/green

This book is set in 10.7/15.5 pt. Sabon by Type-it AS, Norway

Printed and Bound in the UK using 100% Renewable Electricity at CPI Group (UK) Ltd, Croydon, CR0 4YY

For Simon

Whom the gods would destroy, they first make mad.

—ANCIENT PROVERB

PART I

THE ELEPHANT

PIECE 1

The child watched a spider spin its web. It was in the hawthorn bush next to the tree stump where she had been sitting just a short time ago. The leaves of the bush grew dense, acid green and glossy, and the air was rich with the soapy scent of its dying blossom.

The child crouched with her back to the water, watching. It was one of those fat spiders that live in a woven tunnel; a labyrinth spider.

'Labyrinth,' she whispered to herself, turning the word in her mouth.

The child supposed the spider had eggs deep in its tunnel. She imagined the spiderlings crawling to the mouth of the web in the purple of a late summer evening and flying away on long strings of silk. She moved her head closer so she could see the spinnerets.

There were sounds behind her but she didn't turn around because she knew what they were. Soon they would stop.

The smell still hung in the air, sour and repulsive, not quite drowned out by the scent of hawthorn flowers. The child breathed through her mouth. She didn't want to be sick.

Bloody, bloody, bloody, she thought.

Then all was quiet. The spider slid backwards until only its two front legs showed at the mouth of the tunnel.

Slowly the child turned to look across the dark water.

It was still.

Rebecca Wise turned over in bed and covered her head with the duvet. Outside in the street, she could hear a high, rhythmic chanting.

'You're fat, Mum. You're a big fat mum with a big fat mum bum.'

Rebecca heard the mother's answering laugh and the wheels of a scooter scuttering along the pavement.

She opened her eyes.

Woken by nightmares at three or four each morning, she usually fell into exhausted sleep shortly before her husband, Sam, got up for work. The dreams that stalked her nights coloured the succeeding days.

'It's as if I can't shake them,' Rebecca told Sam. 'They come with me.'

'But what are they about?' he asked.

Rebecca shook her head. Something slithered at the edge of her perception; a sound, a sensation that fled as soon as the grey dawn crept over the windowsill and London began to roar.

'I don't remember,' she told him. 'Spiders, maybe. There was one in the kitchen yesterday. It ran at me. I hit it with the broom. I've got PTSD.'

'From what? Not spiders?' Sam picked up his phone from his bedside table to check the time.

4

'It's an elephant, a huge, inescapable, impassive, disinterested elephant and it's crushing me to death.'

'I'm late for work,' said Sam. He had forgotten to charge the Apple Watch Rebecca had reluctantly bought him for Christmas.

'But it's ugly,' she'd said at the time, 'and you have to plug it in.'

'I want one,' he'd replied, but now, as he pushed back the cuff of his shirt and looked at its blank face, he had to admit that she'd been right.

The front door slammed and the house gave an answering shudder.

Then there was silence.

The house, tall, Victorian, with fireplaces and creaking floorboards, retained many of its original features and despite the years they had spent throwing money at it, it had also retained many of its original inconveniences.

'Seven flights of stairs?' said Rebecca when they had seen it first. 'Blown plaster, rotten window frames?'

'They're half-landings. We can mend it. The area's coming up and think how fit we'll be with all these stairs.' Sam was ever the optimist.

They had brought their three children to see the house. Abigail, the eldest at eight, had burst into noisy sobs. Seven-year-old Kit had bagged the room at the very top, which looked east across the City and the marshes beyond. Their youngest, one-year-old Annie, had struggled from her mother's arms and fallen down a small flight of stairs into the filthy basement.

Now, twenty fleeting years later, with the two eldest

5

children living nearby in shared flats and Annie deeply asleep in Kit's old eyrie, Rebecca crawled from the bed and staggered into the bathroom to sort washing as a bitter January wind threw handfuls of sleet at the rattling sash windows.

She folded sheets and put them in the ironing pile. Sam had left a small bundle of dirty washing next to the laundry basket. Rebecca wasn't sure why he hadn't lifted the lid to put it inside. She went through the pockets of his trousers, which were full of loose change and crumpled receipts. Their washing machine was new but the engineer had said that if coins became stuck in the filter, this machine would flood the basement, just as the old one had. Rebecca remembered that the paint above the basement skirting board was still bubbled and peeling from the residual damp.

She must write that down.

It must go on one of the To-Do lists.

Ideally on the mending list because painting was mending, even though picking up dry-cleaning wasn't mending and it was on the same list.

She had better make another list.

Rebecca had asked Sam to empty change out of his pockets before he put his trousers in the wash but he hadn't done so. Sam, she felt, never listened to her anymore. Only yesterday, as they'd sat on the sofa not watching *Escape From The City*, she had told him that their neighbours had eaten their baby. 'They ate it,' she'd said, 'because there weren't any chickens in Tesco.' Sam had merely grunted in response.

The lists were quite unmanageable. There were masses and masses of things on them. They spilled from the desk in the sitting room, were stashed in piles under stones stolen from Cornish beaches and folded quietly into coat pockets. They ruled Rebecca's life.

As a child, Rebecca had been unattractively silent, watchful and, she felt, unwilling to learn the simple skill of lovability, but had grown into a strong, competent woman through sheer concentration. She had even found someone to love her and had had three healthy, able children. She used to feel proud of these achievements, but now, it felt as though she watched herself from above and all she saw was failure.

Betty always said fake it 'til you make it.

Rebecca had tried.

Betty was the name Rebecca had given her inner voice. So named because she was better than Rebecca. She had known Betty since childhood. Although Betty was deeply suspicious and often spiteful, she hadn't always been so unhelpful.

Lately, however, she had become intolerable.

Rebecca felt as though she were lashed to the stern of an ocean-going liner that didn't know or care that she was there. She hadn't the will to free herself, so now she just waited for the inevitable flip, the engulfing wave or the submerged reef. There was something rotten in the state of Denmark, a worm in the apple or at the heart of the rose, a hole in the life raft and a plank in someone's eye.

It's all downhill from here, said Betty. And TBH, you've run out of metaphors.

For once, Rebecca agreed with her. Rage, she thought, does not nourish the soul. She was always angry and her soul was starved.

She *had* hoped that the wine would see her off but in reality she knew, as she walked past the park drunks huddled on benches over their bottles of White Lightning, that it took more than Chardonnay to kill a rich and rested woman. Sometimes she felt like sitting down next to them. She could buy a bottle of Sapphire Gin and they could pass it round. New friends . . . she imagined the faces of the yummy mummies as they passed pushing their Bugaboos and smiled.

Laziness, said Betty.

'Not laziness,' said Rebecca, 'cowardice.' She was stuffing shirts and underwear into the washing machine. She didn't like talking to Betty because it seemed to give her more power, but she wasn't going to be called lazy.

You don't matter, you don't matter, Betty said, matching the rhythm of her words to the action of her arms. Not at all, not one bit, she continued.

I have to make a wall planner, thought Rebecca, standing up and swivelling the dial on the machine to Mixed Load. She made a wall planner each month and stuck it to the kitchen wall with Blu Tack so that she knew exactly what she had to do and what Annie and Sam were doing.

'Just write it on the planner,' she would tell them when they asked if she could do something, buy something, pick something up, reserve a restaurant or make up an extra bed. 'Write it down, I can't remember things.'

'I've got to make a wall planner,' she said aloud.

I gotta make a wall planner, mocked Betty, sing-song.

'Shut up,' Rebecca said. 'Shush. Be quiet.'

She knelt on the floor in front of the laundry basket,

dragging more sheets and duvet covers from its depths. Like guts, she thought. I'm gutting the laundry basket.

She cast her eyes around the bathroom, looking for spiders. She really hated spiders.

This room needed painting, too. She remembered the last time she had done it. She had mixed Farrow & Ball's Savage Ground with Bone to make a lovely warm, buff colour.

She wished Pawel would come for odd jobs, but one had to book him three months in advance. He was back in Poland at the moment.

Rebecca thought she would add *paint bathroom* to her list. If she waited, it would get worse.

She drifted for a moment, trying to imagine Poland. There would be tall grey mountains and deep green lakes fringed by pine forests and there would be silence.

Then she thought of Scruples, her dear little dog, who had slowly coughed her life away.

Why had that happened?

Rebecca had taken her to the vet.

'We don't operate,' the vet had said, as she'd fondled Scruples' long black silky ears. 'It would throw up all kinds of ethical issues, you see.'

Rebecca hadn't seen, nor had Annie when she'd told her.

'What issues?' Annie had said. 'The only issue I can see is that there are dogs being put down every day with perfectly healthy heart valves but our dog has to drown in her own snot.'

'I don't know if it's actually snot,' Rebecca had said.

But there it was.

Scruples had been doomed.

As Scruples had become more ill, Rebecca had gone out less and less. Scruples couldn't walk around the park anymore so she and Rebecca had watched the New Year progress through rain-spattered windows.

The dog had panted through her last day and Rebecca had wished the vet had suggested putting her to sleep. Annie had propped her up on velvet cushions and tried to feed her chicken breasts and Scruples had died.

'She died,' Rebecca had told her friend Megan. 'There was nothing we could do. She was only eight.'

'That must have been very sad for all of you,' Megan had said. 'I'll miss her too. She had a good soul.'

Megan and Rebecca are dog-walking friends. Before Scruples became ill, they walked at least once a week with Scruples and Megan's cockapoo, Charlie. They rarely social-ised in any other way. Megan was a glass-half-full sort of person and Rebecca thought this was probably because she had a strong religious faith.

Now, Rebecca thought about Scruples' soul.

She thought about her own soul.

She waited for her soul to respond in some way, but was met with a brimming silence.

'Anyway,' Megan had said, 'I don't intend to lose you as a friend just because Scruples is no longer with us. We can walk with Charlie or without, I don't mind which.'

The post clattered through the letterbox onto the hall floor and Rebecca shut her eyes. She hated post.

She dropped the dirty laundry onto the bathroom floor and stood staring down at it.

You don't matter, hissed Betty again. Rebecca turned on her heel and left the room, her bare feet pounding out the mantra, you're not a person, you don't matter, you're not a person . . .

She stopped at the top of the stairs, looking down at the black and white tessellated tiles on the hall floor.

Not high enough, said Betty.

'I do matter, you're just trying to get to me,' Rebecca said it as loudly as she could, but her voice sounded thin and high and she knew that actually she had already been got.

There was some vodka downstairs in the kitchen, not much, but enough to stop all this for a while.

Supermarket . . . she must write that down too.

In the kitchen, she poured a glass, emptying the bottle. She could count the beats of the pulse jumping in her throat.

Pomp, the cat, wound his way round her legs, purring loudly. She had forgotten to feed him.

A decision had to be made about the vodka, to gulp or sip? She wondered if people noticed she had been drinking when she answered the door or paid at a till. She was never drunk, not in the daytime, and she cleaned her teeth all the time, but still, she wondered.

They would notice, said Betty. They *do*.

Rebecca turned her head to hear a little better and then shook it.

It was herself, that was all.

It was just herself talking to herself.

She gulped the vodka down in one and sat down at the kitchen table. She put her arms straight out in front of her, rested her face on them and started to cry.

Later that day, Rebecca was talking to her mother on the telephone.

'I feel awful. Like a hamster going pointlessly round and round on a wheel, going nowhere, using up all my energy and no one cares. I've tried to explain, but no one's listening.'

'I know, darling, don't tell me. No one ever does care. So long as the shirts are neatly ironed and folded and the meal is on the table at the right time, they never do care. Anyway I've got to go, I'm meeting Daphne for coffee. Don't worry, just don't do it. Refuse; leave them in their own squalor. Bye . . . bye, bye.'

Rebecca stared at the receiver for a minute or two before replacing it.

The list next to the telephone had thirty things written on it. Thirty.

I have to prioritise, she thought.

If I don't prioritise, I'm lost.

Shoelaces. She picked a Biro up off the bedroom floor and wrote it at the end of the list. I could get those tomorrow, but I'm sure we have some somewhere. Drill bits, she read. Then she dropped the Biro and began twisting her wedding ring around on her finger. Sam had left forty minutes ago and she still hadn't made the bed.

'I haven't got time for this,' he'd said. 'I have a Zoom meeting and I'm already late.' Sam was a production journalist on a national newspaper and he was always late for everything. 'I like deadlines,' he would explain. 'I like to be at the edge of things.'

I'm going to watch *Escape From The City*, Rebecca decided. I'm going to sit in the playroom and finish that bottle of red from last night and watch the presenter, Justin Hammond, trying to look like he even *cares*.

She wished she could escape . . . to anywhere really.

Betty cackled. You're not going to though. Are you? Ever? No one's coming home, not until at least ten. You've got time. Or are you going to drink the rest of that and just sit and then do it all again tomorrow?

'No,' Rebecca said aloud. 'There are three things I have to do this year. Just three. All the other things don't matter.'

The things were:

1. Learn to drive on motorways.
2. Use the above skill to run away to France.
3. Begin new life in France under assumed name.

She thought about it for a moment. A moment that jolted adrenaline down both arms as terror sank its claws deep into her lungs.

You can't go, said Betty, suddenly soft and caressing. It's impossible. There's an alternative . . .

Rebecca knew there was. She had clutched the idea close to her chest for several months now, letting it grow and take form. She felt the hot shame of it slide over her now as she named it to herself.

There would be no blame-filled letter. The ties that held her to her life were pulled taut, a quick tug and they would snap, sending her into the oblivion she craved.

To look for an ending one should, ideally, understand the beginning, but Rebecca could not, so she had decided, or rather had let the idea pool in her mind . . .

That it would be better,
or easier,
on balance,
if she were honest,
not to change her name to Mathilde
and not to go to live in Sarlat or similar.
Continuing was unthinkable.
Not continuing, impossible.
So,
Yes? said Betty.
'I have decided to die,' said Rebecca.

PIECE 2

At their first meeting, Dr Glass holds out a hand, shakes Rebecca's, and smiles a brief on-off, closed-mouth smile. 'Good afternoon, Mrs Wise,' he says. 'I'm Titus Glass. Do sit down.'

Obediently, Rebecca takes a seat. She is in a private psychiatric hospital.

'We can't afford a private psychiatrist,' she'd protested to Sam.

'You're insured. So you're going to see this guy as soon as he can see you. A mental health team is coming to see you this morning, Becky. This is serious. You might have died.'

Now, two days after her son, Kit, had found her and phoned for an ambulance, Rebecca is seeing a psychiatrist. She hadn't meant Kit to find her. She had texted him, telling him not to come over, but apparently she had forgotten to send the text.

Rubbish, says Betty.

When she thinks about Kit finding her, Rebecca feels the adrenaline thump through her. I can't even kill myself tidily, she thinks.

Collateral damage, says Betty.

He's my son, thinks Rebecca.

The doctor's consulting room is white and furnished with two grey upholstered chairs. There is also a dark wood desk with a maroon leather inlay.

Dr Glass is a tall, slim, bespectacled man, wearing a navy-blue suit, a red tie and a startlingly white shirt. He is neither old nor young; neither dark nor fair.

Average, hisses Betty in her ear, but Rebecca thinks not.

The doctor has short brown hair and fine lines around a mouth that turns up agreeably at the corners. He appears benign; the glasses, the white shirt, the smooth, lightly tanned skin are all indicative of a helpful orderliness.

He cocks his head on one side and looks at Rebecca keenly. She stares into his face, holding tightly onto the arms of her grey chair to stop herself bolting from the room.

The psychiatrist takes the chair opposite hers.

'I understand you've been through the mill rather. I'm here to help,' he says. 'Now, tell me what happened, as you remember it.' He picks up a pad from the desk beside him.

Rebecca talks. Afterwards she can't remember what she'd said but all the time she was speaking, Dr Glass had taken notes.

'These voices, are they exterior to you or are they in your head, as it were?'

'It's me talking. It's only one voice. I used to think it was a "her" b-b-because it made it easier to ignore her, but really I know it's me.' Rebecca is starting to shake and she clamps her hands between her knees to make it less obvious.

'Have you ever been under the care of a mental health

professional previously?' The doctor writes a note in the margin of his pad and looks at Rebecca, scrutinising her.

Rebecca realizes that she doesn't understand who he is, what his qualifications are and whether she can trust him. 'How did I end up coming to see you?' she asks, answering his question with a question.

Dr Glass stands up and walks around his desk. 'I can find out. Do you not *want* to see me? Let me just check for you . . . ' He turns to his computer monitor and scrolls through a list. 'A Margo Shriver booked the appointment. Do you know her?'

Rebecca remembers the name because Sam has mentioned her. She's a PA, Rebecca thinks, at Sam's paper. She shakes her head.

'I don't know her; I don't know you. I just wondered. It's all so weird. I don't know what to do.'

'Well, let's see how we go, shall we?' says the doctor, picking up his pad from his desk again and returning to the seat opposite Rebecca. She notices that his glasses are too big for his narrow face. She wonders vaguely if he really needs them or if they are part of his 'look'.

'Can you explain exactly what it was that you felt when you made this decision? Can you clarify for me what it was that you were thinking at the time?' he asks.

Rebecca looks at the floor. 'It was a long time ago,' she says. 'I think I thought that it would be better if I wasn't a factor.' She nods her head, agreeing with herself.

'Mrs Wise, it was two days ago. What do you mean by a factor?'

17

'I think I thought I was counter to their best interests.'

'To your family's best interests? To the best interests of your husband and children?'

Rebecca nods again. It sounds like a reasonable explanation. She darts a look at the doctor and then looks quickly away.

'Look at me, Mrs Wise. Please. Can you tell me what your plans were, had you not come here to me?'

'I didn't have a plan.'

'Can you elaborate, at all, on how you felt that you were counter to the best interests of the people you love?'

Rebecca cannot.

'Try,' the doctor says.

'I felt as though I had been given a green light.'

'By whom?'

'My dog died,' she says. 'My children grew up.'

The doctor shifts in his chair. He says nothing.

'Things collaborated. They colluded with me.'

'Which things made you imagine you had been given a green light to kill yourself? Not your dog dying, surely?'

Rebecca shakes her head. 'The things I just said.' Her mouth becomes completely dry suddenly. The blood sings in her head and she knows what is coming next.

Congealed, Betty yelps, gleeful. Rebecca winces. She sees the doctor noticing. He looks down at his notes.

'So, you took all the pills in the house and you hoped to be beyond help by the time your husband arrived home from work?'

'Not in a dead body way . . . '

The doctor raises his eyebrows. 'There would, nonetheless, have been a dead body.'

Rebecca shakes her head again.

The doctor takes a note. Then he looks at her over the top of his glasses.

'My mouth's gone dry,' Rebecca tells him.

'I know,' he replies.

Then Rebecca rallies. She can't just give in.

'The thing is, Dr Glass, I'm an enabler. I enable my family to succeed, to achieve, in a way that I can't.'

A sharp frown line appears between the doctor's brows. He takes off his glasses and leans forward in his chair. His eyes, slanted like a Siamese cat's, are the same blue as the winter afternoon outside.

'You're not doing a very good job of it, are you?' he says quietly. 'Do you think you understand how much you have almost certainly hurt them?'

Rebecca feels her hair shift on her scalp. Does she understand? She isn't sure. She knows how much her parents hurt her. If she closes her eyes, she can still feel the visceral pain of the injustices that every child in a large family has to endure. But her parents hadn't tried to leave her.

'I was doing well. They were fine before all this. They were doing really well,' she says.

'And now . . . I imagine, they're all feeling like hell, eaten up with guilt and anger.' He puts his glasses on again and the lenses reflect the window back at Rebecca. 'What did you do before you had children?' he asks.

Rebecca shakes her head. 'I was a nanny. I was a nanny

even after I had Abigail but when Kit was born I couldn't do it anymore. I left home too young, I didn't finish school properly. I'm not qualified for anything.'

Dr Glass takes a note in his pad. 'Do you miss having your children at home?' he asks.

Rebecca thinks, then she says, 'No, they live very near. Annie's still at home. No, I don't miss them. It's difficult coming in fifth place in your own life.'

'Behind the needs of your husband and children, you mean?'

Rebecca feels the betrayal. She feels the guilt of saying the unsayable, but they will never know. This doctor will never meet her children or Sam and tell them how she feels. 'Yes,' she says.

'Listen,' says the doctor, steepling his fingers, 'you are exhausted. I'm going to admit you to the hospital. I believe we have a bed. I think, from what I have observed, that we can look after you best if you stay here with us.'

Rebecca stands. 'No,' she says. 'I have to go. I told them in A&E that I wouldn't do anything like that again and I won't. Also, I only have this.' She holds up her small green satchel. 'I haven't got anything with me, my stuff, I mean. I haven't any of it. I can come back on Monday, but I don't need to. It was an accident.'

The doctor remains seated.

'An accident?' he says. 'So how was it that you were found unconscious by your son having downed half a bottle of vodka, wine and several bottles of painkillers? Did you have an especially bad earache, perhaps?'

Rebecca clutches her satchel to her chest. She looks at the

doctor. He looks terribly young, she decides. He probably doesn't understand how hard life can get. His suit jacket is showing far too much cuff and he is wearing amethyst and silver cufflinks.

Amethyst cufflinks before noon, scoffs Betty in her left ear. Betty is the most frightful snob.

'Well, anyway . . . how old are you?' It's out before she can prevent herself.

The doctor shifts in his seat. 'Sit down please, Mrs Wise,' he says, 'and explain precisely what you mean by that?'

Rebecca sits. In fact, she thinks her knees must have given way. 'I mean that you probably haven't experienced much, really, probably . . . ' her voice trails off into silence.

'I can assure you that I am more than qualified to treat you.' The doctor shuffles some papers on the desk in front of him.

'I'm not staying here, though. It's too frightening.'

'That, of course, is entirely your choice. I will write you a prescription to take some of the edge off this anxiety and I would like to see you again at ten on Monday morning. Can you tell me how you are going to get home today? You don't look as though you could manage public transport at the moment.'

Rebecca wonders how one needed to look in order to manage catching a bus. There are a lot of very unwell people on buses, always. Rebecca supposes that Dr Titus Glass has rarely been on a bus.

She glances at the doctor, who is tapping his pen on his lower teeth. 'I'll come back on Monday,' she says, 'at ten. A driver is taking me home. He brought me.' Sam had arranged, through work, for Rebecca to be driven to the appointment and picked up afterwards.

'Good, I'll see you on Monday then.' The doctor stands, strides to the door and holds it open. 'Goodbye, Mrs Wise,' he says.

It had been an accident. Rebecca was sure. She sat in the back of the car, watching London slide past the window. The driver was a Romanian called Viktor. He had a bald head and mirrored sunglasses. When he had dropped Rebecca outside the hospital he'd said, 'You haf my number. When all is finished, please phone me and I will come bek here very quickly.' Rebecca thinks he is probably rather kind.

They drive across London Bridge and Rebecca turns her head to the right to see Tower Bridge and Canary Wharf in the distance and the great brown river flowing fast away from her.

She hadn't meant Kit to find her. If she had meant anything at all, she had meant it to be Sam, when it was too late.

'Don't come over tonight,' she had texted Kit but she hadn't pressed send. Kit had been dropping by to pick up some leftover pasta sauce that she had made. She often gave Kit leftovers because she worried that he wasn't eating properly in his shared flat.

Obviously, she thinks, there hadn't been a plan. Not in any real sense. It was more of an idea that had become too heavy to walk about with. So, Rebecca had just got drunk while watching *Escape From The City*. The presenter, Justin Hammond, had turned to do his final piece to camera and Rebecca had listened with a sense of growing dread.

'Let's hope,' said Justin, 'that Jonathon and Kelsey have finally found their perfect new home in the country; that the mystery house can provide Jonathon with that longed-for man-cave and Kelsey with the perfect village community of which she has so often dreamt.'

And that had been that. Rebecca had pulled herself up off the sofa, dropping her phone to the floor, staggered up the stairs to the bathroom where she had taken every pill in the house. No suicide note; no plan . . . 'Just bleakery,' she would tell Sam, after she came home from the hospital. 'Just a feeling of doom. It was . . .'

'The most self-centred thing I've ever witnessed,' said Sam. 'Thank God we didn't have any paracetamol, that's all I can say.'

Rebecca had woken in their local hospital. A young doctor with a stethoscope around his neck stood by the side of her trolley. Sam stood behind him and her three children were just outside the curtain that shielded her from a Wednesday night in a busy London A&E.

'Ah good, you're awake,' the doctor had said. 'How many paracetamol did you take, Mrs Wise?'

Rebecca had shaken her head.

'Jolly good,' said the doctor, 'that agrees with the bloods.' Rebecca looked down at her arm and saw a plaster in the crook. She didn't remember any blood being taken.

Then the duty psychiatrist had arrived and had asked her if she intended to try to take her life again. 'Because,' said the psychiatrist, a single silver bangle sliding on her slim childish wrist, 'if you cannot tell me that you won't, we will have to admit you to the hospital here. You look angry. Are you angry?'

Sam had taken her home and the children had all gone back to Kit's for the night.

'Are you angry?' Sam had asked her as he'd driven home through the grey dawn light.

Rebecca had sighed. 'Just frightened,' she'd replied.

Viktor drops her off outside the house. 'You take care,' he says and he drives away.

Sam would be at work, thinks Rebecca, as she puts her key into the Yale, but Annie will be here. Annie, she knows, will have been told not to let her out of her sight. Her mobile buzzes while she is still in the hallway.

'Home?' asks Sam.

'Yes, home,' she answers.

PIECE 3

Unlike most children, Rebecca Kelly did not look at the world through round, innocent eyes. She regarded it coolly from behind a pair of National Health glasses in her favourite colour, blue. She was a tall child with an unmanageable tangle of reddish-blonde hair, which she continually pushed out of her eyes or tucked behind her ears. Her mother bought her hairbands.

'You'll get sticking-out ears if you do that with your hair,' she told Rebecca. But Rebecca said nothing, rammed the hairband down over her forehead and decorated it with leaves and feathers.

'What do you think you look like?' asked her eldest brother, Martin.

Rebecca shrugged. 'Hiawatha,' she answered.

She was hyper-flexible and found standing straight difficult, so she stood sway-backed and knock-kneed squinting into the future and not much liking what she saw.

She was born in Cornwall, the only girl in a family of four children. She saw early on the advantages of not having to compete with a prettier or more socially able sister. Her two older brothers, Alex and Martin, took the brunt of their father's unpredictable rages, and the younger, Giles, she could bully or baby at will.

When she was eight, the family moved house. They packed their decrepit Cortina to the roof with their belongings, squeezed the children along the back seat and drove to Suffolk where their father, David, had found a job flying helicopters out to the North Sea oil rigs.

Crossing the River Tamar, which separates Cornwall from the rest of England, had reduced Rebecca's mother to tears.

Rebecca remembered this, because her father had put his hand on her mother's knee in an uncharacteristically gentle gesture and had told her, 'Don't worry, Pen; we'll be back sooner than you think.'

Rebecca's mother was called Pen, short for Penelope.

'Your grandfather named me Penelope,' Rebecca's mother had told her. 'He thought Penelope rhymed with Antelope and he was awfully upset when he found out the horrible truth.'

Rebecca's grandfather had always called her Pen after that.

'Pen, for a female swan,' he'd said, and it had stuck.

That first weekend, after their arrival in East Anglia, exhausted from unpacking and arranging their furniture and belongings in a rented house, Rebecca's parents decided to take the children to the beach.

'We were so excited to see where we would be living,' Pen remembered later. 'But it was so depressing; there were miles and miles of empty plough and the sky was enormous. Occasionally one could see a grey church tower and a row of trees standing on the horizon, but my first impression was one of utter desolation.'

The car had disgorged all six of them, dressed only in jumpers and corduroy trousers, onto a stretch of pebbles that was being pounded by a sea the colour of a slug and the children shrank back in terror at the brutality of the wind and the grinding cold.

'It was late February,' Pen told Rebecca. 'In Cornwall, the weather would have been much softer at that time of year and the wind was never that cold. In Suffolk, the weather blew straight in from the Urals. We just weren't prepared.'

Rebecca remembered a childhood punctuated by those winds. Winters spent under towering skies when she would feel her cheeks numb and her hands, always without gloves, stiffen and turn white: summers when the wind whipped her hair across her eyes and bent the trees against cloud-filled skies, prematurely tearing green leaves from their thrashing branches.

By late spring, the family had found a house to buy.

It was Tudor, long, low and timber-framed, its walls painted a pale Suffolk pink. It stood with its barns in the middle of a potato field, encircled by tall, tangled hedges of hawthorn and hornbeam. In the kitchen was an ancient Aga with rusty hotplates and the counter of the village post office, which had recently closed.

'But it's six miles from the nearest town,' Pen had protested.

'Which is why we can afford it,' David replied and so it was settled.

The children spent the two weeks of their first Easter

holiday in Suffolk gleefully pulling up potatoes, enjoying the smooth hardness in their small soft hands and bicycling around the narrow lanes to meet the few neighbours who lived nearby.

Their parents hacked out the 1940s counter from the kitchen and burned it on the hard-standing in front of the biggest barn.

'I could keep a boat in that barn,' David said at supper one night. He was sitting at the head of the table, his empty soup bowl pushed away from him and, in his hand, was a rummer filled with red wine which he held up to the light. The wine glowed like a jewel. Like a ruby, Rebecca thought.

Pen stacked the bowls. 'I don't know that we have time for a boat,' she said quietly.

I wish I had a pony, Rebecca thought, I could keep a pony in that barn, but she said nothing and spooned more scalding leek and potato soup into her mouth.

Rebecca's parents were not happy. David took the car to work, leaving Pen stranded with the children in the middle of nowhere, knowing no one, with a million chores to do. The rows that resulted were apocalyptic.

Often, Rebecca awoke in the night to raised voices and a crash as something fell or was thrown. She would hear the bedroom door slam, a glass break and once, horrifically, the sound of her mother fleeing down the drive, her Dr Scholl sandals clattering on the gravel.

'And don't bloody come back!' her father roared from the kitchen door.

Would she? Rebecca didn't know. She got out of bed and pressed her face to the window, straining her eyes in the dark to see a trace of her mother. Rebecca would have to make sure Giles was safe if she never returned.

In the morning, she heard the car drive away, and as she helped herself and Giles to breakfast cereal she saw, next to the bin, another empty bottle of wine, and she heard, from above, her mother's despairing sobs.

Sometimes Rebecca woke just before dawn. All would be quiet and then she would imagine that she could smell smoke. Without her glasses she couldn't see very well. She could just make out the top of Giles's dark head on his pillow, a smudge of window and the dark block of the open bedroom door. She would have to persuade herself to lie down and go back to sleep. She pressed her ear hard into the pillow until she heard the blood thumping in her head and imagined its rhythm to be the sound of a child skipping on the gravel below the window.

She pictured an expertly wielded rope in the darkness, feet landing close together as it whizzed below them, missing by an inch or less. The child's hair was flying golden curls, washed silver by the moon, her face a concentrated mask. Rebecca would slide from her bed and tiptoe to the window; but the moment her head left the pillow, the child would gather up her rope and disappear. Rebecca thought the girl could be her twin.

Her night-time twin.

She called her Betty. Rebecca heard her speaking sometimes.

I'll come back, she'd say. Another time. And she always did.

*

The Kellys found a cleaner. She was called Lorraine. Lorraine had bright yellow hair and huge pink arms like hams. She festooned her sturdy wrists with coloured bangles that jingled as she worked. She wore tight tops with no sleeves and tight skirts. She laughed a lot and sang along to the radio while she worked. Rebecca liked Lorraine because she seemed happy.

Lorraine had two sons called Gary and Grime. Gary was almost grown up and had a motorbike and Grime was eleven. The boys didn't have a father, but they had an uncle called Billy Parfitt who lived with them. Uncle Billy had a bad back. They all lived in a cottage a little way down the road from the Kellys.

Grime went to the village school but he appeared to have few friends. Sometimes he played guns or football with Rebecca's brothers but he preferred to go exploring with Rebecca. He knew everything about the countryside and Rebecca came to hero-worship him.

When Grime wasn't at school or busy with some obscure obligation that he would never fully explain, he and Rebecca would take off across country, in search of the wild.

Grime and Rebecca didn't talk, they *did*.

Morning would break and they would be off. Under skies as bright as a robin's egg, they stalked hayfields, searching for the nests of curlews and skylarks. They caught sticklebacks and dragonfly nymphs in the stream that edged the woods of the nearby village of Benham and they climbed trees to the very top where the branches would bend and snap underfoot, sending shock waves coursing through their limbs.

Grime's Uncle Billy was tall, nearly as tall as Rebecca's father, but unlike her father, Billy had stooping shoulders and an aura of defeat.

When he wasn't at work, Rebecca's father wore jeans and a checked shirt. Billy was never at work and he wore an old grey jacket that drooped on his thin back. He had thick, grey hair styled in what was, Rebecca's mother told her, a quiff. His hair was long at the back and nestled in curls at the nape of his neck.

'He probably used to be a Teddy Boy,' her mother explained. Rebecca didn't know what a Teddy Boy was but, if it was something Billy used to be, she was pretty sure she didn't care.

When Rebecca's father was at work, he wore a captain's uniform with gold on the peak of his captain's hat and gold stripes on his shoulders. Rebecca thought he looked like a hero in it. He looked like Richard Attenborough, Lawrence of Arabia or John Wayne.

Rebecca loved old films. When she was not at school, her mother let her lie on the sofa with a blanket and watch them. Mostly they were black and white, but Rebecca didn't mind because she could colour them in with her eyes. She especially liked war films. She liked men standing on the decks of ships, scouring the waves for U-boats. She liked Trevor Howard diving for cover under heavy fire. She liked John Wayne crossing the prairies dressed as a cavalry officer. She liked men who were heroes.

Trevor Howard was in a film called *Brief Encounter*. It was Rebecca's mother's favourite film. It wasn't a war film; it was a love story, about two old people. Her mother adored it and it never failed to reduce her to floods, but Rebecca and her brothers thought it very funny. It wasn't Rebecca's best film but when she grew up and met her husband, Sam, she taught him whole scenes, which they would quote to each other in clipped 1940s accents.

'He's not called Grime,' Pen told her children one day, in exasperation. 'He's called Graham.'

'But he says he's called Grime,' argued Rebecca. 'He should know his own name, shouldn't he?'

'It's an accent,' explained her mother.

'What if saying Gray-ham is an accent?' asked Martin. 'You can't just go around calling people things they're not called and then say it's an accent. We've got an accent. We're posh,' he added reasonably.

'And,' said Alex, 'grey ham would be horrible.'

'We're not posh, I didn't say grey ham and we don't have an accent,' said Pen. She turned back to her chopping board, cutting streaky bacon into thin slivers and tipping them into a frying pan.

Rebecca slid silently out of the kitchen door as the room filled with the delicious aroma of frying bacon. She wasn't sure that one should eat pigs but she hadn't yet come up with a plan to avoid it.

One day, Grime told Rebecca that he had found a rats' nest and asked her if she wanted to watch him kill the babies.

'They've gotta be killed,' he explained to Rebecca. 'Or they get in amongst the stored apples and we can't use 'em.'

'Use them for what?' asked Rebecca. 'Why don't you just eat them when you pick them?'

'Cider,' said Grime. 'Tha're cider apples and we make Scrumpy with 'em. Come'n watch. I kill 'em with a saucepan.'

So Rebecca went with Grime to his house down the road. He laid the tiny naked baby rats one by one on the concrete step outside the back door of their garden shed, then brought a heavy, rusted iron saucepan down on each rat, reducing it to a pink pulp, which he scraped aside with a stick before replacing it with another.

'Do you wanna go?' asked Grime, holding out the saucepan to her.

Rebecca shook her head. 'It's too heavy,' she said, and inside her stomach curled into a tight knot.

PIECE 4

Rebecca was supposed to start school after Easter but her mother wanted her at home. Spring came slowly to Suffolk and summer more slowly still. David Kelly worked long hours flying and he came home stressed and exhausted. The house, though beautiful, had suffered long years of neglect and the list of tasks to turn it into a family home was overwhelming.

'I need her here,' Rebecca heard her mother tell her father. 'She can watch Giles and I can work on the house. There's so much to do. She's way ahead of most children her age anyway. She can read and write beautifully,'

So, while the older boys settled into their new lives, catching the bus from the end of the lane and making new friends at school, Rebecca stayed at home with Pen and her little brother. With Giles on her lap, she nestled against the trunk of an ancient apple tree, next to the pond, and read *Grimms' Fairy Tales* aloud. Pen sanded, painted, cooked and watched from behind the mullioned windows as the world outside turned green and the sky filled itself up with blue.

Rebecca was quite content. She loved four things – Giles, reading, animals and insects. This life gave her all four.

Sometimes, Grime would arrive and stand on the gravel drive and when Rebecca and the boys came out of the house, he would pull a dead animal from a pocket or a sack and display it proudly in his dirty hands. Once he had brought a mole; caught in a mole trap, he'd said. Rebecca had stood just behind Alex and peered, entranced, by the tiny creature. It had smooth, shining black fur and great, naked paws. Its tiny dead eyes gleamed black and its teeth were stained russet with blood.

Eventually Rebecca's parents began to make some friends: a colleague from her father's work asked them over for drinks; a mother from the boys' school invited Pen for coffee; the local vicar called in.

Pen wasn't a person who liked to join things. The jumble-sale committee and the Women's Institute weren't for her, but slowly the Kellys were beginning to become acquainted with their neighbours.

Through Lorraine, they found a babysitter called Mrs Lightwing. She was quite an old lady, Rebecca supposed, perhaps sixty or seventy years old. Rebecca thought she was lovely. She had short, shining, grey hair, a sweet lined face with red cheeks and faded brown eyes. She rode a bicycle with a basket on the front and Rebecca, during her walks, would often meet her pedalling down the country lanes with her black coat flaring out behind her.

'She's a witch,' Grime told Rebecca. 'She knows spells and can make potions. She gave my Uncle Billy a potion once, for his back, but it didn't work. Once, my mum saw her picking toadstools on a full moon.'

'Is Mrs Lightwing a witch?' Rebecca asked her mother.

'No,' said Pen. 'But she is probably a wise woman.'

Mrs Lightwing babysat for the Kelly children when Lorraine couldn't do it, and Lorraine couldn't do it much at all.

'It's because of our Billy's back, you see,' she told Rebecca's mother.

Pen didn't see, but she also didn't mind because Mrs Lightwing didn't sit downstairs reading *Woman's Own* or watching the television; she engaged with the children and seemed to have an especially soft spot for Rebecca.

'She brings her out of herself,' Rebecca heard Pen telling a new friend as they sat drinking tea in the kitchen. 'Rebecca's such a funny, silent little thing. Most people don't really bother with her.'

Rebecca understood that Mrs Lightwing meant to be her particular friend. She would wait until the boys were asleep or ensconced in front of the television, then she would come to sit on Rebecca's bed and gossip to her about the village and the church. She told Rebecca how the vicar's wife had cheated by buying a cake for the WI baking competition and how Denise Styles absolutely refused to do the church flowers since the vicar had banned gladioli.

Rebecca didn't know what gladioli were but she knew she was supposed to laugh, so she did.

Mrs Lightwing read Rebecca her favourite books and gave her boiled sweets to suck, even after she had cleaned her teeth. As an adult, the scent of a barley sugar could still send her spinning back through the years.

When the first primroses bloomed, pushing their way up

through the heavy clay, Mrs Lightwing would pick a honey-scented bunch especially for Rebecca and arrive on her bicycle with the flowers in the basket on her handlebars.

Rebecca wasn't used to being a favourite and initially she found this marked preference uncomfortable. She had none of Giles's beauty, Alex's charm or Martin's confidence. Her mother openly called her a peculiarity and her father took no notice of her at all.

'In my family, we marry daughters, we don't *have* them,' her father said one day. Rebecca imagined it was a kind of joke or an explanation but she also supposed it was true.

Rebecca soon learned to trust Mrs Lightwing and to view her as her own special person. She even told her about the secret place she had discovered at the bottom of the garden where a tunnel led through the hedge into a soft, grassy dell, like a nest that was just big enough for Rebecca to curl into.

'It's probably a place where a dog fox rests up during the day,' Mrs Lightwing told her. 'If you approach very slowly and quietly you might see him.'

Rebecca had spent the next few days walking silently down the long garden, breathing quietly through her nose, making sure that no twig snapped underfoot in the hope of surprising the fox, but she never saw him. She also told Mrs Lightwing about the game she and her brothers would play with the electric fence behind the Cherry Tree pub.

'You hold on to the fence with both hands and the last one to let go is the winner. Martin can hold on forever.' Mrs Lightwing didn't seem too keen on that game. Grown-ups were odd about things like that; sometimes it was better to tell them nothing at all.

She told Mrs Lightwing about the huge dark woods at Benham where Grime had told Rebecca you could see badgers. Rebecca longed to see badgers. 'There's a pond too,' she went on. 'Grime said it has much more fish in it than the one I fish in.' Rebecca had taken up fishing in a pond opposite their house with a bamboo rod that her father had made for her.

'Promise me you'll not go near that pond, Rebecca,' said Mrs Lightwing, laying her hand over Rebecca's. 'You stay nearer to home than that. Those woods aren't safe for a little thing like you.'

Rebecca was quite shocked by her seriousness. She thought nothing could happen in the woods and then she thought of *Snow White*, *Hansel and Gretel* and *Little Red Riding Hood*. She looked down at the two hands, lying together on the eiderdown, one old and rough with big knuckles and green veins, one small, freckled and pale, and she felt a huge responsibility course through her. An adult had never asked her for anything before. They had only issued instructions.

Rebecca shook her head. 'I won't,' she said, still looking at Mrs Lightwing's hand and wanting to pick it up and kiss it.

'Will you read me *Black Beauty*?' She handed Mrs Lightwing an old hard-backed copy.

Mrs Lightwing took the book from Rebecca. 'Oh, it's so sad when Ginger dies,' she said.

Rebecca nodded enthusiastically. She loved that bit.

PIECE 5

'Good afternoon, Mrs Wise. Are you ready for your close-up?' Dr Glass is standing next to her in the waiting room.

At the sound of his voice, Rebecca jumps. Her heart is leaping about and her blood is pounding. Like surf, she thinks. 'Noise,' she says.

'What did you say?' The doctor crouches down in front of her.

'I said, "Hello."' The roaring is loud but she can hear him. It's odd that he can't hear her.

'OK.' Titus Glass stands up in one fluid, quick movement. 'Come with me.'

Rebecca stands and follows him down a corridor, into a room; a different consulting room that looks just like the other one. Had Rebecca been able to think, she would have wondered how it was that grey and white were the very best colours for consulting rooms and waiting rooms but she is unable to think, and her fingers keep stretching out involuntarily so it appears to her that her hands have each developed an independent exercise routine. She stands for a moment in the doorway and pushes her hands into her coat pockets to stop them moving.

'Sit.' The doctor gestures towards a chair. She sits.

Rebecca decides that she likes being told what to do. She likes being told: 'Follow me' or 'sit'. It takes the pressure off. She doesn't have to make any decisions. He sits down opposite her in a chair the same as hers. Between them is a low, pale wood table and behind the doctor is a heavy, antique desk with a computer on it. He is wearing a lightweight charcoal suit with pinstripes. And his shoes are black and highly polished. His paisley tie is pulled up tight to his collar but Rebecca thinks that, underneath it, his top button is undone. She feels as though her eyes are taking photographs. She feels at once distracted and highly concentrated. She is surprised to find that this interests her.

'How long have you been like this? You've been taking two pills at night, thirty milligrams?' The doctor sounds concerned but Rebecca decides that he isn't really.

'I took them for two nights and then I had this horrible feeling,' she says.

'So you stopped?' He reaches behind him and takes his pad and pen from the desk, crosses his legs, puts the pad on his knee and writes. 'How long ago? How many days?'

'It's difficult, yesterday and today are the same day. Since Friday, maybe. I couldn't sleep. My muscles were crunching, all up and down my arms.' Rebecca holds out her arm to show him. 'All the long muscles felt as though they were shortening. It was horrible like, you know, when you touch unglazed pottery or . . . a potato covered in dried mud.'

The doctor frowns. Rebecca can't quite imagine him ever having touched an unwashed potato and she suddenly feels quite convinced that unglazed pottery is beyond his experience too. She feels her face quirk into a smile.

'What's funny?' he asks.

'Have you ever touched an unwashed potato?'

'Shush,' says the doctor. 'Fingernails down a blackboard?'

'What do you mean?'

'The sensation that you describe, is it like fingernails down a blackboard?'

'Probably,' she says.

He looks up from his pad. Rebecca notices that two dimples appear as he smiles. She can feel herself beginning to relax a bit, but her breath is still short and sitting still is almost beyond her. She takes her hands out of her coat pockets and slips them under her thighs to stop them clawing. They feel like those cranes from an amusement arcade, the ones that are supposed to grasp a cuddly toy when you move the levers, but never quite do.

'I bet no one's ever screeched their fingernails down one.'

'Probably not,' the doctor concedes. 'So you stopped taking them altogether?'

She nods. 'Why would they?'

Titus Glass looks up from his pad. 'Why would who, what?' he says.

'Anyone screech their fingernails down a blackboard? Do concentrate. Can I call you Titus, Titus?'

'You can call me anything reasonable with which you are comfortable.'

Rebecca looks at him. 'I'll call you Sir, if you stop this feeling. It's excruciating.' She is jiggling her feet up and down as she speaks. 'I feel like I've accidentally walked into a spider's web.'

'Well, you haven't. And you've been like this ever since? Two days? Two or three? That's a shame. Have you been taking the Tranquiltolam?'

'I've tried not to take three. I've been taking two.'

'Have you any on you now?' He looks at her over his glasses.

Rebecca shakes her head. 'No.'

'Did you drive here today?'

'No.' The roaring is really loud now and she is whispering. 'Viktor brought me.'

'Viktor?'

'A Romanian. He has sunglasses.'

Titus nods. 'OK, I'll tell you what we're going to do. I'm going to write you a prescription right now, then we'll go to the hospital pharmacy together, just down the corridor, and get you some Tranquiltolam. You will take it and then we will wait for it to work. We can't really talk when you're like this. You're in withdrawal.'

'I hoped so.' She tries a smile but it doesn't really work. 'Because if it isn't, it's very dangerous.' Her eyes take a snapshot of the low table between the two chairs. Some of the veneer has cracked away at the far corner. There is a box of tissues placed precisely in the centre in a grey covered box.

They stand and go to the pharmacy.

Back in the room, he gives her a plastic cup of water. 'Take one and try to sit quietly for a few minutes. You'll begin to feel a bit better.'

Within ten minutes, the roaring is considerably quieter. Rebecca clamps her hands between her knees to stop them shaking.

'What does your family think of this? What does your husband think?' Titus is behind the desk, writing as he talks.

'They think that I shouldn't be taking drugs. That I would be OK if I had a rest or a holiday or something.'

'And what do you think?'

'I think I should do what you tell me to do.'

Titus looks up from the pad. He taps the pen against his bottom teeth. It is his black pen, the same one he used before. 'That's a bit too passive for me,' he says.

'I mean, I think that there would be no point in my making all the effort to find someone to help me and to come all this way to ask for their advice and then to ignore what they were telling me,' she clarifies. She feels that it is important that he knows she is trying to be co-operative.

Titus looks back at her, silent for a moment. 'You didn't stay in the hospital,' he says.

Rebecca says nothing. She doesn't think anyone needs to be *that* co-operative. She's looking down at her knees; clenching her hands into fists. She has bitten her nails and their surrounding skin so badly, she can feel the skin weeping into her palms.

'This Jane Austen notion of taking the sea air, a rest cure and all that, is all very well. Look at me, Mrs Wise.' Rebecca looks up at him and sees that his eyes are veiled, like a cat's, the pupils, pinpricks in the blue. Rebecca bets hers aren't. She bets he can read every thought as it careers across her face.

43

'But, of all the branches of medicine most at risk from the influence of old wives' tales, ours suffers the most. Everyone is not an expert, whatever they may imagine to the contrary,' he continues. 'You're feeling a bit better now? A bit calmer?'

'A lot,' Rebecca says.

'Mrs Wise, you have to listen very carefully and understand. You should not have stopped taking your medication without advice. Promise me you won't do that again? Promise?'

Rebecca nods.

'We'll reduce the dose back to fifteen milligrams and see how you are with that. Any more problems, phone me. OK?'

Rebecca wipes her hands on her jeans. They aren't so sweaty now and the roaring in her ears has stopped. 'I promise. Thanks a bunch, Titus.'

The doctor's face lights up suddenly with a wide, white smile and Rebecca feels something unfurl in her chest. The smile is completely disarming. 'Much better, obviously. I'll see you next week. Take care, Rebecca.'

Viktor draws up outside the hospital in his white Prius. He jumps from the driver's seat and opens the rear passenger door for her.

'Thank you, Viktor,' says Rebecca. Titus called me Rebecca, she thinks. Weird.

PIECE 6

'Isn't it funny how Gary looks so like one of the Catchpoles?'
Rebecca was listening to her mother's new friend, Caroline
Gilbert, talking to Pen as they sat drinking coffee in front of
the Aga. The Aga had gone out and they were waiting for the
repairman to arrive but there was enough residual heat in it to
slowly boil the kettle. The Aga was ancient and temperamental
but the Kellys couldn't afford to replace it.

'I've never thought of it,' said Pen, leaning closer to
Caroline. The Catchpoles ran the farm that owned the wood.
Daniel Catchpole was the farmer and he let Rebecca and
Grime play there. Rebecca liked him. He was very friendly
and had sticking-up blond hair and crinkled eyes. Rebecca
left the kitchen but stayed lurking just by the door with the
two women in her line of vision.

'Well, the reason he looks exactly like a Catchpole,' said
Caroline, 'is because he is one.'

Pen laughed.

Caroline looked around the kitchen theatrically. 'Lorraine's
not here, is she?' she asked, dropping her voice so that Rebecca
had to strain to hear.

'No,' said Pen. 'We only have her on Wednesdays and Fridays now. It's just all too expensive.'

Caroline took a sip of her coffee. 'Oh, I know,' she said. 'Staff are such a nightmare.' Rebecca knew that Caroline's husband was very rich and they lived in a Queen Anne house and that they had two cars and their children went to boarding school. Rebecca didn't know what a Queen Anne house was but it sounded better than theirs.

'Anyway,' said Caroline, 'I was talking to Lorraine the other day. We were shelling peas together at the kitchen table. I love shelling peas, don't you? I love sliding my thumbnail along the seam of the pod and then seeing all the dear little peas lined up inside.'

Rebecca suppressed a sigh. She wished Caroline would get on with the story. Rebecca's mother laughed again.

'I said to Lorraine that wasn't it funny how children from the same family can often look so unalike. Like your Rebecca, she looks completely different from the rest of your family, doesn't she?'

'Not really,' replied Pen. 'She looks a lot like her cousins and my father had reddish fair hair.'

'Well, Lorraine carried on shelling peas for a moment and then she said to me, "Do you know what my mother-in-law said to me when I told her I'd fallen pregnant with Gary?"'

'No,' I said.

'She said, "That carn't a bin our Ronald. He couldn't do nuthin' like tha."' Caroline was very good at imitating Lorraine's accent and Caroline and Pen laughed loudly.

'Lorraine says,' Caroline went on, 'that it was her

mother-in-law who broke up her marriage. She and Ronald were married at sixteen and the woman just wouldn't stop babying her son. And it seems Ronald didn't do "nuthin' like tha" because if you look at Gary he's the living image of Daniel Catchpole,' said Caroline.

'And Graham?' asked Rebecca's mother.

'The spit of old Kenneth Tink.' Rebecca's mother had a mouthful of coffee and she choked and spluttered until tears ran out of the corners of her eyes.

Rebecca took a deep breath. She had some thinking to do. She flitted quietly through the house. She let herself out through the scullery door and ran down to the pond. A heron rose silently from the shallow water and disappeared over Grime's apple orchard. Rebecca tried to imagine Mr Tink as Grime's father. She couldn't, but then, she reasoned, nor could she imagine anyone as Grime's father or how she came by her own father. The mechanics of sex were still a mystery to Rebecca and thus far she had no inclination to dwell on them.

While he was squashing the rats, Grime had asked Rebecca if she wanted to bicycle over to Benham to see some badgers playing. Benham was further than she normally went because her bike wasn't very safe.

Rebecca's bike was red and was called Thunder. The brakes didn't work because she had left him lying on the gravel and her father had reversed the car onto him. Rebecca didn't mind about the brakes because, to her, Thunder was a spirited strawberry roan part-bred Arab gelding and brakes were not part of his nature. Anyway, if she wanted to stop she just put her feet down until Thunder came to a halt.

Grime had a Raleigh Chopper but it didn't have a name and it did have brakes. Martin would have loved a Raleigh Chopper but Rebecca's parents said they couldn't afford it.

'How come Grime's got one then?' asked Martin. 'You're a pilot and Grime hasn't even got a dad.'

'On the money we pay Lorraine, I'm surprised that he hasn't got a car,' said Rebecca's father bitterly and Martin knew to drop the subject.

Rebecca really wanted to see the badgers. She had told Mrs Lightwing that she wouldn't go into those woods, but if she did go, just once, Mrs Lightwing wouldn't know . . .

She sat down next to the apple tree where she liked to sit and read to Giles. A frog ducked its head, disappearing beneath the weed and on the opposite side of the pond, she saw Uncle Billy. She wondered why Billy was in their garden. He raised an arm. Waving? Rebecca waved back. She was going to see the badgers with Grime, she decided; she just wouldn't mention Kenneth Tink.

PIECE 7

Ellis is Rebecca's best friend. He is a gay child psychiatrist. Rebecca had met him at the school gates when she was dropping Abigail and Kit off on the first day of term. He had danced up to her saying, 'Ooh, pale and interesting. Thank the Lord for new blood.' And she had been won over instantly.

Ellis had grown up reading poetry in the treehouses of his rich friends in North Yorkshire. Then he'd waltzed through a medical degree at Cambridge as though it were a side effect of having the most fabulous time being the only gay in the college, 'Or at least,' he would tell Rebecca, 'the only one who counted.'

'Darling,' he would say, 'I had a gilded youth but it's entirely paid for, I promise you.' He had messed up by becoming the single father of three children when he was only twenty-six.

'All mine,' he'd told Rebecca when they'd first met. 'And none of them Rod's, so he just pissed off and left me with my offspring.' Rod seemed like bad news to Rebecca and she silently thought Ellis was better off without him.

'And the mother?' Rebecca had asked aghast.

'Went to find herself in India but she only got as far as Budapest and decided that she wasn't a lesbian after all. She's married to a Hungarian farmer and makes goat's cheese.'

Rebecca had looked at him. 'You sure?' she'd asked.

'No, not at all, but she's not around so there's just me and the three going to hell in a handcart and I have no rotting picture in the attic to take the strain, so my face is like a book for all to read what's written on the pages. Frankly, it's a disaster.'

Rebecca adored Ellis but she also knew that he was a bad influence, or rather that they were a bad influence on each other. They met, every week on a Thursday, for 'chip night' with the children. A second bottle of wine would always be opened and as the children, full of fish and chips, grew sleepy and fractious in front of the television, Rebecca and Ellis would gossip and drink until Sam came home from work at ten.

'You're not good for each other,' Sam told Rebecca. 'Can't you go for a walk or the cinema instead of just sitting drinking? You never eat anything together either. You shouldn't drink that much and not eat.'

Rebecca rolled her eyes. 'We can't drink that much *and* eat,' she told him, 'we'd be enormous.' She knew Sam was right, but the pull of a Thursday night spent laughing with Ellis was just too strong.

Ellis had come over to see Rebecca as soon he heard about her suicide attempt. She had seen Titus Glass only twice.

Rebecca felt weird about Ellis. He would have expected her to confide in him but, before her overdose, Rebecca had started to slide from his life and replace him with less interested people. Conveniently, for Rebecca, this had coincided with Ellis getting back with Rod, so he was suitably distracted anyway. Now, it was impossible to continue with any kind of subterfuge.

'What the fucking hell were you thinking?' asked Ellis. He was a consummate swearer and was halfway down a bottle of Casillero del Diablo from the corner shop so was less erudite than usual. 'I'm a fucking psychiatrist, I'm your best friend. Who is this fucker you've been seeing?'

Rebecca took a gulp of water. She had filled a wine glass from the kitchen tap to keep Ellis company. 'Titus,' she said, 'he's called Titus Glass.'

'Titus arse,' said Ellis. 'Where does he work?' Ellis scrolled through his phone. He found Dr Glass on the GMC website. He zoomed in on his photograph.

'God, he's young,' said Ellis. 'Qualified though, same letters after his name as me.'

Rebecca was beginning to feel like a stalker.

'He's almost certainly gay.'

'How d'you know?' asked Rebecca.

'His tie,' explained Ellis inexplicably, pointing at Titus. 'And, anyway, there aren't any straight adult psychiatrists; everyone knows it.'

He scrolled through his phone. 'Private psychiatry should be fucking illegal,' he said. 'Why would a private psychiatrist have the slightest interest in discharging a patient? Their primary concern is to make as much money as they can. Being mentally ill isn't like having pneumonia or breaking a leg.

A private psychiatrist can string the thing out for as long as they think they can get away with it. They can also facilitate massive dependency on prescription drugs, replacing one problem they're not interested in treating with another. Get me your laptop, babe. I'm going to nail this guy.'

'But Ellis—' Rebecca had been hoping that her doctor had a tiny bit of integrity '—they're doctors; they have a code of practice and the Hippocratic oath to stick to, just the same as you do.'

'Yeah,' said Ellis, 'but it only takes one bad apple . . . get me your computer.'

Doubt, like tinnitus, chimed in Rebecca's head. She went into the dark sitting room and found her laptop stuffed behind a sofa cushion. Some unquiet thought slid just beyond her grasp. She picked up her laptop and went back into the kitchen. Ellis was still sitting at the table, scrolling through his phone with his thumb like a teenager.

'I'm sure these wine bottles are getting smaller,' he said, picking up the empty one beside him and looking at the label, owlishly.

'I'll make coffee,' Rebecca said. She knew she shouldn't drink coffee after midday, but she thought she could make an exception, just this once. Ellis took the laptop from her and began bashing at the keyboard.

'He's qualified, that's all I need to know, and I think I like him.'

'Obviously he's qualified, but as a what? All I can find is that weird, smug picture and a paper he wrote eons ago. Why leave them up there? Bloody academic. You know what's wrong with academic doctors?' said Ellis. Rebecca shook her head.

'All cold fish; like anaesthetists. They prefer not to engage.'

Rebecca thought that if Ellis became any more engaged, his head might fall off. 'Perhaps a little distance is helpful,' she said.

'It's the person sitting in front of you that matters, from the way they sit to the way they smell. It's the flesh and blood human being, not some theory you cooked up to get a bit more funding to arse around at university for another year or two.'

'He's quite good at noticing the person.' Rebecca thought for a moment about Titus's cold blue eyes. 'Anyway I can't find this much about you. No pictures, no nothing.'

Ellis rubbed his scalp. He had had a buzz cut and Rebecca longed to rub his scalp too.

'I can't afford to have an online profile; I'd get stalkers. There's not much else here,' he said. 'Sometimes, you know, I worry about doctors, I really do. I mean, so you're at school, you're very, very good at science so you decide to become a doctor. It's not a qualification.' Ellis took a slug of the coffee Rebecca had put on the table beside him and pulled a face.

'Yeah,' said Rebecca, 'but it is really, isn't it? You might need empathy and stuff as well, but science is a good starting point, better than woodwork or something.'

'Being a surgeon is just woodwork and plumbing,' said Ellis.

Rebecca raised her eyebrows; she put her head on one side and she looked at him over her glasses. Ellis upended the empty wine bottle over his empty glass.

'What kind of batshit is that?' he asked.

'Batshit?' said Rebecca.

'Yeah, all that looking over the glasses, head on one side thing?'

'It's what psychiatrists do to undermine people. I've been practising on Sam; it's quite effective.'

'Well, don't do it to me, it's upsetting. D'you know, you really are the most appalling influence on me,' he added. 'I haven't had a drink in three weeks, then I see you and it's all hands to the pump.'

'Not my responsibility,' said Rebecca.

'I'd better go soon,' said Ellis, looking at his watch. 'Your bloody husband hates me.'

'Ellis is gay,' Rebecca had told Sam.

'I'm not jealous,' Sam had replied. 'I just worry that you take each other in the wrong direction.'

'We don't. We're fine. If you were here more often, perhaps I wouldn't need him so much.' Rebecca knew that, essentially, Sam was married to his job. She knew that his sense of self was very wrapped up in it. When she'd once asked Sam, 'Who *are* you actually?' he had replied, 'I'm a journalist.'

Rebecca told him that she hadn't asked, *what* are you? She had asked *who* are you? The two were distinct, but Sam couldn't see the distinction. Rebecca supposed this was because he was so alone in the world as a child, his life so fractured by his parents' divorce and his experiences at boarding school that work became his safe space, long before he had met her. She minded but she also understood.

'Sam won't be back until ten,' Rebecca told Ellis. 'He

doesn't hate you; he likes you. If he hated you, I promise you would notice.' Rebecca changed the subject. 'How's Rod?'

'Oh, you know . . . ' said Ellis vaguely.

'Can I stroke your head?' Ellis leaned forward across the table, offering his scalp. 'It's lovely,' said Rebecca. She ran her hand over his head. 'Your head is a lovely shape.'

'Did you plan this?' Ellis was suddenly serious.

Rebecca reached across the table and took his hand in both of hers. 'Not planned, no. I just felt as though it was something that was going to happen and that really it would be better if I stopped fighting it.'

'Becks, babe, you've got kids. What about Sam? What about all the people who love you?' A tear slid out of the corner of Ellis's eye and left a shining track down his cheek before plopping onto the table.

'I forgot,' said Rebecca. 'I thought they would be happier without me. I thought . . . ' She held her wine glass by its stem and watched the water swirl in the bottom for a moment and then drained it.

'I thought I wasn't a person,' she said. 'Can we talk about something else? I'll go on seeing Titus until he proves he's useless, OK? Now, how long have you had that tattoo? I told you never to have one and I have a quick suicide attempt and, before I know what's happening, you're all inky.'

'It hurt like hell.' Ellis showed her his muscled bicep, girded, now with an intricate Celtic design. 'What do you think?'

Rebecca didn't really like tattoos. At least hair grows back, she thought.

'You look amazing,' she told Ellis, 'but be careful with Rod. He's dangerous.'

'I know,' said Ellis. 'Do you want to come to a pub quiz on Thursday?'

'No,' said Rebecca. 'I can't drink; it wouldn't be fun.'

Ellis shrugged. 'You're not drinking now,' he said, 'but you're still fun. Back to your mad psychiatrist though, no one who gave a shit would tell someone they're not to have a glass of wine. It's positively inhuman. How long are you supposed to deny yourself? Has the incredible Dr Glass given you a ballpark?'

'I don't ever want to drink again,' said Rebecca, standing up from the table to put the kettle on.

'As Amy Winehouse once said . . . ' Ellis was looking slightly cross-eyed.

'Anyway, how's Orlando?' Rebecca decided to change the subject. Orlando was Ellis's youngest and was sliding inexorably off the rails.

'Oh, you know, it's "fucking" this and "fucking" that; anyone would think he'd invented the fucking word.'

'Well,' said Rebecca, 'Kit's not talking to me at all, not since . . . '

Kit hadn't recovered from finding Rebecca lying on the sofa comatose. He'd kicked an empty bottle of vodka further under the coffee table as he bent over her and shook her by the shoulder. He hadn't spoken to his parents since.

'I told him not to come over,' Rebecca had explained to Sam. 'He should have gone straight back to his flat.'

'So that I would have found you, stiff as a board, when

I came home from work?' Sam had been furious with Rebecca. 'If you could only hear yourself.'

'Gosh,' said Ellis. 'I'm not convinced by your method but it must be divine to be sent to Coventry by one's child. So very relaxing.'

PIECE 8

'How does this work, Dr Glass? I mean, what happens? Do I just see you, or could I have to suddenly see someone else?' Rebecca is in Titus Glass's consulting room. She needs to sort a few things out. She is sure he doesn't like her; if he doesn't she should stop seeing him or try to change his mind.

Titus twirls a pen round two fingers. He looks distracted. 'Have you heard from the therapy team yet?' he asks, reaching for his pad and making a note.

'No, I don't need therapy. I need to see you. You can give me pills and talk to me about how stupid I am and then I will get better.' Rebecca thinks the direct approach will work best.

Titus snaps to attention. 'I hope,' he says fiercely, 'that you don't think that I think you're stupid.'

Oh God, she's said the wrong thing again. She backtracks. 'No, no, of course not . . . well, maybe, I don't know. Failing to kill myself was a bit stupid though. I mean, just not trying . . .' He is watching her now with a look of growing incredulity. Rebecca sighs; she's so bad at this. 'I'm not very good at this,' she says. Perhaps flattery will work. 'You suit me,' she adds.

'In which way, exactly, do I suit you?' He focuses on a spot

58

just above Rebecca's head; he pushes his notepad to one side and puts down his pen.

'Well, I think you have a sense of humour. I have one too.' Rebecca realizes that she's grasping at straws.

'So far, you've been singularly unfunny,' says Titus. Rebecca shrinks back in her chair. Then, he rubs his eyes under his glasses with the fingertips of both hands and drags them down his face to cover his mouth. For a moment, he sits with his mouth covered. Manicured nails, Rebecca notices for the first time. It must take Titus hours to maintain this level of grooming, literally hours.

'At home, I'm funny. I want people to like me, so I'm ironic and witty and I make people laugh,' she says.

'Do they like you when you get so drunk that you attempt suicide?'

'No, of course not; that's not fair. That was something I *did*, not something I do. Anyway, it just seemed sensible at the time and, by the way, I don't care if *you* like me or not.'

Titus puts both his hands on the desk in front of him. 'I think,' he says, 'that we both know that that's not true.'

'Which bit?'

'You not caring if I like you or not. I think one of the most difficult parts of your treatment is the tightrope you are having to walk between appearing likeable and telling the truth.'

'Because telling the truth makes me unlikeable?'

'No, because you think it might. Can I assure you that it is irrelevant?'

'You can, but I can't work at getting better with someone who doesn't like me, can I? I mean, if you don't, I need to know so that I can find another psychiatrist.' She stares straight into his eyes. She needs reassurance.

He stares straight back. 'Don't try to take me down,' he says. 'And please don't try to manipulate me. You couldn't do it, so don't try. I'm here to help you, Mrs Wise, and I do believe that you tried to kill yourself.'

Rebecca is quite surprised that he imagines she feels strong enough to attempt taking *anyone* down, or that he could have misinterpreted her intentions so completely. 'Well, help me then,' she says. 'I wanted to die. It felt like a proportionate response. It seemed reasonable. It felt unselfish. Why am I wrong?'

Titus is becoming irritated. 'If it was proportionate and sensible—' here he describes speech marks in the air '—and "unselfish", why fail? Why bother to deliberately fail to die?'

Titus's defining characteristic, Rebecca decides, is irritation. He vibrates with it. Even his eyelids are stiff with annoyance. She does wonder if it is, perhaps, her that he finds irritating or whether it's his default response to all his patients. She sighs.

'Now what's the issue?' he snaps.

'Nothing,' says Rebecca.

'I can't help you if you refuse to communicate,' says Titus. He finds her so annoying he can barely sit still. He raps on his computer keyboard. He crosses one leg over the other and leans forward in his chair.

'Look at me,' he says. 'Mrs Wise, why, if you meant to die, did you decide to be drunk before attempting suicide? So drunk, that you were almost inevitably going to fail in your attempt?'

Rebecca shrugs.

'Why not wait until you were sober? After all, you are sober quite a lot of the time, aren't you? You don't drink all day, you don't drink and drive or stagger round Waitrose swigging from a coffee cup laced with brandy, do you? So why did you have to be drunk to try to die?'

'So, you think I didn't want to die?' Rebecca feels her mouth turn up at the corners.

'As I've said, I don't think you're unintelligent or unable in any way. I believe that had you meant to die, you wouldn't be sitting here, in this room with me.' The doctor leans back and folds his arms.

Rebecca thinks that she has lost an argument. She's not sure how or why but she is pleased that she has.

'Rebecca—' his voice has changed, all the snappiness has disappeared and she finds herself looking into the face of a friend '—I know that you need my help. I understand that your attempted suicide was serious and that the next time you may very well succeed. I would rather that didn't happen. So would you please make an effort and allow me to help you? It's what you want.'

Rebecca doesn't think that she can. She puts her thumb in her mouth and bites down on it until it hurts. She feels the skin on her knuckle break and her mouth fill with the hot, salty taste of blood. She says nothing.

'Rebecca, stop doing that. Look at me.' She hears him get up from his desk and walk round it until he is standing in front of her chair.

Rebecca keeps focusing on her shaking legs and her eyes fill with tears.

Titus crouches down in front of her, carefully taking her hand away from her mouth. He reaches behind him to the desktop box of tissues and wraps one deftly around her thumb.

'Look at me, Rebecca.' His voice is quieter; not gentle but less abrupt.

'You have to help me, it's your job. I had to be drunk because I'm afraid. I was afraid and I still am. I don't know how not to be. I'm afraid to be alive and I'm afraid to die. You're right. I wanted someone to see; I wanted someone to notice, that's all. Maybe I wanted to give myself another chance.' How could she explain that she felt the same way, now, as she had in January, but now, she felt heard? The silent scream into the vacuum of indifference had been replaced with— well, him, Titus. 'No one at home could hear me. I think you do.'

'If you create an elaborate smokescreen, you're hardly in a position to complain when it proves to be effective, are you?' Rebecca wipes her nose with the back of her hand and Titus hands her another tissue.

'Now I know why all the desks and tables here have tissues on them,' she says.

Titus Glass stands up and resumes his seat. 'They are useful, on occasion,' he says.

'You understand what I'm trying to say, even when I'm not able to say it . . . '

'As would be the case with any of my colleagues in this hospital,' he replies. 'Often meaning is found in the silences between the words for those who know how to listen.'

Rebecca shakes her head. 'I feel as though I have plonked

a mass of tangled wires, string, bits of twig and chain on the table and said, "Untangle that if you can? Untangle it and then put it all back together functionally and sensibly and at the same time could you please not be invasive." It's skilful and most people couldn't do it, not without getting right up in my grill.'

The doctor smiles and picks up his pad and pen. 'The adult brain is plastic; it is malleable,' he says. 'If untangling is required then we will untangle. You are the major player; the hard work's all yours. I'll try to continue not to get up in your grill, as you so charmingly put it, to the best of my ability. Now, shall we just carry on with this session and leave all the other stuff to one side for now? I genuinely care about you as I do all my patients. If it honestly makes you feel any better, I'm the doctor assigned to you, until such time as we discharge you. Even though it wouldn't alter my treatment of you, I absolutely don't dislike you. Does that help?'

Rebecca feels her body flood with relief. 'I wish I had a notepad.'

'You do; you have that one with the elephant on the front that you write your appointments down in. Isn't it in your bag?' He holds out his pen. 'Use this.'

She takes the pen and fishes the elephant notebook from the bag at her feet. 'Safe,' she writes and hands him back the pen. She wishes she hadn't bitten her thumb.

The doctor takes the pen and puts it down next to the box of tissues. 'Now to work; how are you sleeping? All good?'

PIECE 9

Pen decided that she and the children should go to church. Caroline Gilbert had told her that church was a very good 'in'.

'So, I've decided to go on Sunday evening,' Rebecca heard her mother tell her father at supper. 'I'll take the children. It will be good for them and they might make a few friends. The boys are OK but Rebecca hasn't got any.'

'She's got Graham,' Rebecca's father answered. Rebecca didn't know how she felt about having no friends apart from Grime. She was trying to eat her supper and was having very little success.

Normally the Kelly children ate their supper separately from their parents. They had fish fingers and Bird's Eye peas or homemade quiche with baked potatoes and salad or soup with cheese and bread. For some reason, tonight they were all eating together.

The boys were eating their food but Rebecca was rolling some crumbs of dry liver around in her mouth and trying to persuade them to go down her throat. They were reluctant.

On her plate remained a mound of cooling white rice and two tinned plum tomatoes leaching their red juice into a pool around the greyish lump of liver. She had only had one small piece of it. She thought the tomato juice looked like blood.

'You would like to come to church, wouldn't you, Rebecca?' her mother asked her. Rebecca swallowed convulsively and her glasses slid down her nose as she nodded.

'It'll be the parish church Caroline's talking about, not the Catholic one,' Rebecca's father said. Rebecca knew her father didn't like the Catholic Church. Sometimes Pen and David had rows about it and although she and the boys had been baptised as Catholics, none of them were confirmed and they had hardly ever been to a church.

'Well, I'm taking the children to the Catholic one in town. I can have the car on Sunday evenings, can't I? I think we need to start giving the children a religious education.' Rebecca's mother picked up her plate from in front of her. 'You don't want any more of that, do you, darling?' she said, stacking it on top of her father's empty one. 'If you're still hungry, have a piece of bread, there's some in the bread bin.' Pen turned and crashed the plates down on the draining board.

There was a beat of silence.

'You can have the car unless I'm on call.' Rebecca's father stood and walked over to the sink to wash up. 'Come on boys, clear the table. Rebecca take Giles up to bed. But I don't think you'll get an "in" round here by going to the Catholic church.'

Giles put his small soft hand into Rebecca's. 'Will you read me a story?' he asked. 'Will you read me *Snow White*?'

*

65

Church was a huge success. Giles stayed at home with their father, who seemed to have conceded his battle with Pen and had agreed to roast a chicken to eat on their return.

Rebecca and the boys piled into the back of the Cortina, bouncing along the scuffed red vinyl seat. Their mother was wearing sunglasses and had tied her hair up with a silk scarf. Rebecca thought she looked very pretty. She and the boys were wearing matching bottle-green jumpers from BHS. Rebecca wore a skirt and the boys wore shorts and their father had polished all their shoes.

Pen told the children that after the service they would shake hands with the priest and say thank you and that, perhaps, they could get an ice cream on the way home.

'This is Rebecca.' Rebecca's mother introduced her to the priest after the service. The priest took her proffered hand.

'All priests are called Father,' Pen had instructed the children. 'Father Francis is a Benedictine monk.' Rebecca knew that St Francis of Assisi was a monk, so she thought that Father Francis probably liked animals as much as she did.

'How lovely to meet you, Rebecca,' he said. She looked up at him. He had a pinkish face with bright brown eyes. Mouse eyes, thought Rebecca. 'Your mummy was just telling me that you love to write stories. I should very much like to read one. Perhaps you could bring one to church next Sunday as a special treat for me?'

Rebecca felt her face grow hot. 'Thank you for the service, Father,' she said, just as her mother had told her, but she didn't know what to say about the stories. They weren't very good.

Outside, Alex and Martin made friends with two other

66

boys and they were all rolling down a grassy slope next to the graveyard, shrieking and laughing.

Pen and the mother of the two new friends started chatting. The other boys' mother wore an ankle-length Indian skirt. Her hair was messy and hung in a blonde tangle to her shoulders and she was smoking.

'This is Miranda,' Rebecca's mother told her.

A small dark-haired girl sidled up and took Miranda's free hand.

'This is Harriet; she's been in Sunday School,' said Miranda. 'She's your age, Rebecca; perhaps you could be friends.'

PIECE 10

One morning, when she was seventeen, Rebecca had left home.

'Tell me about your home life, your childhood,' Titus Glass asks. 'How long have you been married?'

Rebecca shrugs her shoulders. 'I've been with my husband since I was seventeen,' she tells him.

The doctor looks up from his pad. He makes a note in the margin of whatever he had been writing. He takes off his glasses and puts them on the table beside him. 'That's very unusual,' he says.

Rebecca had packed her bag and, rather than catching the bus to school where she had been taking her A levels, she had moved in with her secret boyfriend, Sam.

Sam was a secret because Rebecca's father had become increasingly restrictive as she had grown older and she'd thought it easier, really, not to tell David and Pen about him. She had, long ago, put her childhood self behind her. She had bleached her hair a silvery blonde and worn it in a swinging, shiny bob. She'd worn contact lenses and ringed her eyes with kohl and kept herself as thin as she could. She'd been channelling Debbie Harry.

Each morning she'd caught a bus for the twenty-mile journey to school. Her best friend was Tabitha who smoked and bunked off. Tabitha was small, dark and angry. 'I'm ruthless,' she'd told Rebecca when they'd first met. Rebecca soon found out that she was ruthless in her pursuit of cigarettes and laughter, less so in her pursuit of an education. But she had a plan. 'I don't need much,' Tabitha had said. 'Only enough to get to university, two A levels maybe, to study Divinity. It's easy to get in studying religion – no one wants to – then I'll do a law conversion and be rich.'

Rebecca's parents didn't like Tabitha. They'd only met her once and she'd called David by his first name without being invited to. Pen didn't like her either. 'She's an incredibly bad influence,' Pen said. 'It's all very well, her encouraging you to idle your days away and smoke cigarettes, but your form teacher says you will fail your mocks if this goes on.'

Rebecca had known, though, that Pen and David weren't going to do anything. They were at the end of their marriage and were too emotionally exhausted to take any action either for her education or against her friendship so she'd just rolled her eyes and felt that she didn't care. It wasn't Tab's fault that they were both just so bored and tired of their powerlessness.

At school, Tabitha and Rebecca lounged around the sixth form common room during study periods sometimes reading D.H. Lawrence or, more often, talking about boyfriends and nightlife, neither of which they had. Looking back, Rebecca's overwhelming feeling about that time was the utter tedium with only Tab to relieve it.

'Oh, the sheer dullity, the ennui,' she would sigh to Tabitha.

They had developed their own high-camp language, having devoured Nancy Mitford before discovering Lawrence.

'Yes, darling, the utter, utter tediosity,' Tab would reply. 'Let's not do double French.'

'Bunkers?' asked Rebecca.

'Bunkers,' agreed Tabitha, her wicked little face lighting up, and they would pick up their bags and saunter out into the small cathedral town which, as they had no money and nowhere to go, Rebecca secretly thought even duller than being in double French.

Rebecca's very bones seemed to ache with the longing for real life to start.

Sam, at twenty-two, was five years older than Rebecca and a journalist on the local paper. She had met him in a café where they had both ordered and found there was only one table left. She'd been killing time while waiting for a bus to take her home. Sam had been sneaking a coffee break from his job on the local paper, having interviewed a couple celebrating their diamond wedding anniversary.

'What's the secret of a long and successful marriage?' he had asked the couple as he'd perched on a rickety chair in their tiny sitting room.

'Give and take,' the old lady had said, leaving the room to make tea for the three of them. Her husband, a one-legged survivor of the Somme, had leaned forward and touched Sam on the knee with a calloused hand and had muttered, eyes darting in the direction of the kitchen, 'I can't stand the bloody woman.'

Sam and Rebecca had drunk their coffee. She'd watched him disbelieving as he'd spooned four sugars into his.

'So you're a journalist? Why aren't you in London?' Rebecca had asked.

'I was, but then things went a bit pear-shaped. I'll get back there.' Sam had thought Rebecca looked a lot like Mary Travers. He hadn't told her this because he'd known that she wouldn't know who Mary Travers was. 'Do you want another coffee?' he'd asked instead. 'My treat.'

Rebecca had thought he looked like Jeff Goldblum. 'You look like Jeff Goldblum,' she'd told him and then wished she hadn't.

Rebecca and Sam had known each other for six months when Rebecca moved in. Sam watched Rebecca unpack her suitcase into his chest of drawers with some uneasiness.

'This isn't going to work,' he said. 'You're much too young.'

But Rebecca turned from her task and grinned at him. 'Can we go to bed now?' she said.

'And do you remember why you decided to leave your home, family and your education, I'm assuming, to move in with . . . ' Titus Glass checks his notes, 'Sam? Unless of course this was a Romeo and Juliet scenario.'

Rebecca thinks back. 'I loved Sam. I still do, but I left because I was unhappy. My father was too strict. I wasn't allowed enough freedom . . . '

'A claim that could be made by most teenage girls, I imagine,' says the doctor.

'Yes, it could,' says Rebecca, 'but my parents didn't like who I was becoming. I think they preferred the dull, bookworm oddball I had been. They rowed all the time. They had been fighting for years. They were getting divorced. I didn't want to stay with either of them. Sam made me feel safe. My mother went back to Cornwall where she came from. She took my younger brother; I had nowhere to be.'

'Did you feel abandoned?'

Rebecca thinks for a moment. 'No,' she says. 'I felt freed.'

Titus narrows his eyes. 'But you immediately chose to tie yourself to another person?'

'I didn't choose. It was . . . expedient.' Rebecca is beginning to feel uncomfortable. She really can't account for her seventeen-year-old self.

'So, Sam was convenient?'

Rebecca nods. 'He was but he wasn't just convenient, he was, is . . . kind to me.'

'What happened after you left your family?'

Rebecca's father had come to fetch her home. He had even half-heartedly punched Sam, breaking his glasses, but Rebecca had made up her mind. In bed with Sam was where she felt happy, so in bed with Sam was where she intended to spend the rest of her nights, forever.

'I left school. I got a job in a jewellery shop and a pub.'

'And kept house? Was that enough for you?'

'I was safe.' Rebecca can't really explain what happened, even to herself. She tries. 'It was as much as I could do,' she says.

'And you moved to London when you were how old?' Dr Glass seems intent upon getting her whole life story.

Rebecca pushes her fringe out of her eyes. 'I was twenty-two. Sam got a job on a national. He's still there.'

'And you?'

'I was a nanny. Then I had children.'

'And gave up work?'

'It didn't make financial sense for me to work and Sam needed my back-up. We would have separated if I'd had a career. I'm not qualified anyway.'

Dr Glass puts down his pad on the table beside him. He looks at his watch. 'Do you have any questions?' he says.

I have a thousand, thinks Rebecca. She shakes her head. 'No,' she says.

PIECE 11

The Kellys had friends over for supper so the children had been fed and put to bed early. The evening was light, Rebecca remembered, so it must have been a summer party. Her little brother was fast asleep in bed, his long dark eyelashes brushing his golden freckled cheeks, his pink mouth slightly open and his thick, shining hair damp with sweat. Rebecca watched him snuggled under his pink and grey striped sheet, and her stomach turned over with the love she felt. Rebecca knew she would have died for Giles. She would have welcomed the chance to die for him just to prove that she would.

Rebecca left Giles sleeping and joined her two older brothers on the landing. The Tudor house had uncarpeted, crooked oak planks on the floor of the upstairs passage that ran the length of the building. Where the planks met the beams that bisected the ceiling of the room below, there were gaps and the children could peer through to see which of their parents' friends had arrived for the party.

They all agreed that it was unfair to be put to bed so early on a warm summer evening. It couldn't have been any later than seven o'clock.

Sometimes when this happened, Rebecca and the boys would climb out of Alex's bedroom window, stretching to reach the branches of the laburnum tree, which grew there. They would clamber into its canopy, sliding on the smooth green branches, eyeing the deadly pods with fascination. Then they would drop silently into the garden below and run, in their pyjamas, past the pond to the strawberry beds, to feast while their parents rowed or ate in the kitchen. They would have been in so much trouble had they been caught but Rebecca didn't remember that they ever had been.

'A bloody fox has been at the strawberries again,' their father would complain. 'I'm going to borrow Billy's shotgun and lie in wait if this goes on.' The children would lock eyes across the breakfast table as they ate their Weetabix, silently vowing never to take the risk again.

Now Martin was lying on his stomach on the upstairs passage with his eye trained on a large hole in the oak planks. He had a birds-eye view of the drawing room.

'The Westons are here,' he said, 'and the Blakes.'

Earlier, Rebecca had helped her mother decorate a huge trifle with angelica and toasted almonds.

'It's full of sherry, you wouldn't like it. I'll save you a tiny bit if there are any leftovers,' her mother told her, as Rebecca delicately laid the green angelica strips in the shape of a flower stalk and used the flaked almonds as petals. Rebecca knew there would be no leftovers.

'Caroline Gilbert has had her hair done all fancily,' said Martin, moving over to let Rebecca have a look.

Rebecca could see Caroline Gilbert's dark head just below

her. She saw that she had her hair twisted up at the back in a mass of curls and that her Indian midi dress had a very low neck so that her bosoms rose up out of it, full and white against the dark fabric.

Their father was standing very close to Caroline; he was holding a black pottery bowl of stuffed green olives. Rebecca could see the tiny pieces of red poking out of each hole in each olive. Rebecca's father took an olive; he held it between his fingers for a moment before leaning towards Caroline and putting it into her laughing mouth.

The room was filling up. Rebecca's father said something into Caroline's ear and she threw back her head, laughing again.

'Move over,' said Alex, shoving Rebecca. 'I want to see.'

PIECE 12

Sam was tall with long legs and broad shoulders but, when Rebecca met him, he had yet to grow into his man's body, so moved awkwardly, reminding her of a young giraffe. He had a mobile sensitive face with widely set, downward-turned brown eyes and a hawkish nose above a mouth that seemed always to be on the edge of laughter. His dark hair grew upwards and too fast and was, consequently, always longer than he meant it to be.

His father was Jewish and his mother was not. His mother had taken a close look at him when he was a child and had found him wanting.

'A little too like his father,' Sam remembered overhearing her tell an aunt one day. Shortly after this she had run off with a neighbour, taking a bewildered Sam and his sister from London to live in Suffolk.

'She took most of the furniture, too,' Sam told Rebecca. 'When we went back home to visit Dad, the house was empty. I mean, really. There wasn't even a chair left.'

'Why didn't he buy any new furniture?' Rebecca wondered.

'Shock, I think,' said Sam. 'They never fought. I don't think Dad knew there was a problem.'

Shortly after his mother had left his father, she had presented Sam and his sister with a round, flaxen-haired stepbrother.

'He was so much better than me,' Sam had told Rebecca. 'The moment he was born I was sent to boarding school.'

Sam's sister had upped-sticks in disgust and moved back to Hampstead to be with their father, Abel, in his empty, echoing house.

'What about your stepfather?' Rebecca had asked.

'He was very nice actually but he didn't really stand a chance,' Sam had replied. 'He paid my school fees. I think it was the best thing that could have happened to me, quite honestly. At least I'm educated.'

But Rebecca knew that the reason Sam still slept with the duvet clutched in two tight fists at his chest had nothing to do with keeping warm.

Now, Sam's father, retired from the City, sat happily at his desk in Temple Fortune, studying Lepidoptera. Using tweezers, he turned clouded yellows, death's head hawkmoths and purple emperors in the light that filtered through the dirty nets at the windows of his 1930s semi. Sometimes he would walk up to Golders Green cemetery and drop sad stones onto Jacqueline du Pré's grave, but he didn't go to the synagogue.

Sam had never been to Shul on Saturdays. He knew no Hebrew and there had been no bar mitzvah. His mother had wanted him to become a lawyer but instead he'd become a journalist which, he claimed, was much the same thing if you looked closely enough, both professions holding people to account, as they did. His mother was nothing at all if not forensic in her judgement but here she missed the similarity.

Urban to his bones, Sam's natural habitat was the hills of North London. The genteel streets, crooked timber-framed pubs and massed medieval churches of the Suffolk countryside did nothing for him and were, he felt, merely a stepping stone on his way home to the top of Holloway Road and the blissful diesel-scented chaos of Archway roundabout.

'I know you have an affinity with mud, Rebecca,' he'd said. 'It's OK for you, you grew up with it, but look at these shoes and tell me I'm wrong. Tarmac is better than grass. If it weren't, we'd all be slopping about in Wellington boots and the whole of Northampton would go bust.'

'Northampton?' said Rebecca.

'Loakes,' said Sam.

Rebecca spent so much time not knowing what Sam was talking about that she'd decided to let this one pass.

Sam's mother had died suddenly when he was twenty-two.

'She went down like a ton of bricks in the greengrocer's in Little Worsted,' Sam's father had told him on the telephone and neither of them had found it in their hearts to much mind.

PIECE 13

Rebecca's parents invited Father Francis over for supper. They invited Miranda as well, because Pen had decided that she liked her, and also some people called the Kents who lived down the road. Geoffrey Kent had recently helped David pollard the willow that grew next to the barn. He had a chainsaw and David didn't.

The children were to eat supper with the grown-ups.

'Darling, I simply cannot find a babysitter; there's no one as sweet as your Mrs Lightwing,' Rebecca heard Miranda tell Pen on the phone. Rebecca had picked up the extension and was breathing very quietly, 'So I'll bring the children and we'll eat early, what?' Miranda always said 'what?' at the end of her sentences. Pen said it was probably because she was upper class. Rebecca wasn't sure what this meant but she decided that she liked Miranda almost as much as Pen did and she was beginning to like Harriet too.

Rebecca heard her mother agree. She was very pleased that Father Francis was coming. He had promised that he would teach her and the boys to stand on their heads when he had a moment. Rebecca hoped very much that he would have a moment this evening. Standing on her head was one of her greatest ambitions next to being a trick horse rider in a circus and walking on her hands.

She was also pleased that Harriet was coming because Harriet had seen a film called *The Sound of Music* and she was teaching Rebecca the words to all the songs. Rebecca hadn't seen the film but she was very interested in the idea of a singing nun and mountains. Alex and Martin had decided to stage a hunt in the garden with Harriet's brothers Milo and Inigo.

'No girls,' Alex told her.

Rebecca shrugged. She didn't want to hunt. What would they hunt anyway? Bats? She and Harriet had decided to dress up Giles as the youngest von Trapp girl and to teach him to sing 'So Long, Farewell' from *The Sound of Music* to the grown-ups, before carrying him to bed.

For supper, Pen made a stew called *La Daube de Boeuf Provencal* from an Elizabeth David book. 'It's a stew, so I won't have to stand over it when people arrive,' Pen said.

Daube, thought Rebecca.

'*De Boeuf*,' said Martin wrinkling his nose.

'It's French,' said Pen, 'and it's delicious. This isn't a restaurant; you'll just have to eat what you're given.'

The house soon filled with the scent of beef, bacon, garlic and oregano. Rebecca watched as Pen poured red wine into a pan and swirled it around before setting it alight with a match.

'Steady on,' said David, watching her. 'We need some wine left over to drink.'

Pen poured the sizzling wine over the meat and vegetables and transferred the whole lot into a casserole. 'See?' she said. 'Done.'

It was late summer and the garden was strewn with rustling brown leaves. Wasps and hoverflies hung drunkenly around the plum tree, feasting on the rotting fruit and Michaelmas daisies collapsed over tangled nasturtium clumps in the flowerbeds.

Miranda arrived in the mauve dusk, screeching to a halt on the gravel in her battered Volvo. Her children tumbled from the car almost before it had come to a halt and Inigo and Milo ran with Rebecca's older brothers into the darkening garden, carrying handmade bows and hazel-stick arrows.

'Don't go far, darlings,' Miranda called after them, 'it will be suppertime soon.'

She strode into the kitchen, trailed by Harriet. She bore a bottle of Chianti and an armful of blood-red roses. 'From the garden,' she said, kissing Pen. 'The roses, not the wine.' She laughed. 'Wouldn't that be just too marvellous, what? Wine from the garden. Something smells wonderful, what is it?'

'*Daube*,' Rebecca told Harriet, taking her hand. 'It's French.'

The boys charged into the house at the sound of the supper gong. The adults were seated at one end of the table and the children at the other. The tablecloth was grey and white checks and the glasses and water jugs shone in the candlelight.

Rebecca sat next to Harriet, trying to listen to the conversation at the other end of the table. Her mother looked wan and a bit tired. She was sitting next to Miranda, who was next to Geoffrey Kent, and Rebecca noticed how she kept leaning towards him as she talked, touching his arm and laughing. Geoffrey's wife Mary was next to David and David was next to Father Francis.

David and Father Francis were getting on very well. Father Francis's dark eyes shone with good humour and David filled his glass with red wine again and threw back his head laughing at something the priest had said. It was funny, thought Rebecca, that her father liked a priest but he didn't like Catholics, even though he was one once. Rebecca was sure she would never understand grown-ups.

Harriet was picking through her stew, searching for kidneys. 'They say there aren't any but they often sneak them in hoping we won't notice,' said Harriet. Harriet really hated kidneys.

Pudding was piles of grapes and cheese and biscuits, after which Rebecca and Harriet, who had promised to put Giles to bed, brought him back downstairs again. They had tied his shining dark hair back from his golden face with a green ribbon and dressed him in an old nightie of Rebecca's that fell to his ankles.

The table where the adults still sat drinking wine among the remains of the meal fell silent as Giles sang in a croaky little voice. Then, the two girls took one of his hands each and skipped him around the room before sweeping him out the door to loud applause.

Later, as promised, Father Francis taught the children how to stand on their heads. They cleared some floor space in the sitting room and each child chose a cushion from the sofa.

'You put your head on a cushion,' he said, 'like this . . .' and he did. 'Then you make a perfect tripod using your head and both hands, and then you very gently push your feet up off the floor and straighten your legs, slowly, first one, then the other.' And there was Father Francis, standing on his head in the middle of the room. On his feet, Rebecca remembered, he wore brown boat shoes with red socks, which seemed almost to touch the beams on the ceiling above him.

PIECE 14

Sam told Rebecca he had to go away for a 'work thing'. It was a Thursday evening and they were sitting on the sofa watching *Escape From The City*.

On the television, the house-hunting couple, Ben and Carole, said they thought that Stevenage was getting very busy and that they wanted to find a dual-aspect lounge with a wood-burning stove, within their budget, in Devon. Justin Hammond was doing his best to help.

'You can't go away. It's Annie's birthday. We're having a party.' Rebecca was quite shocked. She hadn't known that Sam was going away.

'I'll leave you to take a look around the upstairs of this little gem by yourselves,' twinkled Justin to Carole and Ben. 'I'll meet you in the garden,' he said. 'There are still a few surprises in store,' he added, looking archly at the camera.

'Why do they always leave people to look around upstairs by themselves?' said Sam, helping himself to a glass of wine from the bottle on the coffee table. The evening light was slanting through the window and, to Rebecca, it seemed as though the air was full of shining dust.

'Because the rooms are too small for a camera crew and the people and a double bed,' said Rebecca. 'You can't leave me to give a party by myself.'

'I told you,' Sam said, 'I have to go to a think-tank in York. It's a team-building thing. Cancel the party or get Kit and Ab to help. Annie's not a child and you're not going to have to deal with a clown or blowing up balloons. I told you I was going. God, Rebecca, you're nuts.'

Rebecca stared at him. 'Yup, and your point is?'

Sam ran a hand through his hair. 'My point is that I told you I was going. I don't mean you're nuts. I mean you'll be fine. You won't need me here. Annie can give her own party; she's grown up.'

Rebecca thought about the idea of Annie being grown up for a second, then she thought about herself at the same age. 'I really didn't know,' she said. 'It's the pills, Sam, they make me forget things.'

Sam put a hand on her shoulder. 'I'm sorry,' he said. 'I know it's horrible for you. It's just that work's been really full on and I'm so used to you picking up my slack. I need you . . . '

'To function?'

Sam nodded. Then he said, 'I've got to go as something quintessentially British. Any ideas?'

'Fancy dress?' Rebecca asked.

He nodded again.

'Please don't go. I forgot, it's obvious that I forgot or I wouldn't have invited all Annie's friends over and I would have thought of something for you to wear.' Sam must know that this is true. There's no way Rebecca would have invited a load of people over and not found him a suitable but dignified fancy dress outfit if she'd remembered he was going away.

Sam took his hand away. 'It's not optional, I'm a team leader.'

'Why York?' she asked.

'Would you rather it was somewhere else? I've got to pack. I'm leaving tomorrow after work and I'll be back on Saturday night.' Sam flicked the television off with the remote and heaved himself from the sofa. To Rebecca, his whole body seemed weary. 'They never buy the house anyway,' he said.

In the bedroom, Sam pulled his small Samsonite suitcase from the top of the wardrobe and chucked it on the bed. 'What do you suggest then? What shall I go as?' he asked. He opened the chest of drawers and threw a couple of linen shirts in the vague direction of the case.

'It's nine o'clock on a Thursday evening and you're asking me what you should dress up as . . . tomorrow?'

'I told you,' Sam said. All the fight seemed to have left him. He turned to Rebecca. 'Please,' he said.

'Go as a Hasidic Jew then, with a big furry hat and a stick-on beard; you've already got the face.' Rebecca thought she needed to humour him. She supposed he had told her he was going to York. Anyway, she couldn't argue with Sam. She needed to keep him onside.

Sam's tired face lit up with amusement and he stuck his tongue out at her before stuffing a filthy navy-blue jumper into his suitcase. Rebecca reached across him and took it out again.

'This has curry all down the front of it and a moth hole in the back,' she said. 'Go as a Sikh. I know, go as a Tory.'

'I haven't got any red trousers,' said Sam, 'or a big furry hat or a turban and I don't think dressing up as a Sikh would go down especially well.'

Sam made a grab for his jumper, which was lying on the bed. Rebecca dived on top of it and turned onto her back laughing and hugging it to her chest. 'You're not wearing this,' she said.

Sam looked down at her for a moment and then he took one of her hands off the jumper and pinned it above her head. Then he took the other and did the same. He lowered himself onto his elbows and pushed her knees apart with his and they lay quite still, breathing each other's breath for a few moments.

'You can't though, can you?' he asked.

'I can, it's still nice.' Rebecca slid one of her hands out from under his and put it behind Sam's head, burying her fingers in his thick dark hair, pulling him close and they kissed. It was still nice but it was also extremely frustrating.

Afterwards, they lay tangled together in the duvet. 'You've got that old bowler hat,' said Rebecca. 'Just wear that with your corduroy jacket and take a black umbrella; that's British.'

Sam pulled her head onto his chest and stroked her hair. 'You're going to have to tell him,' he said. 'It's important, we can't go on like this.'

Rebecca tried to imagine telling Titus that she can't orgasm and she failed. She disentangled herself and sat up. 'I'll see if I can find that hat,' she said.

PIECE 15

Rebecca fished in the pond opposite their house. She caught fish from there using bread pellets on a small gold-barbed hook. She could sit contentedly for hours, watching her painted cork float drift across the glassy surface of the water chased by pond skaters and dancing midges.

If she was hungry, she would break a lump off the damp bread ball in her pocket and crush it against her palate with her tongue, enjoying the soft, salty paste. Then, inevitably, the cork would bob and she would haul in a small, thrashing, silver fish, carefully remove the hook from its gulping mouth and transfer it to the galvanised bucket at her side. When she had caught enough fish, Rebecca would bring them home and empty them into the home pond.

The three older Kelly children could not be kept away from water. They loved the ponds, streams and the sludge-filled dykes surrounding their new home.

That first spring, Martin, Alex and Rebecca collected great clots of frogspawn from beneath the banks of their pond and kept it in jars on windowsills until the tiny black nuclei burst into life and wriggled free. As the year progressed, the boys and Rebecca caught newts, copper-eyed toads, water beetles and water boatmen. They made elaborate plans to trap the great grey heron that stalked the shallows, vacuuming up Rebecca's fish. They rigged up a rope swing to hang from a willow and leapt onto it from the bank, swinging perilously low over the muddy depths. Alex had fallen in once when the rope snapped and he had plodded, wet to the waist, up the long garden in his black gum boots.

'Alex, why is it always you?' Pen had asked him as he'd stood shaking with cold at the kitchen door. 'You're absolutely filthy. Take your boots off. I'll get a towel.'

Alex had removed one boot using the toe of the other and pulled the second one off on the doorstep. It was only when he'd tipped the water out onto the gravel that he'd realized the boot was full to the brim with blood. Pen had come back with a towel to find him out cold on the step. He had cut his knee to the bone.

'Lord alone knows what cut him,' she'd said. 'There could be anything in the bottom of that pond.'

The pond where Rebecca fished had steep sides dropping off into deep, dark water. Rebecca was protected from accidentally slipping in by a couple of rusting posts and a strand of barbed wire, behind which she would sit. 'You'll be safe there,' her father told her. 'Don't go any closer though. Don't climb over the wire; it's very deep.'

'I don't know why I bothered to tell her really,' Rebecca had heard him tell Pen. 'Everything I say to Rebecca goes in one ear and out the other.'

'She's not disobedient, she's just dreamy,' Pen had replied, but Rebecca knew that she only did as she was told if the instruction made sense or the threat of punishment was too great a risk.

The pond was surrounded by hawthorn, grown tall with ancient, twisted trunks. In May, its white flowers filled the air with a rich, sickly scent, and in early summer, among its green leaves, Rebecca found a mass of big-eyed, blue-faced caterpillars, which she took home and put in a shoebox. She watched their glossy ochre and rust-striped bodies undulate as they moved, and she fed them each day with fresh leaves, choosing only the tenderest tips in the hope of raising tame butterflies.

'They're lackeys, they turn into moths,' her father told her. 'They're not very pretty.' But Rebecca found her caterpillars charming. One morning she found the box full of tiny, deflated corpses. Each one with a shiny reddish blob attached to its side. 'I'm afraid they have ichneumon wasps. The larvae eat caterpillars from the inside out; those blobs are their chrysalises,' her father said. 'They'll all be infected.'

From the inside out? thought Rebecca.

She took the shoebox, ran down the garden and emptied the contents into the pond, banging the side of the box to dislodge the very last chrysalis. 'Drown!' she said angrily to the dark water, 'Just drown.'

PIECE 16

'And you were allowed to fish in this pond by yourself?' Titus makes a note in his pad.

'It wasn't dangerous.'

'When you were how old?'

'Eight, nearly nine. Weren't you allowed to go out by yourself when you were little?'

'Not when I was eight.'

'Are you allowed out by yourself now?'

Titus drops his pen onto the table next to his pad. 'I absolutely refuse to have that conversation,' he says.

Rebecca watches him for a moment. 'Titus,' she says.

Titus looks up from his notes. 'What?' he says.

'Hawthorn blossom smells of decay. That's why you're not supposed to bring it into the house. It smells of death. People thought it brought the plague in.'

'Did it?'

'No, really it was just the warmer weather. But it does smell of death . . . and sex.'

'One or the other, surely.'

Rebecca thinks for a minute. 'No, both,' she says.

PIECE 17

Miranda, Rebecca decided, was the nicest word she had ever heard. 'Miranda,' she whispered to herself enjoying the sound. Miranda had golden-brown skin. Her voice was deep and full of laughter. She always wore long Indian skirts and sandals on her rather dirty feet. Rebecca thought that she probably didn't wear sandals in the winter but, so far, she had only seen her in sandals with a toe thong.

Harriet, Inigo and Milo went to the Catholic school attached to the church. Harriet was very pretty. She had a shiny brown bob, a small freckled nose and large heavy-lidded blue eyes. Rebecca thought she looked like a doll, or she would have done had she not always been wearing her older brother's hand-me-downs. Rebecca was jealous of Harriet's clothes. She preferred boys' clothes. Her mother never gave her the boys' outgrown things to wear.

'Miranda is divorced,' her mother told her. 'Harriet's father lives in London.' Rebecca felt sorry for Harriet, but Harriet didn't seem to mind.

'Oh, he's not worth much,' she told Rebecca, shrugging. 'He even forgets our birthdays and Mama has boyfriends now. They're nicer.'

Harriet, it seemed, had embraced Rebecca as her new best friend. She would rush up to her after church and take Rebecca's hand, whispering some piece of gossip in her ear about the other children at Sunday School, or tell her a rude joke in her soft husky voice, which would send both girls reeling with breathless giggles.

Rebecca and the boys weren't allowed to go to Sunday School because, although David had allowed his children to go to church, for 'social reasons', he wasn't, he explained to Pen one evening, going to 'have them indoctrinated into the filthy cult of Catholicism'.

'There's nothing more anti-Catholic than a lapsed Catholic,' Pen had said, and Rebecca had slipped from the room, knowing the storm that would follow. David hated to be called 'lapsed'.

PIECE 18

'When Sam called you selfish, did he mean inconsiderate or inconvenient?' Titus is poking around in Rebecca and Sam's relationship. He seems determined to find cracks.

Rebecca looks at the floor. She grinds the heels of her hands into her eye sockets and wonders what Sam had meant.

'I don't know, stop poking me,' she says. 'It was selfish.'

'I think,' says Titus, 'that I can honestly say I have never yet poked one of my patients.'

That's a shame, Rebecca finds herself thinking.

'Don't be silly,' she says. 'You know what I mean.' Titus is very silly, she decides, but . . . people with fault lines, she thinks, are more *her* sort of people. Things with cracks in are, according to Leonard Cohen, more likely to let the light get in.

She looks at Titus and wonders if the light is there.

Titus looks back at her. 'What are you thinking?'

She shrugs. You're cracked, she thinks. 'Nothing,' she says.

Titus clears his throat. 'If,' he says, 'this were a different sort of hospital and I were a heart specialist, rather than a psychiatrist, would your husband have thought you selfish for being under my care; for seeking treatment?'

'This isn't the same. I didn't know I was ill, I just thought that this was reality. If I didn't know, then how was anyone else to know? How was Sam to know? He's just a man, a newspaper man, Titus. He's not a doctor. This is something I did. I didn't just passively sit there and wait until something bad happened to me. I actively did it.'

'I think that's debatable. I also think it's debatable whether or not everyone else in the family just sat passively and let something bad happen to you.'

Rebecca sighs. 'It was my fault, my decision,' she says. 'Abigail said she didn't think it was that surprising when you consider how I was running my life.'

'Again, the cause is being brought firmly back to you. One can't just take an effect and make it a cause, because it suits one's narrative.'

Rebecca looks at Titus. He is sitting at his desk but he isn't taking notes today. He has left his computer keyboard to its own devices. Rebecca is quite shocked by how well he understands the gaps she has left in her story. He seems able to fill the gaping holes, to recognize the omissions. She has no idea how he does it. It's like watching a street magician perform a card trick. Rebecca wonders if distraction plays any part.

'Titus, how are you doing this? How can you make sense of it?'

'I'm not emotionally involved, I'm the outsider. In the end that's what makes it simple.' Titus swivels round in his chair and turns his back to her for a moment. He picks up his pad.

'Can we do a run-through of your meds now and see how well we think you're adjusting to the Dulsexatine?'

Rebecca watches him tap on his keyboard. She can tell by the set of his shoulders that he is pleased. She can see by the way that his fingers are hitting the keys that his dimples are showing and that he has turned away from her to compose his expression.

PIECE 19

One Sunday, after church, Miranda and Pen were standing smoking, while the boys rolled down the grassy slope at the edge of the graveyard.

'I'm organising a beach party,' Rebecca heard Miranda tell her mother. 'Do come! It'll be such fun, what? And you'll meet the Wilsons. They're an absolute riot.'

Harriet and Rebecca were sitting on a low wall next to the two women. They were making daisy chains. Harriet's slender fingers were quicker than Rebecca's and Harriet crowned her head with a circlet of daisies and sat swinging her legs while Rebecca toiled on with her glasses slipping down her nose. She didn't hear her mother's reply because she had a much quieter voice than Miranda.

'Bring a sharing picnic, bring the children; bring your crusty old husband too if he'll come. It'll be such fun and the weather's going to be fabulous next weekend. We play cricket and swim under the stars.'

Harriet turned her head slowly towards Rebecca so as not to dislodge her crown. 'Do say you'll come. It will be no fun without you.'

Rebecca abandoned her flowers and jumped down off the wall. She took Pen's free hand.

'Can we go?' she asked.

The beach party began as dusk fell. Rebecca's parents parked the Cortina on a small country lane beside a ruined church and she and her brothers tumbled from the car onto the grass verge. Giles had stayed at home with Mrs Lightwing.

'He's so young. He would get tired,' Rebecca's mother said. 'There's quite a walk to the beach too.'

The path to the cove where the party was wound past wheat fields and was bordered by a tangled hedge of hawthorn, hazel and bramble. The boys ran ahead, followed by Rebecca's parents who carried a bag between them filled with picnic food, towels and drinks. Rebecca came last, stopping now and then to admire the under-ripe blackberry clusters, whose weight bowed the bramble branches over the path, and to look for caterpillars.

Soon, the Kelly family stood on a low sand cliff above a small white beach. Her parents dropped the picnic bag at their feet and paused to take in the scene. The westering sun was throwing long shadows. Beyond them were low dunes and, at the edge of a grey sea, Miranda's party were gathered around a driftwood bonfire.

'Well, come on, there's a way down just over there. Let's join the fray.' Rebecca's father picked up the bag and headed down towards the group.

Rebecca followed her father and mother towards the fire. A warm breeze was blowing off the water and up ahead towards the higher sand cliffs she saw swifts or swallows swooping in the clear evening light. Harriet materialised beside her and took her hand. She leaned in, whispering.

'Let's go swimming,' she said. As an adult, Rebecca would remember the beach party as the proper beginning of her friendship with Harriet.

Together, holding hands, they ran down to the water where they splashed each other, kicking up the sea foam. Then Harriet dragged off her wet T-shirt and shorts and ran into the sea, diving through the grey, muscular waves to emerge floating on her back beyond the breakers. Rebecca looked back towards the fire, unsure for a moment if her parents would stop her.

She saw a tall man with grey, blowing hair, standing to hand her seated mother a glass of white wine. The wine in the glass trapped the setting sun so that it flashed gold in the man's hand. Then Rebecca pulled the straps of her sundress from her shoulders and dropped it on the sand, laid her glasses on top and, kicking off her sandals, followed her friend.

Just before the sun dropped below the horizon, it bathed the clifftops in silver light, throwing the beach and the fire into purple shade. Harriet and Rebecca had finished their swim and were wading in the shallow surf looking for amber. Harriet said you could find amber here, and that if you did, you would be rich forever. Rebecca looked up the beach, shading her eyes with a hand, and saw the fire flame orange in the deep shade of the cliff and the spectre-like figures around it shifted and blurred. She saw that their four brothers were playing a makeshift game of cricket using driftwood for stumps and a tennis racket as a bat.

'Come on,' said Harriet, 'let's get dressed. We can catch swallows before it gets dark.'

'How?' asked Rebecca.

'I'll show you,' said Harriet.

So they climbed the treacherous sand cliffs and, shoving their hands down the swallows' nest holes, they pulled the roosting adult birds into the open and threw them into the air to watch them dive and spiral.

As darkness fell, the fire was stoked with more driftwood. A friend of Miranda ladled batter into a blackened pan and made pancakes, passing them round, wrapped in greasy paper napkins. Picnics were unpacked and shared and more wine was poured.

The children pulled rugs up over their shoulders and gazed sleepily into the flames; then as the stars began to pepper the sky with bright points of light, everyone took off their clothes and dashed into the freezing sea.

PIECE 20

Rebecca had seen Sam off to York and then she'd wandered into the kitchen, barefoot, to make some coffee, the cord of her dressing gown trailing behind her. Pomp had followed, tapping half-heartedly at it and thinking of biscuits. Rebecca had ordered an Ocado delivery with as much ready-made food as she thought she could get away with. Abigail had promised to come and help her cook.

'Just make one of those saffron fish stews you do,' she'd told her mother on the telephone. 'Whack in one of those packets of prepared mussels and some tilapia fillets and you're done. You can buy breadsticks and everyone knows you're ill so no one will be expecting much anyway.'

'Thanks,' Rebecca had replied.

She heaped dessertspoons full of ground Colombian coffee into the cafetière and waited for the kettle to boil. She slept so well on all her drugs that it took at least two huge mugs of black to make her feel properly awake in the morning.

'Kit's coming,' Abigail had told her mother. 'I've persuaded him to get over himself.'

Ellis had come over at about four and helped Rebecca put up the canvas gazebo in the garden in case it rained, and Kit had brought the wine and lit the fire.

'Shall I put rugs and cushions out here so people can sit down?' Annie had asked. Rebecca was feeling guilty because Annie had made her own birthday cake. 'Yes,' she'd said. 'What a good idea.'

'Well, you're crap at making cakes, aren't you?' she'd told Rebecca. 'Do you remember all those horrible lemon drizzles you used to make? Every year, a lemon drizzle. I don't even like lemon.'

Rebecca tried to remember making lemon drizzle cakes but she couldn't.

She had chopped onions and roasted red peppers for the fish stew. She'd smashed garlic cloves with the side of her knife and she'd minced parsley and mint leaves. Ellis had brought her a glass of Viognier.

'This,' he'd said, 'is particularly good but I want you to pace yourself. You're not going to have a nice time if you face-plant by seven o'clock.'

'Face-plant?' said Rebecca.

'Yes, it's terribly *now*, I know, but babe, I don't want to be left hosting Annie's dull birthday party all by myself.'

'Face-plant? I'm not supposed to be drinking,' Rebecca had said, spearing a red pepper with her knife and blackening the skin over the hob's gas flame. She knew Ellis hated drinking alone.

'And I'm not supposed to be co-hosting a boring party and I'm certainly not doing it with you sober. Just pace yourself, darling. To face-plant is to fall over, collapse, nosedive, that kind of thing,' said Ellis. 'It's very *de nos jours.*'

'Just so I know,' Rebecca had replied. Apparently she'd ignored him.

Now, the following morning, Rebecca is sitting in the waiting room at the hospital. She doesn't even know how she got here. She feels as though her head has caved in. The skin on her arms is burning and her fingertips itch. Her feet are curling inside her gym shoes and she feels as though her eyes are about to fall out of her head.

Which is not a hangover, says Betty. It's a hangover plus pills. Is he trying to kill you?

There are two other people in the waiting room. 'We've come to see the doctor,' says the man. His wife stares blankly into the middle distance.

'The thing is,' says the man, 'that I'm not mentally ill, I have to explain, not mentally ill, but physically. I'm physi- cally very, very ill.' The woman continues to stare.

Rebecca sits in the corner, trying not to hear him, trying to stop juddering and flinching, trying to breathe.

'Go up, room one-thirty, Rebecca,' says the receptionist.

Rebecca knocks on the door and goes in.

'How are you today?' Titus Glass is sitting at his desk. He is wearing a red checked shirt with mother-of-pearl cuf- flinks and no tie. 'Not good by the look of you; what's been happening?'

'I'm fucked up,' says Rebecca, flinging herself down onto a chair. 'Completely fucked up. I'm screeching with nerves.

I have to go to France soon and I'm screeching with nerves. We booked it last year. I have to go, Annie's coming.'

'How much have you had to drink today?' Titus is looking at her, writing in his pad; writing quickly.

'Why are you writing? You're always writing stuff about me and I'm fucked.' Rebecca puts her head in her hands and tries to catch her breath.

'How much?' Titus puts his pen down.

'Nothing, I had lots last night. I had a party. I was as high as a kite if you want to know, write that down.'

'I ask you because I can smell alcohol,' says Titus quietly. 'Metabolised alcohol. It's from today, not from last night. How soon do you have to go to France?'

'I have to go, that's all, and now I smell like a tramp. I'm going to France smelling like a tramp and with my head falling off. I haven't had anything to drink today; it must be pouring out of my skin from last night.' Rebecca is shaking. She feels as if she cannot sit still. It's as though every part of her body is in rebellion.

'How much?' says Titus, glaring at her, 'and I did not say you smell like a tramp, so stop putting words into my mouth.'

Rebecca lifts her eyes to his face. She wonders why he's so angry.

'Nothing,' she says.

'I think you have but anyway, we'll leave that for now. I have told you that mixing these drugs with alcohol is an especially bad idea, haven't I?'

'How old are you, Titus?' Rebecca decides to wind him up. He is being horrible and he shouldn't be bossing her around.

'We've been here before,' Titus sighs. 'How old do you think I am? Why on earth would you want to know that anyway?'

'You know how old I am. It seems fairer.'

'How old then? A rough guess,' says Titus, folding his arms across his chest.

'I think you're forty-seven.'

'Way out and quite rude, try again.'

Rebecca looks at him silently. He is sitting up in his chair, his notepad abandoned, examining her through narrowed eyes. He takes off his glasses and pinches the bridge of his nose.

'Can we stop this now? It's so depressing.' Titus shifts in his seat, impatiently.

'Have you got a headache?' says Rebecca. She drags some air into her lungs like a swimmer surfacing.

'Not yet,' says Titus. 'So go on, try again.'

Titus has no grey in his hair. For a moment Rebecca thinks it may be dyed, then she thinks it can't be. Hair dye doesn't come in that particular shade of light brown. No one would buy it.

Mouse? suggests Betty. 'OK, mouse,' agrees Rebecca.

'What?' says Titus.

Rebecca shakes her head; she hadn't meant to say it aloud. His hair, she thinks, would have been blond when he was a child. He has lines around his mouth but the frown line between his brows comes and goes and his dimples have yet to carve deep furrows into his cheeks. Titus shifts impatiently.

'I think you're about forty,' says Rebecca. 'And I'm still fucked up because you gave me some stupid overdose.'

'Nearer,' says Titus, picking up his pad. The tension between them snaps like an elastic band. 'The reason that you feel so ghastly is because you drank too much and took drugs at a party. It has nothing to do with the prescribed pills you are taking.'

'I didn't take any drugs, where did you get that from? When did I say I took a drug? I took one once about four years ago but I don't just randomly take drugs at parties, not generally.'

'Oh, I thought you said you were high.'

'On wine, that's all. I don't live in a world where people take recreational drugs.'

'Journalists?'

'I'm not one,' says Rebecca. 'And they don't.'

'I want to see you again tomorrow.' Titus stands up. 'I want you, in here, at ten o'clock tomorrow morning. You look as though that might be a problem. Is it?' He looks furious.

Rebecca shakes her head. 'I like notice,' she says.

'Well, you'll have to forego that just this once.' Titus opens the consulting room door and Rebecca remembers the couple in the waiting room, wanting to see him. Poor Titus.

A short while later, walking fast down Borough High Street towards London Bridge, Rebecca remembers that she did have a drink today. She'd downed a glass of wine while clearing up the party. There had been a bit left in a bottle and she'd drunk it. God, now he was going to think she told lies as well as everything else.

Bloody weird relationship, that's all, she thinks.

It's not actually a relationship, says Betty slyly.

Rebecca feels the familiar exhaustion slide over her like a shadow.

'Shut up,' she says loudly, loudly enough for a man walking in front of her to turn and look at her.

Rebecca hears Betty snigger.

At home, Rebecca reads a copy of an email that Titus Glass has sent to her GP. She has no idea which one of the doctors at the surgery *is* hers so she supposes it doesn't matter if they think she's an alcoholic nutjob.

Unfortunately, the higher dose of Collapsetine has led to increased agitation and an increased startle response. This has been exacerbated by alcohol consumption at a party she threw at home where she drank more than a bottle of wine and went to bed at 2 a.m. She woke at 7 a.m. Consequently, today she is feeling rather unwell. This is a shame after such a good early response.

I have asked that she abstain from alcohol whilst we are titrating her medicines.

I have asked her to reduce her dose of Collapsetine to 50 mgs again and to take Tranquiltolam this evening.

Mrs Wise departs for France soon and I have asked her to see me again tomorrow when I hope she will be more settled.

PIECE 21

'I'm sorry, Dr Glass, about yesterday.' Rebecca is sitting in his consulting room at ten o'clock the following morning.

Titus is tapping on his keyboard. He presses return and looks at her. 'For what? Why are you sorry?' He seems quite calm and friendly.

'I said fuck quite a lot,' says Rebecca. 'It was rude.'

'It's fine; sometimes I say fuck quite a lot too. How are you doing today? You're still pretty uncomfortable by the look of you. Did you take fifty milligrams this morning?'

Rebecca nods her head and the whole room nods at the same time. She is shivering and her shoulders are hunched. She tries to sit up, to sit still, but it's difficult.

'Did you take a Tranquiltolam after you took the Collapsetine?'

'I took it at the same time. I didn't want to give it a chance. I didn't sleep all night.' Rebecca had fallen asleep at about ten but had woken in a pool of sweat at two to find Sam snoring beside her. He must have undressed in the bathroom. She'd groped in the darkness for the glass of water on her bedside table and had swallowed it down but she was still ragingly thirsty. The feelings of dread coursing through her body had been so intense that she'd had to reach for Sam and hold his hand to ground herself. Sam had turned over in his sleep and muttered something, releasing himself from her grip. Rebecca shuddered at the memory. Something scuttled in the periphery, something sinister pulsing at the very edge of the experience, and then it was gone, leaving her with a pounding heart.

'It was like a waking nightmare,' she tells Titus.

'What was? You didn't want to give what a chance?' Titus turns to his keyboard and scrolls down the computer screen.

'I don't know.' Rebecca folds her arms and shudders. 'Nothing probably. Titus, how long have I got to feel like this? I've got to go to France soon.'

Titus stops scrolling. 'How soon do you have to go?' he asks. 'You didn't tell me yesterday.'

'Not very soon, but in a couple of weeks or so . . . '

'Tomorrow you will feel considerably better and the following day you will feel almost no anxiety at all.' He turns to face her. 'Listen to me, Rebecca. Stop trying to be in charge. I know what I'm doing. Trust me. There's no way you can postpone this French trip, is there?'

Rebecca shakes her head. 'No, there are other people involved,' she says.

'Classic,' says Titus. Then he picks up his pen and writes a prescription on the pad on his desk. 'There's enough Collapsetine and Dulsexatine until I see you next, and enough Tranquiltolam for any problems you may have before then, but honestly I don't think you will.' He smiles his sudden white smile.

Rebecca stands to go. 'I'm scared of flying to France,' she says.

'Do it anyway,' he says, handing her the prescription.

'And Titus . . . '

'What?'

'I didn't throw a party. You wrote to my GP that I threw one. I didn't. I gave one like a normal person.'

'Oh, I'm sorry,' he says. 'I imagined that you were the kind of person that threw them. I will make a note that you don't.'

'Will I be all right?'

'Trust me,' says Titus again.

PIECE 22

The badgers had a sett at the far end of Benham Wood where the trees thinned and glimpses of gently rolling countryside could be seen between the grey trunks of the tall ash trees.

'This sett's bin here for a hundred years,' Grime told Rebecca. 'Et's got seven entrances but I know which one they use most. You can tell because of the scrapes.'

Rebecca didn't know what scrapes were but she supposed she would see. They skirted the dark pond where Rebecca was not allowed to fish. Grime told her that the pond was so deep that a tree, an oak, stood upright in its depths without the topmost branches piercing the pond's surface. Rebecca paused on the path to gaze across the water. The trees clustered close to the edge and the pond shimmered blackly in the gathering dusk.

'Et's full of fish,' Grime told Rebecca.

'How did the tree get in there?' asked Rebecca.

Grime paused thoughtfully. 'I 'spect it was there before the pond,' he said, turning back to the path.

Grime left the path and began to weave between the trunks with the edge of the woods to their right. She saw the white scuts of rabbits feeding in the field beyond the trees and she heard an owl hoot and the clattering call of a cock pheasant. The failing light blurred outlines and distances. Rebecca felt as though she was walking underwater and that Grime's darting figure up ahead might suddenly disappear into the green twilight, leaving her stranded.

He turned and signalled, his finger to his lips and she trod carefully avoiding twigs, holding back swishing branches and brambles as she passed.

The entrance to the sett where Grime said the badgers would appear was halfway up a low ivy-covered bank, above the stream that bisected the wood. A long muddy track bordered by heaped leaves led from the entrance, which was wide and low.

'See the scrape?' whispered Grime, pointing towards the track. 'That's from them cleaning out their dens. I found some bones in that scrape, hedgehog bones.'

Rebecca followed him up the bank and they settled quietly against the trunk of an oak tree. 'They'll be out soon,' Grime told her. 'Don't make a noise.'

The badgers appeared one by one. First, a large powerfully built animal paused at the entrance of the sett, raised his striped snout and sniffed the evening air. Rebecca strained her eyes in the gloom as the grey pelt melded with the dark bank. Her heart thrubbed uncomfortably in her chest and she breathed lightly, fearing detection.

Grime had told her that they would sit down-wind of the sett but the evening was still and she could hear the badger grunt as he snuffled in the leaf litter. Four others followed less cautiously. The three kits and their mother romped down the slope, play-fighting and chirruping before disappearing down towards the water. The large male trotted calmly after them and the wood was completely silent again.

PIECE 23

Diagnosis:

1. *Generalised anxiety disorder – severe.*
2. *Major depressive disorder – severe.*
3. *Cluster B and C personality traits.*
Medications: Hifatlatrine 15 mgs.

Rebecca stops reading. Apparently Titus Glass was infiltrating Cryazatine and she wasn't keen on being infiltrated. She wasn't East Germany in the 1970s. She wasn't MI6 or a branch of CND. Why all the weird language? What was wrong with *introducing* Cryazatine rather than infiltrating it?

As if you were at a cocktail party? asks Betty.

It would be less sneaky, thinks Rebecca. Infiltrating!

She looks out of her bedroom window. The silver birch, planted in the pavement outside, is as tall as the house now and its leaves are casting beautiful shadows across the bedroom wall. Rebecca sits down on the unmade bed, draws up her knees and wraps her arms around them. She drops her head onto her knees and grinds her eye sockets into them. She tightens her grip on her legs, then lets go and lies down on the bed, staring at the shifting leaf pattern and wondering if she can find a wallpaper that looks like that. Not moving obviously – that would be very distracting – but something as delicate.

Today, she decides, she would start to recover despite the infiltrating; it was time to get a grip. She couldn't go around sporting personality clusters and having people writing about them. She stands up, opening the sash window an inch to let some air into the room and begins to make the bed. The door to the spare room slams in the draught and Rebecca jumps.

'I jumped about a foot in the air,' she tells Sam, as he climbs into bed with her later that evening. 'I'm being infiltrated and it's doing my head in.'

'Are you sure you should be taking all these drugs if they're making you jumpy? You were jumpy enough anyway.'

'I don't know. I mean, if you ask a professional what you should do and then they tell you, it's probably just as well to give it a go. I might get used to it. I've got to take more Hifatlatrine when I'm used to this dose. I'm a bit worried it might mush my brain.'

'It might turn you into a big, fat, mentally ill cabbage.' Sam laughs into the darkness at his joke. 'Anyway, guess what? Biffo came into the office today. He retired in January. He took voluntary redundancy and he's bored witless.'

'Do you think he's majorly depressed?' asks Rebecca, snuggling into Sam's shoulder.

'Maybe,' he says.

Rebecca puts her hand onto Sam's chest, under his T-shirt.

He is wearing his favourite black T-shirt with a lightbulb emblazoned on the front that glows in the dark. She can feel the reassuring steady thud of his heart beneath his ribs and she takes a long deep breath. 'Sam, do you think I am?'

'What?'

'Depressed.'

'I don't know. I suppose so. That's what you've been diagnosed with, isn't it?'

'Sam, why is Biffo called Biffo?'

'Biffo stands for Big Ignorant Fucker From Oldham.'

Rebecca props herself up on one elbow. 'It doesn't!' she says. 'Does he know?'

Sam pulls her down beside him again. 'No,' he says. 'He thinks it's just a nickname.'

'Sam?'

'Mm?' Sam is falling asleep.

'I will get better, won't I?'

Sam suddenly sits up and turns on his bedside light. He leans over and strokes Rebecca's hair back from her forehead. 'You will,' he says. 'I know you. You are one of the strongest, most resilient, lovely, loving people I have ever met. You will get better. This is like the flu or something and you are going to survive it and look back on it one day not quite remembering what this was really like. I love you, Becky.'

He turns off the light and Rebecca stares into the dark. 'I love you too, Sam,' she whispers.

Rebecca is dreaming. She knows she is dreaming because a dog is sitting on her legs and she can't move them. It is inching up her body, shifting its weight, stealthily. She can hear it breathing. It is panting rather than breathing. Her hands won't move. They are pinned to her sides and her eyes won't open. Rebecca knows that if the dog's face reaches hers that it will tear the flesh from her cheeks with its teeth, leaving naked muscle and twisted blue veins. It will fasten itself to her throat and bite the life out of her. With supreme effort, she tries to move, to make a noise, to warn . . . someone, something.

Sam shakes her awake.

'Becky, you shouted.'

Rebecca turns towards him, feeling his arm encircling her.

'I have to go downstairs,' she says.

'Why? You were dreaming. Go back to sleep, I've got you.'

'I can't sleep, not now. I'll just go and watch TV for a bit. It's too frightening.'

Sam turns over, pulling the duvet up over his shoulder. The curtains are slightly open and she can see the dark hump of him silhouetted against the pale wall.

'OK, but don't be long. You were just dreaming, come back to bed soon.'

Rebecca sits on the sofa and flips channels. She has wrapped a blanket around herself but she is still cold. She finds *Escape From The City* and Justin Hammond is just doing his final piece to camera.

'So we wish them both well in their new life, here, in the beautiful Cotswolds,' he says and the camera pans away over lush green hills, peppered with golden Cotswold stone cottages. Rebecca sighs and the dog inches closer. She can feel the weight of it leaning against her shins and she pulls her legs up off the floor and wraps her arms around them.

Of course, she knows it's only a dream; the kind of dream you have when you are not well.

PIECE 24

Rebecca has started to write. She has decided to write down everything that has happened, so that she has some illusion of control. Rebecca has a notebook. On the front she writes, The Psychiatrist, and inside on the first page she writes, Cyrus Mason.

The doctor, she writes, is a big man, tall and well-covered, rather than fat. He has tightly curled, dark-brown hair, almost black. It grows straight back from a high, wide, unlined forehead. He is standing by a heavy antique desk, as she enters the room, holding out a large brown hand.

'Good afternoon Mrs Marshall. May I call you Emily?' His hand feels cool and dry in hers. 'Do sit down,' he says, gesturing towards a tall wing-backed armchair upholstered in a dark-green William Morris print. 'I'm Dr Mason, Cyrus Mason. I understand that you have been through the mill rather. Do you want to tell me what happened?'

Rebecca hears a person outside in the street break into a snatch of song. She looks at the bedroom door. It is closed. She takes a deep breath before turning back to her notebook.

Emily, writes Rebecca, supposes that Cyrus must be about

sixty but it's difficult to tell. He is wearing a pair of heavy-rimmed Tom Ford spectacles and a dark-brown checked suit. The jacket is open and, underneath, his dark-grey shirt looks as if it needs ironing and the suit trousers bag at the knees.

Emily can see that he is the kind of person who does this to clothes.

She instantly likes him for it.

She also likes his voice, which is rolling and deep with a quiet energy.

She hadn't expected him to be black.

Emily decides that he is quite attractive.

She sits in the armchair. She tucks her hair behind her ears and looks out of the window. A pale-yellow April sun has bounced into the room and it seems to her that its ebullience only serves to emphasise the bleakery of her situation.

Bleakery is not a word, says Betty from the corner of the bedroom.

'Look at me please, Emily,' writes Rebecca. Emily turns her head to look back at the doctor who has taken a seat behind his desk. He is resting his forearms on the desk and has interlinked his fingers. His hands are relaxed. On his left hand, he wears a signet ring and a wedding ring.

Choose! Betty hisses in Emily's ear. One or the other, not both.

'Snob,' says Emily.

'Now, I wonder why you would say that,' says the doctor. He has taken off his glasses and they lie upside-down next to a large notepad. Emily can see that his eyes are such a light brown that they are almost yellow.

Rebecca puts down her pen and reads back what she has written. She imagines that she can shut the book and imprison the experience between its pages.

But you can't, says Betty. It's still happening.

'Please shut up,' she sighs.

Betty laughs.

PIECE 25

Rebecca takes a bus to London Bridge station. She has given up on her driver, Viktor because he is too concerned and it makes her feel responsible for him.

On the bus, she checks her Instagram and she checks her email but her head is chattering so much that she is nearly catatonic. She gets off the bus and walks across the bridge to see if this will help her calm down. It doesn't.

A group of homeless people look up hopefully as she approaches but Rebecca is waving her hands about and her eyes are all big and staring. The homeless people smile understandingly and continue to talk amongst themselves.

Rebecca presses the button on the front door of the hospital. She doesn't hear that she has been buzzed in but, after a moment, she pushes the door and it opens. The waiting room is empty. She takes a seat and checks her Instagram. Pomp is sitting on a rug that very nearly matches the colour of his fur. Someone in Indonesia likes it. Rebecca tries to breathe slowly. She takes long deep breaths. She tries to relax.

Her hands have other ideas so she sits on them. What on earth is the matter with her? It must be association. Coming to the hospital is very, very difficult because she associates it with things that are very, very difficult. She associates Titus with some very difficult things and they are all crowding into her mind and shouting at each other. Rebecca feels overwhelmed by the noise and drama of it all. Really she knows it's the pills. The pills are quite beyond her.

A phone rings and the receptionist tells Rebecca to go upstairs. She walks upstairs but it is very tiring. Every step is at a premium so she walks slowly. Her heart is banging so loudly that she can't hear herself think, which is probably just as well, she thinks.

Rebecca sits down opposite Titus Glass. He is behind his desk. She shoves her hands under her legs again because they are still being unreliable.

'What on earth have you been doing?' says Titus.

Rebecca tries to control her breathing but real Titus is so much more frightening than fictional Cyrus that she doesn't know what to say. So she just says everything. If she tells him everything he might understand how much she is trying and, more pertinently, how badly she is failing.

'I've fictionalised all of this,' she tells Titus. 'I've made it all up and then I come here and I find out that it's real. I'm literally wandering around in my brain.'

'Slow down.' Titus gets up from his desk and comes to sit in the chair opposite hers. 'What do you mean, you've fictionalised all this? What does that mean?'

Rebecca takes a deep breath. Her hands crawl out from under her legs and wander along the arms of her chair. She watches them for a bit, then she says, 'I started to write it all down. I wrote what I said, then I wrote what you said . . . '

'So you're writing?'

Rebecca nods.

Ha! says Betty.

'Shush,' says Rebecca. 'You see, it's not funny. It's like a rain hopper. It's blocked and all the words are overflowing and pouring down the sides. I can't sleep so I write . . .' Her hands make a cup shape in front of her face and then her fingers do sprinkling movements.

'You write at night?' Titus looks worried.

'Yes, because of the paralysis dog and things,' says Rebecca. 'I'm wandering about in my brain . . .'

'You are *not* wandering about in my brain,' says Titus, mishearing her. He stands and picks up his pad from his desk and begins to write.

'Not *your* brain; *my* brain.' Rebecca tries to imagine Titus's brain.

Titus's brain will be full of Roman roads and towns laid out in grids. It will have flat lawns and open vistas, avenues of trees and canals that are as straight as arrows. It will be very Capability Brown. It will personify The Age of Reason and embrace an ersatz naturalism. Things in Titus's brain will lead sensibly from here to there without the tiniest deviation. Rebecca knows that if she were to wander about in Titus's brain, she would feel extremely exposed. She decides to tell him something else because he doesn't like being fictionalised. He is very uncomfortable with the idea.

'It is truly horrible taking Cryazatine. Really horrible.'

'I know,' says Titus. 'I can see that.'

Rebecca holds his gaze. He screws up his eyes. She looks out of the window again. She wishes he would tell her to go away.

'I'm not being difficult. I feel ill. I'm sorry,' she says.

Titus writes a note.

'You do know, don't you, that the side effects you are experiencing are extremely rare?'

Rebecca swallows. Her throat feels tight. 'I don't mind if they're rare; they're unbearable, that's all. Everything you give me takes me up a notch and I need to come down three notches.' She sighs. She can feel him not believing her. 'I'm thinking too fast,' she says.

'So it would appear.' Titus taps his pen against his bottom teeth.

'You can keep up though, can't you? Lots of people can't. It's tiring.' Rebecca hopes he can keep up. She wishes her brain would slow down. Her words are coming out too fast.

'Oh don't, I might feel flattered.'

'You won't. You're trained to keep up though, aren't you? Some people are just slow.'

Titus takes off his glasses and puts them on his desk. 'What does Sam think of all this?'

'I didn't ask.'

'What about your children?'

'I don't know. I think they think I'm the same. I'm just speedier. I talk more quickly. My edit is down.'

Titus looks very worried. 'Could you bring someone with you next time? Perhaps Sam is too busy but could you bring a family member?'

Rebecca thinks. 'I don't think they would want to come.'

She wonders why he thinks Sam would be too busy. She thinks that if Sam met Titus, Sam would be too annoyed, so it is something she would rather avoid.

Titus sighs. 'Mrs Wise . . . '

'Don't call me that.'

'What?'

'Mrs Wise, it's not my name. If I identified as Brian, you would have to call me Brian, wouldn't you? But because I identify as Rebecca, you're perfectly happy to ignore it. It's not right, Titus, really it isn't.'

Titus sighs. 'Mrs Wise,' he says, 'you have to cooperate.'

Betty screeches.

Rebecca feels hideously invaded. She decides to change the subject. 'Does Hifatlatrine make you fat? Does Cryazatine?' she says.

'Hifatlatrine is associated with weight gain but that's because it gives people cravings for sugar and refined carbohydrates.'

'But in themselves they don't make you puff up, like a steroid might?'

Titus shakes his head. 'No,' he says.

'One doesn't have to respond to hunger; one can ignore it,' says Rebecca. 'I was worried about it making me put on weight.'

'If you don't eat junk, it won't,' says Titus. 'I want to see you next week.'

'Next week?'

'Tuesday? Can you do Tuesday?'

Rebecca can.

'Goodbye, Mrs Wise.'

'Goodbye, Mr Glass.'

Rebecca looks back at Titus who is sitting behind his desk, again grinning his big gap-toothed grin.

Smiling damn'd villain, she thinks.

She takes a Tube back home. She sits there and wanders about in her brain.

Rebecca's brain is full of rolling roads, bridle paths, footpaths, switchbacks and dead-ends. It has nooks, niches, crannies and mirages. There are cellars, caches, secret passages and woodpiles. Its ways are cobbled . . . and cobbled together. Tall spires jostle for space with cottages, hunkered down against prevailing winds. Its rivers whoop down gorges. They carve out oxbow lakes, inundate marshes, silt up harbours and flow down to pebbled shores. It is entirely unmanageable.

At home, Rebecca asks Annie if she would come to see Titus with her next week.

'Which day?' says Annie.

'Tuesday,' says Rebecca.

'See you next Tuesday?' says Annie, waving her arms above her head.

'What do you mean? Why's that funny?'

'It just is,' says Annie, dancing around the kitchen.

Rebecca gazes at her youngest daughter. Bizarre, she thinks. Annie slides across the kitchen floor in her socks and executes a perfect pirouette. 'See you next Tuesday,' she says, curtseying.

'Am I weird?' Rebecca asks Annie.

Annie laughs. 'You're really weird,' she says. 'You have

screeches and you listen to the same music over and over and you say weird stuff.'

'Titus wants someone from the family to come and tell him what they think of me.'

'Yeah,' says Annie, 'but that would just be a roast, wouldn't it?'

'Would it?'

'It would be quite hard to tell you why you're weird without it sounding, well, not very nice, wouldn't it? I mean I'd have to say, "She's mad, you're not helping, so . . . Bye!" There wouldn't be much point, would there?'

Rebecca shrugs. Annie takes a bowl of the chickpea curry that Rebecca has made. As she leaves the kitchen, headed for her bedroom, she says, 'I literally haven't done any work today. I was talking to Jay for ages and then I was eating an ice cream and then it was five o'clock.'

'A time-slip,' says Rebecca. When Annie has gone, she starts to think about how weird she is. Then she begins to think about how weird she has always been. Then she eats half a bowl of curry and goes to bed. She takes 10 mgs of Tranquiltolam and falls asleep.

Mrs Wise was unsettled today. Although she put this down to travelling on public transport, it is clear that she is experiencing daily difficulties as well as a degree of insomnia.

She also reported and demonstrated rapid speech and rapid thought processes, which are being noticed by family members.

I have asked her to restart 5 mgs of Tranquiltolam to
help with the agitation and will monitor things more closely
in the coming weeks.

This drops into Rebecca's inbox the next morning. I didn't
put it down to travelling on public transport, she thinks. Why
would he say that I did, when I didn't?

Covering his arse? says Betty.

PIECE 26

Rebecca was fishing in the pond opposite her house. She had been sitting on her upturned bucket behind the strand of barbed wire for some time but the fish weren't biting. She was hungry so her stomach gave an occasional growl and she felt sure that the fish could hear it. She knew that she wasn't allowed to fish from anywhere else but her father had taken the boys sailing at the coast and Pen was digging the vegetable patch so no one would know if she did.

Rebecca scanned the opposite bank. It was thick with bulrushes. A young willow grew sideways out of an ancient tree stump, its branches, ashy grey, were dotted with bright green shoots. She thought that perhaps she could sit on it, perhaps she could shuffle out along one of the branches and sit, legs dangling above the water, and fish from there. She imagined all the perch and rudd huddled together, beneath the willow branches, giggling at the idiocy of someone sitting, fishing on a tin bucket with a rumbling stomach.

Rebecca decided that she had nothing to lose and, even if she didn't catch anything, she rather fancied sitting out above the water, swinging her legs. She knew she would have to be careful not to fall in, because the spiny hawthorn grew right down to the water's edge and she wouldn't be able to get out very easily.

Mrs Lightwing had told her that it was unlucky to bring hawthorn flowers into the house.

'Never bring in the May, ye'll live to rue the day. It's an old saying round here,' she'd told Rebecca, May being an alternative name for hawthorn blossom; but Rebecca thought it would be very nice to sit among the blossoms, inhaling their rich soapy scent for a while.

She had quite a struggle to get to the willow stump. She left her rod balanced on the bucket, the line still in the water. She would have become tangled up, she realized, had she taken it with her. She fought her way through the branches to the water's edge. The twigs tore at her hair as she pushed her way through. At last, she felt the smooth grey bark of the stump beneath her palms and, with a small jump, shifting her weight onto her arms, she scrambled up into the tree. It bent slightly but she enjoyed the springiness and, ignoring a long bloody scratch on her wrist, she sat astride the trunk and began to ease herself out over the water.

The day was warm and Rebecca sat for a while, watching the pond skaters skidding expertly across the surface. Tell-tale bubbles rose from deep shade beneath the bank, so she knew where the fish were, which was somehow pleasing, even though she couldn't get to them. She reached into her jeans pocket and pulled out the lump of damp bread she used for bait. Breaking off small pieces, she rolled them into tiny balls and scattered them into the water below her perch. The fish may as well be fed even if they weren't to be caught. She saw a couple rise in the water, snatch the bread, and turn with a flash of red fin or tail.

Then, suddenly, she felt uneasy. The sun ducked behind a cloud. A blue tit, which had been chatting to itself in the bush above Rebecca's head, was abruptly silent. Gnats danced crazily above the water and, as she watched, a huge mosquito settled on her arm and slid its proboscis almost lazily into her skin. She slapped it away, leaving a bloody smear.

Far away across the fields towards Benham, a cuckoo called.

She felt as though she were being watched. She felt as if invisible eyes were boring into her back. Rebecca did sometimes feel like this, but it was usually in the evening when she was out by herself, and she would always turn for home. Now, she sat in broad daylight thinking of witches, trolls, shadow people and ghosts.

A shudder ran through her.

Then, the sun reappeared and she saw a flash of bright blue out of the corner of her eye and caught her breath. Grime had told her that a pair of kingfishers nested here. She hadn't thought she would see them, not really, but he was right. Rebecca sat as still as a stone and trained her eyes on her bucket across the pond. Again, there was the flash of blue and the bird skimmed low across the pond. She saw its sharp beak skim the surface, its orange breast, then it was gone.

Afterwards it was difficult to tell what happened. She watched as her rod, still resting atop the bucket across the water, gave a convulsive jerk and her cork float disappeared beneath the silver surface. Then the line cut through the water like a cheese wire and the rod fell off the bucket with a clatter.

Though she had no memory of clambering down from the willow, Rebecca recalled kneeling next to the bucket, pulling in her line to find it broken, the hook gone. Then Billy Parfitt was standing over her. She looked up and saw him silhouetted against the afternoon sun.

'A catfish, I expect,' is all he said.

PIECE 27

Rebecca writes.

The house in London was dark but Emily couldn't switch on the lights because she was unsure of what might be lurking in the corners of the room. There were no curtains in the kitchen and switching the lights on would make her visible from the garden and she had a feeling that what was outside was even worse than the thing inside. She also had a feeling that she should have stopped taking the blue pills before she came to this point. Cyrus had said that they might make her sleepy; he hadn't said that they would make her think of tearing Velcro, snakeskin and tomato pulp. Emily knew that she was having a bad reaction to the pills but Cyrus had told her, made her promise, not to stop any medication without first consulting him.

'Promise me,' he'd said, and she had.

'I promise,' she said it aloud to herself now and the skin on her arms shrank and shivered as she folded them.

Phone him, phone his secretary. He had said she should, hadn't he?

Sam was away. He was in America but he would be back

on Thursday. Today was . . . Emily couldn't remember. Annie was with her friend Charlotte. They had gone to see her friend Robin. Robin had a gig in Camden. Abigail was with them.

'I'm not supposed to leave you alone,' Annie had said. But Emily knew that Annie was longing to go to Robin's gig and she didn't think Annie should have to stay at home just to look after her.

'I'll be fine,' she'd told her. 'I'm not your responsibility.'

Then Annie had texted and said she was going to stay at Charlotte's if that was OK?

Emily had texted back and said that was absolutely fine, but it wasn't.

Emily decided to go and sit on the stairs for a while. That way the front door with its opaque glass would be constantly in view and there were no other windows in the hall. Guiding herself with one hand on the wall, she tiptoed out of the kitchen, up the four steps to the hall, turned and sat flinching halfway up the stairs to the first floor landing, facing the front door.

'Halfway down the stairs, is a stair, where I sit/There isn't any, other stair, quite like it.'

Christopher Robin, she thought.

She felt in her dressing gown pocket for her mobile, pulled it out and looked at her screensaver, a photograph of a French sun setting over a sea of sunflowers. God, France seemed a million years away. She didn't imagine she would ever go there again. She rested her head against the wall and tried to remember, but it was like trying to catch pouring water with her bare hands.

She looked at her phone again. She swiped the screensaver

left; scrolled down her contacts, touched the green phone icon and let the phone dial Cyrus.

She heard the phone ring and then divert and ring again. It rang out. She pressed the red phone icon and put the phone back in her dressing gown pocket. She decided to stay where she was and rested her head against the wall again. Sam might be home tomorrow, she thought; some time tomorrow. She shut her eyes.

'Hello, Dr Mason's secretary, can I help you?'

Emily was holding the phone to her ear. Her heart was somersaulting in response to the sudden buzz of her ring tone. She took a deep breath.

'Hello?' she said. She tried to steady her voice. There was a delay as if she were on a transatlantic call. 'Hello?' she said again.

'Hello, this is Dr Mason's secretary.' The voice was louder this time.

'I need to speak to Dr Mason,' said Emily. 'I'm having a reaction to some medication and I need to speak to him.'

'Who's speaking please?' The secretary sounded bored. She sounded as though she couldn't quite be bothered.

Emily squinted at the time in the top right-hand corner of the screen. 20:47, she read. The secretary had probably been hoping for a quiet evening.

'Emily,' said Emily. 'He said that I should phone him. He made me promise.'

There was a pause at the end of the line. Then, 'I'll see if I can get a message to Dr Mason. Can I call you back on this number?'

'Yes,' said Emily and the secretary rang off.

Emily rested her head against the wall and shut her eyes again. She slid her phone back into her dressing gown pocket and put her hands on her knees, feeling them burn as skin touched skin.

She jumped awake to the sound of the doorbell. Blood roared in her ears and her heart was flopping like a stranded fish. She could see a shadow outlined against the front-door glass by the orange glow of the street lamp. Emily sat very still, hoping it would go away.

The doorbell rang again, tearing through the silence. The shadow stood back from the door and Emily imagined the person looking up, scanning the house for light or movement. She took her phone from her pocket; it was dead. Slowly, leaning on her right hand, she rose. Her legs were stiff and cold and she stood breathing heavily for a moment before she walked one step at a time down the stairs towards the front door. The shadow stood, outlined in the glass.

Rebecca decided she may as well open the door. It was dark but she didn't want to sit shuddering on the stairs waiting for the person to go away. It was probably . . . someone she knew.

Cyrus Mason was standing on the doorstep. He jumped back slightly as the door opened, then stepped forward into the dark hallway.

'God, Emily,' he said. 'You frightened the life out of me. You shouldn't creep about in the dark like that. Where's the switch?'

Cyrus put out his hand and the hall flooded with light. Emily stood still, dazzled and shocked. What the hell was he doing here? How did he get here? She took her phone out of her pocket and stared at the blank screen.

'Come.' The doctor took her elbow and steered her into the sitting room. He crossed the darkened room and flicked on a table lamp. 'Sit,' he said.

Emily sat down on the sofa and Cyrus, looking around, drew up the tapestry chair that she and Sam had brought back from France the previous year.

'I was on my way back from a . . . meeting, a thing, at this end of town,' said Cyrus. 'My secretary phoned me and said you sounded odd. I couldn't get you on your mobile. Are you alone?'

Emily nodded.

'Are you OK? What's happened? You've never rung me before.'

Emily stared at him for a moment. 'What time is it?' she asked.

Cyrus pushed back the sleeve of his coat. He was wearing a grey wool car coat. He looked at his watch. 'Ten-twenty,' he said. 'So, what's going on? Why are you all alone, creeping about in the dark?'

'You told me to phone you if I needed to. I didn't think you would come here to the house.' Emily still couldn't quite believe her eyes.

'I told you. I was passing. I just happened to be nearby. I had a meeting at the hospital just down the road.' Cyrus rested his forearms on his knees, leaning towards her, maintaining eye contact. 'You're having some kind of reaction, aren't you? Have you stopped taking the pills I gave you?

I did tell you not to stop without speaking to me first, didn't I? You promised.'

Cyrus smelt of outside; of the crisp early autumn night. His dark hair was damp and he had taken off his glasses and was holding them by one arm in his left hand. Emily had never seen him out of context before. He seemed different, much less big.

'That's the point,' said Emily. 'I phoned to ask if I should stop taking the blue pills. They are making my skin hurt and . . . ' She took a deep breath. 'Why are you here?' she ended miserably.

Cyrus sat up in the chair and put his glasses back on. He steepled his fingers, narrowed his eyes and examined her. 'I'm going to stay with you,' he said, 'You can stay there and I will stay here, until someone arrives home to be with you.'

'No one's coming,' said Emily. 'No one's coming all night.'

Cyrus let out a long sigh. 'Oh, right,' he said quietly, almost to himself. Then, 'Can I make a pot of coffee? Do you want a cup? Where's the kitchen?'

Cyrus stayed all night. He found the cafetière, he ground the beans and he came back into the sitting room where he had left Emily hunched on the sofa.

'I've brought you this,' he said, handing her a blanket. 'It was on the chair in the hallway. And coffee. It's black; I don't know if you take milk.'

Emily took the blanket and wrapped it around herself, drawing her knees up to her chin. Cyrus put the coffee down on the low table in front of her and sat down again in the tapestry chair.

'When will I stop feeling like this, Cyrus?'

'You will stop feeling like it, I can assure you, but prescribing these drugs is far from an exact science. I wish it were. The thing you have to learn, Emily, is that how you feel is distinct from how things actually are. For instance, you said your skin was burning, but it's not, is it? Not really.'

Emily looked at her forearms. She stretched her arms out in front of her and turned them in the lamplight. They were perfectly normal.

'No,' she said.

Cyrus stood up and handed her a coffee. 'Drink this,' he said, 'Drink it and concentrate on the taste and the heat and the feel of the mug in your hands.' He picked up his mug and sat back down in his chair.

Emily began to talk. She told Cyrus how Kit and Annie and she had buried Scruples in the garden and how they had been crying so much that they could barely speak to one another. She told him how Kit had said it was ridiculous and that he'd said, 'What would I do if you died if we feel like this about a dog?'

Cyrus said nothing.

'We put Scruples' favourite treats into the hole with her. We wrapped her in her blanket and covered her with nasturtium flowers,' Emily said.

'Why was she called Scruples?' asked Cyrus.

'She had none,' said Emily. 'She told tales on Pomp when he licked the butter by barking at him. She wasn't allowed on the beds but, whenever we went out, she would go straight upstairs and curl up on one and when we came home, she would be back in the kitchen like lightning, leaving a dog-shaped nest where she had been sleeping.'

'Why is the cat called Pomp?' asked Cyrus.

'We had two kittens called Pomp and Circumstance but Circe went missing two years ago so now we just have Pomp.'

'How's your coffee?'

Emily drained the mug and noticed that her hands were not so shaky.

'It's good,' she said. 'Are you going soon?'

'No,' said Cyrus. 'I'm staying here. Just here.'

Emily watched him settle back in the French tapestry chair. He rested his big head on one of the wings and the lamplight hit the side of his face.

'It's very difficult,' she said, 'to understand that one's sense of reality is so skewed. I didn't know that all the things I believed, leading up to January, were wrong. I really thought that everyone would be better off without me.'

'And now?'

'Now I question my thinking more often. I ask myself whether the things I think are true or whether I am, perhaps, giving these thoughts a meaning that doesn't belong to them. It's difficult when I get physical reactions though. If you feel physically terrified, then it's hard to imagine there is nothing to be afraid of.'

'But you have insight, now,' said Cyrus. 'How's the burning?'

'Much less. Cyrus, you can't just stay there all night. I can go to bed in a minute.' Emily pushed her hair back from her face and looked at him. His face was impassive, the dark, straight brows above his shadowed eyes betrayed nothing.

'I'm staying,' he said. 'You shouldn't be alone.'

He stayed until Rebecca had fallen asleep on the sofa, then he made himself some more coffee in the kitchen. The house was beautiful, he thought. There was a huge vase of Michaelmas daisies on the big kitchen table and a dresser stood against one wall full of patterned, vintage crockery. Paintings hung on the white walls and French windows looked out onto the dark garden. Cyrus thought of his 1930s flat in Maida Vale, of the blond parquet floor, the Eames furniture, the carefully selected prints on the grey walls and the bitter silences, and he sighed.

He sat in the tapestry chair until the dawn filtered through the curtains and the street lamp switched itself off, then he stood up and walked quietly from the room, closing the front door after him with a gentle click.

Rebecca puts down her pen and closes her notebook. She sits back against the headboard of her bed and thinks for a moment, then she opens her notebook again and begins to write.

Boundaries, she writes, cannot always be reinstated, once they have become blurred or broken. Experience can carve too deeply into the psyche, forming paths and expectations that cannot be easily denied. One cannot retrace one's steps. She thinks of Hansel and Gretel. They couldn't go back because the birds had eaten all the breadcrumbs; she couldn't go back because . . . she imagines herself turning round in a dark wood; behind her are the clear marks of her passage to this point. Couldn't she just retrace her steps? No, she doesn't think so; she doesn't think she wants to.

She stops for a moment, chewing the end of her Biro, wondering what she is getting at. The early sun slides through the curtains branding the floorboards with slices of gold. Outside, a robin throws his soul into the morning air. She takes a deep breath and lets the peace of the sleeping house envelop her.

No one will care, she writes. They never do.

PIECE 28

Rebecca studies Titus Glass sitting at his desk, so neatly and quietly in control, and she minds. Last time she'd seen him, she had been quite bonkers. She wonders if it's possible to come back from that or if he will think she's a mad woman from now on.

She hands him a printout on a piece of paper.

'What's this?' he asks.

'I wrote it all down, the last meeting we had. I know I wasn't making sense so I wrote it all down so you could read it.'

Titus glances at the paper. 'I don't say, "What on earth?"' he says.

'It's fiction,' says Rebecca.

'But it isn't, is it? Are you writing a book?'

Rebecca shakes her head. 'I just wanted you to . . . oh, I don't know. I think I'm a bit mad.'

Titus raises his eyebrows. 'You know you should be in hospital, don't you?' he says.

'I don't know why I should,' says Rebecca.

Titus begins to explain something to her but she stops listening. She watches his face; he is quite absorbed in what he is saying, she thinks. She notices that he ties his tie with a Windsor knot. Today his tie is silk and has a paisley print. He isn't wearing his mother-of-pearl cufflinks; he is wearing garnets.

Garnets! scoffs Betty.

'Consequently . . . ' says Titus.

'Thus,' says Rebecca.

Titus sighs. 'Mrs Wise, what are we doing?'

'Simplifying. Can you call me Rebecca?'

'Obviously I can but nonetheless my point stands . . . Rebecca.'

'It usually does but I didn't hear what you said.' Rebecca had stopped listening to the words and had concentrated on the quality of the voice.

He frowns. 'I'm sitting here, right in front of you, with three feet between us. How is it that you didn't hear? Perhaps, rather, you didn't understand.'

Rebecca thinks she had been listening, but she had been listening to the voice rather than the words. Titus has a very distinctive voice because it is so anonymous. Most people she knows could be recognized by their voices. Titus could not. It is mid-toned, without accent, without verbal creak and thus is distinctly indistinct. Such a voice must be a very useful tool, thinks Rebecca.

'I would have understood,' she says. 'I *was* listening but could you say all that again, Titus?' She sees that the doctor minds her using his first name and, obscurely, it pleases her.

Titus Glass folds his arms.

'No,' he says. 'I could not and you have to tell the truth.' He chucks his pad onto the desk beside him.

146

'I'm not telling lies,' says Rebecca. 'Do you think I tell you lies?'

'I think telling lies is over-stating what you do. I think, however, that you obfuscate, you avoid answering questions and you continually try to take control of our sessions.'

Fair enough, says Betty.

Rebecca says, 'I'm taking all these pills, aren't I? I'm doing my best. I mean, you must know that whoever walks through that door is going to be a bit more complicated than average so couldn't you just run through the main points of whatever you just said again so I have the gist of it?'

'No,' says Titus. 'I could not.'

'You're so intractable. Can't you be a bit more accom-modating? I mean . . . ' says Rebecca, who knows she means something. 'You must know I am trying to cooperate.'

'You didn't stay in the hospital.'

'You know I couldn't. I didn't have any stuff with me.'

The doctor sighs. He pushes a hand through his tidy cap of brown hair and it springs neatly back into shape, Rebecca feels herself recoil. Neatness in men is anathema to her. Sam is specifically not neat.

Titus peers at her over the top of his glasses.

'Mrs . . . ' he says.

'Brian,' she interrupts.

'OK, Rebecca.'

'These pills make it very difficult for me to concentrate. Normally, I'm good at concentrating and one of these pills is fucking me up.' Rebecca puts a hand over her mouth. 'Sorry,' she says. 'It's removed my edit, too.'

'How was your edit before you were on medication?'

'I find this unbearably intrusive,' says Rebecca. 'I don't know you.'

'Look, this isn't some drinks party where you and I present ourselves in our best light and go away, relieved that we haven't blown our cover.'

'Unless we have,' says Rebecca.

'Do you feel as though you have?'

'Of course I have. I've leaked the blackest parts of me all over the floor and you're wading about in it all, cherry-picking. I feel very judged.'

'That's not what's happening and I am not judging you.' The doctor turns and picks up his black fountain pen from his desk and holds it by both ends. 'You have to trust me,' he says. 'It's important. I care about you, as I do all my patients.'

'Why should I? I don't normally go around trusting people I don't know.'

'You have very little choice.' He puts down his pen on the desk and removes his glasses. He puts them beside the pen and regards her for a long moment.

Rebecca looks back at Dr Glass, Titus Glass; the doctor assigned to her until her discharge, until she is quite well again.

Once, when she was a child, Rebecca had picked a bumble-bee from a clover flower and squeezed it between finger and thumb until it had died. It had stung her but it had died. Rebecca looks at Titus and decides to squeeze.

'Titus,' she says. 'Titus, are you a twin?'

The doctor sits up and folds his arms across his chest again.

'Why do you ask?' he says.

'Are you one though? I find twins fascinating. Are you one?'

'It's none of your business and I'm not here to fascinate you.' Titus is becoming annoyed.

'You have a very narrow head.'

Rebecca had told Sam that Titus Glass could squeeze his head through park railings had he a mind to. It wasn't true but Sam was suspicious of the whole psychiatrist thing, even though he'd arranged it himself, and Rebecca used humour to placate him. Sam was very proud of his own broad brow and wide Russian cheekbones.

'Actually,' says the doctor, 'I don't have a particularly narrow head. It's no narrower than anyone else's. Now, could we get back to the point of your being here?'

Rebecca is not to be diverted.

'I thought it might be because you're a twin,' she says.

'Because they have narrow heads?' Titus pinches the bridge of his small tidy nose.

'They might do.'

'They don't.'

'They might though.'

'They do not.'

'How do you know?'

'Because I'm a doctor.'

'Is your twin a doctor, too?'

'Rebecca . . . you're doing precisely what I have just said you do in our sessions.'

'I *am* not. I'm just interested. Are you and your doctor twin identical?'

'If you continue with this, I'm leaving the room.'

Rebecca smiles. 'But I thought I was meant to talk to you.'

'Well, at the moment you're not.'

'Have you changed the rules?'

'Rebecca, be quiet.'

'I'm trying,' she says.

'The thing is, you aren't, and we—' Titus pushes up the cuff of his shirt to look at his watch '—are out of time. I'll see you on the tenth. Write that down or you'll forget.'

She fishes for a pen and her notebook with the elephant on the front from her bag. She draws a smiley face emoji.

Rebecca lets herself out of the hospital and hears the door clunk behind her. She stands, for a moment, breathing in the cold, blue air of Borough High Street. She decides to walk to Southwark Cathedral. She steps down onto the pavement. The ground feels unexpectedly slick beneath her feet, like oiled glass. Rebecca hesitates and puts a hand out to feel the reassuring solidity of the bricks behind her. Messages shoot up her arm, from her fingertips to her brain. 'Rough, cold, hard,' they tell her. She can feel her toes curling up inside her boots.

Broken feet, bound feet, club feet, she thinks. She reaches out and grasps the handrail next to the step. Her fingers close tight. Don't let go, they say.

PIECE 29

It was Rebecca's birthday party. She was standing at the kitchen table in front of a red Habitat calendar, which said April at the top. She was wearing a brown striped dress and no glasses. She was looking straight at the photographer, smiling a happy, gappy smile. The pendant lampshade had obscured half her face but the photographer had taken the picture anyway. Rebecca supposes that the photographer had been her father.

There was a birthday cake on the table, small and brown with the candles lit. Around the table sat her brothers and a girl. The girl had straight long brown hair and was wearing an Alice band. Rebecca doesn't know who she is. She is guessing that she knew at the time but now she doesn't. The girl is not Harriet.

At the end of the table stood Pen. Pen had her long dark hair tied back in a ponytail and she was wearing a pink jumper and pale-pink trousers to match. Pen had turned her head to face the camera. Her eyes looked large and startled in her white face. Rebecca thinks she looked sad and was trying to look happy.

Rebecca turns the photograph in her hands. There is nothing written on the back of it. She turns it again to look at the picture. She imagines that this must have been her ninth birthday. She wonders why Harriet isn't there. It's strange, she thinks, how this piece of paper retains a memory that she has lost. It's also difficult for her to understand why she, as a little girl, had felt so awkward and uncomfortable. She was a very pretty little girl with slanting dark-blue eyes and tumbling golden curls that hung below her shoulders although, obviously, in this picture one could only see one blue eye. Maybe it was her eighth birthday, thinks Rebecca. The back of Giles's head is in the way of half the cake so she can't count the candles.

Rebecca can't remember when children usually lose their front teeth but she thinks it's before they are nine. She peers harder at the calendar to read the year, pulling her glasses away from her nose to magnify the numbers. Oh, she must have been seven. That's why Harriet isn't there. She didn't know her then.

Rebecca suddenly recalls a cuckoo calling far away but she doesn't know when. She has a feeling that she had been by herself.

Grime had shown her a cuckoo once, sitting fatly in a blackbird's nest deep in a holly bush.

'But where are the blackbird's eggs?' she had asked him.

'The cuckoo hatches first and then kicks all the other eggs out of the nest,' Grime had told her.

Rebecca remembered looking down and seeing a sad scattering of bright turquoise eggshells against the trunk of the bush.

Why was she thinking about cuckoos? She was looking at a picture of a birthday party, discovered a few minutes earlier between the last pages of *Jane Eyre* and thinking about cuckoos. Why? She must be completely potty.

PIECE 30

RE: Rebecca Wise
DOB 23/04/1965

DIAGNOSIS:
    Generalised anxiety disorder – severe.
    Major depressive disorder – severe.
    Cluster B and C personality traits.

MEDICATIONS:
    Hifatlatrine 15 mgs.
    Dulsexatine 60 mgs.
    Collapsetine 140 mgs.

PLAN:
To remain abstinent from alcohol.
To continue current medication.

Mrs Wise continues to improve, which is lovely to see. She is abstinent from alcohol. However, today she mentioned the onset of abdominal pain located along her costal margin

that feels like acid. She also has a bitter taste in her mouth.
I wonder if perhaps this may require further investigation?

Rebecca reads this and runs her tongue across her dry lips. She has just learned a new word – 'costal' – and she is experiencing a new sensation: stomach pain.

Great, she thinks.

She is sitting on the sofa in the sitting room with her laptop open. Emily, she thinks, is probably braver than her or maybe she's just less inhibited. Rebecca believes that had she been born better looking she may well have been less inhibited herself. Emily, she decides, had been born better looking.

Emily has shining dark-red hair and sapphire-coloured eyes. She is like Dolly Parton's Jolene, with ivory skin and a smile like a breath of spring or . . . something.

Anyway, however you look at it, Emily is more self-assured than Rebecca.

She begins to write.

'These fun drugs you've prescribed have made me almost entirely unresponsive.'

'In which way?' says Cyrus.

'Like a lump of marble.'

'What sort of lump of marble?'

'Oh, I don't know, Michelangelo's *David* for instance.'

'He has rather disproportionately large hands, as I remember,' says Cyrus. 'And is a depiction of a male.'

Emily looks at her hands. That morning she had painted her nails a pearlescent pink. Her nails look nice, she decides, also her hands appear to be in proportion which is a good thing and they are not clambering about with a mind of their own, which is another good thing.

'I was trying to think of something quite attractive that is made of marble,' says Emily. 'The *David* was the first thing that came into my head. I hope you're not going to start analysing me about that.'

'You could have said the *Venus de Milo*,' says Cyrus reasonably.

'She hasn't got any arms,' says Emily, stretching hers out in front of her, 'and I have, you see.'

'So you have,' says Cyrus. 'And if I'm following you, and to be frank I'm not at all sure that I am, you are having trouble . . . you are unresponsive to . . . ?'

'Yes.' Emily sits up straight in her chair and folds her arms.

'Are we, perhaps, talking about sex?'

Emily is breathing very carefully through her nose. She must not let Cyrus tip her off balance. She is a mature and confident woman. 'We are,' she says.

'You could have said, "as unresponsive as a lump of wood", rather than Michelangelo's *David*,' says Cyrus.

'Mm,' says Emily, 'but I think I've developed a superiority complex since I stopped drinking. I've been out so many times and noticed how stupid and red in the face drunk people are so, in comparison, I think I'm rather fabulous. You've caused an enormous amount of damage now I come to think about it. Maybe I should take up vodka again.'

'I doubt that that would improve matters.' Cyrus reaches behind him and picks up his pen and his notepad. 'Can you be any more explicit?' he says.

Rebecca shuts her laptop with a snap. She doubts she'll get that far with Titus. Anyway, she won't today because, today, she's not going to address the sex issue and if she *has* to talk about sex to Titus, she might die.

Which would be ironic, giggles Betty.

Rebecca has had nothing to eat today because everything tastes like earwax. She wonders how she knows what earwax tastes like, then she stops wondering. The earwax taste comes from a new pill. The acid pain comes from a new pill. She knows this but she can't imagine persuading Titus. She takes a bus to the hospital.

'How long is this going to take? How many months?' Rebecca is feeling cross. She doesn't like the open-ended nature of this process.

'How long is a piece of string?' says Titus.

'Don't do that.'

'What?'

'Clichés.'

'Listen to me, this isn't . . . it can't be a silver bullet.'

Rebecca stares. 'You're literally doing it on purpose now. What actually is a silver bullet? I mean I've always thought silver bullets had to do with werewolves. I'm not a werewolf. This whole thing isn't a werewolf.'

It's an elephant, whispers Betty. Rebecca turns to remonstrate but she's gone.

'What was that?'

'What?' asks Rebecca.

'Are you still hearing voices?' Titus, she sees, is sitting forward watching her closely.

'No,' says Rebecca. 'My mouth tastes of . . . ' she nearly says 'earwax' but heads herself off at the pass and says 'dandelion stalks' instead. Then she realizes this won't mean a thing to Titus. 'And I still have a stomach pain,' she adds.

'Detail,' he says. 'Why are you so endlessly entangled in detail? I imagine you think it gives you more control but, you know, what you should be looking for is less control. Hand a bit over, see what happens.'

Rebecca thinks that if she hands over any more control she could be officially recognized as a robot. She shakes her head. 'If we are going to use clichés, if that's what we're doing—' Titus raises his eyes to the ceiling '—if that's what's going to happen, I would like very much to draw your attention to the expression "the devil is in the detail".'

'Touché,' says Titus. 'Well done, do you feel any better now?' He picks up his pen and removes the lid.

'And,' says Rebecca, 'I feel as though I am captaining a tea-clipper, running down-wind in light airs and that all the crew have abandoned ship.'

'Very good.' Titus swivels in his chair to face his computer. 'Do these images just come to you or do you practise them on the way here?'

'Which images?'

'That one . . . the one where you say you have no idea whether you are on foot or horseback. The other one, I believe, had something to do with a jack-knifed lorry. You know you do this to evade questions, don't you? You know that, all this time, you have almost entirely avoided facing or even looking at what brought you here and that if I push you, you push back twice as hard. That you ask me where I live or if I'm a twin and you must know, that I know, that you don't care about any of those things. You're just evasive. You do know that, don't you?'

Rebecca opens her mouth to speak and then closes it again.

'Maybe we're getting somewhere.'

'Because I shut up?'

'It's a change.'

'You're rude. I'm just a person sitting in front of another person asking him to help her and you won't.'

'I will if you let me.'

'You poison me.'

'So, you don't trust my clinical judgement. You've decided that I am too young, tidy, urban or something or other, to help.'

'Funny,' Rebecca says.

'And for your information, I'm none of those things.'

'I don't care if you are. I don't care if you're all of them.'

The doctor considers her for a moment. Rebecca wishes that he wouldn't do that and she sits as still as she can but her eyes dart around the room.

'And you're thinking what?' says Titus.

Mind your own business, thinks Rebecca. 'Nothing,' she says.

'I think you are thinking something,' says Titus.

Rebecca glares at him.

'It's not my job to mind my own business,' says Titus. 'Your business is my business as far as this—' he gestures to himself and then towards her '—is concerned.'

'I'm going,' says Rebecca, standing up.

'Do,' says Titus. He is sitting very still. His face is expressionless.

Rebecca stands outside the hospital. Her head is thumping. How does Titus do that? How does he know what she's thinking? It's uncanny and it's unnecessary. It's a trick. She is sure it is. He's one of those face readers. He's a Chinese face reader.

Rebecca looks up and down the street. The wind is chill and the traffic at a standstill, belching exhaust fumes. She can smell the river underneath the smell of petrol and hot metal.

A man crosses the zebra crossing. He looks neither left nor right and a taxi slams on its brakes with a screech. The man, small and Asian, his hair blowing in black feathers over his large forehead, turns left towards the hospital. Rebecca thinks that maybe he is a patient, maybe a member of staff. She waits on the hospital steps, clutching the iron railing in her left hand. The man stops at the bottom of the steps and looks up at Rebecca. He is holding a John Lewis bag. It appears to be empty.

'Land is always on the mind of a flying bird,' he says to Rebecca and then he is gone.

PIECE 31

Rebecca is sitting on her bed at home. She has her laptop open and she is writing. Pomp is stretched out at her feet. Despite the wind thumping against the sash windows, she feels very peaceful.

Emily sits in the doctor's consulting room, writes Rebecca.

'So,' he says, 'how've you been?'

Emily looks him up and down. He is wearing a grey-checked waistcoat with notched lapels over a dark-green shirt. His Harris tweed jacket hangs on the back of his chair. Emily bites her bottom lip.

'What?'

'Are you going as a cowboy?' says Emily.

'Going?'

'Wherever you're going next. Have you got a hat?'

'Emily . . .'

'Cyrus?'

'What?'

'Have you got a horse?'

'So I assume by your general demeanour that you're fine.

All good. Taking your medication like a good girl and feeling quite cheerful. Am I correct?'

'I feel quite normal but I fell downstairs,' Emily tells him. She tries to concentrate on his socks but she's finding them rather entertaining too.

Cyrus takes off his glasses and narrows his eyes. 'Why?' he says.

'Am I looking at your socks? Well, they are red and green. It's not Christmas.'

Cyrus puts down his pen and turns his chair to face her. 'Did you fall downstairs?'

'Yes, I just told you I did.'

'Why then?'

'Because I was looking at my laptop and wearing socks, normal-coloured ones, and I slipped.'

'But you're OK?'

'No, I'm all bruised. My ribs hurt but I saved my laptop, which is the main thing, and I'm not screeching.'

'Actually, you are,' says Cyrus.

'Well, I was a bit early so I bought a coffee on the way here and I had to drink it quite quickly, so I'm a bit screechy but I wasn't before the coffee. I'm feeling very strange though, rather too up, if you see what I mean, and your waistcoat might be the last straw.'

'No coffee after midday, I've told you that. In fact, I believe I've told you that repeatedly.'

'I've turned my mobile phone off, that's obedient.'

'No coffee,' says Cyrus, 'and I don't want obedience. You're not a dog.'

'I love it when you're prescriptive,' says Emily.

Cyrus writes something on his pad. 'I know you have a tendency to giggle things away but I'm serious.'

'But is your waistcoat?'

'What's wrong with it? It's new.' Cyrus looks down at himself. He has left the bottom button of his waistcoat undone, which is quite correct but he is wearing a signet ring and a wedding ring, which is not.

Tell him, says Betty in Emily's ear. Emily shakes her head.

'I thought you had to be called Laurence Llewelyn-Bowen before you were allowed notched lapels on waistcoats.'

'Well, clearly and demonstrably you are wrong,' says Cyrus, 'and don't ruin it for me; I was liking it. It's new.'

'Sorry,' says Emily. She stretches her fingers as wide as she can. 'Can I go now?'

'Have you enough Tranquiltolam and enough Dulsexatine for the next two weeks?'

'I haven't got any. I gave up the Dulsexatine three weeks ago.'

Cyrus puts his head in his hands, then looks at Emily again while tearing a page from his prescription book. 'Why on earth would you do that without consulting me?'

'I told you I couldn't put up with it and you wouldn't listen so . . . '

'So you just stopped? Cold turkey?'

'No, thanks, I'm a pescatarian.'

Cyrus chucks his pad back down onto the desk. 'I give up,' he says.

'Please can I have a prescription for Tranquiltolam? I'm

still taking that and the Collapsetine. I've got lots of it but I'm still taking it.'

Cyrus sighs and picks up his pad.

'How's the writing going?' he asks, handing the prescription to Emily. 'Does Sam read it?'

'It's going well. The trouble is, you absolutely refuse to do anything interesting and I have to make the whole thing up, which takes way longer than reportage. Can't you be even a bit nutty so I have something to write? You're far too grounded.'

'If I were grounded, I wouldn't make a very good psychiatrist, would I? I wouldn't even make a good doctor; one needs a level of empathy, you know.'

'So you're not?'

'Not very, no.'

'So you don't have a bastide town and a motorway in your head?'

'I don't believe so, no. Although, obviously, it would help if I had the slightest idea what you were talking about.'

Emily reaches into her bag and pulls out her elephant notebook. 'Can I borrow your pen?' she asks.

'What have I done?' Cyrus asks. He is trying not to smile.

'Been interesting,' says Emily. 'Revealing.'

Cyrus hands her his fountain pen.

Emily writes. 'Thanks, that was very useful,' she says, handing the pen back.

'Why do I feel that there's something rather the wrong way round going on here?'

'Because there is,' says Emily. 'Remember, I'm awfully bright.'

'Did I say that?'

'You did,' she says.

'I really must be more careful.'

'You must,' says Emily.

PIECE 32

Rebecca had asked all the children to come for supper. She wanted them to know how well she was and she wanted to mend her relationship with Kit. Abigail had forgiven her for her horrible behaviour, she thought, because Abigail forgave everyone, but of Kit she was less sure. Annie, she felt, had almost forgotten about the whole incident.

She'd been peeling potatoes at the kitchen counter with Abigail beside her. Annie and Kit were playing a game on the computer upstairs and Sam had promised to come home early from work. It felt as though things might be returning to normal. It would be, she hoped, a happy family gathering.

Rebecca remembered a long-ago family mealtime. It was unusual because her mother and father were at peace. Maybe they hadn't always been rowing; maybe she had misremembered.

The family were all sitting together in the garden in Suffolk. It must have been a special occasion, perhaps a birthday. They sat on a rug spread on the lawn and she could picture a glass jug of lemonade, a cake and Giles sitting on their mother's lap, holding a big red rubber ball.

Rebecca's family, the Kellys, had been Irish originally but

none of them remained in Ireland. They left long ago during the famine. She remembered that her father had been discussing this. He was propped up on an elbow, wearing a blue shirt with rolled-up sleeves, his dark hair ruffled by the wind.

It was like looking at a photograph, a moving photograph, she thought.

'They left or they died,' David told his children. 'If some brave great-great-great-granny of yours hadn't picked her man out of the pub and packed up her children and her house and got on a boat, none of you would be here, not one. You should all be grateful to that woman.'

'So they went to Cornwall?' Alex asked.

'Maybe they did, maybe they went to Wales first. We don't know, but you should be proud to be Irish. The Irish are fighters and survivors and it's where you get your pretty hair from, Rebecca.' Rebecca blushed with pleasure. Her father rarely praised her and never her appearance.

'I thought we were Cornish,' said Martin.

'You're half Cornish,' said Pen quietly. Her family had fished the deep green waters of the Fal and farmed the rich soil of the Roseland Peninsula for generations.

'But it's the ones that move on that make a difference. Steel is forged in fire and it is risks that reap rewards,' said their father. 'Like us moving here to Suffolk. If we'd just stayed living in Cornwall, we'd still be in that tiny cottage, all squashed up together instead of in this beautiful place.' Rebecca could picture him sweeping his hand out to indicate the wide green garden and the long, low timber-framed house.

Now, Rebecca picked up a potato and deftly began to peel

the speckled golden skin with a sharp paring knife, revealing the firm white flesh beneath.

Abigail had just arrived home from a trip to Dublin and was telling her mother all about it. Rebecca had never been to Ireland.

'I was in a taxi going to the airport,' Abigail said, 'and the driver asked me if I got my red hair from my Irish ancestry. I didn't want to get into Dad and all that Jewish thing, so I just said, "Yes."'

'So, what's your name?' the taxi driver had asked.

'I told him Kelly,' said Abigail, 'and he said, "Aaah so you'll be the bastards that took the soup."'

'What does that mean?' asked Rebecca.

'He said that we'd dropped the O, you know like in O'Connor or O'Reilly, which meant we'd taken the soup from the English to feed our children. He said that's why we were in England at all, because the Irish wouldn't accept us after that. He said we were worse than the Ulster Scots.'

'Bit rude,' said Rebecca, tipping chopped onions into the pan on the hob.

'No, he was being very funny,' said Abigail.

'I'd do it again,' said Rebecca, recalling, as if the memories were her own, the ditches piled high with blighted potatoes, putrefying, where the good, clean harvest had lain.

Abigail picked up a knife and stood next to her mother, peeling carrots. 'Do what again?' she asked.

'Take the soup.'

Abigail slid her eyes sideways towards her mother. 'I know you would,' she said.

PIECE 33

'Mrs Wise.' Titus is standing in the doorway of the waiting room. He doesn't smile. 'Follow me,' he says. Rebecca follows. He stands aside at the door to his consulting room, ushering her in ahead of him. Today he is wearing a black suit with a blood-red tie. The tie has a Medusa motif at its widest point. Versace, thinks Rebecca.

Titus sits down behind his desk and scrolls through something on his laptop. This is unusual. Titus must have moved deliberately, to put the desk between them.

'Sit,' he says, without looking up from his computer screen.

Uh-oh, I'm in trouble, something's just come along to burst my bubble, thinks Rebecca. She sits.

Titus stops doing whatever he is or isn't doing. He sits back in his chair and folds his arms across his chest and looks at Rebecca. 'So?'

'What have I done?' says Rebecca.

'You tell me,' says Titus.

'Umm, not much,' says Rebecca. 'I got Pawel to put up a shade sail on the balcony. I wrote an awful lot. I had a very happy birthday, yesterday. Thank you for asking. We went to see the Vanessa Bells at the Dulwich Picture Gallery. I've been to Charleston so—'

Titus puts his hand up to silence her. 'I'm referring to your medication,' he says. He looks at her over the top of his glasses, then he pushes them up onto the bridge of his small neat nose with his forefinger and Rebecca shrugs. 'Nothing,' she says.

Titus runs a hand through his hair. 'That's not true, is it?' he says. 'Why have you stopped taking your Cryazatine without first discussing the matter with me?'

'Oh that,' says Rebecca. How does he even know? she thinks.

'Yes, that,' says Titus.

'It made me screech,' says Rebecca. 'It made me want to take down the screeches with alcohol and it made me wonder why you had prescribed it for me.'

Titus picks up his pad. 'Meaning?' he says.

'Did you wear that outfit today specially to tell me off? I have to say, it's frightfully menacing.'

'I don't choose my clothes with you in mind, no,' says Titus.

'Oh good,' says Rebecca, 'because, what with the Medusa and the black . . . '

Titus sighs. 'Stop it, Rebecca,' he says.

'Well, you started it,' says Rebecca.

'I invaded Poland?' says Titus.

'I love it that we share so many cultural references, but no, I was going to say that you prescribed me a really foul drug that obviously didn't suit me. You seemed determined that I should keep taking it despite what I believe you would call clear contra-indicators. So, you started it.'

'So you thought you had better stop it?'

'Yup,' says Rebecca. 'I began to question your motives.'

'Why do you think I might have wanted you to stay on Cryazatine? I did tell you that the chances of recurrence of depressive illness is high in patients who stop taking prescribed anti-depressants within a year but you appear to be implying something else. What exactly are you saying?'

'Your interest, your field of study, is functional somatic syndromes, isn't it?'

Titus folds his arms more tightly across his chest, then he unfolds them and rests his hands lightly on his desk. 'Yes, and?'

Like a book, thinks Rebecca. Really Titus would have been better served to have paid more attention to body-language studies. 'You are also interested in striatal motivational salience, aren't you?'

'You have no idea what you're talking about, do you?' says Titus.

'I think I have a rough idea,' says Rebecca.

'Not good enough,' says Titus. 'Now if you would like to get to the point . . . ' He looks at his watch. 'I have a very busy afternoon ahead of me.'

'I think that you realized, quite early on in our acquaintance, that I'm not very ill. I think that maybe you were interested in my tolerance of a drug, which is almost exclusively used to treat fibromyalgia . . . '

'If you knew how paranoid you're beginning to sound, you would probably stop this right now.' Titus stands up. 'Mrs Wise, whatever you may imagine to the contrary,

I am not a monster and at no point have I used you as a guinea pig. Now, I'm very busy, so . . . ' Titus walks over to the door.

'I'm not going yet,' says Rebecca. She puts both her hands on the arms of her chair as if she believes that Titus might leap across the room and attempt to forcibly eject her. 'I want you to tell me why you wanted me to take Cryazatine so badly and why you are so upset that I stopped.'

Titus turns and looks at her. 'I thought, I genuinely thought that it would help you. I think it was helping you. I can't imagine why you don't trust me.' He leans his back against the closed door and briefly closes his eyes. He opens them and looks at her. 'Why don't you?' he says.

For the first time since she's known him, Titus appears to have dropped any pretence.

Rebecca sees that his face is pale, that there are dark shadows under his eyes. He looks vulnerable and exhausted.

God, she thinks. What am I doing? 'I'm just so confused,' she says.

'What do you find confusing? Which bit? I'm your doctor. You are ill. I prescribe medication. You refuse to trust me. I am on your side, you know.' Titus is still leaning against the door.

'The part where the more you do something you don't like doing, the better you will become at it. That pill was driving me round the twist. I didn't want to get better at taking it.'

'It most certainly wasn't,' says Titus. He walks across the room and sits behind his desk again. He pushes his glasses up onto his forehead, puts his head in his hands and grinds the heels of them into his eye sockets. Rebecca feels a sudden rush of empathy for him. He looks up at her.

'Is there any chance, do you think, that you are wrong, that I thought Cryazatine may have been helping you and that I had no other motive than that? Why don't you trust me?'

'I don't even trust me,' says Rebecca. 'I trust myself with other people's well-being but not with my own. Why would I trust anyone else?'

Titus shakes his head wonderingly. He says nothing.

'What about the people who steel themselves for an experience they can't bear and then steel themselves to repeat it and find it equally difficult? How many times are they supposed to have a go? How do they know that repeatedly experiencing something horrible isn't consolidating it? Piling it up until it becomes too much, until it becomes something they must avoid at all costs and in all circumstances?'

'You're talking about Cryazatine?'

'Oh Titus, of course I am. It was too much. I couldn't bear it.'

Titus looks at her for a long moment.

Rebecca cannot imagine any other situation in which she and Titus would have made any connection. Each would have dismissed the other, she is sure of it; yet here they are, eyes locked. She talks about Titus a lot, to friends and to family. She is sure he doesn't talk about her at all to anyone.

'When you first came to see me, you were afraid of me. You said so repeatedly. How do you feel about me now? Apart from exasperated, obviously.'

'It wasn't actually you. I was afraid of what you represented. I'm not exasperated. I'm confused.'

'Do I not still represent all that stuff?'

'What?'

'Whatever it was. Authority, getting up in your grill, space-invading, whatever else you want to call it?'

'No, but you still can't expect me to trust you.'

Titus takes off his glasses and puts them on the table beside him. 'Why?' he asks. 'Haven't you become used to me and to what I do? Honestly, have I let you down?'

'Yes, no, I don't know. I'm literally incapable of trust. I do like you, though. Can you imagine that? It must hardly ever happen.'

Titus almost smiles. 'To me in particular or to psychiatrists in general?'

'You.'

'Why me? Am I repulsive?'

'You know you're not.'

'So why me especially?'

'Because of your armour; the suits, the elaborate politeness, the weird classless voice, the glasses used as a prop . . . all of it. You keep people at arm's length. You mean to.'

Titus pushes his hands through his hair again. He rests his elbows on his desk and turns for a second to look out of the long sash window. It is a late summer day with high white clouds and shifting shadows. When he looks back at Rebecca, he looks much older.

'I don't keep people at arm's length, but as I have explained before, a professional distance is essential in order for me to do my job properly. And I will tell you again, I am on your side, I have no ulterior motives and I wish you would believe me.'

'Cryazatine made me feel like a hamster, in a cage, on a wheel, on crack,' says Rebecca.

Titus smiles. 'There she is,' he says.

PIECE 34

Harriet and her family lived in a large Georgian house three miles away from Rebecca's. The house, approached along a gravel drive flanked by paddocks, was tall and pantiled. It was washed yellow and had a bottle-green front door. From the gloom of the lofty hallway, a grand galleried staircase led to the upper floors. To the right of the hall was the kitchen breakfast room and, to the left, a huge drawing room, and beyond that a snug.

Outside, the garden encircled the house in a wild green embrace. Yew trees studded the lawns where a small flock of red hens scratched for worms. A weeping willow grew far too close to an ancient, crumbling A-framed barn and the borders groaned under the weight of hydrangeas, hollyhocks, lupins, clumps of iris and weeds. Beyond the barn was a large pond upon which Aylesbury ducks idled.

Miranda, standing in the kitchen, drew on her cigarette and looked out of the window. 'I have a gardener,' she said, 'but he's worse than useless, what?'

Rebecca and her family were visiting for the day. Her parents sat at the large oak kitchen table after lunch, drinking red wine. They had eaten jugged hare with mashed potato and red cabbage followed by apple crumble. Rebecca had only eaten the vegetables because she thought hares were too beautiful to eat.

'But Rebecca, darling,' Miranda had remonstrated, 'Milo shot it with an air gun, up in the top paddock; it was dead anyway.'

Rebecca had shaken her head. 'No, thank you,' she'd said, but the kitchen was full of the wonderful scents of gravy, herbs, wine and juniper. Miranda was a very good cook.

Earlier Harriet had shown Rebecca around.

In the barn she kept a pony called Ambrose. He was a small bay with a white star on his ill-tempered little face.

'Don't touch him, he bites,' Harriet had told Rebecca, swerving his snaking head as they'd walked past his stall. 'You can't ride him, he's too difficult for beginners. I'll ride him later on, if you like. He has a huge jump.' She'd gestured towards the stacked hay bales at the further end of the building. 'We have to hunt for the hens' eggs in there,' she'd said. 'They hide them in the hay, then they sit on them. Of course they'll never hatch. We don't have a cock.' Rebecca had paused for a moment, breathing in the musty darkness, the slanting shadows and the silence. Behind her Ambrose had snorted.

'Stop wool gathering,' Harriet had said. 'It's nearly lunch-time.'

Wool gathering? What's wool gathering? Rebecca had thought. She knew she was supposed to ask, so she didn't.

Now Harriet made two glasses of Ribena, filling them from the kitchen tap, and Rebecca listened to the adults talking.

'Well, why are you putting up with him?' Rebecca's mother asked.

Miranda took another cigarette from her packet, lighting it with the stub of the previous one and let the smoke trail from her nostrils. 'Oh, Patrick's rather a sweetie,' she said. 'It's youth really, you know, the *energy* levels? I find that terribly attractive, if you see what I mean, what?'

Rebecca's parents laughed. `

'Come on,' said Harriet, passing Rebecca a glass of Ribena. 'Come and see my bedroom.'

Harriet's room overlooked the barn. Faded crewelwork curtains hung to the lime-washed oak floorboards and a rug the colour of sunshine lay next to her tall brass bed, which was stacked high with pillows, rag dolls and balding teddy bears. A cream-painted armoire took up one wall and against another, on a low table, stood a doll's house, the front of which hung open revealing a chaos of tiny furniture and mismatched dolls. Rebecca walked slowly towards it.

'Don't touch that,' said Harriet, 'It's antique.'

PIECE 35

Rebecca is lying in bed next to Sam. 'You have to tell him,' he says. 'I know it will be embarrassing but you have to.'

Rebecca feels her face flush at the thought. 'If it was the other way round, you wouldn't tell a doctor.'

'I wouldn't *want* to,' Sam agrees.

'No, you just wouldn't. Can you imagine? "Oh, by the way, Dr Thing, my penis has gone all peculiar and non-functioning. Any suggestions?" Anyway, maybe we could do something about it. Perhaps we could do something different. Maybe it'll be better in France. Perhaps we're too tired.' Rebecca hopes this is true.

'I don't mind for me, I really don't, but it's not normal, not for us, is it? Am I pressurising you? Is that it?' Sam sounds very stressed.

'No, you're not. You just wouldn't. Maybe I'm pressurising me.'

'It was fine before you started taking these pills and it says in the directions that if you experience sexual dysfunction that you should tell your doctor. It says that, doesn't it?'

Rebecca breathes slowly in through her nose. She doesn't answer.

'Maybe this is a sign that you shouldn't be taking them.'

Along with all the other signs, she thinks.

'I don't mind. I mean, I do a bit but there are worse things.' She does mind though; she minds quite a lot. She and Sam haven't had any sexual issues before now and she has always been secretly pleased about how high functioning her body is. It had babies, it never had a bad back, it had put up with everything she had thrown at it over the years . . . except SSRIs. 'I've probably got too much serotonin. It's probably ruining my vagus nerve or something,' she says vaguely. She had read somewhere that one's vagus nerve is very important for mental health and that eating lentils or similar made one's vagus nerve happier. She really wished she didn't have so much crap in her head.

'What are you talking about? What's a vagus nerve?'

'I don't really know,' she says. 'It's a thing I read about somewhere and it can feel things.' Rebecca props herself up on one elbow. 'I just can't quite get there.'

'You're nowhere near,' says Sam.

Rebecca lies down again. She wonders if it's psychosomatic or idiopathic then she thinks she really must stop Googling things.

'It's that ridiculous brain doctor of yours. He's probably doing some study on sexless marriages and divorce. He's probably lecturing on it at this very moment to a load of gaping students.'

Rebecca picks up Sam's arm and looks at his Apple Watch

glowing in the dark. 'It's twenty to one, so I don't think he is,' she says.

'Well, I think you should talk to him.'

Rebecca lies on her back and blinks into the inky dark. She says nothing. Soon she hears Sam's breathing change to a low rhythmic snore and tears begin to trickle out of her eyes and back into the pillow.

She is afraid to sleep. Her eyes are sore with the lack of it, the lids heavy and red during the day, flinching against sunlight and aching to close each afternoon, but her dreams are too terrible.

'My dreams are horrific,' she'd told Titus last time she'd seen him. 'Why are they? I've never watched a horror film. I can't see how I make these things up. How can I?'

'You're welcome,' he'd said. 'The dreams are almost certainly a side effect of your medication.'

'I'm not thanking you. I'm afraid to sleep. Why am I having such revolting thoughts? What's going on in my head?'

Titus had considered her for a moment. 'Well, anything to do with the brain . . . ' he'd said.

'I don't so much wake, as surface.'

'Surface?'

'Yes, I'm sort of tossed onto the shore of the morning like a shipwrecked sailor, dragging the remnants of my dreams like entrails.'

'Gosh, did you make that up?'

'That's what I'm saying, does one make anything up?'

'How do you mean?'

'Can one, I mean?'

'I'm sure *you* can.'

'Did you like it?'

'I liked the entrails, but on the whole I found the image rather overblown.'

'You don't have my dreams. Titus, I don't watch horror films. How can I come up with such gruesome imagery?'

'Why don't you watch horror films?'

'They're horrible and they would get stuck in my brain. You know when you accidentally put your hand in dog poo?'

'No, but go on . . . '

'I mean, if you did?'

'It wouldn't happen.'

Rebecca knew it wouldn't. 'The point is, you could wash it off,' she'd said, fixing him with a fierce stare. 'If it's in your brain, it's there forever.'

'Dog poo?'

'It's an analogy.' He was being obtuse.

'Of course I understand your point. It's a bit scatological but I do understand. You do know it's the drugs, don't you?' he'd said.

Now, Rebecca thinks of diving into a filthy swimming pool to save a drowning anorexic. She can feel the girl's bones sliding between her desperately clawing fingers and swims to the bottom of the pool to find only bloodied bobbing breasts. She thinks of Titus lying on a therapist's couch in a room lined floor to ceiling with ancient crumbling books and parchment scrolls while moth larvae munch through his fine woollen suit and burrow into the white skin beneath his crisp ironed shirt.

'Are they really that bad?' Sam had asked.

Rebecca had nodded. 'Offensively so,' she'd said, 'even when I'm awake sometimes.' That afternoon, she'd been in the kitchen washing up her coffee mug when she had been quite sure that the flesh had melted from her hands and that her skeletal fingers were scratching at the stainless steel beneath the soap suds. Pulling her hands from the water had been a mammoth task. She had stared at her pink, flesh-covered fingers for a good two minutes to ensure they were solid.

The sleep paralysis dog had been bad but things had developed.

Spiders swarmed in the dark.

The devil, a seven-foot-high, goat-footed, horned manifestation, carried a child, its face contorted with wide-eyed malice, into the abyss.

Her body bulged and exploded hot guts.

A baby, unexpectedly slippery with blood, slid from her grasp into the mouth of a great grinning frog.

Every night she awoke with a hammering heart, wet with sweat that dried rapidly in the warm summer nights leaving her shivering in damp pyjamas.

Normally, she decides not to try to going back to sleep. Now she leans over and kisses Sam's head. 'I'm just going downstairs,' she says.

PIECE 36

As the day wears on, Rebecca becomes more and more restless. She had woken at six. Today she has to see Titus. Sam has already gone to work. Rebecca hates seeing Titus; that is all there is to it. There are so many problems attached. How to get there, bus, Tube, taxi, drive? What to say when she does get there. 'I'm fine. I'm not fine. I sweat all the time. I feel useless in bed with my husband. Can I take less of this pill? Can I take none?' Or any of the above.

She gets out her laptop and sits on her bed, propping it on a pillow in front of her.

'So, how exactly do you experience this compromise that you describe?' Cyrus Mason leans back in his chair, steepling his fingers, she writes.

Emily watches him. He tilts his head, waiting. Not how *roughly* but how *exactly*, she thinks. 'I'm very bad at being exact,' she says.

'But you can try,' says Cyrus.

Cyrus has crashed in through her front door, made himself a cup of tea, rearranged her sofa cushions and now he is in her bedroom, rifling through her underwear drawer and he wants to know '*how exactly*'. Emily feels compromised.

Rebecca leans back against the headboard and takes a deep breath. Did everyone respond to Titus like this, she wondered, or was it just her?

Emily decides that Cyrus is stupid, writes Rebecca. Then she realizes he isn't, then she understands that he knows precisely what he is doing.

'I don't want you to know what you know,' she says. 'I don't like you knowing that I cry, that I'm confused, that I'm afraid, that I became ill.'

'Me in particular or anyone?' says Cyrus.

'You, you're not my friend, you're not my family. I have a front to keep up and you keep pushing it over and trashing it.'

Cyrus smiles. 'Do I?' he says. 'I don't mean to.' He looks as though he doesn't care.

You, you in particular, thinks Rebecca, closing her laptop.

She decides to drive to the hospital. At least her car has air conditioning. Outside, the sun is strafing the streets with shards of heat that bounce off the dusty pavements and the stucco-fronted houses. The plane trees are shedding curled brown leaves and the sycamores spitting sticky sap onto the cars beneath them. Even the blackbirds have given up singing and now they tetchily chirrup warnings to one another instead.

Rebecca doesn't know where her car is. She had lent it to Kit and now he is stubbornly refusing to answer her texts or to pick up his phone. She decides to walk up to Hawksmoor Road where Kit usually leaves it. Hawksmoor is the nearest road to his flat within her parking permit area.

Rebecca double locks the front door and steps out into the heat. She scans the road, crosses it to avoid the workmen in high-vis jackets who are digging a mega-basement under the house on the end. They always seem to be in the midst of some kind of technical crisis and spend an inordinate amount of time shouting into their mobile phones or sitting on the pavement holding their heads in apparent despair. Rebecca thinks it likely that, at some point, the entire terrace will collapse into a vast chasm.

A wave of sweat washes over her, and her Ray-Bans slide down her nose. Her entire face is wet. What kind of pill did that? How could that be helpful to anyone? Having thought that, she thinks that perhaps it was, instead, the menopause suddenly deciding it was time to launch a proper assault, rather than the odd mood swing or griping headache or perhaps it was just the relentless pounding heat of the city. She rings Kit again but there is no reply.

Her car isn't on Hawksmoor Road. The nursery is just releasing its inmates as she arrives and she dodges whizzing scooters and yummy mummies, two abreast, pushing their Bugaboos. She presses her key fob at a few black cars that look likely, but none are hers. Why do all cars look the same? What is the point of that? Cars, thinks Rebecca, are proof that there is no such thing as evolution in nature. If there was, all animals and birds who live in similar environments would look the same, too. How could a blue-footed booby be the result of evolution? Blue feet were pointless, gaspingly useless and, in some circumstances – here Rebecca's thoughts become less acute – probably a hindrance. Yet male boobies' feet were overwhelmingly blue and the bluer they became and the more the booby waved its feet about, the more likely it was to secure a mate. Explain that to me, you bloody scientists, she thinks savagely. Then she thinks about Titus and she knows that were she to ask him, he would explain it to her with inarguable clarity, and that she would understand and that it would be irritating. She decides not to ask him about evolution when she gets to the hospital.

She turns and heads back towards home, tapping out Kit's number on her mobile one more time. He answers.

'No, I've got the day off. I worked all weekend,' he tells her. 'I left the car about three doors down.'

'From home?' asks Rebecca. A bus thunders past, whipping up dust and leaves in its wake.

'From home?' she asks again but Kit has been cut off.

The car is where Kit said he had left it. Rebecca has twenty minutes to go before she has to leave for her appointment and she lets herself back into the cool shade of the house, fiddling with the Yale to release the lock. That's going to need looking at, at some point, she thinks. I'm going to get locked out one of these days.

Upstairs in her bedroom, Pomp sleeps stretched out on the unmade bed. Rebecca looks in the mirror and another wave of heat hits her, dampening her scalp. She drags her hair back into a ponytail, grabs a clip from her bedside table and clips it up onto her head. The sensation of it sticking to her neck is unbearable. She looks in the mirror again. She supposes she looks reassuringly un-mad, which is a good thing. She feels almost unmanageably unhinged. At least now, she knows where the car is and at least she has enough time to cross the river and get to the hospital, leaving the obligatory half an hour extra that she will need to find a parking space.

'Dr Glass?' says the hospital receptionist when she walks into the waiting room. 'Take a seat. I'll tell him you're here.'

Rebecca sits in the corner of the room. Her stomach rumbles because she has forgotten to eat again. She spends a lot of time forgetting to eat. Eating, she has decided, is optional for the time being and probably best avoided. Sam and she have been invited to a party at the end of September. The invitation demanded she wear something glittery. Rebecca hasn't anything glittery so she will have to buy something and buying something means being stupidly thin or else she will look like a glitterball. So for now, eating is off the menu.

Opposite her, sitting next to a sleek air-conditioning unit, is a woman with a bloated, pallid face. Her limp, colourless hair is dragged back in a ponytail. It is difficult to guess her age. Rebecca is worried that if she keeps taking medication that she, too, will become a remnant.

The woman is eyeing Rebecca with unabashed interest. Rebecca stands and walks out of the room. She reads a leaflet about a meeting for the families of long-term patients at the hospital. She walks along the passage to the hospital entrance and then turns and walks back into the waiting room. She flexes her hands and counts her fingers, then takes a seat out of the eye-line of the woman. A wave of heat hits her and she feels beads of moisture form on her upper lip.

The receptionist's phone buzzes. 'You can go up now,

Serena,' says the receptionist and the woman lumbers to her feet. Rebecca wonders if, perhaps, it is helpful to look so ill if one is ill or if it just makes things worse.

'Rebecca.' Dr Glass is standing beside her, smiling his interested smile. 'Come with me.' She hasn't seen Titus for three weeks. When she does actually see him, sometimes he is more nerve-wracking than she imagined and sometimes less. Today, she thinks, as she takes a seat, he isn't too bad. He looks friendly and she thinks she might be able to evade all the questions and perhaps get her way about some of the pills.

'So,' says Titus, 'what's the problem? You look as though there might be one.'

Rebecca drops her bag from her lap to the floor. 'Why?' she says. 'Why does it look as if I have a problem? I mean, I know I have a problem but what am I doing that makes you think I have a specific one right at this moment?'

'Don't you?' Titus puts on a concerned expression.

'I'm a bit . . . it's all just a bit . . . '

'Have you mucked about with your dosages? Have you been sticking to them?'

'I've been taking all the pills, in exactly the way I'm supposed to, but I don't like this anti-depressant. It disables me. I just feel a bit flat that's all. I don't like this pill. Can I take less of it?'

Titus sighs. 'That,' he says, 'is entirely illogical.'

Rebecca widens her eyes. 'How?' she asks.

'You feel flat and disabled so you want to take less of an anti-depressant? I would be inclined to suggest more. How are you disabled? Explain.'

'I sweat.'

'It's very hot outside.'

'No, it's random. I suddenly get all sweaty for no reason.'

'You have hot flushes?'

'No, I mean, how would I know? I've never had a hot flush. How would I know if it was one or not? What do hot flushes feel like?'

'I've never had one either, believe it or not.'

'It's that pill,' says Rebecca.

'How are you disabled? Not by feeling sweaty, surely? I really can't help you if you won't explain what seems to be the problem?'

'Seems, madam? Nay, it *is*,' says Rebecca. 'I know, not seems.'

'All right, if you insist, what *is* the problem?' Titus Glass has very little Shakespeare.

Rebecca pushes a hand through her hair. 'I can ski, I can ride a horse well, I can swim, at a push I can do plastering.'

Titus puts his head on one side. 'So, how are you disabled?'

'I feel all wobbly. I feel weak. I just feel as if I can't do things. I can't do things I ought to be able to do.' Then she decides to derail the conversation. Titus is too interested.

'Have you got a bicycle?' she asks.

'Have I got a bicycle? Why? Where did that come from?'

'I just wondered if you had a bicycle; you look like a MAMIL.'

'MAMIL?' he says.

'You know, Middle-Aged Man In Lycra.'

'Can you imagine me in Lycra?' He is wearing a beige

lightweight summer suit. The jacket is hanging on the back of his chair and he is wearing an ironed white shirt with his amethyst cufflinks.

'Anyway, the thing is, I've had three babies,' says Rebecca. 'I mean, I work. I know my brain is a bit whatever, but physically, I worked before I took this pill. Now I don't.'

'How? And what do babies have to do with it?'

Oh, for fuck's sake, Rebecca thinks. Then she says, 'Sam preferred me on Hifatlatrine.'

'It would be very odd if you had another baby.' He looks at her quizzically. Rebecca wishes he would just try, so she wouldn't have to spell it out. 'Why did Sam prefer you on Hifatlatrine?'

'Sex,' says Rebecca. And it's like jumping off a diving board. She feels her face flame. 'I'm not saying any more. It's too awkward.'

'So, you don't want sex or you can't have sex?' says Titus.

Rebecca looks at the floor. 'What's the difference?' she says. 'Why can't you just give me HRT instead?'

'I'm not qualified. You don't have to have sex if you don't want to, you know.'

Rebecca does know. 'So why can't you?'

'Prescribe HRT? It's not my area of expertise.'

'You're a doctor.'

'Thanks for noticing. Now what exactly are we talking about here? Are we talking about orgasm? Could you sometimes reach orgasm before you took this pill and now you can't? Are you sure it's the pill, not just Sam being a bit, well, useless? Is there nothing he could do to improve things?'

Rebecca drags her eyes up off the floor and looks at Titus. What on earth could he be suggesting? She certainly isn't going to ask him, she decides. Imagine if he had some ideas.

Then she says, 'It's not Sam. I could before and now I can't.'

'Always?'

Rebecca drops her head. What does he mean by always? Why not always? Imagine if she thought he only orgasmed sometimes. Just because I'm a woman . . .

A middle-aged woman, says Betty.

OK, not a young woman. Why does *that* mean that she doesn't want sex, doesn't know she can say no to sex and only sometimes orgasms? She knows without raising her eyes that he will be looking all interested and switched onto the subject.

'Yes, always,' she says.

She can almost hear his silent whistle of disbelief. She looks up at him. Titus has taken off his glasses and is holding them in his right hand. Her face is burning. He turns to his computer. 'I could add more Dulsexatine to your prescription,' he says. 'This might be stress related.'

'I won't work if you keep adding things. Why are you always adding stuff instead of taking it away?'

'It's not a question of your "working".' Titus makes speech marks in the air. 'You shouldn't be feeling this kind of pressure. You are unwell and a side effect of the medication that is improving your mental health has caused a certain amount of sexual dysfunction. I think, on balance, that your husband should be more understanding.'

Rebecca sighs. Titus is always rifling about in her relationship with Sam.

'You're always rifling about,' she tells him. 'And it's not Sam putting pressure on me; it's me wanting to be who I am, rather than some drugged-up facsimile.'

Fatsimile, laughs Betty.

'What on earth does that mean?'

'You need to stop poking me, I don't like it.'

'I don't poke, I challenge. You have some very entrenched thinking that you *should* question. Sex is not all about orgasm, you know.' Rebecca can hear the smile in his voice.

Rebecca is still looking at her pink Kenzo trainers. She snaps her head up to look at him. He ducks his, to hide the smile. She doesn't know why she lets him get away with it.

Silly, says Betty.

It might be silly, thinks Rebecca, and if I wasn't me sitting here, I might think it funny, but I am here and it's not.

'Mrs Wise,' says Titus. 'Are you or are you not under pressure to somehow perform in bed?' Again, he uses his fingers to form speech marks.

If she is any more explicit she thinks she might die of embarrassment. Titus is determined that Sam is some kind of useless-in-bed sex pest. 'No, I am not under any pressure. I am in a long-term relationship which, prior to all this garbage I've had to wade through, was sexually fine and now it's not. Please can we stop talking about it?' she says. 'There's obviously no point so please?'

'I don't respond to begging,' says Titus. Then he reaches behind him and picks up his prescription pad. He writes and he hands the piece of paper to Rebecca. 'A present for Sam,' he says, smiling. Sometimes Titus is literally beyond toleration.

Rebecca walks back to her car. She sits in it for a moment before starting the engine. It is overwhelmingly hot. She pulls her Ray-Bans out of her bag and pushes them up her sweaty nose. She turns on the ignition and the air conditioning whoops into action. On the passenger seat beside her is a prescription. Dulsexatine 30 mgs, it says.

'I'll see you at two on Monday,' Titus had said as she'd left. Outside the hospital, she'd stood gasping on the pavement for a minute and then she had thumped her palm hard on the hot bricks beside the door.

As she drives home, Rebecca ignores the satnav. For some unknown reason, it's speaking French and she hasn't had the energy to sit with the car's handbook on her lap to change it back to English. She doesn't need the satnav anyway because she's going home in the manner of a homing pigeon and she will get there.

She negotiates jumbles of Japanese tourists looking at their phones as they cross roads. She watches a snake of Germans, in trainers, wearing knapsacks, queuing outside the Museum of London and realizes she must be lost.

'*Tournez à droite et après continuez tout droit pour cinq kilomètres,*' says her car, bossily, in a Parisian accent.

'You're mad,' she tells her car. 'This isn't Paris. Are you sure you've got the right map?'

'*Faire un demi-tour où possible,*' replies her car.

'Now you're just being inconsistent,' Rebecca says. She

turns left. Islington is nearly always left unless she goes to Shoreditch when it's nearly always right. She hardly ever goes to Shoreditch in the car though because there is nowhere to park, ever.

'*Prenez le deuxièm chemin à gauche et ensuite, prenez le premier à droite,*' says her car audaciously.

Rebecca turns off the satnav. Ha! I'm going to *prenez*, whichever route I like, she thinks. It is a small victory but a victory nonetheless. Rebecca wishes all people had an off switch.

'Are we talking about orgasm?' she hears. She wishes her brain had an off switch.

PART II

FRANCE

PIECE 37

Rebecca got on the plane to France without an alcoholic drink. Annie took her to a coffee shop at the airport. 'It's really cool here,' she told her mother. 'They only employ boys, really good-looking boys.'

'I think that's illegal,' said Rebecca, looking at the boys. All of them looked about fifteen.

'In London, they only employ really, really good-looking boys,' said Annie. 'Once I ordered a medium latte and I was given a large one.'

'The one who served us was quite sweet-looking,' said Rebecca. She sipped her flat white. It was disgusting. Rebecca thought for a moment about a large cool glass of Chardonnay. Then she remembered the last time she had a large cool glass of Viognier at Annie's party and decided to drink her coffee. She drank it with a Tranquiltolam.

Sitting on an aeroplane sober was surprisingly very much like sitting on one while slightly drunk. Annie kept up a steady stream of chatter to distract her mother as the plane took off but Rebecca didn't feel particularly bothered. She supposed it must be the Tranquiltolam taking effect, but she also supposed that being drunk while doing something one didn't really want to do was unlikely to make one feel vastly better anyway. The thing about being Rebecca, Rebecca decided, was how relentlessly stupid she was capable of being.

She sucked a breath of foetid aircraft air into her lungs and looked over the shoulder of the man sitting next to her at the world spinning far below. France was spread out like a green and gold patchwork quilt. The man next to her put his hand on her arm.

'*Avez-vous peur de voler?*' he asked. '*J'ai quelque-chose qui va vous-aider.*'

Rebecca said nothing but watched as he took a white leather box from his jacket pocket. He opened the box to reveal a sugar lump, which he handed to Rebecca. Underneath was a small screw-topped bottle about one inch high. He took it from the box, opened it and, indicating that Rebecca should hold out the sugar lump, he poured the clear liquid onto it.

'*Tenez,*' said the man, smiling sweetly. Rebecca looked at his friendly, lined face. At his grey curls and then down at the sugar lump in her palm.

'*Ça vous aidera,*' said the man. Annie was deep in a game on her phone. Rebecca ate the sugar lump.

'I cannot believe you did that.' Annie was furious. 'Why would you do that? It could have been anything.' They were at Bergerac Airport.

'I think it was alcohol,' said Rebecca.

'Why would you, though? Imagine if I'd done that, you would have gone mad.'

Annie and Rebecca had left the plane and walked out

across the single runway to the terminal building. A warm southerly wind was blowing and the sky was dotted with the kind of white fluffy clouds that children draw. They queued and showed their passports. A notice at the entrance to the terminal said:

Nous nous excusons pour tout retard à cause des contrôles de sécurité accrus à cet aéroport en raison de la menace terroriste et nous vous remercions votre compréhension.

There was no delay. Rebecca imagined that attacking Bergerac would be a doddle; in fact, she thought she would be able to attack Bergerac Airport with a wooden spoon all by herself. But as soon as they left the building, she saw two Gendarmes armed to the teeth with machine guns held across their broad French chests and handguns rammed into their rather attractive leather holsters.

'Oooh, robocops,' said Annie.

'Shush,' said Rebecca. There had been similarly armed police at Stansted Airport when they'd left England but then, as she'd passed them, Rebecca heard one saying to the other, 'I know, absolute nightmare, and you should have seen the queue at Lidl on Saturday. It took me forty minutes and I only went in there for some Liebfraumilch,' which she'd felt rather spoiled the effect.

Michel picked them up. Michel was the gardener and caretaker at the French house they had rented. They had been renting it for years.

'Go to France, Becky,' Sam had told her. 'Take Annie and go. You know how the whole thing works and at least you'll be away from London.'

As Michel loaded the two suitcases into the boot, Rebecca felt the warmth of the sun on her face and she knew that Sam had been right. Michel took off his baseball cap and kissed Rebecca and Annie on both cheeks. '*Ça va?*' he said.

'*Bien merci, très bien*,' said Rebecca, climbing into the car beside him. As they drove, the Dordogne countryside unfolded before them like a green silk scarf.

Thirty minutes later, they arrived at the French house, which stood foursquare, facing the forest, under a sky the colour of bluebells and Rebecca felt the silence seep into her bones.

'*Le frigo ne marche pas*,' Michel told Rebecca as they drove. Rebecca glanced in the rear-view mirror and saw that Annie was looking out of the car window at the fields of sunflowers and the tall black tobacco barns and realized that she didn't care about the fridge. She smiled across at Michel, who looked rather stressed.

'*Pas de problème*,' she said, and she felt that, for once in a very long time, she was telling the whole truth.

At the house, the car thermometer read 40°C.

'Forty,' said Rebecca, showing Annie. 'I have to go to pay M. Legrange the rent,' she said. 'Do you want to come with?'

'To Velines?' asked Annie.

'*Oui*,' said Rebecca.

'*Non*,' said Annie.

'*D'accord*, I'll have my mobile on me but if anything happens, go to Francois.' Francois was a neighbour.

'Like what?' Annie asked, wrapping her towel around her rolled-up bikini in preparation for a quiet afternoon by the pool. Rebecca got into the car. She was wearing denim shorts and the seats were so hot that she had to sit forward so the vinyl didn't burn the skin on the back of her thighs.

'Earthquake, hurricane, pervert, dog attack,' said Rebecca.

'Trust me,' she heard in her head and she nodded.

'What did you say?' said Annie. She had put her towel under her arm and was watching her mother as she put her foot on the clutch and pressed the ignition button on the dashboard.

'Nothing,' said Rebecca and she reversed out of the drive, leaving Annie standing on the gravel in the white haze of the early afternoon.

That evening, Rebecca walked to the end of the field beyond the swimming pool. Michel hadn't cut the grass recently and Rebecca curled her bare toes into the soft turf and breathed in the wild mint and purple flowering thyme as she crushed it underfoot.

A blackbird sang, sweet and low.

The field beyond had been left fallow and was a haze of poppies and daisies. The colours smudged at the dark line of trees that edged the forest. Rebecca focused her eyes and saw the tiny shapes of two roe deer, heads up, alert to her presence even at this distance. It's like a Seurat landscape, she thought. Or it might just be that my eyes are unused to horizons. Then she realized that they were filled with tears of relief and wonder.

A green-striped hammock hung between two hornbeams. She lay in it and watched the leaves shift against the blue sky and fell asleep.

When she woke up, she found Annie still by the pool.

'Listen,' said Annie. 'I think I heard a hoopoe.'

Rebecca wrote a list. '*On a besoin de beaucoup des choses*,' she told Annie.

'Like what?' said Annie.

'*Des DVDs, de l'eau gazeuse, du fromage, du pain . . .*'

'We can watch Netflix,' said Annie.

'*De tout façon, beaucoup de choses*,' said Rebecca.

'Stop speaking French; you're murdering it,' said Annie.

'Just practising,' said Rebecca and she wrote on her list.

On the terrace, all the pot plants were dead, even the rosemary plant had given up and turned wizened brown spikes up to the pellucid sky. The grass was still green but the leaves on the cherry trees drooped long and copper-edged. Rebecca resolved to replace the pot plants and nurture them through the summer so when the year turned, they would be strong enough to survive the winter.

'You won't even be here to see,' said Annie.

'I like to imagine it,' Rebecca replied. So she stood in the field and imagined.

In the evenings, the muntjac deer barked warnings. During the days, the hunting red kites called to each other as they wheeled overhead and the sun went down every night behind the fields of sunflowers, but the nights were still bad.

At night, drenched in sweat, Rebecca dreamed of children hacking limbs off one another with machetes; of tidal waves and hurricanes and of the dog that lay across her body, paralysing her.

One night, she dreamed a cold, hard hand gripped her by the foot and dragged her down the bed. Rebecca felt the fingers, tight on her instep, her leg pulled straight and the damp sheet beneath her rucking as she slid. She was unable to move but, as she lay there, she heard a voice hiss into her straining ear, '*Qu'est-ce que tu fais ici?*'

'I knew that if, when I opened my eyes, I actually was at the foot of the bed, that we would have to go home,' Rebecca told Annie the next day.

'And were you?' said Annie.

'No, I was lying with my head on the pillow, just as I had been when I went to sleep.'

'Oh, good,' said Annie. 'It's spooky though.'

Rebecca told her about the dog.

'That's an urban myth,' said Annie.

'What's an urban myth?' Rebecca was chopping up plum tomatoes, warm from the sun, in the kitchen. A neighbour had come round with a basketful.

'*On en a trop*,' he'd said, but Rebecca knew it was a welcome.

Later, she would stir them, with fresh basil and spring onions, into a bowl of steaming couscous and season with chillies, sea salt and olive oil.

'A dog that sits on your body when you're asleep and paralyses you,' said Annie.

'I knew it was a dog but I couldn't open my eyes and I couldn't move at all.'

'A ghost dog,' said Annie.

'I suppose,' said Rebecca. Annie was fiddling with the television, trying to get Netflix.

'Does that work yet?'

'Yup,' said Annie. 'We're going to watch *The Indestructible Matty Smith*.'

They sat eating couscous and drinking fizzy water and they watched Matty overcome almost everything with a big grin and a can-do attitude.

'I can put up with anything for ten seconds,' shrieked Matty happily and he counted slowly to ten. 'And when that ten seconds is up, you just start counting again, one two three four five . . .'

'I think I'm going to be sick,' said Rebecca, but she found the notion of counting to ten oddly helpful.

'Happy arms!' said Annie, throwing her arms in the air, like Matty.

'I know where you get it from but it's not so funny when someone else does it,' Rebecca told her daughter, seeing herself through someone else's eyes.

Outside, the sun dipped behind the sunflowers turning them to molten gold but Rebecca and Annie were in the kitchen smiling insanely at each other and waving their arms above their heads, so they didn't see.

Annie's friend Charlotte came to stay. She flew into Bergerac with Sam. Rebecca and Annie drove to the airport to pick them up.

Rebecca always felt France was her and Annie's special place. She understood the silence.

'You understand it,' she often told her.

'I get it. D'you get me?' said Annie.

'You get it, I get it. D'you get us?' they asked Sam, in unison.

'You're like Clarice and Cora,' said Sam.

'You're like Steerpike,' Rebecca told him. Sam was waving his phone around looking for Pokémon. 'Charlotte, you can be Fuchsia.'

'I get it,' said Charlotte, looking out at the lines of vines climbing the muscular rolling hills, 'but who's Fuchsia?'

'*Gormenghast*,' said Rebecca.

'All I can get is a Pidgey,' said Sam.

For supper they had *tarte aux oignons* scattered with rosemary leaves and great creamy lumps of goat's cheese. They baked some of the neighbour's tomatoes with whole garlic cloves and they drank pale Provençal rosé under a sky the colour of a blush.

'Mum, I thought you weren't drinking,' said Annie.

Rebecca shrugged. 'I'll be all right now,' she said. 'Sam's here.'

Rebecca wasn't all right though. She wasn't even slightly all right. She swam in the pool in the cool of the morning. She ate no breakfast or lunch. She cooked and shopped and sang along to Amy Winehouse on the way to and from the supermarket, choosing the scuffed CD from the car's glove compartment.

Sam sat exhausted in the salon and watched Netflix.

He had work to do.

'Just one interview to write up,' he told Rebecca, but it took him days.

Annie and Charlotte drifted around the pool in the heat of the afternoon while Rebecca lay in the shade of the grapevine that rambled over the pergola. She tried to read a book while watching the small grey lizards hunting flies until she fell asleep, lulled by the girls' laughter and glass after glass of wine.

Rebecca couldn't go home. It was a hopeless situation. She couldn't go back to London. She would die if she went. She didn't know how to be there.

Or anywhere actually, whispered Betty.

She couldn't go, though. Her stomach turned to concrete at the thought.

Sam shrugged. 'So what will you do? Stay here for the winter?'

At night, Rebecca poured with sweat. She drank water from a bottle on her bedside table and when her body succumbed to a drug-induced sleep, she dreamed of quicksand and death.

One afternoon, they all piled into the hot car, wound down the windows and went treasure hunting in the local brocantes, buying embroidered, hand-loomed linen sheets and admiring ancient carved dressers.

'*C'est très vieux, de l'époque d'Henri II*,' they were told as they gazed in admiration at a particularly ornate example in heavy, caramel-coloured walnut.

'It's older than God,' said Sam, turning to an astounded Rebecca.

'It's bigger too,' she said.

'That,' said Annie, 'is the ugliest thing I've ever seen.'

Sam ran his hand over the age-scarred cupboard doors and opened the drawers one by one. 'Look,' he said. 'It has all its keys with tassels.'

Afterwards, they drove to a bastide town that had been entirely colonised by the English and sat in the square eating omelettes and frites.

'It's really weird,' said Charlotte. 'Even the shops are owned by the English.' One shop stocked only English food, from Marmite to sherbet fountains with liquorice straws.

'Imagine if a load of French did this in Oxfordshire,' said Sam. 'Imagine the uproar.'

'They've done it in South Kensington,' said Rebecca, topping up her wine glass. 'Did you know, there are four hundred thousand French people living in London?'

'It's not the same, though, is it? Not when it's a country town.'

They looked around at the English with their blond hair and plump pink shoulders.

'Shall we go?' said Annie.

A week later, Sam and Rebecca took the girls to Bergerac to catch a plane home.

'London!' said Annie gleefully, as she waved goodbye.

'I do get it,' said Charlotte, 'but it's very quiet.'

The temperature was climbing steadily again into the late thirties and the stone house began to warm up.

Hunting spiders stalked the walls of the barn and the salon. When she woke in the night, Rebecca wandered through the house, saying, 'Don't look left, don't look right,' to herself. One had to be very sure where one was headed because the spiders perambulated up and down the walls with dreadful purpose.

'What did you say?' asked Sam as she swung her legs from the bed and planted her feet on the warm stone floor.

'Don't look left, don't look right,' said Rebecca.

'Stay here,' said Sam.

'I need more water. I think there's a drowned spider in my glass.'

'There isn't. I can get you more water if you like.'

'I'm too hot,' said Rebecca, standing.

'The stones have warmed up,' said Sam.

'Like a pizza oven,' said Rebecca. 'I'm thirsty because of the wine.'

'You shouldn't be drinking,' said Sam. 'Drinking isn't solving anything.'

'I know,' said Rebecca. 'But it's numbing and I have to go home.'

'You know you'll pay for it in the end,' said Titus, but she knew he wasn't there, so she ignored him.

The neighbours had their grandchildren to stay and Rebecca took them swimming in the pool. Sam listened to his music, cooked or sat with Rebecca drinking wine as the sky flamed behind the sunflowers. They were buff-coloured now with wizened stalks, their seed-laden heads bent and heavy.

On their last evening, they walked to the edge of the forest, which echoed with a heavy, autumnal silence. Brown leaves spun to the ground in the still air.

'I can't go home,' Rebecca told Sam. 'I don't know how to live there. I feel as if I'm going to die. I want to die,' she said. 'If only I could die.'

Sam took her hand. 'But darling, if you died, you'd forget me and I want to be remembered.' They were being Laura and Alec from *Brief Encounter*.

Rebecca put her other hand in his, facing him. 'It will be all right, darling, won't it?' she asked.

'It'll be fine,' said Sam. 'I'll pack. You must come back; you can't stay here. Your whole life is in London. This isn't real, you know, and anyway you have to see Titus.'

'You know I hate seeing Titus, don't you? I don't hate him. I hate that I have to see him.'

Sam pulled her into a hug. 'I *do* know, yes,' he said. 'You've been so brave about it.'

'And you know I've tried really, really hard to get better?' Rebecca said into his chest. 'And I think Titus is trying to poison me.'

'I know you've tried,' said Sam, 'and I don't think it's especially likely that he's trying to poison you.' Rebecca heard the amusement in his voice. 'But sometimes, I think, giving yourself time to reflect without actively doing anything can be a way of recovering. Just the process of getting there, the sitting down in a room with someone who is paid to listen, the talking about it might help.'

'It's not happening,' she said.

Sam pulled away from her and held her by her upper arms so that he could look into her face. 'Becky,' he said. 'Even if you never get better, I am here. I will always be here and I will never leave you. You know that, don't you?' He hugged her again. Rebecca felt safe in his arms. 'But you will get better; you just need more time. You need to concentrate on it and stop trying to live normally. Be ill if you need to be. Take to your bed if you want to. We're all here for you.'

Rebecca felt tears start behind her eyes and the creeping dread of the coming night and she said nothing.

That night, she felt a massive, late summer spider land on her upturned face as she slept, catapulting her from the bed to crouch, screaming, in the corner of the room.

'Becky, you're dreaming,' Sam told her. 'Come on, come back to bed.' He got up and hugged her. 'It's nothing.' He flicked on the bedside lamp and searched the floor. 'There's nothing here, it was a dream.'

Rebecca knew it wasn't a dream though. She lay awake until dawn with her hands clutched to her face, pressed hard into Sam's side so that the sweat ran between their bodies.

The next morning Sam packed up the house and closed the shutters against the day. As Rebecca sat shaking and drinking wine on the bedroom chair, a spider, the size of a mouse, with broken twisted legs crawled up the wall beside her.

'You hit it pretty hard then,' said Sam.

PART III

SPIDER, SPIDER

PIECE 38

During her time in France, Mrs Wise emailed me, requesting
a reduction of her dose of Dulsexatine.

Today, I had a telephone conversation with her husband.
It seems her health has deteriorated and that she has been
self-medicating with alcohol since the family returned to
London.

Consequently, I have arranged for her to be admitted to
the hospital at the beginning of September and will refer
to you again when she is discharged.

Rebecca is in hospital. She is in hospital because Dr Glass
says she has to be.

They'd been home from France for two days and Sam was
at work. Rebecca had been talking to Annie in the kitchen
when the bad feeling had started. Suddenly, Rebecca had
felt as though she was speaking with her fingers in her ears
and that everything she'd said was being repeated by a high,
mocking voice.

'It's like feedback on the telephone,' she'd told Annie. But
it was worse, she'd thought.

It's me, Betty said.

'What is?' said Annie.

'Something,' said Rebecca. 'I'll make supper. You go. Go and do some of your summer project. Phone someone. I can't talk at the moment. Do you mind?'

Rebecca had wanted Annie to go away so that she could open a bottle of wine. Her limbs were stiff from the journey home and the evening was stretching ahead of her like a piece of elastic pulled tight. Rebecca had known she was unravelling and she needed Annie to leave the room.

Annie had phoned Charlotte. She was going to art school too.

'Mum, I'm going round to Charlotte's,' she'd called and the front door had slammed.

Rebecca had gathered up her keys from the hall table. Outside, the rain had been falling, drifting in a thin veil, drenching the dry lavender hedge and the exhausted gauras in the front garden.

She'd bought some wine, four avocados and some basil from the corner shop and then she'd walked up the road to the Turkish supermarket where she'd bought some more wine and some dog biscuits. She'd forgotten that Scruples was dead.

Back at the house, Rebecca had switched on Radio 4. She'd emptied the washing machine and chopped up some onions, then she'd opened a bottle of wine. The wine had been called The Accomplice. Rebecca tried to smile at the name but her lips slid up over her teeth and gums in a grimace.

Rebecca had drunk the first glassful and had topped it up

immediately. She'd drunk the second glass and poured a third, then she'd begun to feel better.

Later on, she hadn't remembered exactly what happened but she'd thought she might die. She'd thought she should take all the Hifatlatrine and all the Cryazatine but she'd laid herself down on the kitchen floor unable to move. The blackness had pooled around her like blood.

Then Sam had come home from work. He'd picked Rebecca up from the floor and helped her upstairs to bed.

'What happened?' he'd asked. 'I phoned your bloody doctor. You have to go to hospital. He says it's the only way.'

Rebecca lay awake far into the night. She could not imagine staying in the hospital. She couldn't imagine talking to Titus about how badly she'd messed up and she couldn't imagine what good it would do. At three she'd tiptoed downstairs and made a cup of tea.

She'd watched Amanda Benson on *Escape From The City*. Rebecca generally preferred Justin Hammond to Amanda but, in this episode, when the house-hunters had said how very little they cared for a dual-aspect lounge and didn't *need* a wood-burner, Amanda had lain down on the kitchen floor and she'd said, 'Here's my dead body. Climb over it.' Rebecca had thought that quite funny. Then she'd thought, No . . . here's mine.

Then she'd gone back to bed and stared into the darkness, thinking about how horrible it would be to see Titus. Sam had drawn in great shuddering breaths and Rebecca had wished she could be better at everything.

PIECE 39

Sam drives Rebecca to the hospital. He carries her suitcase and they are shown to a room on the ground floor. It has a double bed and an en suite shower room. Briefly Rebecca thinks of Justin Hammond, then she stops herself. She doesn't want to be completely potty.

There are ironed white sheets on the bed, which has a blue suede headboard. At the end of the bed, against the wall is a grey chenille-covered chair and, next to that, a modern teak-effect table. Under the window is a pine-effect chest of drawers. Rebecca sits on the bed and a psychiatrist with an eastern European-effect accent comes to see her. He sits heavily on the chair. He is very tired. Rebecca wonders if he is really tired or if he is just being affected like everything else in the room.

'Do you hear voices?' he asks.

'Yours?' says Rebecca.

'Do you take any drugs other than those prescribed for you?' he asks.

Rebecca notices that he has quite short legs.

'How much do you drink a day?' asks the psychiatrist.

'An apple a day keeps the doctor away,' says Rebecca. If you throw it hard enough, she thinks. 'Spiders,' she says.

An Irish nurse takes Rebecca's blood pressure and gives her some vitamin B. Actually, Rebecca thinks the Irish nurse is quite nice. Sam tells her not to take all Rebecca's things away and the nurse takes her chargers for her Kindle and her phone and she takes her hair straighteners. She also takes her computer charger, her hair clips and her tweezers.

Sam tells the nurse, 'Rebecca can't really not have her stuff.'

The nurse is very sweet and tells Sam that she will make sure everything is given back to Rebecca after it has been tested.

How exactly does one *test* tweezers? asks Betty.

Rebecca can't say anything. She can feel her nerves jangling. She is shivering.

'Are you cold?' asks the psychiatrist.

'I feel like a dog that's been taken to the vet,' says Rebecca.

'We'll check you every fifteen minutes,' the psychiatrist tells her.

Rebecca says nothing.

Sam looks at his watch. 'The car parking is running out,' he says. 'I'll have to go.'

'Sam?' Sam turns round in the doorway. 'Don't tell anyone I'm here, unless you have to. Tell the children and Ellis when he's back from Greece, but don't tell my parents. They don't need to know.' Rebecca tries to imagine the humiliation of her parents visiting her here. The attendant pity and shame and she can't bear it.

'They won't know,' says Sam. 'No one will know unless they need to; I will make sure of it.'

They all go and Rebecca is left alone. She paces round the room. She throws her bag onto the chair and lies on the bed, scanning the room for spiders.

She uploads an update onto her computer. She installs Word for Mac. She tries to play Candy Crush and she listens to a group of patients talking below her window as they take a cigarette break. They drag out their vowels so that their voices are a low whine in the still air. They laugh loudly at a joke. They all sound quite mad or quite stupid.

Rebecca is worried about her brain. She decides to write everything down on her computer as evidence.

Evidence of what? asks Betty.

'Bugger off,' says Rebecca aloud. Then Titus walks into the room.

'Good afternoon, Mrs Wise,' he says. He picks up her bag from the chair and drops it onto the table. He sits down. Rebecca is sitting on the bed with her bare feet tucked under her. She shuts her computer.

'If we're going to do this . . . ' she says.

'Which we are,' says Titus.

'Can you always call me Rebecca, please? When you call me Mrs Wise, I keep thinking you are talking to someone else. No one calls me Mrs anything.'

Titus looks at her over the top of his glasses. 'I'll try but I forget,' he says. 'And you can call me Dr Glass,' he adds.

'Or, Sir?' asks Rebecca.

'*Comme tu veux*,' says Titus.

'Oh, you speak French,' says Rebecca.

'I don't,' he says. 'Tell me, now the niceties are over, what's been going on? What on earth have you been doing? I hear you were lying on the kitchen floor saying everything was awful. When was this? Yesterday? And why are you shaking like a leaf?'

Titus has a tan. His thin brown face looks relaxed after his break in . . . Tuscany, Rebecca decides. She imagines him in a navy linen shirt with the sleeves rolled up and faded red chino shorts. He has fine Achilles tendons and he wears boat shoes.

'I'm probably shaking because I'm scared of you.' Rebecca takes a deep breath and tries to stop shuddering. It's stupid.

'I love it when you say that.' Titus grins and Rebecca finds herself smiling back. He's so funny. Rebecca remembers now that this is what she likes about him but she's never sure if she is laughing at him or with him.

It's not a good reason to put up with crap, says Betty.

Then Rebecca tells him what happened. She tells him that she gets awful screeches at four o'clock in the afternoon and that she drank nothing at all for the first nine days in France, that she had been on the aeroplane stone-cold sober.

'How was that?' asks Titus.

'Fine,' says Rebecca. Then she tells him about the man and the sugar lump.

'Oh Lord,' says Titus. 'Why would you take it?'

Rebecca shakes her head. 'I don't know why I did. He was being kind. Maybe it's because I knew he was being kind.'

'Maybe he was being creepy. Thank God your daughter was

221

there. How has your medication been? Are you still taking the Hifatlatrine?'

'No,' says Rebecca. 'I think I made a mistake. I think maybe the screechiness was caused by the Hifatlatrine.'

'Still screeching then?'

'Worse than ever. Did you go to Tuscany, Titus?'

'I'm not answering that,' he says. 'And you didn't have screeches before you took the Hifatlatrine?'

'Umbria?'

He sighs.

'OK, I stopped taking the Hifatlatrine and took twice as many Dulsexatine. I thought that would work but it didn't. Puglia?'

Titus shakes his head, 'So, you thought you would alter your medication without advice and drink, I understand, copious quantities of wine just to be absolutely sure the whole thing would kick off again.'

'A spider landed on my face. It was huge. I felt its legs and its abdomen on my face. I was asleep. It frightened me.'

'In France?'

'No, in Umbria . . . Of course, in France! It did it on purpose. It was an attack.'

'Oh Lord,' says Titus.

'It did! It's something to do with electricity. They can tell you're frightened by reading your electricity. Anyway, they've taken away my hair straighteners,' says Rebecca. 'I'll have to go home.'

Titus rolls his eyes. 'They may have done but that's *not* a reason to leave,' he says. 'And spiders cannot *read* your electricity. I'm quite sure they are generally known to be illiterate.'

'I need my straighteners,' says Rebecca.

'You don't,' says Titus.

'Please make the hospital give them back. I really need them.'

'I won't be here tomorrow,' says Titus, standing up. 'But I'll see you on Thursday.'

Five minutes later, Titus comes back into the room with Rebecca's GHDs. He throws them on the bed. 'Don't say I never do anything for you,' he says and then he disappears.

Sam is coming to visit Rebecca in the evening and he is going to conceal some tweezers in his pocket.

'I'm not going to sit in a hospital and grow a menopausal beard or huge hairy eyebrows,' Rebecca tells him on the phone. 'I'm not happy about being here and I'm not going to have out of control facial hair if I have to be.'

'What?' says Sam. 'I can't hear you very well. The signal's bad.'

Rebecca repeats herself. 'I'll text you,' she tells him. 'Yes, I know the signal's terrible.' She texts.

Sam texts back that he quite understands. He says he will smuggle some tweezers into the hospital when he comes.

Rebecca can't quite believe that she's in hospital. She has never been in hospital before except to have babies and now she's in one because she is mad and nurses have to check on her every fifteen minutes. She's a bit confused about the fifteen minutes because she could easily kill herself in a fifteen-minute gap, especially now that she has her GHDs. She decides, however, to read a book instead. She pulls *Humboldt's Gift* from her bag and opens it. She may as well try to educate herself while she's here. The print is tiny.

Rebecca puts the book aside and phones Sam back.

'Titus gave me my straighteners back,' says Rebecca. 'And the nurses have stuck a sticker on my phone charger telling me it's safe.'

Sam tells Rebecca that he loves her but he can't hear her and hangs up.

PIECE 40

At six, the nurses change shift and they come to Rebecca's room to introduce themselves. Rebecca has had a shower and she has dried and straightened her hair and is sitting on her bed in her pyjamas, writing on her laptop.

'Have you any special dietary requirements?' asks one of the nurses.

'I eat fish but not meat,' says Rebecca.

'Someone will bring your food to your bedroom quite soon,' says the other nurse. 'Do you want to look at the menu?'

'I don't mind, not really,' says Rebecca.

'You mustn't close your bedroom door,' says the first nurse. 'We need you to leave it ajar. We bring your medication at about nine; is that all right for you? And we'd like to take your blood pressure.'

Rebecca wonders what would happen if she decides that she wants her supper at ten and that she prefers to keep her blood pressure to herself, but she rolls up the sleeve of her pyjama top and offers her arm.

At nine, just as Rebecca has finished listening to *The*

Archers on her laptop, a nurse knocks and comes into her room. She has a small plastic cup with five pills in it.

'What are they?' asks Rebecca.

'Vitamin B, Tranquiltolam, Hifatlatrine, Dulsexatine and Collapsetine,' says the nurse. 'We will check you every fifteen minutes.'

'All night?'

'Yes, all night.'

'You might keep me awake.'

'We won't, I promise,' says the nurse.

Rebecca hopes she will remember to ask Titus why she has to take vitamin B next time she sees him. She drinks the pills down with a glass of water and gets into bed. She falls asleep instantly.

In the morning, Rebecca wakes to find herself lying in the exact position in which she went to sleep. She is on her back and the bedcovers are tucked neatly under her arms. She tries to lift an arm but it's too heavy. She swivels her eyes around the room. The curtains are drawn and a grey daylight is creeping through the gap at the top.

There is a knock at the door. She turns her head. The door is slightly open, she notices.

'Come in,' she says. Rebecca thinks her voice sounds curiously not like her voice. Higher? Deeper? No, just not the same.

A woman is standing in the room. She is wearing a beige uniform and she is holding a tray.

'Breakfast,' says the woman. 'I'm Mary,' she says. 'Do

you want me to help you sit up?' She puts the tray down on the teak-effect table and walks over to the bed. 'Sometimes, it takes people like this,' she says. 'You get used to it, but sometimes the medication does this.' She pulls Rebecca into a sitting position. Rebecca wants to close her eyes.

'I'll be back shortly,' says Mary. 'Your breakfast is just there.'

Tell her not to call you Shortly, says Betty.

Rebecca crawls from her bed and walks barefoot across the grey carpet to the table. On the tray is a plate of brown toast, some butter in a small white dish and three tiny pots of jam. Next to that is a cafetière and a small jug of milk and a mug. Rebecca pours herself a cup of hot black coffee.

A different nurse knocks on her bedroom door – the bedroom door which she has been told must remain ajar.

'A team will come to assess you later on this morning,' she tells Rebecca.

'Team of what?' Rebecca asks. She is not very good at teams, being more of a solo artist. She always got picked last for teams at school but that was largely because she couldn't run and she couldn't hit a ball or even a slow-moving shuttlecock. Now she prefers not to associate with teams because she is sure that in her spiteful, cold heart, she doesn't care about other people as much as she should.

'A team of therapists will assess you for group therapy.'

'I'm not going to do that,' Rebecca tells her.

On the afternoon of her second day in the hospital, Titus comes to see Rebecca in her room. Rebecca has just made a very nice cup of coffee in a cafetière. She found it in a cupboard in the ward kitchen.

That morning, she'd been to Sainsbury's with a mental health nurse boy. She had tried to go by herself but the man on the door at the hospital said she had to go with someone and they sent the mental health nurse boy with her. Rebecca thought he looked about eighteen.

She'd bought eight bottles of fizzy water. She'd picked up some glass bottles but the boy said that she wasn't allowed glass. Rebecca didn't know how she felt about being restricted. She'd also bought some Colombian coffee. The boy had bought some cigarettes and Rebecca had said he wasn't allowed cigarettes but he took no notice of her and bought them anyway.

When she'd returned to the hospital, Rebecca had made herself a lovely cup of black coffee. She'd sat on her bed and opened her laptop.

Outside her window, she'd heard a group of patients laughing. They'd gathered there to smoke and laugh. She'd wondered if they were the same ones, every day.

'Why are you shaking like a leaf?' Rebecca had written.

'Because I'm afraid of you.'

Suddenly a door outside her room had slammed and she'd heard a girl scream.

'You're the fucking devil,' the girl had screamed.

'Come on, lovely, you know that's not true,' she'd heard one of the nurses reply.

'You're fucking Satan,' the girl had sobbed.

Rebecca had closed her laptop, got off the bed, crossed the room and quietly pushed her bedroom door shut.

PIECE 41

It was the summer holidays. Harriet was riding Ambrose round the paddock. Patrick the gardener had helped her to tack him up.

'Ambrose is really cowardly,' Harriet told Rebecca. 'Last week, he bit Patrick's arm so Patrick punched him and now Ambrose does everything he says.'

Patrick was stocky with shirt sleeves rolled up to reveal thick, brown forearms. He'd kneed Ambrose in the stomach and pulled the girth up tight. He'd clanked the bit against the pony's teeth when he'd put the bridle on and, turning, had picked up Harriet as if she were a kitten and plonked her in the saddle.

'He'll be good as gold now,' he'd said, clapping the pony on the rump and walking away.

Now, Rebecca sat on a five-bar gate and watched Harriet try to canter around the perimeter of the field next to Ambrose's paddock. Rebecca wished she could ride.

The field was full of long swishing grass that rippled in the breeze. It should have been cut for hay but Miranda had forgotten to arrange it. Tall poplars stood sentinel along one side of the field and a mixture of blackthorn, beech and hawthorn hedged it.

Harriet was wearing her usual jeans and gumboots with a checked-shirt that had belonged to one of her brothers. She looked like a cowboy and she rode well. Her hands were light on the reins and she was entirely still in the saddle as Ambrose cantered sideways, jibbed and chucked his head about but, underneath her crash cap, her face was set and white.

She's frightened, thought Rebecca.

'Got a lovely little seat on her, hasn't she?' Patrick was suddenly at Rebecca's side leaning on the gate with his elbow touching her thigh.

'She's good at riding,' said Rebecca. 'I would fall off if he did that with me on him.' She looked down at Patrick. His dark, waving hair was swept back from his forehead and his narrowed eyes were watching Harriet intently. Like a black cat, thought Rebecca, watching a bird.

Just then, Ambrose gave three enormous bucks, which sent Harriet sailing through the air to land heavily in a crumpled heap. Patrick vaulted the fence and ran across the field. He scooped Harriet up off the ground and carried her towards Rebecca, who stood slightly breathless with shock just in front of the gate.

'Broken something, I shouldn't wonder,' he said.

Harriet lay still in his arms. Her face was colourless and her eyes, huge, were fixed on Rebecca's with a look, which Rebecca read as triumphant.

'Can you catch that little sod and put him back in the barn? I'll take this one up to the house.'

Rebecca walked slowly towards Ambrose, who was grazing. He hadn't moved since Harriet fell.

'Ambrose?' Rebecca held out a quivering hand. She clicked her tongue. 'Come on, Ambrose,' she said.

The pony put back his ears and shook his long black mane at her. Rebecca reached for the reins that lay on the ground in front of him. She picked them up, holding them by the buckle and turned to walk towards the gate. There was a slight resistance as she heard him take one last mouthful of grass. Then he followed her.

PIECE 42

Titus is sitting on the grey chenille-covered chair next to the teak table at the end of Rebecca's bed. He is wearing a navy-blue suit and a pink tie. He had walked into the room, dropped his pad on the table and taken a seat, crossing one long leg over the other and exposing his socks, which were brown with red cuffs. He had taken off his glasses and put them next to the pad.

'All the furniture in this hospital is covered in this extraordinary material,' he says, running a hand along the arm of the chair. 'I wonder why?'

'It's chenille,' Rebecca tells him.

'Oh,' says Titus.

Rebecca sits on the bed and looks at him. She notices for the first time that he is wearing a signet ring. She wonders if he has just bought it or inherited it or if it has been there all the time and she just hadn't noticed.

Titus notices her examining him.

'What?' he says.

You couldn't buy a signet ring, says Betty in Rebecca's ear. You just *couldn't*. Rebecca agrees.

'Nothing,' she says to Titus. 'Did you know that chenille means caterpillar in French?'

Titus shrugs. 'Caterpillar?'

Rebecca nods. 'It feels like a shaved Muppet, doesn't it?'

'Yes, I suppose it does.' He rubs the arm of the chair thoughtfully. 'How odd,' he says. Then he says, 'How are you? How did you sleep?' He picks up his glasses and holds them by one arm. He is wearing black leather-soled shoes. He is rather handsome in a geeky way, Rebecca decides. His teeth are very sensible today, apart from the gap between the two front ones.

'I slept very well,' she says. 'I'm not sure it actually counts as sleeping because I took the pills the nurses gave me and then I passed out.'

'When did you wake up? At what time?' asks Titus.

'About six,' says Rebecca.

'What did you do yesterday?'

Rebecca looks out of the window. For a second she feels as if she's not really there.

'I'm over here,' says Titus.

Rebecca looks back at him. 'Why do I have to do group therapy?' she asks. 'What's it for?'

Titus sits up in the chair. He looks like a physical oxymoron sitting in it. Rebecca wonders if she should tell him and decides not. She's feeling quite proud of her edit today. It's not as if it hasn't every reason to have gone AWOL but it appears to be functioning adequately.

'I have absolutely no idea,' says Titus, putting his glasses back on.

Rebecca sits up and crosses her legs. She feels like she's nine and at school. In a moment, she might put her hand up to ask a question.

'How can you tell me to do something when you don't know what the thing is?' she asks.

'Rebecca, it works. It's not my area but the professionals whose area it is are very proficient.'

'You give your opinion very decidedly for so young a person. Pray, what age are you?'

Titus looks at her over the top of his glasses. 'What are we doing?' he says.

'I'm Lady Catherine de Bourgh and you're Elizabeth Bennet,' says Rebecca. She'd been wrong about her edit, clearly.

'Oh, of course,' says Titus. 'Obviously. What have you eaten today?'

'Nothing,' says Rebecca.

Titus frowns. 'Why?'

'I don't eat breakfast, ever, and I can't go down there to the café and eat by myself. You do realize, don't you Titus, that this whole place is full of absolute nutjobs?'

'I think if you did go down there and eat, some of those "nutjobs"—' he describes quotation marks in the air with his fingers '—might talk to you and you would find some of them fairly normal. There's a no-smoking area.'

Rebecca doesn't believe that the people she hears outside her window are normal. 'Is there a no-smirking area?' she asks.

Titus sighs.

'Is there a grey area?'

'I believe you would find either of those two places very uncomfortable.'

Rebecca smiles. 'Thank you,' she says.

'Any other questions?' says Titus.

Rebecca sits up straighter. She pushes her hair back from her forehead. 'How long?' she asks.

'How long is a piece of string?' says Titus.

Rebecca imagines a piece of string. Then she imagines that he's taking the piss. Then she looks at him and imagines that he's not. He must be half-witted, she thinks. Then she realizes he's doing it on purpose so she decides to ignore it.

'An admission for a week is practically unheard of. Getting your dosages right in a managed environment usually takes a minimum of three to four weeks but that's just an estimate,' Titus tells her. 'It's about how you are physically, about what triggers your drinking, about dealing with and managing those triggers.'

'I know what triggers them,' says Rebecca. 'The moment I walk through the front door of my house I know. I feel ensnared.'

'Ensnared?'

'Yes, you know like when a rabbit is caught in a snare?'

Titus shakes his head.

'Wrong reference; of course you don't. If a rabbit, caught in a snare, struggles, the noose tightens. If it lies still, the noose won't kill it. It can't escape because escape isn't possible but it can survive.'

'By lying still?'

'Yes.'

Titus runs a hand through his hair. 'So what are you going to do about it? Obviously *I* can't do anything.'

'Me neither.'

'So, you're stuck?'

'Yes.'

'In a snare?'

'Yes. It's not horrible because I'm not being hurt.'

'I think you are.'

'Well, I am a bit but everyone has to compromise.'

'It's the extent to which you're having to compromise that worries me. It's unreasonable and your use of the snare as an image is particularly troubling.'

'Why?'

'There is a very real threat of death.'

'No one is trying to hurt me.'

'I know that you don't believe your life to be in danger, at least not from anyone other than yourself, but surely your history tells you the lengths to which you're prepared to go in order to escape?'

'I know I can't escape. I know I have to tolerate what's happening.'

'I wouldn't say tolerance is your strong point. There'll come a point where you can't tolerate it anymore and then where are you?'

Rebecca sighs. 'I might be able to. I could learn to. You said I had a plastic brain. Maybe I will learn how to cope.'

'You won't.' Titus leans forward in his chair.

Rebecca holds his gaze. She likes his face. She feels as though he's on her side but she knows he can't help her. 'So you see,' she says. 'It's environmental and you can't help. You can medicate me so that I don't care too much but I'm still trapped. I'll always be trapped. Anyway, I'm not going to drink anymore. It didn't work.'

'You can say that again.'

'No, it didn't so I'm not going to.'

Titus gives her his special professional 'I don't believe you' look. He says nothing.

PIECE 43

At eleven, a nurse comes to take Rebecca to group therapy. At group therapy, there are four people and there is Rebecca. Three of the people are mad and one is the therapist upon whom the jury is out.

The room is small, grey-carpeted and square with a large north-facing window. There is a low pine table in the middle of the floor with a box of tissues just off-centre. Rebecca wants to lean forward and push it two centimetres to the right with her forefinger but she doesn't.

'Please could you leave the room. I feel that this group is not suitable for you at the moment,' says the therapist to one of the mad people. The therapist is small and dark-haired. Her tumble of hair is secured back from her hawkish face by a brown tortoiseshell clip.

The mad person has a yellowing bruise around one eye. He has a swollen jaw and he has scabbed arms. Slowly he peels a scab from his forearm and Rebecca begins to shake and her fingers stretch as wide as they can. She balances her bag on her lap and shoves her hands under her thighs.

'Please leave.' Rebecca hears that the therapist is Greek. She has fierce dark eyes.

The mad person looks out of his swollen face at the therapist. 'I feel that I ought to be allowed to stay here,' he says calmly. 'I have a problem with the way this hospital is treating me. The communication isn't good and I can't really manage being told to leave a group like this one without adequate explanation and without notice.' He has shorn fair hair and the light from the window is catching the tips of it, gilding his head.

Rebecca is finding it quite difficult to stay in the room. Opposite, a tall thin man with large grey eyes is sitting looking at the floor. Rebecca can see his eyes from the side because they bulge slightly from the sockets. A woman, about the same age as Rebecca, is running her eyes around the moulding at the top of the room. Rebecca wonders if she is looking for spiders.

'Carl, I am not going to attempt to physically remove you from the room,' says the therapist, 'but I would like you to leave voluntarily.'

So, she's not wholly mad then, thinks Rebecca. She tries to imagine this slight woman trying to remove Carl from the room and she can't.

Carl says nothing. He doesn't move.

The therapist looks around the room at the other two mad people and at Rebecca.

'Well,' she says. 'I suppose we had better begin this session with Carl in the room with us.'

Rebecca can feel waves of antipathy radiating from Carl. They fill the room. His fury is everywhere.

'Good afternoon everyone,' says the therapist. 'My name is Maria and I will be spending the next hour and a half with you. Could each of you introduce yourselves? And Carl, could you please stop picking at your scabs? Thank you.'

The woman who was looking for spiders turns her devastated face towards Rebecca and then turns to the man with the grey eyes. 'Hello,' she says, 'my name is Alice. I am coming to the end of my time at the hospital and I hope that I will be able to manage but I'm really not at all sure that I will.' She drops her head so that it hangs on her long thin neck like a snowdrop.

The thin man looks up from the floor. He has very big feet and is wearing some very ugly trainers that look slightly too small so that his feet bulge out through the leather at the toe joints. He has rather a sweet face.

'Hi,' he says. 'I'm called Darren. I have tried to harm myself – actually to kill myself – and I have been coming to the hospital for six months. At the moment, I am an in-patient.' He has a soft South African accent.

Maria turns her eagle gaze on Rebecca. 'Are you OK?' she asks. 'Are you finding this difficult?'

Rebecca thinks she is going to be sick. Her fingers clench and scrabble under her legs. Her bag slides off them onto the floor. Luckily she has zipped it up. Rebecca stares at her bag for a few seconds so that her eyes can take a snapshot of its helplessness, then she looks at the therapist. 'I'm called Rebecca,' she says. 'I came here yesterday. I'm very shy. I can't talk.' She draws in a huge breath and thinks she may not be able to let it out again.

'I'm Carl,' says Carl. His voice is low with menace. 'I'm

here because I want to be in this room and because I'm not prepared to be thrown out just because you, Maria, don't like me.'

Maria looks at Carl. Rebecca thinks they may all be about to be held hostage. She decides that there is nothing Carl won't do.

'I find it interesting that you say you think I don't like you,' says Maria to Carl. 'What makes you feel that way?' Maria puts her head on one side, the corners of her mouth turn up a little, but her eyes are still fierce.

'You've just tried to remove me from this group,' replies Carl. Rebecca slides her eyes sideways to look at him. He is jiggling a foot and a scab on his forearm is raw and bleeding.

'I feel,' says Maria, 'that you are not really benefitting from these sessions but there is no question of my personal feelings being involved in that decision one way or the other. It is purely a professional opinion. Now,' she says to the room at large, 'who would like to say something about their experience? Who would like to share with the group?'

Darren looks blandly round at the others. Rebecca thinks he may be over-medicated. She wonders if perhaps she should be over-medicated too. It looks fun.

'I tried to kill myself,' says Darren, blandly.

'What exactly did you do?' asks Maria.

'I slit my wrists,' says Darren, displaying broad red tracks on his broad strong wrists, 'and I stuck a knife in my stomach.' Rebecca is still staring at the wrists. Darren's hands are resting on his lap. His wrists are broad but they are also thin with

241

pronounced knobs where they join his hands. Rebecca can see the veins beneath the scars.

'So, you really meant it?' asks Alice. Rebecca thinks she might laugh and she bites the inside of her cheeks.

'I self-harm. I have lots of scars,' says Darren. 'My scars are the scars of my battle. I haven't the right to break what has been given to me. I know that now.'

'It's interesting that you say you have no right,' says Maria, forming speech marks in the air with one hand, using just her forefinger and her little finger.

It's not at all interesting, it's insane, thinks Rebecca, but she's impressed with the speech marks. She has never seen that done before, not with one hand.

Later, Rebecca is back in her room. Her lunch is sitting under a silver cloche on the table. She walks over and picks up the cloche. A slice of hot smoked salmon sits pinkly next to some crushed new potatoes and a small pile of wilted baby spinach. On a separate plate is a triangle of apple tart. She puts the cloche back over the food and goes to sit on her bed. She opens her laptop. Then there is a knock on the door.

Rebecca hasn't shut her door. She has left it ajar so that the nurses can do their fifteen-minute checks without knocking.

'Rebecca?' A nurse called Miriam puts her head round the door. Miriam is about the same age as Rebecca. She is Nigerian and wears her hair in tight cornrows. She comes into the room.

'I thought you might like a chat,' she says. 'It's probably

all a bit strange for you, being here, therapy and all that. You went to therapy this morning, didn't you? How was that?'

Rebecca tells Miriam all about therapy. 'I thought it was horrible,' she says. 'I didn't understand it at all.'

Miriam smiles a slow, wide smile showing large white teeth. Her eyes dance when she smiles. Rebecca is quite shocked. Miriam has one of those rare smiles that turn an otherwise unremarkable face into something quite extraordinary. Rebecca gazes at her. You're beautiful, she thinks. She manages not to say it aloud. Then she watches as Miriam's smile fades and her face becomes normal again. It's as though a dimmer switch has been turned down.

'You'll get used to it,' says Miriam. 'It's all a bit strange at first but lots of people find group therapy very helpful after a while. Aren't you going to eat any lunch?'

Rebecca shakes her head. 'I'm not hungry,' she says.

'You have to think of food differently while you're here, sweetheart,' says Miriam. 'You're taking quite a lot of medication and you have to eat for it to work properly, for your body to adjust. Do you see?'

Rebecca wants Miriam to smile again. 'I'll try then,' she says. Miriam smiles and the room is filled with dappled sunlight.

When Miriam goes, Rebecca picks up her computer, puts her headphones on and scrolls through her iTunes account.

'Are you lonesome tonight?' croons Elvis. Rebecca really hates Elvis. She doesn't understand why the algorithm on her iPhone thinks otherwise.

She takes off her headphones and lays them on the bed

next to her. She opens Word. She had copied all her notes from her Elephant notebook onto Word because it's quicker to type.

The small blonde woman shakes her head violently, she types. 'No, I didn't mean to kill myself. I really didn't. I wanted a release. It's the same reason I do this.' The woman pulls up the sleeve of her blouse revealing a cross-hatching of raised scars, some grey, some white and some fresh, scabbed and red.

Emily feels her body recoil, writes Rebecca. She feels herself shrink back into her chair. She stares down at her knees. She looks at her bag lying next to her feet where she had dropped it. She feels the image of the white-skinned, slender arm with its brutal carvings etch into her retina and she wonders what group therapy is for.

Rebecca shuts her laptop. Her arms are throbbing at the wrists. Her eyes feel too big for their sockets and her toes are curling inside her sandals.

Toe-curling, she thinks.

Rebecca walks to the nurses' station. 'I just want to run to the top of the hospital,' she tells Miriam.

'Why?' asks Miriam.

'To run upstairs. I have too much . . . something,' says Rebecca. 'I need to burn some of it off.'

Miriam looks puzzled. 'Too much of what?'

'Screechings,' says Rebecca. 'I get them. It's the drugs, it's all this . . . ' she gesticulates.

'Do it,' says Miriam. She smiles her beautiful smile. 'But be careful and don't fall over.'

Rebecca runs as fast as she can, taking two steps at a time. On the fourth floor, a man comes out of the ward.

'Are you lost?' he asks.

'No, I'm running,' says Rebecca.

'Your ward may be looking for you,' says the man.

Rebecca takes a deep breath. 'They know I'm here,' she says and takes off down the stairs. Back to her room.

PIECE 44

Alex and Rebecca took their bicycles and rode towards Bluebell Wood. On the other side of Bluebell Wood was a steep hill called Devil's Dip. The only other hill nearby was Shooter's and it wasn't nearly as steep and it hadn't nearly such a good name. In the winter, the children took sleds and skimmed right down the middle of the road on the frost-crusted snow.

'Well, if the road's all snowy then no one can drive up it, can they?' reasoned Martin.

'And we could always jump into the hedge if something did come,' said Alex.

Rebecca thought that only Alex would come up with that solution. She could just imagine him launching himself into a hedge to avoid a tractor but she thought Martin was right. No one could drive up Devil's Dip when it was covered in snow. It would be impossible.

Today, she and Alex had decided that they would go to Devil's Dip because it was fun to bicycle down the hill as fast as possible; to feel the thrill of the wind whipping through their hair and to grip tightly onto the handlebars, steering on the loose grey grit as the road swept around a corner and ended up with a stomach-whooping humpbacked bridge at the bottom. Rebecca experienced an added sense of jeopardy because Thunder had no brakes, but the bridge slowed him up and she would put her feet down if he threatened to get out of control.

Alex was faster than Rebecca. He was heavier and his bicycle had bigger wheels. She watched him disappear around the corner ahead of her and she put her feet down. Alex always mocked her for doing this but he didn't understand how fast Thunder would go otherwise and, anyway, he couldn't see her if she was behind him. She remembered putting her feet down. She remembered the foot nearest the verge turning over and the sickening swerve that followed and, just before she fell, she saw Alex standing on the bridge still astride his bicycle, looking back at her.

Rebecca lay on the ground with her head on the grass verge, watching Thunder's front wheel turning lazily against a sky full of white scudding clouds. Her leg was stinging and she felt tears of shame trickle backwards into her hair.

'I'll get into trouble now.' Alex stood over her, lifting Thunder off his sister. 'They always blame me when something happens to you or Giles. Why do you always have to put your feet down? Typical of a girl.'

Rebecca remembered sitting up and seeing that she had grazed her left shin from top to bottom. She had been wearing shorts and small sharp grey stones had stuck to her knee. The prickles of blood were growing and had begun to run down her leg onto her sandals.

After that, she remembered being alone. Rebecca pushed

Thunder along beside her. She was hobbling slightly and she dragged the bicycle up onto the bank near the humpbacked bridge and dropped him in the cool green grass. The water beneath the bridge had dried to a trickle and she slid through the drifts of cow parsley, narrowly avoiding being stung by a clump of nettles, and jumped down onto the dry riverbed. Beyond the bridge, the water almost reached the apex of the arch and a grass snake swam through swaying weed, its collared head held just above the surface.

'And you say that the river had quite dried up?' asks Titus.

'I couldn't have stood in it otherwise.'

'But on the other side of the bridge the river was full?'

'Yes, that's how the snake was swimming. It was as if there was a glass screen between me and it, like looking into a fish tank.'

Titus shakes his head. 'You know that it's not possible, don't you?'

'Of course I do, I'm just trying to show you how unreliable my memories are. I don't think you're going to find them helpful. I obviously make things up.'

Titus smiles and shakes his head again. 'Could you possibly try not to?'

'I'm not trying to. As far as I'm concerned, that's what I saw. I would swear to it.'

'So?'

'I probably don't remember things and I probably misremember things. If I can remember all that, in all that detail and it's not true, maybe I didn't fall off my bike. Maybe I wasn't there. Maybe I was somewhere else doing something completely other. Maybe I was sitting up a tree reading *Black Beauty*. I could have been doing anything, do you see?'

'This level of depression does not, in my experience, come out of the blue. It must have context. I would like to know what it might be in your case. Do you have any diaries, anything at all like that, which might verify some of the things you are telling me?'

Rebecca thinks. 'Not from when I was eight,' she says. She looks at Titus. The sun is shining through the window. It is hitting the side of his face. She scans it quickly. It's his experience that bothers her.

'This is what I do, Rebecca. I've been doing it for a comparatively long time. You really shouldn't judge a book by its cover.'

Oh God, he was doing that mind-reading thing again. It really was most inconvenient.

'I didn't say anything.'

'You didn't have to. But back to the point, you almost certainly were there but your memory is in some way distorted. In this case, you have probably muddled up seeing the snake swimming in the full river with standing in the dried-up riverbed. Does that make sense?'

Rebecca tries to imagine that it does. She pushes her fringe out of her eyes and looks round the room. Titus is sitting, watching her. Her bag is on the floor next to the bed. Will she remember this moment or will it muddle and mix with other days?

'It doesn't, no,' she says.

'Why not?' Titus leans forward in his chair. His feet are

planted firmly on the floor. His forearms are resting on his thighs. His hands are clasped between his knees.

'Because I saw the snake from below. To see it swimming like that, I would have had to be standing underwater. I would have had to be standing fully clothed underwater with my eyes open.'

Titus sits up straight. He is suddenly brisk and efficient. 'I still want you to read your diaries if Sam can locate them.'

PIECE 45

Rebecca stared into the black.

Harriet had told her that if she didn't get confirmed, she would go to hell.

The devil would get her.

He would carry her down to hell if she died.

She wasn't good.

She prayed in church but, at home, she forgot.

God wouldn't hear her because she wasn't confirmed.

He would hear Harriet.

Harriet could be as horrible as she liked because she could go to confession but Rebecca would die with all her sins hanging from her like chains and the devil would take her.

Rebecca sat up. She groped for her bedside lamp and switched it on. In his bed, across the room, Giles muttered in his sleep and turned over.

Betty fled before the light caught her and Rebecca looked round her room.

Her chest of drawers stood against the far wall, topped by a Victorian swing mirror. In the corner stood her velvet armchair, covered, as always, with discarded jumpers and jeans.

A bookshelf overflowed with worn copies of her favourite books.

A low table housed her shrine to Our Lady complete with votive candles and a postcard from Walsingham.

An orange rag rug lay rumpled on the oak floorboards and, at the window, there was a tiny gap between the pulled curtains.

Rebecca could see a glimpse of the night between them and a red-rimmed eye that watched her. Unblinking.

She ran from the room, pounding down the passageway to her parents, flinging herself through the door and into their bed.

'The Devil,' she sobbed, burrowing into her father's arms. 'The Devil.'

PIECE 46

'So,' says Titus, 'new meds. How's it going?' He is sitting on the shaved Muppet chair, watching Rebecca. She has just made herself a cafetière of black coffee, which sits on her bedside table with her mug beside it.

Rebecca is on her bed, cross-legged. She has decided to be very co-operative and intelligent. She needs Titus to like her but she doesn't think he does at the moment. Rebecca imagines she probably has the skills to turn this around. Titus may believe it's not relevant but really she can't be comfortable with someone who finds her annoying.

So don't be so bloody annoying, says Betty.

'I'm not going to be,' says Rebecca.

'Not going to be what?' says Titus.

'Annoying,' says Rebecca. 'I don't like new meds,' she adds. 'And I don't like group therapy or being inside all the time.'

'How are you physically? I hear you've been drinking an awful lot of coffee. That's not the best idea on your medication.'

How is she physically? Rebecca imagines her body as a bag of skin stuffed with lungs that if laid out one cell thick would cover a football pitch or stretch as far as the moon. A liver shot with fat, kidneys bloated, blood vessels twining for miles, shit and piss and her wet bones slipping against muscle . . . and coffee, black, bitter and a bad idea swilling about in it all.

'Fine,' she says.

Titus takes off his glasses. He puts them on the table. 'Has Sam been to see you?' he asks.

'Yes, he came yesterday. He comes every day. He's very stressed. He can't really manage life without me.'

Titus sighs. 'How did he find you?'

Rebecca can't stop herself. 'I think he used satnav,' she says.

Titus glares at her.

'You always make me feel as though I've just been caught smoking behind the bike sheds,' she adds.

Titus runs a hand through his hair. 'Why?' he says. 'Just tell me why I bother?'

'It's a vocation,' says Rebecca, 'like being a nun.'

'I'm pretty sure it's nothing like being a nun,' says Titus.

'It might be. All that self-flagellation and frustration. It could be similar. I was taught by nuns,' she adds, lying.

Titus examines her again. His eyes are like two grey pebbles. Rebecca can see that her charm offensive is not going to plan.

'I'm not at all surprised,' says Titus. 'I would have expected nothing less.'

'They were awfully frustrated,' says Rebecca.

'I don't want to talk about nuns,' says Titus. 'I want to talk about you. Now, tell me what you don't like about the new medication?'

Rebecca thinks for a minute. 'I don't like the restlessness. My limbs feel restless.'

'All the time? Now?'

'I am trying . . . but they do, especially at three-thirty. And everyone at group therapy is frightened or frightening.'

'Three-thirty in the afternoon?' says Titus, ignoring the group therapy bit.

Rebecca nods.

Titus gets up and walks to the window. Rebecca watches him. Her heart is jumping. He turns and sits on the windowsill so that he is silhouetted against the pewter sky.

'You need to try,' he says quietly. 'You need to give your treatments a chance before you decide they're not working.'

'I am trying,' Rebecca says again and she shuffles backwards up the bed, away from him, and leans against the blue suede headboard.

'You're extremely trying,' says Titus. He doesn't move but Rebecca thinks his voice has softened. She thinks she might be bringing him round. 'Rebecca, we are here to find out what brought you here. We are not here to play games, to prevaricate or to engage in a battle of wits. I want you to take this seriously. Do you think you can or are we just wasting each other's time?'

Not bringing him around at all then, she thinks. She says nothing.

'Rebecca?'

'I'm tired,' she says. 'I think I've tried everything. I feel like Townes Van Zandt.'

'What?'

'Townes Van Zandt,' says Rebecca. 'He's dead now.'

Titus moves, quickly across the room. He snatches up his pad from the table. His eyes are blazing. 'I don't think you have, quite honestly,' he says. 'I am not some amusing hobby with which you can entertain yourself for a few minutes each day. I am a consultant psychiatrist at the top of my profession and your inability to take this situation seriously could be catastrophic for you, indeed it already has been. I am not prepared to let that happen again. Do you understand?'

Rebecca smiles. She doesn't mean to but she can't help it. 'So, you *care* about me?'

'Of course I do. What kind of doctor would I be if I didn't?' He sits in the chair again. 'Listen, I can shut you down. You do know that, don't you? I can call another doctor into this room and have you put on a section.'

'You can't shut me down. I'm not a sub-post office and, anyway, you need a policeman.'

'What?' says Titus again.

'To section someone. Don't you need a policeman?'

Titus stands up. 'I'm going,' he says. He points at her cafetière. 'And I don't want you to drink that.' And he goes.

Rebecca draws in a great long slow breath. She looks out of the window at the thin grey clouds. Then she jumps off the bed and runs into the bathroom where she throws up and up.

PIECE 47

Harriet hadn't broken any bones as a result of her fall from Ambrose but she had hurt her back.

Miranda and Pen were sitting at the kitchen table, smoking, and Rebecca was waiting for Harriet to wake up.

'She gets up for a couple of hours a day,' Miranda was telling Rebecca's mother, 'but she likes a rest in the afternoons. Patrick is an absolute darling with her. He sits on her bed for ages and tells her stories.'

Rebecca slipped out of the kitchen door and headed for the barn. She thought she may as well go and see Ambrose. She had some carrots in her pocket. He might like that.

The barn was still and dark. In the stall next to Ambrose's hung his bridle and his saddle was propped on its pommel against the wall. Two large feed bins stood next to that. She heard Ambrose snort and turn so that his head appeared over the door of his stall.

'Hello,' she said, reaching into her pocket. 'I have carrots.' The pony stamped a foot and put his ears back.

Rebecca stood very still in front of him. Cobwebs festooned the small high window at the back of the stall which let in a shaft of pearly sunlight. A hen clucked contentedly in the haystack to her right and Rebecca breathed in the sweet smell of dusty hay and horse. She held out a flat hand just below the pony's nose, offering him a small wizened carrot that she had found that morning in the bottom of the fridge. He snatched it and turned away from Rebecca, crunching and rolling his eyes.

'Come on,' Rebecca spoke quietly. Ambrose nodded his head up and down and snorted again. 'I've got another one.' She held out her hand and he took the carrot but this time he paused for a second to breathe her in.

Far away, Rebecca heard her mother calling. Harriet must be awake. She reached out towards the pony, pushing her hand into his forelock and Ambrose let her give his poll a quick scratch. 'See you soon,' Rebecca said.

She sat on Harriet's bed. Harriet was in a funny mood but Rebecca supposed that it was because she had hurt her back.

'What've you been doing?' Harriet was propped up against a pile of pillows. She looked sulky.

'When?'

'Just now, where were you?'

'Talking to Ambrose.' Rebecca absently picked up a rag doll and began playing with its long black woollen hair.

'He'll bite you.'

Rebecca stood up, still holding the doll. 'He didn't,' she said.

Harriet shuffled irritably. 'Why are you wearing a blue jumper with a green shirt? Why are you all dressed up?'

That morning, Rebecca had chosen a blue Aertex shirt and

a sea-green jumper. Now she looked down at herself. 'What's wrong with it?'

Harriet grinned. 'Blue and green should never be seen without something in between,' she chanted.

Rebecca had thought she looked quite nice. 'Anyway,' said Harriet, 'you can't make a silk purse out of a sow's ear.'

Rebecca dropped the doll back down onto the bed. 'Why are you being mean?' she asked.

'I'm not but friends should tell the truth. You wouldn't want me to tell you lies, would you?' Harriet widened her large pale eyes.

Rebecca shrugged. She could feel her throat tightening and her cheeks growing warm.

Harriet picked up the rag doll and began to plait the woollen hair. 'Did you see Patrick?' she asked.

Rebecca shook her head.

'He's being really kind to me.'

Rebecca shrugged again.

'Yesterday he brought me a KitKat. He says that when I'm better he'll take me shopping and he'll buy me a present.'

Rebecca nodded. 'I've got to go now.' She looked at her watch, lying. 'We have to be home by four, Alex has a friend for tea.'

At home, Rebecca sat and looked into the mirror on her dressing table. She pushed the shrine she had made to Our Lady to one side, knocking over the votive candle and the small framed picture of the Virgin, and she looked.

Hail Mary full of grace, she prayed, forgetting what came next. The face looking back at her was flat. Freckles trailed haphazardly across the bridge of her nose and scattered over her cheeks. Her eyes behind her blue-rimmed glasses were blue, too, but considerably lighter than the plastic. Her mouth was wide and had a tendency to turn down at the corners.

'You have a lovely wide smile,' her mother had told her. Now, Rebecca smiled at her reflection and saw only big square teeth in a face too small for them. Around her face, her hair stood out in a wild yellow bush. She picked up her hairbrush and dragged it through the tangled mass, which appeared to make it worse.

She thought of Harriet's sleek brown bob, of her small plump mouth and proportionate teeth. She took off her glasses and laid them next to the upended picture of Mary. Now, her reflection blurred and she blinked and tried to focus. She leaned forward and peered at her face again. She looked better without the glasses. She took a handful of her hair and twisted it into a ponytail, pulling it to one side. She looked better without all that hair. She thought of Harriet and wondered why Harriet was her friend. If she were Harriet, she probably wouldn't want to be Rebecca's friend.

She stood, standing the candle upright again and balancing the picture against her mirror. She would ask her mother to help. She would ask her to buy some clips. She left her glasses on the dressing table and went out of the room.

Pen was in the kitchen. The sink was full of muddy carrots and Pen was washing them under the cold tap with a sponge scourer.

Rebecca came and stood next to her. Her mother's hands looked sore and red.

'Mummy?'

Pen turned off the tap and put the scourer down on the edge of the sink. Rebecca didn't often start a conversation.

'Yes?'

'Can you buy me some clips?'

'What sort of clips? For what?'

'For my hair. I think if I wet it and then put clips all down the sides, it might dry like this.' Rebecca pulled both sides of her hair flat against her face.

'You mean hair grips, not pretty ones, the brown ones you get in the chemist?'

Rebecca nodded.

'Why do you want your hair to be different, it's lovely.'

'I want it flatter, that's all.'

'Have you lost your glasses?'

Rebecca shrugged. 'No, they're upstairs. They're . . . blue. I don't need them just for walking about and stuff.'

Pen looked down at Rebecca. 'I'll get you some clips the next time I go into town,' she said.

PIECE 48

'How's the writing going?' Titus is sitting in the Muppet chair. He takes off his glasses and puts them on the arm, balancing them precariously. 'The nurses tell me you're writing most of the time. Well, most of the time that you're not running up and down stairs in precisely the way that I asked you not to.'

Rebecca thinks that he probably feels guilty for being so cross with her last time he'd seen her and is trying to appear nice and interested . . . but she's not going to fall for it.

'Oh, it's good,' she says. 'It's very good.' She ignores the running comment. After all, if you lock up polar bears, they go nuts, and if you lock up Rebeccas, they run.

'Tell me what it's about,' says Titus.

'It's about a psychopathic psychiatrist and his lovely sane patients,' says Rebecca.

'Is it a book? Are you writing a novel? I thought perhaps it was a diary.'

'I couldn't write a diary; nothing's happening. I have to make lots of things up to keep myself entertained. Don't you get bored just hanging around in here for five days a week? I would die of boredom.'

Titus ignores the question. 'So, this book is based on your experiences here? Is it going to hurt my feelings?' he says.

'No—' she shakes her head '—it won't because you're a psychopath.' Then she decides to change the subject because Titus is looking a bit anxious and it doesn't suit him. Also he might get cross and frighten her but then he changes the subject for her, which is unexpected.

'I would like to try something with you,' he says, sitting up straight.

'What?' says Rebecca.

'Some inner child work,' says Titus.

Rebecca snorts with laughter.

Bloody *hell*, whispers Betty. He's lost it.

Titus holds up a hand, 'No,' he says, 'bear with me. This could be interesting.'

'It could be embarrassing.' Rebecca shifts uncomfortably on the bed. 'I don't want to work,' she says.

'No,' says Titus. 'You want to play verbal ping-pong, you want to bat away any help that might be offered and you want to turn everything into a joke. Nonetheless, I would like you to accommodate me.'

Rebecca can feel her breaths beginning to shorten. Titus isn't cross. He is quite calm but he is dominating the room. She can feel the force of his personality and she doesn't like it.

'Now,' says Titus, 'close your eyes and imagine yourself as a child.'

Rebecca closes her eyes. She can't imagine herself. She opens her eyes. 'To look at? What do you mean?'

'Close your eyes, imagine yourself as a child. Imagine yourself aged eight or nine. She is sitting on the bed, here, now. She is unhappy. What do you think you want to say to that child?'

Rebecca closes her eyes again. She can feel little Rebecca sitting next to her. She can feel the weight of her small body and she can hear that little Rebecca is breathing lightly so no one can hear her. She wants to move away from her. She breathes in through her nose. 'I don't want to talk to her.' It is the truth, she doesn't.

'Why not?'

'She would hate it. She doesn't like talking to people.'

'Any people, even someone who cares about her?'

'No, she would be too shy. She doesn't like people seeing her.'

'Do you care about her?'

Rebecca considers this. She has spent most of her adult life trying to bury sad little Rebecca. She shakes her head. 'No,' she says.

'OK, open your eyes.'

Rebecca opens her eyes. She looks at the bed where little Rebecca had been sitting. She can still see her tangled yellow hair and her fixed white face.

Titus is looking at her with his arms folded. 'You have absolutely no compassion,' he says. There is no triumph in his voice. He is just stating a fact.

Rebecca stares at him. 'I have.' She can feel tears starting to burn behind her eyes. 'I'm very kind. I help people all the time.' Titus keeps looking at her, his arms folded. 'I have children. I'm kind to them,' she adds.

Titus looks around the room. 'Really?' he says.

Rebecca shakes her head. She has no words.

'You have no compassion for yourself,' says Titus. 'Why do you think that might be? Are you really worth so little?'

A tear falls from her lash and drops onto the bed. Betty hisses in her left ear.

'Some children don't learn how to read other people. They cannot project themselves into the minds of others and imagine how they feel,' continues Titus. 'They don't learn because the people around them feel unpredictable and are read by the child as dangerous or unreliable, so they shut down. They avoid contact and they don't learn how to interact fluently. In the short term, this may be a good coping strategy but as life progresses and the person has to cope with the normal pressures of adulthood, they become chronically maladjusted. They are unable to cope. Children learn compassion by being able to put themselves in another person's shoes and to walk a few steps in those shoes. If they feel that other people are not trustworthy, instead of learning as other children do, they immerse themselves in books or animals or whatever else they feel they can trust. Does any of this feel familiar? I think you have spent your whole life being avoidant. You secured yourself in a safe and unthreatening marriage with a man who hasn't asked too many questions, nor made many demands.'

'He's really demanding.' Rebecca's heart is thudding and she has given up trying not to cry. Her face is full of streaming tears. She feels Betty get up and flounce out of the room. Rebecca thinks of all the things she has to do for Sam. She thinks of all the things he can't do without her. Then she thinks, I can't bear Titus.

'He hasn't asked you for anything that you have not been willing to give.' Titus is twisting the knife.

Rebecca gets off the bed. Titus remains sitting. She walks past him into her shower room. Her face in the mirror is smeared with tears. 'He hasn't,' she says quietly to her reflection. 'He never has.' She turns and looks into the bedroom, at the back of Titus's neat head. 'But *you* have,' she says.

The next morning, Rebecca goes to a Cognitive Behavioural Therapy group. She has washed her face but her eyes are still all piggy. She supposes no one will notice as all their eyes are piggy with prescription drugs anyway.

Rebecca thinks CBT might work better than the session with Maria. She thinks that she might be able to learn something and then she might be able to leave the hospital. She hasn't digested what Titus had said to her that morning and she is trying not to think about it.

The CBT group is at 11 a.m. on the second floor. Rebecca takes a lift with Blessing, who is a nurse.

'It's quicker in the lift,' says Blessing, but Rebecca thinks that Blessing prefers the lift because she puffs when she walks. Blessing pushes her fingers up under her black curly wig to scratch. The wig shifts slightly and settles lopsidedly. Blessing has a very beautiful face, all smooth dark curves with full lips and soft, friendly eyes.

On the second floor, Rebecca meets Alice. There is no one else there, initially. Alice and Rebecca say, 'How are you?' simultaneously and then they sit down side-by-side on a sofa.

A thickset man in his late fifties arrives. He has powerful shoulders and heavy dark-grey hair. He is wearing a pair of combat shorts. Rebecca thinks he is a bouncer, that maybe when Carl turns up, this man will bounce him from the room, but he takes a seat opposite her and Alice.

A boy arrives, his eyes are shining and he is singing gleefully to himself. 'Hey, man! Now I'm really livin',' he sings, slapping his thighs to an inner beat as he sits down on another sofa. Another boy, slender and dark, slips into the room behind a woman carrying a clipboard. The woman gestures for the boy to take a seat. 'Sit here, Siva,' she says. Siva sits and then the woman looks round at the others.

'I'm Morwenna and I am leading the session today,' she says, smiling round at the group. She has smooth dark hair held back from her forehead with a hairband. Her face is smooth too, untroubled and open. Like a friendly egg, thinks Rebecca.

'So to begin,' says Morwenna, 'shall we all introduce ourselves and, if we would like, give some information about what we would like to achieve during our stay here? Would you like to start, Alice? You're coming to the end of your time with us, so you will be the most used to this process.'

'Hello, my name is Alice,' says Alice obediently. 'I have learned during my time here that I am something of a people-pleaser and I have also learned that I don't have to live up to other people's expectations.' She takes a deep breath and looks at the carpet. She makes a note in an exercise book which she has open on her lap. 'I'm going back to work next week,' she says, 'and although my colleagues have been understanding and supportive, I'm a bit worried about it. I spent all of yesterday answering work emails.'

'How do you feel about the fact that you felt that they felt you should be doing that?' asks Morwenna.

Rebecca folds her arms across her stomach. She starts to shake and her breath becomes short.

'Well, the person that I'm most concerned about is my team leader,' says Alice. 'I feel sure that he feels that I should be able to pick up where I left off but I don't really feel that I can.'

Siva shifts in his seat. The boy with the shining eyes smiles broadly.

'Well, we'll leave that for a moment and return to it after we have all introduced ourselves,' says Morwenna. She looks at Rebecca. Rebecca thinks she is going to sneeze.

'My name is Rebecca,' says Rebecca. 'This is only my second ever group therapy and I don't think I understand the language. I don't think I understand how all this works.'

'Is Carl coming today?' asks Alice.

'No,' says Morwenna.

Rebecca feels her lungs relax slightly.

Morwenna turns to the smiling boy. 'You're coming to the end of your time here too, aren't you, Frank?' she says. 'How do you feel about that?'

Frank runs a hand through his filthy hair. His eyes dance and he taps a foot to his internal beat.

'It's all great,' he says. 'I'm not going to go back to breaking down and I'm not going back to uni. I have other stuff to do. I'm going to kick back and take it easy. I'm going to lead. I'm going to live my life, not let it live me.'

The thickset man introduces himself as Kostas. 'I've been everywhere,' he says. 'I thought I'd seen everything. I've been a mercenary for twenty-three years. I've been to Iraq and Kosovo. I've seen combat in Sierra Leone and Rwanda but this—' he gestures with an upturned palm '—is the roughest place, full of some of the toughest people I've ever met.'

Rebecca looks at Alice. Alice looks at the floor. Morwenna writes 'TOUGH' on the whiteboard.

Oh God, thinks Rebecca.

'Now,' says Morwenna, 'I think we need to check our boundaries. Do you understand what boundaries are, Rebecca?'

Rebecca shakes her head. 'Fences, walls, hedges?' she says and then she realizes how facetious she sounds, but she still thinks group therapy is ridiculous.

'Alice?' says Morwenna, ignoring Rebecca, which makes Rebecca feel even sillier.

Alice puts her book neatly onto her knees. 'The ability to say no without qualification, guilt or apology because saying no is what works best for you,' she says.

'So,' says Morwenna, 'if I were your boss and I said to you one day after work, "Hey, Alice, can you stay for an extra hour; I'm really up against it this week," and you really didn't want to or, indeed, *couldn't* give that extra time, what would your answer be?'

Alice picks up her pen. She grips it quite tightly and then she says. 'Now, I would say, "I'm afraid I won't be able to do that for you this evening, Stephen."'

Morwenna smiles encouragingly. 'And how would you feel about being able to say that?' she asks.

'I think I would feel a bit guilty but before I came here, I would have said, "Yes, absolutely," every time.'

Rebecca feels herself beginning to take an interest. It's as if something in her brain has switched on.

A lightbulb? asks Betty.

Yes, thinks Rebecca.

Rebecca walks back to her ward. She takes the stairs and gets lost. Two doctors approach, discussing something earnestly, heads together.

'Are you here for the meeting?' one doctor asks Rebecca.

Rebecca looks from one to the other. 'I'm on ward seven,' she says. 'I'm one of the mad people.' The doctors direct Rebecca back to her ward. She heads straight for the kitchen. She pours Colombian coffee into the cafetière straight from the bag, adds hot water and carries it to her room. Sod Titus, she thinks.

At 3.55 p.m., Rebecca's screeches start. They are less vicious than they had been the day before, so Rebecca lies down on her bed and stretches her feet towards the ceiling to stop her muscles cramping. She flexes her fingers. She lies on the floor in the pose of The Child, which is the only yoga pose she knows. It doesn't work, so she opens her computer and searches Spotify for Townes Van Zandt. She puts on 'Waiting Around To Die' and lies on her bed in the darkening room, staring at the ceiling. Sometimes her muscles cramp.

There is a rap on the door and Titus walks in. 'Oh,' he says,

'I feel as though I have just walked into a teenager's bedroom. Sit up, please, Rebecca, and look at me. What on earth are you doing?' He sits down on the Muppet chair.

Rebecca slams her laptop shut and sits up. 'I'm sorry,' she says. 'I've got the screeches. It's screech o'clock.'

Rebecca pushes her hair out of her eyes and looks at Titus. He puts his head on one side.

'Screech o'clock? Really, Rebecca?'

Rebecca feels a bit irritated 'Well, I *am* screeching,' she says crossly.

Titus sighs. 'Where are we with that?' he asks. 'Have you taken a Tranquiltolam? Have you been down to the nurses' station and asked them for one?'

'No,' says Rebecca.

'Why?' asks Titus.

'Because I was trying to manage it without drugs.'

'Whilst listening to someone singing about dying, in the dark,' says Titus, reaching behind him and switching on the light. 'I think we should shed some light on the subject. I believe that's my job.' Rebecca had hoped he hadn't heard Townes.

'If you were in physical pain, you wouldn't try to manage it by yourself, would you? You'd be down there like a shot asking for codeine. It's not different, you know. What is it with all my patients today? Any minute now, you'll all be asking for homeopathic eye drops or some such twaddle.'

Rebecca smiles. 'I wouldn't,' she says.

'Good,' says Titus. 'Any questions? Apart from, how long is a piece of string?'

'I can't get a signal in here,' says Rebecca. 'I have to stand on my bed on one leg and wave my phone in the air. Is there somewhere better to pick up? At the moment, it's all about texts and you know how easily misunderstood a text can be.'

'You can get one in the no-smoking area in the courtyard,' says Titus, standing up. He walks to the door. 'Go and get a Tranquiltolam,' he says. 'Have a lovely weekend, missus, and don't drink too much coffee.' Then he is gone.

Rebecca gets off her bed. She walks across the room and opens the door. She walks down to the nurses' station. Titus is standing there with his back to her, talking to Miriam.

'I just thought you ought to be aware,' he is saying. 'I don't know but she might just try it.'

Rebecca walks over to them.

'I would like a Tranquiltolam, please, Miriam,' she says.

PIECE 49

Rebecca drinks too much coffee and then Ellis comes to visit. He whirls into Rebecca's room like a maelstrom. He is high and happy but also despairing. He is wearing white ripped jeans. His hair has grown a bit and is tipped blond by the Mediterranean sun.

'What in the name of fuckery are you doing in here?' he asks, flinging himself down on Titus's chair. 'I go away for a two-week holiday and when I come back, you've got yourself banged up. What the fuck is going on?'

Ellis is just back from Greece where he has been helping some friends move a yacht from here to there.

Ellis is very hyper. He has fallen in love again and *not* with Rod. This is good but it is also complicated.

'This is my friend, Ellis Scupper,' Rebecca tells the nurses at the nurses' station, just in case they think Ellis is another patient. 'Ellis is a doctor, a psychiatrist for children,' Rebecca tells them. The nurses look at Ellis and they smile understandingly.

'Show me a photograph of him,' says Rebecca. 'How was the yacht? How was the sailing?' It is such a relief for Rebecca not to talk about herself. Rebecca wishes she had been in Greece too. She loves Greece. She imagines a wine dark sea, white pebble beaches, crystal water and silver-green olive groves.

'The yacht?' says Ellis.

'Yes, weren't you going to move it from here to there?'

'Oh, it was an absolute nightmare, force six Meltemi at the very least and none of us can sail, not really.' Ellis looks around her room. He gets up and puts his head into the bathroom. 'No ligature points,' he says. 'How entertaining. Are you mad?'

'North, north-west,' says Rebecca. 'When the wind is southerly, I know a hawk from a handsaw.'

'Good, good,' says Ellis.

'Tell me about Greece,' says Rebecca. 'I'm bored here. If you can't be entertaining, then I'm afraid you will have to leave. I'm very busy being bored.'

'Are you still seeing that doctor?' says Ellis, sitting down again. 'The one with the chemistry set?'

'He hasn't got a chemistry set. *I'm* his chemistry set. Greece. Now!' says Rebecca.

So Ellis tells her.

'We sailed together. Our thighs were touching and at night we slept side-by-side in a white tent.'

'What happened?' asks Rebecca.

'I can still see his brown hand on the white jib sheet, his strong, corded forearm, his biceps, a thin tracery of blue veins at his wrist. I was the helmsman.'

'Shut *up*!' says Rebecca.

'Isn't that enough?' says Ellis.

'No,' says Rebecca. 'Sex, what about sex?'

'Oh, sex,' says Ellis. 'If you had had more, you would understand. This was a meeting of souls. You know the kind of thing, eyes locking, hearts thumping.' He clasps his hands under his chin. 'It was *so* up my boulevard. I literally can't tell you.'

Rebecca hasn't had sex with anyone but Sam, it's true, but she wouldn't light up like a firework if someone touched her leg.

'So what then?' she asks. 'Is he coming to see you in London?'

'No, he's all about Seattle. He loves the rain,' says Ellis.

'Seattle?' says Rebecca. 'Do you want some coffee? Ooh, am I free associating?'

'Love some but stop that. It's weird and once you've picked up all the language in a place like this, it's difficult to get rid of it,' says Ellis. 'What's the matter with you? What's all this with the hands?' He waves his hands about in an imitation of Rebecca.

'Screeches,' Rebecca tells him. 'I thought I had a lid on them. Seeing you has made me all excited.'

'Screeches?' says Ellis. 'Bizarre, what are you on?'

'Collapsetine, Dulsexatine, Washingmachine,' says Rebecca.

'Coffee, where?' says Ellis.

'Kitchen,' says Rebecca. 'Follow me.'

They sit in Rebecca's room drinking black coffee and they talk of bays dappled green and blue and white pebble beaches.

They remember silver-green olive groves and vine-shaded tavernas and they wonder about the call of Seattle.

'Have you got a picture?' asks Rebecca.

'In my heart,' says Ellis.

'Jesus,' says Rebecca.

'No, not at all,' says Ellis. 'He's more Jonathan Miller but soo much younger.'

'How much?' asks Rebecca.

'He's thirty-eight,' says Ellis.

'Unattached?' asks Rebecca.

Ellis takes a gulp of his coffee. 'Hope so,' he says.

'Jewish?' asks Rebecca.

'Don't know,' says Ellis. 'Can you keep your hands still at all? It looks terribly affected.'

'Come and have a look at my drugs sheet. I expect they'll show it to you, then you can tell me which drug is making me all antic.'

'Won't Dr Whatever-the-Fuck tell you?'

Ellis looks at Rebecca's drug sheet. 'It all looks fine,' he says, 'but of course it's not my speciality.'

Rebecca adores Ellis. He's so funny.

PIECE 50

'I remember once there was a full moon,' Rebecca tells Titus. 'The sea was full of phosphorescence. Have you seen it?'

'Yes, although not in this country,' he says.

Rebecca is telling Titus about her childhood.

'It might be helpful to understand some of your history,' he tells her. 'I believe there may be some childhood issue that is driving the way you are feeling now.'

Rebecca looks at him, narrowing her eyes. She really doesn't want him to push her again. She doesn't feel up to it.

'It will be something we're not yet aware of.' Titus is being very friendly. Rebecca isn't sure she trusts a friendly Titus. She thinks she prefers him when he is very cross with her. She looks at him now, sitting in the Muppet chair. He is wearing a blue-checked shirt with no tie with lightweight, navy-blue suit trousers. Outside, the sun is bouncing off the pavements.

'What are you thinking?' he asks.

Rebecca shakes her head again. 'Nothing,' she says. Sometimes, she thinks he is nice to lull her into a false sense of security so that she will be more confiding and she really doesn't want him to make her do any more 'inner child work', so she must be on her guard.

'Tell me more about these beach parties. Were you and this . . . ' he looks at his pad, 'Harriet, the only children there?'

'My brothers were there. So were Harriet's. Anyway, every wave was tipped luminous green.' Rebecca remembers standing thigh deep in the water, splashing her hands and sending flashes of green light skittering across the surface.

'Look at me,' Harriet called. As usual she was further out. 'Look!' and Rebecca saw, as she dived through a wave, that her whole body shimmered and that she trailed green-gold ribbons like a mermaid.

'And you all swam naked? The children and adults together?'

'It wasn't weird to be naked. It was nice.'

'How old were you?' asks Titus.

'I don't know . . . eight, maybe nine.'

'And you were naked with . . . ?'

'All the people at the beach party. Nothing weird happened.'

Titus sits back in his chair. 'Didn't it? It sounds weird to me,' he says. Then he says, 'It's odd, I've noticed that you've said several times, "I was about eight or nine", when recounting your childhood. Did anything happen before or after that age?'

Rebecca shakes her head as if she has water in her ears. 'I grew up,' she says.

She knew she shouldn't have talked to him so unguardedly. She remembers swimming through the deep, dark water, salt on her lips, the drag of the current, the stars winking overhead, a huge, buttery moon, Harriet by her side.

Harriet's whisper.

'Did you see Tony Wilson's willy? It's huge.'

PIECE 51

It was a Saturday and Rebecca was going to be dropped off at Harriet's. Harriet was feeling better after her fall. She didn't spend the afternoons in bed anymore. Pen was going to drop Rebecca off on her way into town. Pen needed to do some shopping and she would pick Rebecca up on the way back. David was staying at home with the boys.

Rebecca sat in the passenger seat while Pen drove with her seat pushed back, with her arms straight out in front of her. She was wearing a pair of rusty-red velvet trousers. Her sunglasses were perched, as usual, on top of her head and her dark hair was tied back from her forehead with a turquoise Indian silk scarf. She'd kicked off her clogs before she got into the car and Rebecca saw that she had painted her toenails a dark plum.

'I can't drive in these,' Pen told her, chucking the clogs onto the back seat with her tasselled, suede bag. Her mother, Rebecca thought, was very beautiful.

The day was hot and dull. A fretful wind tugged at the hedgerows. The great grey East Anglian sky sat low over the trees, shutting in the heat like a lid. 'There'll be a storm tonight,' Pen said. Pen was afraid of storms. Rebecca hoped that they would be safely at home when the storm broke.

At Harriet's house, Pen opened the glove compartment and rifled inside. She retrieved a lipstick and, using the rear-view mirror, painted her lips a deep red. Rebecca wished she was going shopping too. She watched the Cortina turn on the gravel drive and disappear in a cloud of dust.

Harriet's house reared up before Rebecca. Its pale yellow face seemed obscurely forbidding, the windows staring down at her, unlit, like blinded eyes. She hadn't really felt like spending the afternoon here. Harriet wasn't very nice.

Yesterday, just before bedtime, Rebecca had washed her hair, rinsing it under the cold tap until her scalp shrivelled because Mrs Lightwing had told her that rinsing hair in warm water would set the soap. Then, using the grips that Pen had bought her, she had clipped her wet hair all the way down both sides of her head. She had slept on it like that. It wasn't very comfortable but, today, her hair hung down each side of her face in two strawberry-blonde curtains. She knew Harriet would notice and she knew that she wouldn't be nice about it.

Now, standing in the drive in front of Harriet's house, she took off her glasses and pushed them into her jeans pocket.

'You don't need to wear spectacles all the time. In the long run, spectacles weaken your eye muscles. Try wearing them just for school or reading,' Mrs Lightwing had told her.

'Boys don't make passes at girls who wear glasses,' Harriet sang, the last time she had seen her.

'Four eyes,' a boy at school had said.

Rebecca wasn't sure if having passes made by boys was

a good thing and she knew she had only two eyes but Mrs Lightwing was usually right about things and Rebecca was wearing her glasses less often.

Harriet was sitting at the kitchen table doing her homework when Rebecca let herself into the house. 'Why aren't you wearing your glasses?' she asked. 'How many fingers am I holding up?' she said. 'Why is your hair all straggly?'

Miranda stood at the kitchen sink, peeling potatoes for supper.

'We're having potato dauphinoise,' said Harriet. 'Do you want to stay for supper? Do you want to stay the night?'

'Mummy, can we go and school Ambrose in the paddock? Rebecca can help me put up jumps, if she can see what she's doing.' Miranda leaned across to the windowsill behind the sink and turned on the radio. A Haydn cello concerto trickled into the room.

'You can stay if you like, darling,' she said, half turning to speak to Rebecca, 'but you'll have to leave first thing as we're going to church and then straight over to the Holbrooks' for lunch. Val Holbrook has roped me in to the hunt ball committee. It's such a bore, what? But darling Virginia is such a lovely friend for Harriet and they're taking Communion classes together.'

Rebecca wondered why Miranda was wearing sunglasses to peel potatoes.

'And they have a tennis court,' said Harriet, running a finger down a column of figures in the exercise book in front of her. 'Finished, Mummy. Can we go to school Ambrose?'

*

In the barn, Harriet and Rebecca tacked up Ambrose together. Ambrose was in a very bad mood.

'Be careful, Rebecca, don't slam the saddle down on his back or he'll bite me.' Harriet was holding Ambrose's head and Rebecca was trying to approach him with his saddle but he kept barging sideways, pulling Harriet with him.

Rebecca put the saddle down on its pommel and felt in her jeans pocket for a carrot or a piece of apple. She usually had one or the other. Instead she found her glasses and a squashed ball of ground bait. She picked up the saddle with one arm and held her free hand out flat with the bait in her palm.

'Come on, Ambrose, come on boy.' Rebecca kept her voice low. The saddle was very heavy. Ambrose turned his head, pricking his ears. 'Come on, old boy, come on, ugly mug,' she sang softly.

Harriet loosened her grip on the reins and Ambrose took the bait from Rebecca's outstretched hand while, with the other, she slid the saddle onto his back. She bent quickly and pulled the girth under his belly, cinched it and Harriet led him from the barn.

Harriet led Ambrose through the orchard next to the barn. Red apples studded the trees and the grass was long. Rosebay willowherb grew pink against the black clapboard and the scent of wild marjoram, crushed beneath the pony's hooves, filled the air. Rebecca ran ahead and opened the gate to the paddock and, once inside, helped Harriet to mount.

Sitting on the five-bar gate watching Harriet, Rebecca wondered why Harriet bothered. Riding Ambrose was very unsatisfactory.

First of all, he resisted being tacked up. Then, when the saddle was on, following bribery and several vicious nips, Harriet would put a foot in the stirrup and he would whirl round making her hop desperately on one leg until she could, if she was lucky, pull herself up and throw herself onto his back. Today, Rebecca had held him by the bridle, pinning him against the gate with her body and Harriet had been able to scramble aboard but normally she had to manage by herself or ask Patrick if he wasn't too busy.

Now, Harriet was trying to trot around the perimeter of the field and Ambrose was star-gazing and cantering sideways at the same time while she sawed ineffectually at his mouth.

'Try to make him walk,' called Rebecca from the gate. She knew immediately that she should have kept quiet or perhaps said, 'Well done,' as they passed her.

Harriet pulled up by standing up in the stirrups and hauling on the reins with her whole body weight. She turned sideways in the saddle, throwing a leg over Ambrose's neck, and slid to the ground. Rebecca saw that her face was white with fury. She punched Ambrose on the side of his nose and led him over to Rebecca.

'You think you're better than me,' she said, hissing the words through clenched teeth. 'You think you know everything. You think if you brush your hair all nicely and write stories to Father Francis and bribe my pony, that you're something, that you can tell me how to ride or what to think. Well, you can't. You're nothing; you're not even a proper Catholic. You're going to burn in hell fire forever.'

PIECE 52

It is Sunday and Rebecca has agreed to try to eat her lunch in the cafeteria with Anya, the charge nurse. She can't really see the point of eating in the cafeteria but, as she has decided to be compliant, she supposes it's better if she complies, if only for consistency's sake. It is 12.30 p.m. when Anya knocks on Rebecca's door. 'Come down to the cafeteria with me,' she says, smiling. Anya is very sweet. She has only been back at work for two months, having had her first baby. Rebecca looks at her gentle, untroubled face and her heart hurts. Poor Anya, she thinks. Rebecca follows her downstairs to the cafeteria. She runs her hands along the wall as she follows Anya through the double fire doors. She taps the wall twice before going into the cafeteria.

'Take a tray,' says Anya, pointing at a pile of stacked trays. Rebecca takes a tray,

'What's this thing on it?' she asks. Her heart is beginning to jump and she is darting looks to her left and right. There are people sitting at tables here and there talking and eating.

'It's a paper mat, to stop your plate slipping and to catch spills,' says Anya. She looks a bit confused.

Anya stands in front of the salad bar. She spoons coleslaw and tomatoes onto her plate. She adds couscous. She turns back to Rebecca.

'You can help yourself,' she says. Then she looks worried. 'You can choose anything you like. It doesn't have to be salad. There are lots of main courses over there and cheeses, too.'

Rebecca grabs a small bowl. She fills it to the brim with cucumber, then she says, 'I can't do this. It's frightening me. I have to go back to my room.' Without waiting for a response, she puts the bowl down on the floor and bolts. The fire doors clap shut behind her and she runs up the stairs and past the nurses' station. She runs into her bedroom and throws herself on the bed and then realizes that she is crying.

Later Anya brings her a printout.

Patient Care Plan, reads Rebecca.

PROBLEM/NEED

Rebecca's level of anxiety has been steadily increasing. Rebecca reports feeling overwhelmed by her responsibilities and to-do lists and failing to prioritise and consequently she fails to sleep.

She has said: 'I couldn't possibly eat a meal in a dining room full of people. The very idea makes me feel sick.'

INTERVENTIONS

Rebecca has agreed to meet with her key nurse three times a week to discuss/review her stated needs.

1. Rebecca is to eat her lunch in the ward kitchen with her nominated nurse.
2. Allocated staff to escort Rebecca to the dining room to choose her meal at lunch time, which she will then eat in the ward kitchen.
3. Rebecca to start writing lists in order of priority.

Oh bum, thinks Rebecca.

'This eating thing, Titus, it's not working. I mean, it can't,' says Rebecca.

'Why?' asks Titus.

'Because,' Rebecca says, 'the reason I'm here at all is because I lost control of everything.'

'Drinking,' says Titus.

'Yes, if you like.'

'Not "if I like",' says Titus. 'As a fact.'

'OK,' she says. 'But the loss of control was about drinking, so it wasn't about eating.'

'But you are restricting your eating.'

'I'm eating as *I* eat and I'd like to be allowed to continue to eat like that. I'm not underweight and I'm not obsessing about food but I don't want the tiny bit of self-determination left to me, while I am at the hospital, to be taken away from me.'

'You're drinking far too much coffee,' says Titus.

'Too much for what?' asks Rebecca.

'It's making you agitated.'

Rebecca says nothing.

'Isn't it?' he says.

'Is there such a thing as coffee rehab?' she asks.

Titus grins. Then he says, 'You are here to address your anxieties. You are clearly anxious about eating in a cafeteria. Or eating at all, it seems.'

'I eat.'

'As little as possible.'

'I'm worried all these pills will make me fat.'

'And I've told you that they won't.'

'I don't have to do everything I'm anxious about, do I? I mean, I'm really frightened by spiders but I don't have to pick one up to overcome arachnophobia, it's not necessary. I just avoid them.'

'Eating is rather more necessary than picking up spiders.'

'In my life, I'm far more likely to have to pick up a spider than to eat in a cafeteria,' says Rebecca.

'Lucky you,' says Titus.

'So can we leave the food thing? Please, Titus, please?'

'You will gain nothing by begging,' he says.

'I got my GHDs back by begging.'

'I think you caught me at a weak moment.'

Rebecca picks up her glasses from her bedside table. She puts them on, raises her eyebrows and looks at him over the top of them.

'Very funny,' says Titus.

'So can we leave it?' asks Rebecca. 'I don't have an eating disorder.'

'No,' says Titus. 'Your problem is social anxiety and the eating issue is a symptom of social anxiety and, as such, is part of the problem.' He stands up, and then he says, 'I don't want to hear that you have drunk any coffee past midday. And if you do, believe me, I will hear.'

Then he is gone.

Rebecca sits for a while on her bed. She wonders why Titus is allowed to tell her what to do. She must be consenting to it, otherwise how would he be doing it? It is really very odd. She has a very strong urge to go and make herself a cup of coffee.

Rebecca follows Miriam to the kitchen. On the kitchen table is a plate covered with a metal dome and a creamy pudding in a pot sitting next to it.

'Do you want me to warm it up for you?' asks Miriam.

'No,' says Rebecca. 'It's fine like that.'

Rebecca and Miriam eat their lunch together. Miriam tells Rebecca about Nigeria, how she lived by the sea there and how her mother would buy great baskets of big juicy prawns from the fishermen as they beached their boats on the golden sand. She tells how the sun shone and how she and the other children from her village played in the deep green sea and the white surf.

'We weren't supposed to get wet,' she tells Rebecca, 'but we did it every day. It was so beautiful, so tempting.' Rebecca pictures Miriam as a child, her black hair escaping from its ties, her beatific smile rivalling the sunlight and her dress wet to the waist with clean, salty water.

'We didn't have eggs like the ones you have here,' says Miriam. 'The chickens ran around in our back yard. The eggs had deep yellow yolks and thick brown shells because the hens ran free and foraged for themselves. I don't like the eggs you can buy in the supermarket here. They're not the same thing.'

When they have eaten their lunch, Rebecca tells Miriam that she had better make a pot of coffee, quickly, before her doctor turns up.

Miriam smiles and sunlight pours into the room, then she leaves.

Rebecca is standing in the kitchen. She wants a drink of water so she walks over to the sink and turns on the cold tap, looking around for a glass at the same time, but there isn't a glass and no water comes from the tap.

She sighs.

Turning back into the room, she sees that the table is in the wrong place and that the chairs around it are not their mid-century, Danish ones but a mismatched set of varying colours and sizes. She walks over to the table and sits down on a large pink chair with curling arms, which appears to be made of plastic. In the middle of the table is a cake stand and on the stand is a cake which Rebecca can see, without reaching out to touch, is made of plaster. The plaster icing is pink and is studded with vermillion strawberries.

She doesn't know where she is, she thinks, but she feels curiously unperturbed by this.

Under her fingers, the table feels plastic too. It looks like wood, but it isn't. Their table, at home, had been made by her younger brother, Giles. Giles is a carpenter. Their table is made of European oak and is bigger than this one.

Giles had been so proud of the table. Rebecca remembers him running his strong hands over the surface, pointing out to her how he had laid each single plank so that the grain alternated and the table would not split even when the wood shrank or expanded with temperature or age.

Rebecca remembers, too, that his hands are scarred.

'All wood-workers have scars,' he'd told her. 'Some have missing fingers. The odd lapse of concentration when you're using a chisel or a circular saw, and well, you can see what might happen.'

Rebecca could.

'One day, this table will be an antique,' he'd said, smiling his quiet smile.

Rebecca stares around the unfamiliar kitchen. There was a window, but it had the shutters closed and the light was dim. It smelt funny too; musty and forgotten.

This room really is very peculiar. Rebecca thinks she might leave it. She walks over to the kitchen door and tries to open it. It seems to be stuck, then she understands that it isn't stuck, rather, that it is being held shut from the other side. Someone is pulling the door against her.

Her heart begins to bang.

She pulls with all her strength. All of a sudden, the room is ablaze with light. Rebecca sees that the front of the room, where the shuttered window had been, is gone and that a huge hand with bitten, black-rimmed fingernails is blindly groping for her, knocking over the table, scattering the chairs.

Then she wakes up.

Rebecca is standing in the middle of her dark bedroom in the hospital. She doesn't move because she thinks she can't.

'Come along, get back into bed.' Rebecca feels Miriam guiding her gently. 'Come on, just a little sleepwalk,' she hears.

She gets into bed and she falls asleep.

Then it is morning.

A slab of grey light has come through a gap in the curtains, turning the chenille chair from grey to a gloomy blue. Rebecca knows she has been dreaming but she can't remember the details of her dream. 'A doll's house,' she says to herself aloud. 'Giles,' she says and she sits up slowly and leans against the headboard.

No one has told Giles that she is ill in hospital. She told Sam to tell no one and mostly he hasn't. He told Ellis because Ellis would have wanted to know where she was. He wouldn't just let her disappear. He told Megan because Megan had wanted to go for a walk round the park and had been wondering why she wasn't answering her calls. The children know, of course, but everyone else has no idea.

If Giles knew, Rebecca is sure that he would have jumped in his van and driven all the way to London from Cornwall, just as he had when he'd delivered the table. 'Table,' she says. 'A dream about a table?' No, she can't remember.

Dear Giles, she thinks. It is a long time since she has seen him. If she gets better, she will go to see him, she decides. She will stand in his workshop next to his cottage and talk to him while he works.

It was in his workshop that he had made their table, hand-finishing its tapered legs with fine sandpaper and oiling the oak. Rebecca loved Giles's workshop. She loved the smell of the sawdust, the curls of blond wood on the cobbled floor and the stacked planks.

Giles used to give her offcuts of wood which she took

home and piled up in the spare room. She had been planning to paint on them one day, pictures of vases full of phlox and irises or perhaps oils of her children staring seriously out into the future. She would have left the wood backgrounds natural and varnished the oils to enhance the grain of the walnut, pine or chestnut. She had never done it though. The wood had just gathered dust and now she thought there were, probably, just too many images in the world.

Giles had married a Cornish girl with black hair and a huge laugh and they lived near the sea. Their small, granite cottage had been a wreck when they'd found it but Giles and Tamsin had worked hard, replacing the roof, laying new slate floors, building window seats in the deep window recesses so that you could sit and stare at the big sky, the hills and the wheeling gulls.

They had two children, Ben and Clara. But they were much younger than Rebecca's children. Clara was probably still only sixteen. Rebecca couldn't remember.

Sometimes, over the years, Sam and Rebecca had taken their family to visit Giles's and to see her mother who lived a mile or two up the road with her latest man. The last one had been a potter called Julian. Rebecca had found him rather effete but he liked her mother . . . until she didn't like him anymore.

Rebecca suddenly feels very sad. She gets out of her bed and walks across the room to pull the curtains back. The light outside is flat and grey and everything feels flat and grey inside too.

Maybe she should have told her family. Maybe they would have liked to know. Sam could have told them not to visit.

Rebecca is pretty sure Alex wouldn't have visited anyway. He was a Lowestoft fisherman with a very tangled love life and a gift for accidental children. He was always too involved to get involved. And Martin? Martin would have sent her a hamper from Fortnum's and promised he and Pilar would visit soon. 'As soon as we can,' she could almost hear him saying, knowing that it wouldn't be soon at all and that Madrid was a long way away.

Rebecca rests her forehead against the window. It is still too early for the smokers to have gathered and the courtyard below is silent. I'm so tired, she thinks. I sleep and sleep and I'm still so tired.

PIECE 53

Rebecca was standing in front of her father. He was telling her off. Her heart was going very quickly because he was angry with her.

'How many times have I told you?'

Rebecca shook her head. She didn't know how many times. She hadn't ever counted them. Now, he was standing there, brandishing a milk bottle at her.

'How many?'

Pen had told Rebecca that Daddy got cross quickly because he had a very dangerous job. She looked up at him and pushed her glasses more firmly onto her nose. Rebecca wasn't sure that her father shouted because of his job. Sometimes she thought that it was because he had too many children or because of Pen being sad or because he hadn't got enough money.

'Ten?' she guessed.

'God give me strength. Are you half-witted?' The veins in his forehead were standing out, Rebecca noticed. He slammed the milk bottle down onto the kitchen table, splashing milk onto the floor. 'Get out of my sight. Go to your bedroom and don't come back downstairs for the rest of the day,' he shouted.

Rebecca fled. She felt the tears pouring down her face as she ran. She stumbled up the stairs and ran down the passageway to her and Giles's bedroom, where she threw herself sobbing onto her bed.

It was Giles who had used the cream off the top of the milk. He had gone downstairs early and had made breakfast for himself and Rebecca.

Rebecca had said he could come fishing with her if he did exactly as she told him so that he stayed safe and didn't fall into the water. So, he had risen early and crept into the kitchen to make her breakfast as a surprise. He was going to take it upstairs for her to eat in bed.

Giles hadn't remembered to pour the cream from the top of the milk into a small jug so that their father could have it on his cornflakes. He'd just poured it straight onto their Weetabix.

When Rebecca had spooned her cereal into her mouth, she had known straight away what had happened.

'Giles, you used the cream,' she'd whispered, her eyes wide, and had watched as the colour had drained from his cheeks and his bottom lip had begun to tremble.

So, she had said she'd done it. For Rebecca, the thought of Giles being in trouble was quite intolerable.

'I'll say I did it,' she'd told Giles. 'Don't worry,' she'd said, taking his hand. 'Daddy won't know.'

That afternoon, Rebecca sat at the top of the stairs listening to her parents talk. She was very hungry because she hadn't had any lunch and she was wondering whether, if they stayed in the sitting room, she might be able to get to the kitchen and grab some bread from the breadbin without them noticing.

'I don't know if she's stupid or just insolent,' her father was saying. 'She just looks at me gormlessly whenever I tell her to do anything and then goes off and does exactly what she wants to do.'

Rebecca heard her mother reply but she couldn't hear the words. Then she heard the sitting room door shut and the sound of the record player. She slipped off the top stair and tiptoed downstairs.

PIECE 54

Rebecca spoons coffee into a cafetière. She adds hot water as Titus walks into the kitchen.

'I think this is what we call being caught red-handed,' he says. 'Is there any point, Rebecca, at which you think you may be able to follow the simplest pieces of well-meaning, well-informed advice?'

Rebecca feels her cheeks grow hot. She is holding the cafetière in one hand and her mug in the other.

'Do I have to chuck it?' she asks. Titus makes her feel about fourteen. She wonders how he does it.

'Nope,' says Titus, 'but I guarantee it will make you feel worse.'

Titus and Rebecca walk back to her room together. Rebecca can't help feeling that some of the pleasure she had anticipated from drinking the coffee has dissipated. She puts the mug and the cafetière on the chest of drawers and sits on the bed.

'Shall we begin?' says Titus. 'Do you have anything, any particular worry or concern, that you would like to talk about today?'

Rebecca thinks for a minute, then she says, 'Titus, I think

298

I have transference issues.' Rebecca had Googled it but she wasn't sure how to address the subject without annoying him.

Titus smiles a wide slow smile. 'Do you?' he says. 'With me?'

Rebecca knows she is on shaky ground because she had Googled, 'Psychiatrist Stockholm Syndrome compliance', which isn't very exact and she had come up with transference, which she thinks means reacting to someone as if they are someone else. She has decided that she reacts to Titus as if he is her father, which accounts for all the obedience, apart from the fact that it had never occurred to her to obey her father.

'Yes, I think I am reacting to you as if you are my father,' she says.

Titus puts his pad on the teak table. 'You do?' he says. 'In which way exactly?'

Rebecca has thought about it. 'Not exactly as if you were my father but as if you were the father that I might have wanted had he been taking care of me through this process.'

'So, a father figure?'

'It's the only reason I can think of that might explain why I should do as you tell me.'

'Which would all add up, if you actually did do anything I told you to do. I really wish that my patients wouldn't Google things. Your knowing very little about something as complicated as transference could be extraordinarily unhelpful.'

Rebecca thinks about this for a moment. 'Well, I may be actually transferring my relationship with my actual father on to you because I never did what he told me to do either.'

Titus sighs.

'To employ some knight's move thinking . . . ' says Rebecca.

'Knight's move thinking is not something one can employ,' says Titus.

'No, I Googled it,' says Rebecca. 'It's a quick way of arriving at C from A without having to visit B.'

'No, it isn't,' says Titus. 'It's a disrupted and illogical thought process. What is your point?'

'Oh,' says Rebecca. 'Umm . . . oh yeah, that I am reacting to you as if you are my real father which is why I can't do what you tell me to do.'

'Could you try not to react to me like that?'

Rebecca rolls her eyes. 'Obviously,' she says.

'Do you know,' says Titus, 'this is the first time you have mentioned your father to me?'

Rebecca thinks for a minute. 'Is it?' she says, knowing that it is.

'Yes, it is. You've told me about your brothers . . . the fisherman, the carpenter, the teacher in Spain. Your mother lives in Cornwall near your youngest brother Giles. That's right, isn't it?'

Rebecca nods.

'But nothing about your father at all, except now, that you found it difficult to take instruction from him. Do you know why that might have been?'

Rebecca takes a deep breath. 'I think,' she says, 'it was because, ever since I was very young . . . '

Titus leans forward in his chair. 'Yes,' he says.

'That I thought my father didn't really understand what was going on.'

'And *you* did?'

Rebecca nods again. 'Not *all* of it, but he didn't seem to understand any of it. He was confused, I think. It made him cross. As if everyone else was in on a secret and he was being left out.'

'And now?'

'Oh, he knows *now* but, at the time, I don't think he had a clue.'

'What didn't he know,' asks Titus, 'that he knows now?'

'About love,' says Rebecca. 'It's a really terrible thing to be married to the wrong person. It's terrible for both people.'

'I imagine it is,' Titus says.

'She sails,' says Rebecca.

'Who does?' he asks.

'His proper person, his second wife. She sails and they love each other.'

Titus sits back in his chair and looks at Rebecca. 'I'm glad,' he says.

PIECE 55

Harriet and Rebecca were sitting on top of a haystack.

So, was it August? asks Betty.

'Or July,' says Rebecca aloud. 'It was a haystack not a straw-stack.'

She is sitting in her bedroom, in the hospital, remembering.

The haystack was in the middle of a field and all around it the grass had grown long and green. The grass rippled like water in the warm summer breeze and the sky above was powder-blue with white clouds.

The hay smelt sweet.

Harriet and Rebecca had climbed up on top of the stack by hooking their fingers through the baler twine and finding footholds between the bales. They were very high up.

Rebecca could see across to Benham Wood on her right and, to her left, she could see Ambrose grazing in his paddock, Harriet's house and the barn beyond it and a line of blurry poplars turning grey and purple on the horizon.

Harriet and Rebecca were having an argument.

It was about palmistry.

Harriet had told Rebecca that she had learned to read

a person's future from the lines on the palms of their hands. Rebecca had never heard of such a thing, nor, she'd said, did she believe it possible and, she had added, where had Harriet learned to do it?

Harriet had been vague on the where but was very definite that she could tell Rebecca's future. She grabbed hold of her wrist, twisted it so that her palm faced upwards, and told Rebecca to 'hold still'. Then she bent her sleek head over the palm, which she suddenly dropped with a high-pitched shriek, as though burned.

'What does it show?' Rebecca felt suddenly frightened.

Harriet shook her head, refusing to speak or meet Rebecca's eyes. 'Doom,' she muttered so quietly that Rebecca almost didn't hear her.

'What?' Rebecca reached out and pulled at Harriet's upper arm, digging her nails in.

Harriet screeched, then threw her head back and laughed, cackling her glee through her small even teeth. 'Got you,' she gasped. 'Got you!' Then, abruptly, she stopped laughing and pulled a piece of hay from the stack and began to chew the end, gazing out across the field. 'Don't you ever mind being so stupid?' She turned to look at Rebecca as she added, 'Milo says you're stupid.'

Rebecca liked Harriet's older brother. Milo was tall with long legs and dark hair like Harriet's. He had the same sleepy blue eyes and, when he laughed, which was often, they looked almost triangular. She felt her cheeks flame.

'Believing people isn't stupid,' said Rebecca, trying to steady her voice. She knew she was more upset by Milo thinking her stupid than by anything else Harriet had said.

'Milo says that if you go on not eating meat, you will go bald with malnutrition. All your yellowy hair and your teeth will fall out and then you will look even uglier.'

Harriet often commented on Rebecca's physical shortcomings. Rebecca tried hard not to concentrate on them herself but Harriet seemed to think them important. Sometimes, she wondered if Harriet would be her friend at all if they had been at the same school or if she would have been too ashamed of her.

Rebecca dragged her hair behind her ears with both hands; she could feel heat behind her eyes. 'If I'm so ugly and stupid, I had better go home then,' she said. She got onto her hands and knees and began to climb down the stack backwards.

Of course she missed her footing and of course she fell, winding herself and biting her tongue so that her mouth filled with blood and the tears in her eyes flooded down her cheeks in a wave of pain and self-pity.

She remembered looking up and seeing Harriet's dark head silhouetted against the glimmering sky and hearing her crow of laughter.

Cow, says Betty.

'She was,' agrees Rebecca, 'but I loved her.'

PIECE 56

Sam comes to visit Rebecca. He comes every day on the Tube in his lunch hour. This time he brings a plastic bag full of her saved letters and her six teenage diaries. He drops them on the bed.

'These are all I could find,' he says. 'They were where you told me they would be, in a shoebox, in the cupboard at the top of the stairs.'

He looks exhausted. The plains of his face have changed. The muscles have slackened or bunched beneath the skin, bringing tension to his mouth and brow while sinking his eyes deep in two striated pockets.

'There aren't any others,' says Rebecca. She makes him lie on the bed and she strokes his hair. Sam had been out for dinner with Kit the previous evening.

'He hates his job,' Sam tells Rebecca. 'He says he'll quit.' Kit is working in a wine shop and says he spends most of his time grabbing shoplifters before they can bolt into the Tube station opposite. 'If he quits, he won't be able to pay his rent and he'll have to move back home.'

'Like a boomerang,' says Rebecca. Then she says, 'I'm

really worried about coming home. Everything might just be the same and I might just go back to the same patterns and get the same results.'

'I've done my best,' says Sam. 'What else can I do?' He turns his palms upwards in a gesture of helplessness. 'Have you understood the impact all this has had on the family?' Sam is very cross with Rebecca. 'At which point do you take responsibility? I'm exhausted. I'm getting ill again.'

'I have to tell you what I need,' Rebecca tells him. She keeps stroking his head. Sam has very nice hair. Rebecca quite wishes she had hair like Sam's. It is smooth like feathers. 'I have all this therapy and Titus tells me where I have to draw a line, how I have to be succinct and to the point about my needs, so I am and then you just get cross.'

'I'm not cross. I'm fucking worn out,' says Sam. 'And I'm fed up with Dr Bloody Titus. When did he become your guru?'

Rebecca knows he is worn out. She knows he can't do his job properly without her.

'He noticed. He believed me. He put me in here. You didn't notice; you just let me fall.' Rebecca thinks that sounded worse than it was supposed to.

'Rebecca, *I* put you in here. I did know. I told you *he* insisted on it because I thought you were more likely to agree. No one knew how unwell you were before your overdose. Did Ellis? Did the children?'

Rebecca thinks about Titus. 'If you create an elaborate smokescreen, you're hardly in a position to complain when it proves effective, are you?' He'd said that when she'd first met him. She shakes her head. 'No one knew, did they?' she says sadly.

'No,' says Sam. 'It was exactly the same as when you had babies, with you just lying there silently in agony so everyone thinks you're doing really well and hardly hurting at all. Why didn't you scream? How are people supposed to know if you're in pain? We're not mind-readers. Afterwards, it's all about post-traumatic stress and blame.' Sam is sitting up now. His eyes are full of tears. 'I have to go back to work now,' he says, 'and I've had nothing to eat.'

'Neither have I,' says Rebecca. 'Let's walk to the Tube via that sushi place and you can pick up something there. They will probably let me go if you are with me.'

'What about you?'

'I don't care if I eat or not,' says Rebecca.

They sign themselves out of the hospital. As they leave, a clatter of anorexics arrives at the door, chattering excitedly. They all look about eleven years old.

They walk back to the Tube together. Rebecca puts her arms round Sam and hugs him. Sam is her best friend and she loves him. Really one ought not to let one's best friend down. They stop off at the sushi place and sit at one of the tables. Sam has spicy salmon rice and eel sushi. Rebecca has some salad. Outside the Tube station, they hug goodbye.

'I'm supposed to walk you back,' says Sam.

'I'll pretend you did,' says Rebecca.

'You're too thin,' Sam tells her. 'Will you promise me you'll try to eat more. Eating is always the first thing that goes with you. Any stress and you're not hungry.'

Rebecca is secretly pleased. It's about time she was thin, but she says, 'I'll try if you want me to.'

'I do,' says Sam. He kisses the top of her head. 'I'll see you tomorrow,' he says.

'I think I'm allowed to stay the night at home,' says Rebecca.

'Good,' says Sam. 'We've missed you so much. Pomp will be ecstatic.'

Rebecca walks back to the hospital. She picks up an *Evening Standard* on the way. MAN CRUSHED TO DEATH IN LIFT SHAFT, shouts the front page. MAN CRUSHED TO DEATH BY WIFE'S INEPTITUDE, thinks Rebecca.

She sits on her bed. She goes into the bathroom and puts on some more mascara. She brushes her hair. Rebecca has decided that she must be in charge of Titus. It's a long shot but it will be easier if she looks good. She looks in the mirror. She does look quite nice actually, she thinks.

There is a double rap on the bedroom door and Titus walks in. Rebecca is sitting on the bed cross-legged reading *Humboldt's Gift* with her glasses on the end of her nose. Her hair is slippery clean and very shiny and she is wearing her new jumper, which makes her eyes look bright blue. Carefully, she lays her book aside and takes off her glasses, holding them by one arm. She hasn't had them on very long so they haven't left red dents on each side of her nose.

'Hello,' she says quietly. 'How are you?'

Titus sits down.

'You've just missed Sam,' Rebecca tells him.

'How did he think you were?' asks Titus. He takes off his glasses and holds them by one arm too. He looks friendly.

'You are coordinating so well with the room,' he says. 'Your jumper and your eyes are almost exactly the same colour blue as the headboard on the bed.'

Rebecca smiles. 'Well, you must have noticed how I claw the air to coordinate. It's my major preoccupation,' she says.

Titus grins. He really does have rather an adorable smile, thinks Rebecca.

'So, how does your husband think you are?' he asks again.

'It's how *he* is that's worrying,' says Rebecca. 'He's on his last legs.'

'And, he's not my patient,' says Titus. 'Didn't he say how he found you? And don't say satnav, just don't.'

'I think he used the satnav,' says Rebecca.

Titus sighs.

'OK,' she says. 'He was upset that I said I was worried about going home. He said he'd done everything he could think of to make it better but what could he honestly do when he's out of the house for twelve hours a day? I told him I was coming home on Saturday and that I could stay the night . . . '

Titus puts his hand up. 'No staying the night,' he says. 'Baby steps, one thing at a time. I want you back here by six on Saturday evening.'

'I thought I was going to spend the night at home and come back on Sunday.'

'Well, you're not,' says Titus. 'Night time could be very difficult for you and I need you back here by six so that you are here when the nurses change shift; otherwise they won't know who I'm asking them to give the medication to and I'll have to get cross with them.'

'Gosh, I bet that *terrifies* them,' says Rebecca.

'I'm very much afraid that it doesn't,' says Titus, taking Rebecca's words at face value. 'I don't seem able to really put the fear of God into people.'

It's the dimples, thinks Rebecca.

'Have a nice weekend, missus,' he says.

'You too,' says Rebecca, and he disappears. Misses, she thinks.

After he's gone, Rebecca decides to sneak a cup of coffee. She thinks Miriam has gone on a break so, if she moves quickly, she may be able to get one in before anyone notices. As she passes the nurses' station, she sees the man from the waiting room with the catatonic wife, the man who'd said he was physically extremely ill but mentally fine.

'I've told the doctor,' the man is telling a nurse. 'She's had loads of ECT. After the first two, she was well again but look at her now.' He gestures behind him to where his wife slumps, pale as death, against the wall. Her mouth and eyes are swollen and her hair a brown mat.

Rebecca can smell metabolised alcohol as she passes. Poor Titus, she thinks.

PIECE 57

Rebecca is trying to remember her childhood so she can tell Titus about it next time he drops in. She can't really imagine that the bag of letters Sam has brought her will help Titus understand her any better, but she supposes she should read some of them just in case. Maybe there will be a prompt and she will have a flash of breath-taking clarity. She doubts it but she supposes she shouldn't dismiss the idea out of hand.

In the bag are some letters from friends and relatives and a few spiral-bound notebooks containing her teenage diaries. The diaries, Rebecca thinks, are almost certainly too embarrassing to read.

Some of the letters are from her friend Tabitha. She hasn't contacted her in ages. Tabitha doesn't even know she is in hospital. Pen had thought Tabitha awful, Rebecca remembers, but Rebecca had always kept in touch. Now, Tab runs an art gallery. Rebecca thinks she wouldn't mind if Tabitha knew.

Harriet doesn't know either because she has gone to live in Caracas with a man she met on Tinder. Harriet is always doing things like that. She has never married or had children so Rebecca supposes that she is freer than the average middle-aged woman. She also knows that she would never do any of the things Harriet did, however free and single she was.

'Guess what?' her mother told her on the phone when Rebecca was six months pregnant with Abigail. 'Miranda tells me that Harriet's shaved her head and gone to live in an ashram.' Or, when she and Sam were fighting a chemically driven war against the cat fleas in their stair carpet, 'Harriet's bought a smallholding in Wales. She's going to live organically, entirely off grid, with a Masai warrior.'

A separate bundle is made up of letters from Father Francis, the Catholic priest. They are held together by a thin brown elastic band. Rebecca picks them up and turns them in her hands. She had forgotten she still had these. She pulls the elastic band and it snaps so the letters slide between her fingers onto the bed. She picks one up and begins to read. Father Francis had the most beautiful handwriting, she notices.

My very dear Rebecca, she reads.

It was so kind of you to write me such a long and interesting letter. Your spelling is improving but I always think that spelling is overrated anyway. It's content that's important, isn't it? And I have to say, the content of your letters is so fascinating that I really cannot imagine that your spelling could possibly have any real impact upon anyone but the most extraordinarily dull pedant. If you don't know what a pedant is, you are a very lucky girl. I come across them in my line of work with predictable regularity. Enough, we are all

God's creatures, even if some of us are more interesting
than others. (Lucky YOU!)

I do so like your stories. The one about the caterpillar,
who would much rather stay as a caterpillar when all
his friends so long to be butterflies, was so interesting.
I'm sure that being a butterfly cannot really be all
that one supposes. Imagine having to manage such
a long tongue! Imagine having to spend one's entire
life fluttering when, perhaps, some days, one would
so much rather not.

I believe I shall never look upon a caterpillar with
quite the same level of indifference, ever again.

I am glad to hear Giles has settled so well at his
new school. It must be lovely for him to have you
there as well to look out for him. I think, however,
dear soul, that you are going to have to let go of his
hand at some point and let him find other little friends
of his own age.

I so look forward to seeing you in church this Sunday.
Do tell Harriet to come too, if she can, and then we
will arrange another expedition, just the three of us.

Until then, I remain your LOVING Father Francis

Rebecca folds the letter carefully and replaces it in the plastic
bag. Caterpillars, she thinks. She can't remember much about
caterpillars. She used to collect them when she was small
and feed them until they would pupate. It is true, she thinks,
that she had always preferred the caterpillar to the butterfly.
Butterflies, she supposes, are inherently unsatisfactory.

Then she thinks about Giles and how, after that first long summer in Suffolk, they had both started school together and had spent each playtime holding hands while staring with a mixture of fascination and horror at the other children playing football and hula-hoop or just charging mindlessly about in the playground. She never did quite recover from that late start. School had always felt challenging.

Rebecca remembers going swimming with Father Francis. These were the expeditions he had referred to in his letter. He would take Harriet and Rebecca to swim in the pools of his richer parishioners while they were away on holiday.

'I have the keys, the means and the ways,' he told them. 'A Catholic priest has special dispensation from the Pope himself to swim in anyone's swimming pool should he feel the urge. Any good swimming pool-owning Catholic knows this rule, so all it takes is a quick phone call and we're in.'

He would arrive, usually without warning, at Rebecca's house.

'Harriet's in the car, my sweet girl. Run and get your stuff, we're going swimming.'

He had a *Deux Chevaux* and encouraged the girls to stand up on the back seat and put their heads through the sunroof as he drove. 'Duck if you see any low branches,' he would say, flooring the accelerator.

Rebecca remembered that once she had seen a water boatman rowing itself determinedly around the edge of a pool, swivelling its huge eyes in search of prey.

'Don't interrupt him,' said Father Francis. 'He's on a serious mission.'

Rebecca looked at him. Father Francis had just dived into the deep end, so the water was choppy. He'd swum over to her in a flashy crawl and now he trod water beside her.

'What mission?' she asked.

'Well, actually, it's for a mission,' said Father Francis. His grey hair was plastered to his round head and his brown eyes were dancing. He turned in the water and Rebecca watched him dive to the bottom of the pool, tap it with both hands and then come up again, to surface beside her.

'You're really good at swimming,' she told him.

'Not as good as Nigel,' said Father Francis.

'Nigel?' said Rebecca.

'Yes, Nigel. He's doing a sponsored swim, you see.' Father Francis gestured towards the storm-tossed water boatman.

Rebecca nodded enthusiastically and her hair nodded shortly afterwards. It became especially difficult if mixed with chlorine. At the other end of the pool, Harriet executed a perfect swallow dive, her dark bob slick against her head. Like a sea lion, thought Rebecca, watching as she slid silently past them underwater.

Stories were Rebecca and Father Francis's special thing. She wrote him a new one each week to give to him after church services. This conversation wouldn't include Harriet.

'I do see,' she said.

Father Francis watched the water boatman for a minute. 'He's doing a sponsored swim for distressed gentle water boatmen, for The Mission for Distressed and Impecunious Gentle Water Boatmen,' he concluded triumphantly.

Rebecca nodded again. 'He was chosen because he is the world champion water boatman rower,' she said.

The surface of the pool was quieter now and Harriet was sitting on the edge, dangling her feet in the shallow end. The water boatman rolled his eyes dramatically and set about his task with renewed vigour.

'Exactly,' agreed Father Francis.

'So, two little girls, a swimming pool and a Catholic priest,' says Titus. He is sitting in the Muppet chair, trying to make sense of Rebecca's childhood.

'Where did you grow up, though?' says Rebecca. 'Surrey, tell me. I bet it was Surrey.'

Titus ignores her. 'This happened when you were how old?'

'Eight or nine,' says Rebecca. 'Father Francis used to write letters to me. Sam brought them to me. They were in the box that has my diaries in it. I wrote stories for him, too.'

'Eight or nine again,' says Titus. He makes a note on his pad. 'And you say there were no other adults present?'

'No, we went when they were out. We didn't know the owners of the pools,' says Rebecca. 'It doesn't sound good, does it?'

'It sounds textbook,' says Titus.

Textbook, laughs Betty.

PIECE 58

Rebecca was lying in bed with her eyes open but it was so dark that she could see nothing, not even the ceiling above her. She was listening to a bird singing outside, singing in the dark, night-time garden. Which bird did that? Rebecca didn't know.

She knew bats flew at night. At dusk, she would hear their sharp, high calls as they tumbled like ash from the outbuildings next to the lavender hedge. She knew owl hoots and calls and she had heard the shriek of a vixen and the clatter of a cock pheasant but this sound was new.

The bird had a low, whistling song like a blackbird but sweeter and more complex. It soared, then dropped suddenly to a low pneumatic rustle before building again to an impossibly high cascade of notes.

Rebecca groped under her pillow for her glasses and switched on her bedside lamp. Giles slept peacefully on. Purple and red patterns swirled in her eyes as they became used to the light and the room swam slowly into view. The pink gingham curtains were drawn close across the window. Rebecca sat up and the bird sang. She got out of bed, crossed the room in a few steps and drew back the curtains so that light spilled out into the night. Afterwards, Rebecca didn't know why she did this. It wasn't as if she was going to be able to see the bird, the sky was starless and as dark as pitch and no light from her bedroom would pierce it.

Underneath the bedroom window, the pantiled roof of the kitchen sloped away down towards the gravelled drive. Sometimes, on sunny evenings, Rebecca would climb out of her window and sit on the roof, leaning back against the sun-warmed bricks of the house and gaze across the garden to the fields opposite, feeling high up and otherworldly.

Now, she opened the casement and peered into the darkness, inhaling the damp summer night as her ears filled with the magical song that had woken her. She put a leg over the sill and climbed gingerly down onto the tiles, pushing the window to behind her without latching it.

The bird was suddenly quiet.

Rebecca sat still on the roof for some moments feeling the tiles, still warm from the day, under her feet. At her back, she sensed the house weighted with her sleeping family and the silent night expanded around her with a breathless, expectant quality.

And then, again, the air was filled with the tumultuous, tumbling sound and there was a sudden rustle of wings in the dark, a thud and the bird fell, hitting the top of Rebecca's head and brushing her face with its wings before landing in her lap.

Rebecca had been sitting with her hands on each side of her, resting on the warm roof. She lifted them to find the bird soft and pliant under her fingers. She shifted slightly so that some of the light from the room splashed down onto her legs and stomach and she saw that when it had flown into the window pane it had broken its neck.

PIECE 59

Titus sits down in the Muppet chair. 'So new medication today,' he says. 'How's it going?'

'Same,' says Rebecca. She didn't know she had new medication. Frankly she couldn't keep track of it all. 'I'm really bored. I'm not used to doing nothing. I've got cabin fever,' she says.

'Go for a walk,' says Titus. 'There are groups you could join.'

'I don't do groups.'

Titus smirks. 'Of course you don't,' he says. 'Go by yourself then.' He looks at Rebecca for a long moment. She can't read the look.

'Outside?' says Rebecca.

'Yes, *outside*,' says Titus, imitating her.

'By myself?'

'Yes,' says Titus.

'Can I go and get my nails done?'

Titus stands up. 'Yes, why not?' he says, then he goes, closing the door softly behind him.

Rebecca signs herself out of the hospital. She opens the heavy outer door and steps onto the street alone. She has been in hospital for such a short time but the noise is still overwhelming. She almost turns to bolt back inside but then, beneath the traffic fumes, she catches the scent of the river on the early autumn breeze and, thus encouraged, she takes a deep breath of outside, and heads for Borough High Street.

Rebecca has blue nails. They look as though she has coloured them in with poster paints. Do poster paints still exist? she wonders.

The woman sitting next to Rebecca in the nail salon is having her toenails painted light red. Rebecca thinks it looks as though someone has stamped on her toes. She has white feet and puffy white ankles. She is on the phone. Rebecca thinks she must be someone's PA. 'It's absolutely huge,' she says into her iPhone. 'It actually says on the office wall: Do NOT take this job. Anyway, I've found someone dumb enough to think they can get it to Sotheby's. What? I know, absolute nightmare. I'm just taking some time out and then I have to dash off and explain to Gerard that it's impossible to get four canvases to California by tomorrow afternoon. Dreading it. *Ciao*.'

The PA ends the call and stares into the middle distance. Rebecca slides her eyes sideways to look at her. She has had some rather bad work done and her swollen lips look a bit like those of a breastfeeding baby.

Back at the hospital, Blessing admires Rebecca's nails. Rebecca is pretty sure she will be going down to Boots soon, to buy some nail polish remover but at least they are a nice shape. She opens her bedroom windows. They only open a crack because otherwise Rebecca will fling herself out and down into the courtyard in a fit of pique. She hears a man in the No-Smirking Area talking on his phone.

'I just think it's time that advert came down,' he says. 'It's losing impact and I can't do anything while I'm in here. Pardon? God knows. How long is a piece of string?'

Rebecca picks up her book. She takes out her lenses and puts her glasses on.

Here I am with a brain the size of a planet, she thinks.

Rebecca hears another phone call from the courtyard below. It's more interesting than her book. She is still reading *Humboldt's Gift* or she is still *not* reading *Humboldt's Gift* because she hasn't the concentration.

'Hi,' says the woman on the phone. 'Yeah, sorry, I've just been taking some time out. No, she's not back from Corfu yet. I had to take a break. Everything got a bit much. Helen is in charge at the moment but I should be back next week. We've got the Polonsky contract to deal with. I know, it's awful, but we'll manage somehow.'

Rebecca lies down on her bed. She imagines all the people putting down their piles of stuff and walking away like she has. She imagines the Polonsky contract falling through and she imagines an advertisement peeling piece-by-piece from its hoarding and losing impact. The huge thing would never get to Sotheby's if it weren't for people like the PA in the nail bar. If she were in here, the huge thing would just rest, pointlessly against a wall somewhere. Rebecca thinks it may be time to go home for good.

PIECE 60

The girls come to visit. They text first and they tell her that Kit says he will come separately.

It is afternoon and the sun is casting long shadows through the window. Rebecca is sitting on her bed, writing on her laptop.

Annie runs in first. She bounces over to Rebecca, sits down next to her and rests her head on her mother's shoulder. 'I miss you,' she says.

Abigail stands in the doorway for a moment, taking in her surroundings. Rebecca sees her notice the teak-effect table, the blue suede headboard and the view of the courtyard wall. 'It's nicer than I thought it would be,' she says. 'A bit basic but nice.'

'Come and sit down,' says Rebecca. Abigail puts her hands in her coat pockets. She is wearing a Black Watch tartan coat that Rebecca and Sam had given her for Christmas a year ago. Her dark-red hair is tied on top of her head. The coat looks too big for her and her face, its expression usually intelligent and incisive, is suddenly childish and vulnerable.

'We want to go for a walk with you along the river,' she says. 'Can we?'

'There's a really nice cocktail bar near Tower Bridge,' says Annie, sitting up. 'We could go there and have virgin cocktails because we're not drinking, in solidarity.'

Rebecca stands up. She walks over to Abigail and hugs her. Abigail is smaller than Rebecca and Rebecca remembers reading somewhere that only two per cent of daughters are shorter than their mothers. She thinks that Abigail almost certainly falls into the top two per cent of every good category there is. She kisses her daughter's head. Top two per cent clever, top two per cent empathic, top two per cent beautiful, she thinks. She looks over at Annie who is still sitting on the bed with her long legs splayed out in front of her. Top two per cent lovely, top two per cent gifted, top two per cent kooky, she thinks, and her eyes fill with grateful tears. She turns away so that they won't see.

'That sounds so nice,' she says. 'Yes, let's do cocktails.'

They sign themselves out of the hospital and walk to the river. Rebecca walks between the girls, holding their hands. She feels a bit afraid to be outside but she thinks she is getting better at it.

'Ooh, Borough Market,' says Annie as they pass by. 'We must buy some bread on the way back. They have the best sourdough. Can you smell it?'

Rebecca sniffs the air and smells petrol and cheese, the dankness of the river, the tunnels beneath the bridges and, far beneath, perhaps a tiny scent of baking bread. 'Maybe,' she says.

The sun is dipping in the west as they sit cradling their cocktails outside the bar. It isn't warm and Rebecca isn't wearing enough clothes but she doesn't mind. She is looking up at Tower Bridge.

'Your grandfather put those twiddly gold bits on the top of the towers,' she tells the girls. 'He had to lower them down using his helicopter. It was very dangerous. He said that if the load had started spinning, he would have had to drop it and flatten a press photographer who was right underneath him.'

'Are you better now, Mum?' asks Annie.

Rebecca tears her eyes away from the bridge. 'I'm getting there,' she says. Then she says, 'Thank you for coming.'

Annie spears a piece of pineapple out of her cocktail with her tiny orange umbrella and eats it. She puts the umbrella into her hair just above her left ear. 'Good?' she asks.

Rebecca leans over and adjusts it slightly. 'Very good,' she says.

PIECE 61

Rebecca is sitting on her bed. She is reading a letter from Father Francis. She really wishes she had kept more of them.

My dear Rebecca, it begins.

Thank you so very much for your long and interesting letter. It's very nice to know that you are learning to cook. I find cooking rather a bore myself but I am sure that is because I refuse to put in the practice and, as we all know, practice makes perfect. Would you be so kind as to make me an omelette the next time I come to visit? Un omelette aux fines herbes, as they say in France. I believe they are meant to be quite delicious.

I liked your story very much, all about the little Matilda who is so poor that she will never afford a pony, but she prays to God and finds one abandoned in a field with a matted mane and curling hooves and nurses it back to health.

No wonder the pony came to love her so much. No wonder he tried to escape the circus after his

kidnapping. Ponynapping? Who knows?? No wonder
he saved her from the burning big top, carrying her
through the flames on his broad, sturdy little back.

Dearest girl, I found it so exciting. I'm not sure that
God gives a pony to every child who prays for one but
little Matilda certainly deserved hers.

Your writing is becoming very neat and easy to read
too. Well done!

I hope I shall see you and Mummy in church this
Sunday. Harriet is preparing for her confirmation. I'm
not sure if you will join the classes or not but you must
ask Harriet to teach you the Hail Mary off by heart.
You would love it. I find it so comforting after one has
a nightmare or some such disaster.

Until then, fondest LOVE dear one.

From your Father Francis

'Titus, do you play the viola?' Rebecca doesn't know what to
say to Titus today so she has decided to wind him up a bit.

Titus looks at her over the top of his glasses. 'Why?' he
says.

'All doctors play an instrument to grade eight,' says
Rebecca.

'Do they?' says Titus severely.

'In a string quartet?' says Rebecca.

'No,' says Titus. He puts his pad down beside him on her
table.

'Trombone?' asks Rebecca. 'In a brass band? Grade eight
piano accompanying an LGBT choir?'

'Shush,' says Titus.

'It's quite disappointing really,' says Rebecca. 'I mean, you do play an instrument, don't you? You really ought to use it. Think of all those hours you spent practising for nothing.'

'How do you know I play an instrument?' Titus is looking cross. He folds his arms across his chest, then carefully unfolds them and tries to look relaxed. He fails.

'You're a doctor,' says Rebecca.

Titus tries to stare her down.

Rebecca smiles at him. 'You know that one of the side effects of taking Dulsexatine is death, don't you?' she says.

'One of the side effects of life is death,' says Titus.

Rebecca looks him up and down. It's like pulling strings on a puppet. 'Oh, bingo!' she says.

'What?' says Titus.

'The psychiatrist in my book says exactly that. I wrote it down last week.'

'So I'm not particularly original. Is that your point?'

'Grade eight flute and you never use it,' says Rebecca.

'Clarinet,' says Titus.

It takes about three minutes for either of them to stop giggling. Rebecca gets hiccups.

Titus takes a deep breath and picks up his pad. 'So,' he says, 'have you died at all this week?'

Rebecca shakes her head and hiccups.

Titus makes a note.

'Can I get a drink of water?' she asks.

'By all means.' Titus stands up. He gives her a long, appraising look. 'Goodbye, Rebecca,' he says softly.

When he has gone, Rebecca gets off her bed and stands in her bathroom. She looks at her face in the mirror, then she puts both arms in the air.

'Happy arms,' she whispers.

PIECE 62

Rebecca was asleep. She could hear Betty skipping on the gravel but she couldn't move because her covers were too heavy. She thought she would probably be in trouble with Betty if she didn't move but she was paralysed.

Then, she opened her eyes and Harriet was standing by her bed in the dark. Rebecca could see her because her bedroom door was open and the landing light was shining into the room.

'Can you move over, sweetheart?' Pen was speaking. Rebecca saw that she was standing just behind Harriet. 'Harriet's going to sleep with you,' her mother whispered. Rebecca moved over and Harriet slid between the sheets, shivering. She was wearing only a thin cotton nightie. Harriet cuddled up to Rebecca and snaked her arms around her neck. Her face and hair were wet.

Rebecca's mother turned and left the room. She pulled the door to, without shutting it completely.

'What happened? Why are you here?' Rebecca could feel Harriet's cold body against hers. She was shaking with convulsive shivers and Rebecca realized that her hair and face were wet from crying.

'Patrick,' whispered Harriet. She buried her head into Rebecca's shoulder and Rebecca couldn't hear her very well.

'Patrick what?'

'He went mad,' said Harriet. 'He hit Mama and he smashed up the house.' She drew in a great shuddering breath.

Rebecca pulled away slightly. She could just make out the light oval of Harriet's face.

'Did he smack you?'

Rebecca felt Harriet shake her head. 'No, he loves me.'

'Where are Milo and Inigo?'

'They're sleeping end-to-end on the sofa downstairs.'

Rebecca put out a hand and stroked Harriet's head. 'Is your mama all right?' she asked.

She felt Harriet nod.

'Let's go to sleep,' she said.

PIECE 63

Rebecca spends the whole afternoon reading. She reads *Humboldt's Gift*, she reads *Lolita*, she reads *Madame Bovary* and she reads *Mount!* by Jilly Cooper. Nothing holds her attention. She drinks four cups of thick black coffee and she runs to the top of the hospital. She eats four Brazil nuts and a Gala apple and then she goes to her CBT group.

At CBT group, Darren is smiling blandly into the middle distance. Alice is wafting about taking books from the bookshelves and listlessly putting them back again. Carl is holding his head in his hands and there is a new person sitting in the corner. The therapist is late and the group starts watching the clock. Siva gets up and leaves. Rebecca is surprised he can see where he is going because his blue-black hair falls directly into his eyes.

'When I got back to my room yesterday, I thought about what was said at CBT Group,' says Rebecca to Darren, 'and frankly I think I have hardly ever heard such a pile of crap in my entire life.'

'What was said?' asks Darren. 'Was it the thing about piling books and water coolers on top of someone until they collapse?'

'We're all carrying books and water coolers,' says Rebecca. 'We can't just put them down. We all have people relying on us. We have mortgages and lives and careers and relationships. Can anyone seriously imagine that a group of high-achieving, intelligent, connected people could just put all that down and walk away because it's too much. I have at least six people relying on me to pick up their slack all the time, every day, and I bet everyone else here does too.'

'Six is my favourite number for a dinner party,' says Darren.

'I like twenty,' says Rebecca, 'then I'm too busy to talk to any of them. Once, I sat next to a man at a dinner party who said, "Hi, I head up Asia, what do you do?"'

'Why did you invite him?' asks Darren.

'I didn't. He was just there.'

Darren smiles gently. 'I head up the Northern Hemisphere,' he says, 'but I try not to mention it at dinner parties.'

Rebecca is jiggling up and down on the sofa. She looks at the clock. Alice wanders out of the room. Rebecca wonders how one can wander wistfully, but Alice can.

Carl leaves holding his head. He has a head injury. Yesterday, he tried to escape by banging his head through a window, only all the windows have toughened glass, even tougher than Carl's toughened head. He ended up in A&E.

'They won't let me go,' he tells Rebecca, 'I'm on a section.'

'I can't stay,' says Rebecca to Darren. 'I can't sit still.' She jumps up and walks out of the room. She runs to the top of the hospital. She runs up each flight of stairs and then down and then up and then down until she reaches the ground floor.

Oh God, she thinks.

She goes back to her bedroom and finishes her pot of cold coffee. Fuck-a-doodle-doo, she thinks, and sits on the bed with *Humboldt's Gift*.

The day stretches out featureless in front of her. No one is coming to visit. Titus is coming but she feels too exhausted to talk to Titus and she falls asleep on the bed. When she wakes up, Titus is sitting in the Muppet chair.

'Jesus,' says Rebecca, sitting up.

'No, guess again,' he says.

Rebecca is wearing her glasses because she can't read the small print in *Humboldt's Gift* with her lenses in. She sits up and looks severely at Titus over the top of her glasses.

'How long have you been there?' she asks.

'As long as you like,' says Titus.

'Titus, my ancestors took the soup. Did you know that?' asks Rebecca.

'I haven't the slightest idea what you are talking about,' says Titus. 'Explain,' he says.

So Rebecca tells him how the Kellys took the soup from the English, during the Irish potato famine, and had to become Protestants and drop the O'.

'But you said your parents were Catholics,' says Titus.

'They dropped the O' but they kept the Catholicism,' says Rebecca.

'Perhaps it would have been better to do it the other way around,' says Titus. 'Anyway, Rebecca, how are you? Any more screeches?'

Rebecca pushes her glasses up onto the bridge of her nose. She notices that there are too many buttons undone on her shirt and that her bra is showing. She also notices that she has a long yellowing bruise on her collarbone which she has no memory of causing. She does up the buttons and shrugs her shirt forward.

'No screeches,' she says. 'Can I go out this afternoon? I'm getting cabin fever in here. I went to CBT Group yesterday and I've never heard such a load of hooey in my entire life.'

Titus grins again. Rebecca knows that Titus has a finely tuned hooey radar.

'You can go home this weekend, for a little while,' he says. 'Would you like that?'

Rebecca doesn't know if she would like it or not. 'I don't know,' she says. 'I like being here,' she says.

'Isn't Sam looking forward to you coming home?'

Poke, thinks Rebecca. She shrugs. 'I expect so, and I wouldn't like to go home if he's not there. I would like to see the children,' she says. She imagines them all sitting round the table looking at her as though she were an unexploded bomb.

'So, what's the problem?' asks Titus.

'I don't know,' says Rebecca.

Titus leans forward. 'Rebecca, you can tell me whether you want to go or not tomorrow but, at this point, I don't want you to feel forced into anything.'

Rebecca watches him. He takes off his glasses and puts them on the table beside him. He is wearing a light-pink shirt that shows off the remains of his summer tan. His hair is flopping over his forehead because it needs a cut and his eyes are a calm sea blue. He's quite attractive, she decides. Then she realizes that *that* is exactly what he wants her to think.

'Wow,' she says.

The elephant in the room, laughs Betty.

Titus sits up straight. 'What?' he says.

Rebecca shakes her head. 'Nothing,' she says. Why? she thinks. Betty laughs again in her left ear.

'Tell me,' says Titus, sitting up straighter and fixing her with his glacial stare. He pushes his hair back from his forehead and puts his glasses on. 'Rebecca, are you still hearing voices?' he asks.

Rebecca shakes her head and stares at Titus. Why would he want? she thinks. What for? She bites her bottom lip.

'It's not at all funny.'

Rebecca has decided that it is.

'Tell me why you feel that you have to be in charge of every single conversation we have.'

Rebecca shakes her head.

'Tell me,' Titus says again. He is glaring at her.

'It's quite sexy when you do that,' she says.

Titus holds up a hand. 'Stop that right now,' he says, but his dimples are beginning to show. 'God, you're a pain,' he says.

'I am, aren't I?' she answers.

When Titus goes, Rebecca lies on her bed and tries to make sense of it all. Perhaps she had imagined it. It's possible but unlikely. Perhaps it's normal and he's just trying to gain her trust or to become more intimate with her so that she will open up to him more easily. After all, it's not very different from the tactic she had been using on him. It's just one way of getting someone onside.

Rebecca thinks she loves Titus because he saved her. She would far rather he was a fireman and that he had saved her from a burning building, but she didn't get to choose, and he is a psychiatrist who has saved her from her burning self, so loving him is probably normal.

But you don't want to touch him, says Betty.

I don't, agrees Rebecca. It's not that kind of love.

Outside the sky is darkening. A nurse knocks on Rebecca's door and she sits up. 'Come in,' she says. The nurse puts her supper tray on the table.

'Try to eat,' she says.

PIECE 64

Rebecca woke early. There wasn't room in Rebecca's small single bed for both her and Harriet and she found herself squeezed against the wall with only a corner of the sheet. Harriet sprawled like a starfish across the rest of the mattress, her eyes closed peacefully, her long dark eyelashes brushing her pink and gold cheeks.

Rebecca scrabbled under her pillow for her glasses and put them on. Harriet turned over, muttered something unintelligible, pulling the covers with her, and Rebecca slid silently from the bed and left the room.

Downstairs in the kitchen, she opened the larder door, found a packet of Weetabix and the sugar bowl and put them on the table.

The kettle began to sing on the Aga. Someone else must be up already. Rebecca wondered who. She looked at her watch: 6.03 a.m. It was probably her father or maybe Miranda. Had Miranda stayed the night too? She didn't know. Rebecca lifted the kettle off the hotplate, closed the lid over it and put the kettle at the back of the Aga. It would boil quickly enough when whoever had put it on turned up.

She walked across the room and opened the back door. The milk stood there in its crate as usual and as usual the blue tits had pierced the silver tops and had a tiny taste of the creamy contents.

Rebecca left the door ajar. The morning was soft and warm and a robin was singing in the plum tree next to the lavender hedge.

She took a cereal bowl, a spoon and a small milk jug from the kitchen dresser and returned to the table and sat in her father's chair. She took two Weetabix from the packet in front of her, shaking the small brown mouse droppings back into the packet, and put them in her bowl. She and the boys had discovered, to their distaste, that if they left the droppings and poured milk on the Weetabix, the milk would go a very unattractive brown.

'Not chocolatey,' said Alex.

'No,' agreed Martin. 'Pooey.'

Rebecca poured the cream from the top of the milk into the milk jug to save it for her father, added milk and sugar to her bowl and, picking up her spoon, shovelled an enormous piece into her mouth.

'Hello, darling girl.' Miranda stood at the kitchen door. She was wearing Rebecca's father's dressing gown and had bare feet. 'It's such a lovely morning, I went for a walk.' Miranda stepped into the room. 'Oh, you are sweet,' she added. 'You took the kettle off. Would you like some tea?' She walked across the room, leaving wet prints. 'Look,' she said, turning to point at them. 'Dewy footprints. The lawn is soaking wet. You would like some tea, darling, wouldn't you? What?'

Rebecca watched Miranda lift the lid and put the kettle back onto the hotplate. She watched her walk across the room to the dresser and select two mugs from the hooks that studded the second shelf and she watched her as she picked up the bottle of milk from the table. All the time, Rebecca held the Weetabix in her mouth.

Miranda's face was red all down one side. Her upper lip was split and one of her laughing brown eyes was swollen shut.

Miranda spooned tea into the pot and poured boiling water into it before replacing the lid.

'Do you want milk and sugar, sweetie?' she asked.

PIECE 65

Rebecca is writing.

Cyrus Mason is sitting at the foot of her bed. Emily is sitting on the bed, watching him. Today he is wearing a charcoal pinstriped suit with a paisley tie. The top button of his shirt is undone and the tie is twisted slightly to one side. His shoes need polishing and he sits heavily, leaning forward slightly, shoulders rounded. Emily thinks he looks exhausted.

'So,' he says, 'what's the problem?'

Emily shrugs. She pushes her hair behind her ear. 'Why do I have a problem?' she says. 'What am I doing that looks like I have an issue? Well, obviously I *do* have an issue—' she gestures at the room '—I'm in here but what am I doing specifically that makes you think I have a problem right this minute?'

'It's not a precise science,' says Cyrus, 'but I have become adept at reading body language. Would you care to share?'

Would she? Emily isn't sure.

'OK,' she says. 'You wrote to my doctor. Mostly I didn't read what you wrote before I came here but, yesterday, I was even more profoundly bored than usual and I scrolled back through all your letters.'

Cyrus sits up straighter. 'Did you?' he says.

'Yes,' says Emily.

'And?'

'You wrote that when I was in France, matters were "less than optimal". You said that I had been self-medicating with alcohol . . . '

'You had,' says Cyrus.

'I know but you told my doctor and now they're going to think I'm an alcoholic.'

'I did not say that you were an alcoholic. I don't believe you are one but I felt I should tell your doctor that you have a propensity to self-medicate and that this has resulted in your being admitted to hospital.'

Emily puts her hands on her knees. 'Dear Emily's doctor,' she says. 'My patient drinks herself into oblivion at the drop of a hat and then she goes all mental and ends up in hospital. Kind regards, Cyrus Mason McPsyche HKLP.'

Cyrus smiles. 'Not an exact quote,' he says. 'What's HKLP?'

'Holds knife like pen. I don't know what all those letters after your name mean.'

Cyrus sits back in his chair and folds his arms. 'They don't mean holds knife like pen,' he says. Emily can see that he's trying to look serious.

'They might,' she says.

'They don't . . . and I don't anyway.'

'What?' says Emily.

'Hold my knife like a pen.'

'That's a relief,' says Emily.

'Snob,' says Cyrus.

'It's not snobbism. It's the same as holding a cello like a banjo, just wrong. Anyway, I think you should write another letter to my doctor telling him or her or whoever they are, that France was very specific, that a spider attacked me and that I'm not an alcoholic.'

'I believe,' says Cyrus, 'that it is what I did. It's not McPsyche either, by the way.'

Emily shrugs. 'Can I go home?' she asks.

Cyrus examines her for a moment. 'You've been here three weeks,' he says.

'Yes, I have,' she says, 'and I'm a bit fed up. I keep falling asleep and, when I'm not asleep, I get screeches and I have to run up and down stairs and my hands won't stay still. My hands always stayed still before. Now look at them crawling around and flexing.'

Cyrus looks. 'That,' he says, 'is a side effect of your medication. I was hoping it would have subsided somewhat before I allowed you to go home. Some of your side effects occur in only one in a hundred patients.'

'I'm not doing it on purpose. What if I'm *one* of the one in a hundred who die?'

Cyrus laughs. 'If one in a hundred died, we really would be in trouble.' He stops talking and looks at Emily. She looks back at him. She likes him, she decides. She trusts him.

You shouldn't, hisses Betty. Betty has been much quieter recently. Sometimes Emily thinks she will never come back.

Cyrus fixes his strange, yellow eyes on her and Emily thinks

343

that she wouldn't be able to pull hers away even if she wanted to. She finds that she doesn't want to. She knows what she is seeing, she can feel it. It is a long time since a man has looked at her like this. She takes a deep, slow breath.

'I would like you to stay,' says Cyrus. 'I think there's a little more to do before I would be happy for you to return home.'

After he has gone, Emily sits on her bed cross-legged. She stares at the chair where Cyrus had been sitting. Her stomach is flipping. He's my doctor, she thinks. He's not supposed to . . . but what had he actually done? She shakes her head. She jumps off the bed and goes into the bathroom. She looks at herself in the mirror.

Same face,

bit thinner,

clear skin, its summer freckles fading,

dark blue eyes,

smooth, rust-coloured hair, grown long these past few months . . .

What had he done?

Emily shakes her head.

She's developed a crush, she decides.

It's not surprising Cyrus is the fireman who saved her from a burning building. She is enthralled by his heroism.

She has Stockholm syndrome. She has come to love her captor.

She is on drugs. Her decision-making and perceptive powers are compromised.

Her hands stretch very wide. She watches her long thin fingers claw the air.

She's a nutter; yes, that's it.

She's mad.

Emily turns and looks back into the bedroom. She sees herself sitting on the bed next to her closed laptop. She is looking into Cyrus's eyes.

He looks back at her.

It is unmistakeable.

Rebecca closes her laptop and gets off the bed. She walks into her bathroom and stands where Emily had been just a few moments before.

She looks in the mirror.

Dark-blonde shoulder-length hair, not yet grey,

slanted, dark-blue eyes,

a pale heart-shaped face, with a scatter of freckles across her nose, cheeks and forehead,

and a wide mouth with a tendency to turn down at the corners.

Age hadn't done her any favours but equally it had done her no harm.

Her face, though blurred at the edges and lined beneath the eyes, was essentially as it had always been.

Funny looking, said Betty.

Rebecca shakes her head. She's not sure she saw anything at all.

PIECE 66

The children ran down the garden to play Kick The Can. The adults stayed drinking wine around the kitchen table. Father Francis was there. Miranda had phoned him and asked him to come.

'When a disaster strikes, one simply *can* rely on one's priest,' Rebecca hears Miranda telling Pen. 'And Patrick is an absolute disaster and he certainly *struck*, didn't he? What?'

'Would you be a darling?' Rebecca heard her say on the telephone. 'We've had the most frightful shock. What?'

Within an hour, Father Francis had arrived in his *Deux Chevaux*. Rebecca heard it screech to a halt on the gravel and she and Harriet ran to meet him, swinging on his arms as he walked towards the house.

Now, she was crouched by the back door, watching Alex flit from gooseberry bush to gooseberry bush as he tried to get near enough to The Can without Milo seeing him. She couldn't see Inigo or Martin. Rebecca was hoping that when Alex broke cover, Milo would be distracted enough for her to make a run for it. Her heart was throbbing. She was not very good at running.

Rebecca could hear the adults talking in the kitchen. She heard Miranda snort with laughter and her mother's, 'No, you shouldn't laugh, it's absolutely not funny.'

Father Francis said something she didn't catch, then she saw that Alex was very near the nearest gooseberry bush but Milo was just standing by The Can, erect, ears pricked. Like a hare, thought Rebecca. He was listening.

Out of the corner of her eye, she saw Harriet flatten herself against the plum tree and roll commando style into the lavender hedge. Alex turned slowly in her direction.

'I watered all his stupid cannabis plants with boiling water. He'd planted about a hundred in my greenhouse. Bloody cheek.' Rebecca heard Miranda laugh again.

'Is he still there?' asked Rebecca's father.

'I've no idea. We had to get out of there. He was wild.'

'You must have been terrified,' Rebecca's mother said.

'Shall I open another bottle?' Father Francis was speaking. 'Listen, Dave,' he said, 'why don't you and I drive over there now and beat the living shit out of him? No one would believe him if he reported it. I'm a Catholic priest and you're a helicopter pilot.'

Milo was walking towards the nearest gooseberry bush, craning his neck.

Rebecca heard the adults laughing again now. Father Francis had been joking, she realized.

She imagined her father and Father Francis smashing up Patrick and kicking him until his face looked worse than Miranda's and she began to giggle. At first, she tried to be quiet but she couldn't control herself. She leaned back against the door and laughed until her sides ached. Milo turned towards her and then back towards The Can as Harriet and Alex broke cover together.

Alex kicked The Can, which bounced off his foot into Harriet's path, who kicked it high into the air.

Rebecca stood weakly against the back door as the other children approached her. She looked up at them. 'I'm sorry,' she said. 'I've got hiccups.'

PIECE 67

Rebecca goes home from the hospital for one night. Sam picks her up on Saturday morning. She feels very excited.

Sam opens the car door for her. He puts her overnight bag on the back seat. Titus had finally agreed to let her stay overnight as long as she promised – 'I mean seriously promise,' he'd said – not to muck about with her dosages.

'I do promise. I'll promise anything you like as long as I can just have one night at home,' Rebecca had told him. And he'd agreed to let her go.

'I hope it's all going to be all right for you,' Sam says. 'I hope it's not too messy. Abigail came over. We tidied up. We can get a takeaway.'

On the kitchen table, in a cobalt-blue jug, is an enormous bunch of flowers. There are rusty chrysanthemums, white gauras, orange gerberas and yellow Michaelmas daisies. Sam is very good at flowers. Rebecca stands and takes it all in while Pomp winds his way round her legs, purring as loudly as he can.

The autumn light slants low and golden through the French windows. It bounces off the white walls, washing them a pale ochre and, upstairs, it bathes her and Sam's bedroom in a veil of saffron.

Kit and Abigail come over. Annie and Rebecca walk down to pick up an Indian takeaway.

'You won't eat any of it,' Sam tells her. Rebecca is sure she won't but she wants to be normal and Indian takeaways are normal.

'Hey you,' says Ahmed, poking his head out of the kitchen as they place their order. 'Where you bin?'

'Cornwall,' says Rebecca.

'I thought you were going to tell him,' says Annie as they walk home.

'I don't think he'd get it,' says Rebecca.

At home, Sam has lit candles. The kitchen flickers. Outside, the indigo evening glows. Abigail has laid the table with the crockery Rebecca and Sam had found in a French brocante the summer before it all went wrong. Kit pours red wine. Rebecca drinks water and likes it.

Before bed, Rebecca tips Cryazatine, Dulsexatine, Tranquiltolam and Thiamine onto the vintage kantha throw covering the bed and drinks them all down with some San Pellegrino fizzy water. She falls asleep the moment she is under the duvet.

Back at the hospital, Rebecca dumps her bag onto her bed. She feels quite depressed. Hospital is beginning to wear a bit thin. At three, Titus comes to see her.

'So,' he says, 'how was that? How did your husband feel about you being home? How did it go?' Rebecca thinks Titus is overly interested in how Sam feels.

'He was very happy to have me there,' she says.

'Because he'd put aside lots of things for you to do? A few lists perhaps?' says Titus. Today he is in very high spirits. He is leaning forward, smiling happily.

'Because he loves me,' says Rebecca.

Titus sits up abruptly. 'That made me sound terrible, didn't it?' He colours slightly.

Rebecca just looks at him. Mousetrap, she thinks inconsequentially.

'Do you think you would like to leave the hospital altogether? There's no real point you being here if you can manage at home.'

Rebecca can hardly believe what she is hearing. 'Altogether? Just leave?'

Titus nods.

'And you would pass me on to my GP and I wouldn't have to see you anymore?'

Titus shakes his head. 'No, you would have to see me. I would like to see you next Friday at three. You will keep seeing me until I'm absolutely sure that you're going to be OK.'

'Forever then,' says Rebecca. She wants Titus to go away so that she can dance around the room.

'No alcohol though,' says Titus.

'I've added it to the list,' says Rebecca. 'Spiders, people, Velcro . . . '

'I didn't know about the Velcro,' says Titus. 'But there's really no need to be afraid of wine. You're not an alcoholic. The odd glass of wine with a meal will be fine for you eventually but not while you're taking all these drugs. Wait until you're a bit steadier.'

Rebecca shakes her head. 'One drink's too many and two's not enough,' she says.

'Did you hear that at CBT?' asks Titus.

'No, my father's cousin told me.'

Titus gets up and goes to the door. 'Take care, missus,' he says. 'I'll see you next Friday at three.'

Titus closes the door behind him. She jumps off the bed and pulls her suitcase from the top of the wardrobe.

I'm actually going home, properly, she thinks. She puts her suitcase on the floor and sits on the bed for a moment. She picks up her phone and scrolls through her Instagram.

She sees all the lives that have been going on since she has been in hospital. She sees that Abigail's friend has had a baby, that Tabitha has been in LA and that Kit has been in Jersey. She imagines all that life passing her by. She stands on the bed and jumps up and down on it, bouncing the pillows onto the floor.

The door opens and Titus is standing there, watching her. 'Three-fifteen,' he says and closes the door.

After Titus has gone, Rebecca texts Sam. 'Coming home today, for good,' she writes. She still can't get a signal in her room.

Rebecca packs up her room. She bags up her shoes and shoves her jacket and jumpers into her suitcase.

She can hear the girl in the room opposite, crying, an abandoned sound like a child wanting her mother, and suddenly she misses Annie.

Home, she thinks.

PIECE 68

Rebecca is writing. She is sitting on her bed at home, writing about Emily and Cyrus and also about Mrs Lightwing.

Mrs Lightwing's mother had killed herself, Rebecca writes.

She stares out the bedroom window. The day is colourless and still, neither warm nor cold, neither bright nor dull. The houses on the other side of the road are bathed in a kind of flat non-light. From here, they look like a stage set, a backdrop and yet there is no drama taking place onstage. The actors huddle breathless and silent in the wings.

Rebecca feels as if she is in a state of flux, that a hiatus has arrived, that catharsis approaches, but then she thinks it's just the weather, just the weather and the pull of the moon.

Mrs Lightwing's mother had taken her own life, writes Rebecca, when Mrs Lightwing was a baby, by throwing herself into the pond at Benham Wood. As far as Rebecca is aware, this is true.

The rest is hearsay.

Mrs Lightwing's mother had drowned herself because Mrs Lightwing had been born out of wedlock and the shame of having an illegitimate child had been too much for her to bear.

Rebecca knows this story because her mother had told it to her.

The weight of the girl's long skirts had dragged her down into the dark water and whether she had thought of her baby, or the man who'd fathered it as she'd drowned, is not recorded. If she had cried for help, no one would have heard because the woods were deep and the trees surrounding the pond muffled sound and kept secrets.

Now, Rebecca thought about the pond. She remembered it well. She had seen it first when Grime had taken her to see the badgers. They had slipped quietly by, glancing sideways across the black water. Rebecca had paused on the path, thinking of fish. Grime had told her that the pond was deep, she remembered, deep and full of fish. Then he'd said, 'C'mon or it'll be too dark to see the badgers,' and they had continued on their way.

Mrs Lightwing sang in the village church choir. She rode her old black bicycle with a wicker basket on the handlebars and she lived alone in a cottage, in a neat terrace, in the next village. Rebecca had been there once, when Mrs Lightwing had invited her to tea.

A coal fire had glowed in the grate of the cosy sitting room and Mrs Lightwing had fed Rebecca Victoria sponge cake on a flowered china plate, white bread jam sandwiches with the crusts cut off and orange squash. Rebecca had never had sandwiches without crusts before and she had made a mental note to eat only crustless sandwiches when she was grown up.

When her mother arrived to pick Rebecca up in the Cortina, she had wished Mrs Lightwing a happy birthday and handed over a hastily wrapped box of chocolates. Only then did Rebecca realize that she had been the only guest at Mrs Lightwing's birthday party.

'Mrs Lightwing asked me not to tell you. She's seventy, you know,' Rebecca's mother had said as they'd driven home through the winding country lanes. A barn owl had swooped low in front of the car and her mother had pulled onto the verge so they could both watch it float across the wheat fields, to disappear into the dusk.

Emily, writes Rebecca, is telling Cyrus about her childhood. He seems to think it interesting. She has yet to understand why.

He had arrived in her room, chucked her copy of the *Guardian* from the Muppet chair onto the bed. 'Now,' he'd said, 'tell me about your country childhood, tell me about all the incest and intrigues. I could do with cheering up.'

So she had started to tell him about Mrs Lightwing. Cyrus looked stressed, his eyes were deeply shadowed. 'Are you tired, Cyrus? Are you having a horrible day?'

He ignores the question. 'Tell me more about Mrs Lightwing,' he says.

'You look really tired, that's all.'

He shrugs. 'What time of year do you think this was? This birthday party? The fire being lit would have indicated a winter afternoon, wouldn't it?'

Emily doesn't know. Sometimes fires were lit in May. The timeline is confusing her. It has to do with her doll. She's not sure. She is sitting on the bed. Cyrus is sitting on the chair opposite and she has a distinct feeling of vertigo.

'Did you go fishing in the winter?'

Emily shakes her head. 'Too cold. Much too cold sitting still next to a pond.' Doubt blooms in her head. 'You know, don't you, Cyrus,' she says, 'that in remembering a memory, you lose the original. You're effectively just remembering the memory of the memory. I might be making all this up.'

Cyrus smiles. 'I do know that, yes,' he says. 'And it wouldn't surprise me at all if you were making it all up. Nonetheless I would like you to continue. Why do you feel that this afternoon is significant?'

Emily looks at her hands. They are resting on her knees. Her knees are flexing, first one, then the other. 'I didn't say it was.'

'Try to sit still, Emily. Breathe slowly and try to sit still.' Cyrus is suddenly switched on. 'Keep going, what happened next?'

'My mother told me about Mrs Lightwing on our journey home. She sighed as the owl disappeared and shook her head as she started the engine, and I said, "What's the matter?"'

'And she said?'

'Poor Mrs Lightwing, she must have had a terrible childhood and look at her now, she's so kind and she's an absolute pillar of the church.'

'Did you ask her to explain?'

'I didn't say anything because I was thinking about Mrs Lightwing being a pillar. Then my mother told me that Mrs Lightwing had been born to unmarried parents and that the man, whoever he had been, had refused or been unable to marry her mother. "So," said my mother, "according to

Lorraine, after the baby was born, the poor girl took herself down to Benham pond and threw herself into the water. She was a Victorian, so she would have been wearing a long dress."'

'She drowned herself?'

Emily nods.

'And your mother just came out with that on the drive home?'

'She probably didn't realize the effect it would have on me.'

'Which was?'

'I became obsessed with the pond at Benham. I kept imagining this little girl in a flowing flowered dress throwing herself into the water and the dress billowing out and then slowly becoming water-logged and dragging her down into the blackness.'

'Why a little girl?'

'I don't know. My mother said Mrs Lightwing's mother had been a girl so I suppose I imagined a child. I imagined that her dress became entangled with the oak branches underwater.'

'Oak branches?'

'There was an upright oak tree submerged in the pond, its petrified branches like grasping fingers reaching up out of the depths.'

Cyrus has put his glasses back on. He looks at her over the top of them.

'It's true,' Emily protests. 'Everyone knew about it.'

'It isn't true,' says Cyrus.

'Well, you said I had to entertain you.'

'I didn't say that, but go on.'

'I didn't sleep for weeks. Now, I think of her as a bog body. Pond water can harden skin; it incarcerates ghosts. I imagine her twisting in the water, tethered by the tattered remnants of her dress.'

'Unlikely when you think of the passage of time and, anyway, wasn't the body recovered?' Cyrus ignores the ghosts.

'I don't know. I was only nine when my mother told me about it. She didn't tell me that the body wasn't there anymore.'

'So you became obsessed, how?'

'I had a doll . . . '

'Called?' asks Cyrus.

Emily thinks. 'Hattie,' she says.

'After your best friend?'

Emily feels confused. She shakes her head. 'Ellis is my best friend,' she says.

'Your best childhood friend?' says Cyrus. 'Hattie is short for Harriet.'

'Oh,' says Emily. She's not at all sure she can continue with the story. Then she says, 'Harriet was horrible to me.'

'Go on,' says Cyrus.

'OK, umm. I drowned Hattie.'

'Where?' says Cyrus.

'Benham pond, in the woods,' says Emily.

'You know that you can't drown a doll, don't you, Emily?' says Cyrus.

'I drowned her. She was wearing a long, red velvet dress.'

'What exactly happened?' Cyrus's voice is very quiet.

*

Emily is walking in the woods. She has circumnavigated the electric fence behind the Cherry Tree pub because there are giblets in the field where the cows used to be. Yesterday, Alex showed her.

'There's a whole pile of giblets in the field on the way to Benham woods,' he told Emily. Emily had only the vaguest idea what giblets were, but she agreed to go with Alex to take a look. Giblets, it turns out, were pretty disgusting. Alex took a stick and poked them. They were just lying there in the middle of the field without explanation, a mass of shining red, white and black insides of something big. A cloud of bluebottles rose up as the giblets wobbled.

Emily found herself focusing on the iridescent backs of the flies, on the sound of their wings, on the tall row of giant hogweed growing along the far border of the field. Then she was sick.

'Did you eat three Weetabix for breakfast again?' asked Alex.

Anyway, Emily isn't going anywhere near the giblet field ever again. She's holding the doll in her arms. It is wearing a red dress and Emily has brushed its hair and plaited it in two neat plaits. She looks down at the doll's impassive face, at her unperturbed blue eyes, and she feels the soft weight of the velvet dress against her fingers. The doll doesn't know what is going to happen, so it's fine.

Getting near to the pond from the far side of the woods isn't easy. The path is overgrown with brambles and nettles. Emily is wearing cords and gumboots and a Shetland jumper over a grey T-shirt. Several times she slips and once she falls because she is holding the doll. 'Bloody!' she says loudly as she clambers to her feet. She charges through a copse of hazel. Long experience has taught her that hazel is best tackled head-on. Emily leaves several strands of red hair hanging in the branches but that's OK because she has lots of it. A hazel twig nestles behind her ear and she can feel it scratching her scalp as she walks onwards.

At the pond, Emily follows the path round the edge. The sun is shining through silvered clouds high above the trees and the pond reflects them, white in its sombre depths.

'Time of year?' says Cyrus.

'Spring,' says Emily. 'Before the bluebells.'

The doll doesn't sink immediately. Emily throws her hard into the middle of the pond and stands breathless to see what might happen. She looks down and watches a fly land on her bare arm. She has taken off her jumper and it's hanging on a branch beside her. The fly is delicate with a long brown body and bulging copper-coloured eyes. Its legs rise up above its thorax and are as thin and delicate as cotton threads. Emily watches the fly clean its head, running its forelegs along its antennae, then she watches as it plunges its mouthparts into her arm.

'And the doll?'

'She's spinning because I threw her. I can't get her. She's too far out. Her plaits are floating but her dress is dragging her down.'

'She sinks?'

Emily rakes her fingernails along her forearm. 'She drowned,' she tells Cyrus.

PIECE 69

Rebecca has been home for a week. She is seeing Titus for the first time. She feels fine apart from a small issue with her dose of Dulsexatine, which, she decides, she may or may not bring up as the situation demands. She sits down in one of the grey upholstered chairs and asks Titus, 'Why are you so available on Facebook?'

Afterwards, at home, Rebecca is writing again. She is sitting on her bed. Downstairs a pasta sauce is puttering on the hob, the washing machine turning contentedly in the laundry room and Pomp lying at her feet, purring.

Cyrus narrows his eyes, writes Rebecca. He looks very pissed off. He takes off his glasses and puts them on the desk beside his computer. He looks at her and his pupils suffuse the yellow iris with darkness.

Emily is pleased she has annoyed him. She's decided that he has no improper interest in her and his reaction now seems to confirm that.

'What?' Cyrus asks crossly.

'My friend Megan looked you up on Facebook.'

'And my question is?' says Cyrus.

'What?' says Emily.

'Why?' says Cyrus.

'Look you up?' asks Emily.

Cyrus runs a hand over his hair. He doesn't say anything. He puts his glasses back on and Emily sees the spectre of the seventy-year-old Cyrus looking back at her. He leans back in his chair and locks his hands behind his head and looks up at the ceiling.

'Well,' says Emily, 'you know I told you that the picture of you in the hospital brochure wasn't . . . ' The picture in the hospital brochure didn't even bear a passing resemblance to the man sitting in front of her.

'As you say,' says Cyrus, still looking at the ceiling.

Emily knows that were she talking to Cyrus and looking at the ceiling at the same time, she would be given short shrift.

'Why are you looking at the ceiling? Are you dissociating?' she says.

He keeps looking at the ceiling, leans back on his chair and puts his feet up on his desk and crosses his ankles. He is wearing green socks today, with red cuffs. The soles of his shoes are worn and need replacing. She nearly tells him and then she decides not to.

'Last year, Kit leaned back on his chair, exactly like that, and it tipped over. He had to spend four hours in hospital, waiting to be stitched up,' says Emily.

'Did he?' says Cyrus, without moving.

'Yes,' says Emily, 'and he has a scar on the back of his head where the hair won't grow back. Luckily he's got masses of hair so it's not a problem.'

Swiftly, Cyrus puts his feet back onto the floor and stands up. He walks to the window and looks out into the gathering gloom beyond the toughened glass. It is 3 p.m. and the clocks have gone back. By 4.30 p.m., it will be dark outside. Emily watches him. His shoulders are tense beneath his baggy tweed jacket. He puts his hands up to the windowpane and splays his fingers as if he might push it from the frame. Emily feels she may have gone a bit far. Cyrus's hair is thinning slightly at the crown. Emily knows that Cyrus must be finding that quite challenging.

'Cyrus?'

He turns away from the window and faces Emily but he doesn't come back to his chair.

'What?' he says.

'It was entirely innocent,' she tells him. 'I said that you didn't look like the picture in the hospital brochure. Megan asked me, "Why not?" and I said, "You just don't, that's all." So she said she'd look you up on Facebook.'

'I don't mind. I really don't.' He looks as if he does.

'Megan just wanted to know what you really look like—'

'Why,' interrupts Cyrus, 'did this Megan want to know what I look like?' Cyrus is very skilled at finding the nub of an issue. He has no truck with obfuscation.

Bugger, thinks Emily. She says nothing.

Cyrus comes back to his desk and sits down.

'So?' he says.

'Well,' says Emily, thinking fast and finding no escape, deciding to tell him the truth, 'I talk about you quite a lot.'

Cyrus looks at her over the top of his glasses. He is unflinching in his examination and Emily flinches in response.

'Sam has been getting jealous,' she says.

'Of?' Cyrus says.

'Do we have to? Can't we change the subject? I could tell you how I've halved my dose of Dulsexatine without asking you and you can tell me off and then I can leave.' Emily thinks it's worth a punt.

'No, I think we have to finish this conversation before the delights of that one are examined.' Cyrus turns from his computer and gives Emily his full attention.

'You've hinted at this before,' he says.

'Have I?' says Emily.

'Yes,' says Cyrus, 'In your CBT group, and I quote, "My husband is being a pillock. He's quite possessive of me."'

'I hope you don't do that at home,' says Emily.

'What?' says Cyrus.

'Quote things back at people that they may have said in the heat of the moment. You'll get divorced. No one could put up with that.'

'You did say it. I have a note of it.'

'That's even worse. Writing stuff down and then accurately quoting it back at them is practically unforgivable.'

Cyrus sighs. 'I'm given a report from all our CBT therapists on any concerns they may have about my patients. That's all. I don't go around randomly quoting irrelevancies back at my family. Nor do I habitually take notes.'

Emily is glad they've sorted it out. 'Because you'll get divorced,' she says again.

'Are you or are you not having trouble with Sam?' asks Cyrus. He puts his pad back on the table beside him.

'He was just stressed. He is quite possessive. Sam loves me but he gets jealous,' she says. Emily really wishes that what happened in CBT stayed in CBT. Cyrus probably knows that she has theories about socialism and Canadians. She decides to be less forthcoming if she ever goes to CBT again.

Cyrus sighs again. 'He was jealous of me personally?'

'Well, he was, but I said he didn't have to be and showed him the hospital brochure picture of you.'

'I had no idea it would prove so useful.'

Emily is beginning to feel idiotic.

'Then what happened? Why is Megan so interested in my appearance?'

'Well, I always tell her what you said . . . and you're all over Facebook.'

'I'm not all over Facebook,' says Cyrus.

'A bit,' says Emily. 'Megan says psychiatrists never have a social media profile.'

'My profile is private.'

'Not very. You're a psychiatrist though.'

'Thanks for noticing.' Cyrus rarely uses sarcasm. 'I'm beginning to lose the will to live,' he says. 'Just to wrap this up, do I look more like me on Facebook than I do in the hospital brochure? Or do I look less like me?'

'You look older,' says Emily. She doesn't want to tell him that he looks silly because even though, in the picture he has a big goofy grin, he's not actually very silly at all.

'I *am* older,' says Cyrus. 'Which you think backs your argument that Sam shouldn't be jealous, I suppose? Did you show Sam the Facebook page you found?'

'No,' says Emily.

'Why?'

'Because, I felt like a stalker looking at it. I didn't want to show it to anyone else.'

'So, you left Sam with the picture in the brochure to mull over?'

'He wouldn't mull it over.'

Cyrus raises his eyebrows.

'Well, he might. Can we change the subject? I love Sam,' says Emily.

'What does this Megan think about Sam being jealous?' says Cyrus, ignoring her. 'Does she think it's reasonable?'

'She thinks I talk about you too much. She thinks I'm a bit obsessed with you.'

'And you used my hospital brochure picture to debunk that theory too?'

'I've halved my dose of Dulsexatine.'

Suddenly, Cyrus's teeth flash white in his tired face. 'Have you though?' he says. And again the long slow look.

Rebecca closes her laptop.

No, she really doesn't understand any of it.

None at all, she thinks.

PIECE 70

Rebecca was clanking through Benham Wood. She was clanking because she was carrying her rod and her galvanised bucket. Her rod was over one shoulder with the line wound neatly around her hand and the hook tucked tightly into it so the barb didn't catch her fingers. The handle of the bucket was loose and with every step it hit the top of Rebecca's gumboots and it clanked.

It was spring and, under the trees, clumps of wild daffodils glowed yellow in the occasional shafts of sunlight penetrating the canopy of tangled branches overhead. The trees were beginning to put forth tiny yellowish green leaves. Close to, they appeared as deeply asleep as they had been throughout the long winter but, if Rebecca had raised her eyes from the path, she would have seen that the woodland was frosted palest apple-green. Rebecca didn't look up though. The path was slick with mud and the debris of winter. In a tree, a chaffinch was idly twittering its repetitive song. It wasn't quite geared up for spring yet and its song had a more than usually desultory air about it. There really should have been a second part. Blackbirds, at least, appear to finish what they have to say. Chaffinches just repeat.

The pond, when she reached it, was as still and dark as a pool of tar.

Rebecca eased her hand out of the carefully wound fishing line and laid the line and her bamboo rod gently on the ground beside her bucket. Now she must pick her spot and lace the water with ground bait. She surveyed the slippery banks. Here and there, moss and lungwort grew. The lungwort flowered with pink and white blooms but the shadier parts of the bank were slippery with dark-greenish algae. Daddy said the pond was like a quarry. The banks looked as though they had been cut into the clay earth and there were no dappled shallows for rushes or bog iris to grow. She thought briefly of Mrs Lightwing's mother whirling in the deep, cold water, of her fleshless body entangled in the grasping branches of the sunken oak and the tiny fishes resting in her streaming hair, oblivious. Then she pushed the thought away with a shudder.

On the far side was a fallen sapling, which Rebecca thought might make a seat. Its sinuous trunk bent out over the water but maybe the base was anchored to the ground still, and maybe it would be wide enough for comfort. She was determined not to sit on her upturned bucket if she could avoid it. Apart from being very uncomfortable, she was sure it magnified every sound she made. She realized she was breathing very lightly at the top of her lungs so she took a great long lungful of air and let it out slowly. Then she picked up her bucket carefully with both hands so that it wouldn't clank. She left her rod where it was and began to make her way to the far bank.

When she arrived, she crouched at the edge of the pond, holding the handle of the bucket with her left hand and reaching behind her for a branch to steady herself. She felt her fingers close around one and turned her head, testing it for strength. It felt firm. Leaning forward, she dipped the bucket into the dark water and lurched forward as it filled. It was very heavy. Her fingers tightened on the branch and she braced herself as she dragged the bucket free.

Half a bucket would do, she thought. I'll never be able to carry a full bucket home. She sat down on the bank and carefully poured half the water back down the bank into the pond.

Slippery, said Betty.

The sapling was good. Its grey trunk was dry, free of moss and comfortable enough to sit on. Rebecca placed her bucket quietly on the ground and sat, testing that the roots were firmly anchored and that the tips of the branches wouldn't disturb the water if she moved. From her perch, she looked across the water to where she had left her rod and felt a thud of alarm in her chest.

There was a man standing there. He was standing right next to her rod, looking across at her. Rebecca's first thought was that he was going to tell her off for fishing here. Then she saw that he was Grime's uncle Billy, Billy with the shotgun, only he wasn't carrying it now and it wasn't his pond. It belonged to Catchpole Farm so he couldn't tell her not to fish here. She watched as he bent stiffly to pick up her rod. Billy had a bad back. That's why he didn't go to work. Grime had to do any lifting that needed doing.

'Ef ut's heavy, me un Mum gotta lift ut,' he'd told Rebecca after he'd finished crushing the baby rats beneath the base of the iron saucepan. Rebecca couldn't imagine a big man who was unable to lift things. In her experience, men could chuck hay bales onto trailers, haul boats up slipways and lug furniture up stairwells. Even Alex and Martin were stronger than her and they weren't much older.

Billy put his forefinger to his lips, signalling 'Shh', and held the rod out towards Rebecca. A question. She nodded slowly. He could bring it round to her. She hoped he wasn't going to start talking. She slid from her seat and reached into her jeans pocket for the ball of bait she kept there. It was wrapped in greaseproof paper. She unwrapped it and began to break off small pieces, rolling them on her palm into tiny balls to seed the water. She was aware all the time that Billy was approaching with her rod.

'Then what?' says Titus.

'I expect he gave me my rod,' says Rebecca.

Titus looks at her. He narrows his eyes.

'Look, I'm better. Despite being used as your own personal chemistry set, I'm way better. Stop looking at me like that. I'm not scared of you anymore. I'm not scared of the High Street. I'm fine now,' she says.

'Because, not despite,' says Titus.

'What?' says Rebecca.

'Because, I have used you as my own personal chemistry set. Or rather because I have accurately prescribed appropriate drugs for you and continued to care whether you are well or not, for over a year.' Titus still has narrowed eyes. Rebecca bites her lip. When Titus gets irritated, nowadays, she always has an urge to laugh.

'OK, "because". I will allow you "because", and I'm extremely grateful, really I am.'

'What happened next?' says Titus. 'Can you remember?'

Rebecca can't. 'I expect he gave me my rod,' she says again.

Billy walked quietly round the edge of the pond towards Rebecca. She could see that he was breathing through his mouth and that his cheeks had flared red. She could see this, even from across the water.

Stupid, said Betty.

'I could have got it myself,' Rebecca whispered.

You would have. It's not like he's helping, said Betty.

Rebecca could hear a note in Betty's voice that usually signalled trouble.

'If he's quiet, it'll be OK,' she soothed, but she knew that their four eyes were all trained on Billy with contempt. Rebecca didn't usually get to choose how they felt, because Betty's feelings were stronger.

'Try to remember.' Titus is leaning forward in his chair.

Rebecca tears herself back to the present. 'I expect he gave me my rod,' she says again.

PIECE 71

Rebecca is writing.

Emily is walking towards the hospital. She is walking across the Millennium Bridge.

She had taken a bus from home to St Paul's. She had climbed, passing through the Whispering Gallery, right to the very top of the dome and she had stood for some minutes leaning on the parapet, trying to catch her breath. There had been a few people there today but not too many as the weather was cold and the wind was full of freezing drizzle.

To her right, the river had cut west through the city like a silver blade. She'd seen London Bridge below, the Shard opposite, tiny Tower Bridge to her left and, beyond that, Canary Wharf stood like an exclamation against the grey sky. Somewhere down there, across the river, was Cyrus. She'd wondered what he was doing. Was he sitting opposite someone, taking them down with his cool yellow glare? She did hope so.

Now, she is walking across the bridge, watching the Thames swirl brown beneath her feet. If she fell in, Emily knows she would be swept away within seconds, enveloped in the river's ancient, filthy embrace. She would be found, floating like Ophelia, her long red hair spread around her head like russet seaweed at . . . Tower Bridge, she decides. At Tower Bridge moorings, she would posthumously ruin someone's afternoon and simultaneously give them something to talk about at dinner parties for the rest of their lives.

Every cloud has a silver lining.

Emily rings on the hospital doorbell and is buzzed in.

Rebecca stops typing. She reaches down and strokes Pomp, who is, as usual, sleeping propped against her leg. To work things out, she thinks. Is that what the writing is for? She needs a cup of coffee. She thinks everything is OK again.

PIECE 72

Rebecca is feeling fine. All is well.

Titus Glass has prescribed her Tranquiltolam and a new red pill, the colour of red clotted blood. It has worked. She feels entirely normal and she catches a bus to her appointment. She gets off the bus and walks in the spring sunshine across Tower Bridge. A bitter east wind is blowing up the river from beyond the Thames Barrier, through Greenwich and Silvertown from Tilbury docks and the Essex mudflats. Rebecca's hair cracks in the wind and she feels the cold sting on her cheeks and remembers the grey North Sea of her Suffolk childhood. She smiles to herself.

For once, she finds that she doesn't mind the Japanese tourists stopping dead in front of her to take terrible photographs of each other, the towers on the bridge, the Shard and anything else they can see through their iPhone viewfinders.

The river swirls beneath and, behind her, the Tower of London stands squarely just where it always has, and all is well. She is early for her appointment and decides to have a coffee.

She walks into a crowded, steamy café on the south side of

the river and asks for a flat white. She still has no idea what all the other coffees are. A skinny latte? A mochaccino? But she knows enough to know that drinking cappuccino after midday is not acceptable and she thinks a flat white is just a coffee, like one she might make at home. Like the ones she drank when she was in hospital. Only they were black because she didn't have any milk. The coffee she is given to take away looks normal and she reaches across the counter and fixes a plastic lid with a hole in the side to her cardboard cup.

'To go?' the barista had asked.

Coffee to go, Rebecca thinks. Weird. Coffee was getting weirder than the internet, as weird as drones and virtual reality. Imagine wanting virtual reality when real reality was so overly complicated.

She walks up Tooley Street, carrying her scalding drink. She negotiates a gaggle of French school children wearing jeans and trainers, flicking long brown fringes out of their long brown eyes.

She gulps back the remains of her coffee at the hospital doorway and casts about for a bin to chuck the cup into. A teenage girl is sitting on the hospital steps, eating a packet of crisps with all the concentration of a confirmed anorexic. 'That's not recyclable,' she tells Rebecca. 'They say they are but they're not because they're lined in plastic. They need specialist recycling facilities and there aren't any.' She has a pronounced lisp. Rebecca looks down at her empty cup for a second, then turns and crosses the road to put her cup into a bin outside the newsagents opposite. When she looks round, the girl has disappeared and her empty crisp packet is cartwheeling along the pavement. Rebecca rings the bell and is buzzed into the hospital.

'And you're here to see?' The receptionist looks up at Rebecca. 'Ah yes, Rebecca, of course, the doctor is expecting you.'

'Dr Glass?' says Rebecca to the receptionist. The anorexic girl is curled into a chair in the corner of the room with her knees drawn up and her feet under her, shuffling furiously through a copy of the *Evening Standard*. 'Idiot,' she says loudly, to no one in particular.

The receptionist looks across the room at the girl, then back at Rebecca. The phone beside her buzzes and she picks it up.

'Marianna, Dr Fury will see you now. Just go up.'

The girl unfolds herself and stalks on long thin legs across the room without looking at the receptionist. She pulls the sleeve of her jumper down over one hand before opening the waiting room door and slamming it shut behind her.

Rebecca wonders what on earth Dr Fury could say to her that would be at all helpful. Perhaps they just sit and have a staring contest. She could imagine the girl saying, 'You blinked, I thaw you. Thtop cheating,' before flinging herself out and back into her contracted, little life.

'Rebecca, please go up,' says the receptionist.

Rebecca is telling Titus about her week and he is sitting opposite her, listening. She thinks he's listening, then she realizes that he isn't.

'What's the matter?' she asks.

Titus shrugs. 'You seem very happy.'

'I'm better, aren't I?'

Titus picks up his pad.

'Don't write. Listen,' says Rebecca.

'I can do both.'

'No, you can't, you're a man.'

'Bit sexist.'

'A bit, maybe but still true,' says Rebecca. 'The thing is, I think that what I did . . . '

'Attempting suicide?'

'Yes, I still think it was proportionate. I was carrying too much of the load and I buckled.'

Titus looks at her. 'I think,' he says, 'you're better placed to know that than I am.'

'Titus, I think this should be the last time I come. I am better,' she tells him. 'I feel well.'

'Well enough to just walk out of here? Well enough to manage your dosages and any further decisions about your medication without me?'

Rebecca isn't sure about that. 'For now,' she says.

'And when you want to reduce your medication and perhaps withdraw some of it, will you manage that alone?'

Titus is sitting opposite her as he has done for a whole year. He is giving her his full attention. She doesn't think anyone has ever looked after her as he does. He listens to her endlessly, issues instructions, forbids her to do things. 'Doctor's orders,' he says, as if that could make any difference. Rebecca doesn't take instruction. She barely takes suggestion. But Titus saw her, when no one else could. He saw the awful, hopeless mess that was Rebecca Wise, but she can't give him the answer he seems to need. She doesn't have it.

She needs to go back to her life.

'What do you think?' she says. He is watching her in that intense way he has. She feels pinioned. She would love to be able to pinion people with a look. She wonders how it's done.

Titus is sitting forward in his chair with his hands between his knees, his mouth slightly open and his eyes are fixed on her. She can feel his tension. His relaxed body language can't disguise it. She capitulates. 'Just tell me what to do,' she says.

Titus sits up. 'I think you have spent far too much of your life being told what to do. This has to be your decision,' he says. 'You obviously want to discharge yourself but I think you know my opinion.'

Rebecca thinks. She thinks about how far she's come. How able she is now compared to a year ago. How she can do things that used to terrify her. How she no longer wakes with a cloying feeling of self-disgust. She is better, she is sure of it, but can she do without Titus? She doesn't want to but eventually she will have to.

'If it be now, 'tis not to come. If it be not to come, it will be now. If it be not now, yet it will come – the readiness is all,' she quotes.

Titus folds his arms across his chest. His Shakespeare really is negligible.

Rebecca shakes her head.

'We still don't know what brought you here,' says Titus.

'Do we need to?'

'I think it might clear things up.'

'I can't remember. I remember wrongly.'

'Given time, you will remember.'

378

Time? thinks Rebecca. Has she time? 'I'm quite busy,' she says. 'My life is nearly normal at home. Everything has gone back to normal.'

Titus looks at her over the top of his glasses.

'I have boundaries, it's not the same.'

'Rebecca . . . ' Titus pins her again.

'You make me feel like a frog in the headlights.'

Titus smiles but his eyes remain fixed on her. 'Rabbit,' he says.

'OK, I'll come back.'

'Sure?'

Rebecca is sure she has no choice.

Rebecca is writing.

'No, like a frog, all bulgy-eyed and ugly,' she writes.

'I make you feel ugly?'

'Well, exposed. You're always looking at me. I can feel you reading me. It's very uncomfortable.'

Cyrus takes off his glasses and puts them on his desk. Emily looks at him. She sees the dark hair growing back from the high wide forehead, the straight nose with its wide bridge, the dark brows above the strange yellow-brown eyes.

'It's my job,' says Cyrus. His entire body appears tense. Emily watches him for a minute. It's as if he can hardly bear to sit there, opposite her.

'Now who's reading whom?' he says quietly. Emily sees the eyes soften. 'What do you see?' he says.

Emily knows what she thinks she is seeing but she can't articulate it. She shakes her head.

Cyrus sits up and puts his glasses on again. He runs a large hand over his hair. He turns to his computer and scrolls down the screen. 'Emily, you know as well as I do what has happened. This can't go on. I can't.'

Emily feels her spine shift and her hands stretch as wide as they can. She pushes them under her thighs. Cyrus isn't looking at her. He seems engrossed in his computer screen.

Then he looks back at her. 'I think you know what I mean,' he says.

Emily feigns nonchalance. 'How open to misinterpretation is that? How easily could that be misunderstood?' she asks. She thinks she knows what he means but she might be wrong and to be as wrong as that would, without doubt, be disastrous.

Cyrus sighs. 'It couldn't be. It isn't,' he says. 'We both know exactly what's going on here.'

Emily decides that she doesn't.

Liar! Betty screeches in her ear.

'Emily, some things are intrinsically dangerous. One needs to be afraid of them. One ought to be.' Cyrus has turned from his computer.

'Aeroplanes?'

Cyrus shakes his head. 'No,' he says. 'Guess again.'

'Spiders?'

'Try harder.'

Emily looks at him. She tucks her hair behind her ears. He is gazing at her. 'It's a simple matter of self-preservation,' he says. 'Something, it turns out, that I'm not terribly good at, after all. Emily, you have to understand and I'm sure that you do. I'm at the very edge of what I can tolerate.'

She feels for a second what he feels. 'I thought I was imagining it,' she says, meaning it. She'd meant him to feel what he feels and now that he does, she doesn't know what to do with it. Had there been a plan, now would be the time to implement it but there hadn't been one.

To be the boss of him? hisses Betty, her voice sly.

'To be the boss of me,' Emily says aloud. She feels as though a great hand is pressing down on her chest. 'Cyrus, I'm sorry.'

Cyrus folds his arms. 'You need to rid yourself of her,' he says.

Emily nods. 'I will,' she says. She looks down at her pink Kenzo trainers and wonders why she has always liked ridiculous shoes.

'Emily, do you understand? I can't see you again. I can pass you on to a colleague but I've had enough.'

Emily doesn't answer. She can feel the sick pain of it in her chest. She can feel the slow rush of heat through her body and the steady thump of her heart against her ribs. She shifts her eyes from her shoes to her hands. They are resting loose and relaxed on her lap. She looks back up at Cyrus and, for one millisecond before he ducks his head, she sees his eyes.

Emily stands. 'I'm sorry,' she says again. 'Of course, thank you, Cyrus. Thank you for everything. You saved me.' She picks up her bag from the floor and snatches her coat from the back of the chair. 'I'll go.' She feels, suddenly, rudderless. 'Can I take you with me?' she asks. 'I mean in my head?'

'I'm not sure that that's my call,' says Cyrus.

PIECE 73

Harriet was lying on her bed. Rebecca was tidying up the doll's house. She was kneeling on Harriet's yellow rug, putting all the furniture back in the right rooms and adjusting the clothing of the doll's house family. Harriet was watching her.

'I miss him though,' she was saying. 'Mama did a very bad thing, killing all his plants. He had been growing them for ages and he watered them every day. He was nicer than Dad. He bought me this.' Something lands on the rug beside Rebecca and she picks up a delicate seed pearl bracelet with a heart locket as a catch.

'It's really pretty but he's still not allowed to hit people, whatever they did,' said Rebecca. 'And it is your greenhouse, not his.' She put the bracelet down beside her. 'Do you want this toy cat in the kitchen or the bedroom?' She turned, holding up a miniature ginger cat between finger and thumb.

'Ambrose misses him too. He's much naughtier since Patrick left.'

'That's only because Ambrose was afraid of him.' Rebecca put a tiny, lace counterpane onto a four-poster bed.

'Rebecca, do you know Billy Parfitt?' Rebecca turns from the doll's house.

'Grime's uncle? Not really, why?'

'He lives near you.'

'I know.'

'Do you know him? He's a friend of Patrick.'

'Is he?' Rebecca hadn't considered that Billy might have friends. She stood up, stretching. 'I think that's finished,' she said. The doll's house was very tidily organised.

'It looks really good, Rebecca, thank you.'

Rebecca picked up the bracelet and brought it over to Harriet on the bed. 'Is it real gold?'

Harriet draped it over her wrist, admiring it. 'Rebecca,' she said, keeping her head low, seeming to concentrate on the bracelet, 'don't ever let Billy Parfitt . . . go near you.'

'He wouldn't. Why would he?' Rebecca remembered Billy standing over her when a catfish took her bait. 'He's just Grime's uncle,' she added.

Harriet fixes Rebecca with her large pale eyes. 'Don't let him anywhere near.'

Rebecca nodded and Harriet sat up on the bed, suddenly distracted by the need to adjust her pile of pillows and teddies.

'I won't,' said Rebecca.

Emily is writing, writes Rebecca.

'So I don't need you?' writes Emily.

'I don't know if you do or not,' says Magnus. He swivels in his black leather chair and taps on his keyboard. Hannah has the feeling that he is avoiding eye contact. She wishes she had a swivelling chair too. She would spin it round and round if she had. Perhaps it's as well that she hasn't one, she concedes.

'Hannah,' says Magnus, 'you really haven't been the easiest of patients, have you? It's taken us an awfully long time to agree on your medication; you've refused CBT.'

Hannah interrupts him. 'CBT is for children,' she says. 'I told you that before. If you don't know all that stuff by the time you're my age, you might as well give up and lie down on the floor, covered in a duvet, for the rest of your life.'

Magnus ignores her. 'And,' he says, 'there's been a certain amount of game-playing, hasn't there?' He turns from his keyboard and stares at her. He looks pale. Hannah supposes he doesn't get outside much. It would be difficult if you had to work five days a week in a consulting room and then take a Tube back to Lewisham or wherever he lives. He'd have no time for outside, she supposes, except for at weekends.

Game-playing? she thinks. Jesus-stand-between-me-and-all-harm. 'When?' she says. 'When did I play a game? Obviously, I've been playing the In Which Sad South London Suburb Does Magnus Live? game but that's just to entertain myself. I mean, the whole thing would be a bit dry otherwise, wouldn't it?' Well, he started it.

Magnus picks up his fountain pen. 'Dry?' he says.

'Yes, dull,' says Hannah. 'Boring.' She sees Magnus flinch slightly. Minutely, but she sees it. 'And I haven't been at all subtle about it, have I? I didn't think you minded.'

Magnus smooths his fair hair back from his high patrician forehead with a large white hand. 'Mind?' he says. 'I don't mind.'

'Maybe it's because you're so young and over-sensitive.' Hannah smiles up at him.

'Don't take the piss. We're not so very different in age, as you very well know. I am neither young nor over-sensitive, but those emails you sent me from France . . . '

'The ones where I needed your help because I wasn't sleeping?'

'No, Hannah. The ones where you wrote an elaborate story with me as the main character and fictionalised our conversations. Well, I've deleted them.'

'Did I do that? Did I send you my story? I'd forgotten I did that.'

'Well, you did and I've been unable to think of anything else since so I've deleted them.'

Kerching, thinks Hannah.

Emily sits back from her keyboard, writes Rebecca. She puts her hands on her knees and takes a deep breath. She looks out of the window. Outside, the wind is blowing steadily from the east and the apple trees in the garden are whipping their bare branches against a silver sky.

He can't delete my emails, she thinks. It's not possible. I still have them.

PIECE 74

Emily has a flame mahogany box on her lap. The windows of the spare room are open and a warm spring wind is drifting through them, bearing the sweet sound of a blackbird singing in one of the apple trees. She'd found the box in the attic. Cyrus said she should look there.

'Where else are you going to find it?' he'd said. 'Attics petrify time, they incarcerate ghosts.'

Emily laughs. 'Funny,' she says.

Emily's mother had given her the box. She is sitting on the bed, running her hands over the smooth, glowing surface, admiring the brass hinges, the flare of the grain and the dovetailed joints.

'Open it,' says Cyrus.

Emily knows he isn't really there but she feels safer with him sitting on the bed behind her. If she turns she won't see him but she doesn't need to. She has brought him with her.

It's safer really, she thinks.

Her heart is beating with a low painful thrum like a loose guitar string. The wood shines warmly, under Emily's hands. Carefully she unclips the brass catch and opens the box. The lid is lined with emerald green felt. She empties the box object by object. She takes out a small silver tankard tarnished with age, a silver spoon in a satin lined case and a prayer book.

She opens the book and finds scrawled large across the frontispiece in her childish hand:

'Here comes a candle to light you to bed. Here comes a chopper to chop off your head.'

She listens. It's a long time since Betty has spoken to her. Rebecca waits for the cackle of delighted laughter. There isn't one. Elsewhere in the book, every spare piece of space is covered in a minute and meticulous script. Prayers. There are prayers for her mother and prayers for Giles. There are prayers for herself, prayers asking for safety and prayers for forgiveness. There are pictures and scraps of scriptures. 'How ye swath so shall ye reap,' says one. 'I will fear no evil,' says another.

From the box, Rebecca takes a blue glass eyewash dish. She holds it up to her eye and sees the world turn blue. A thimble, a small rubber baby doll. She turns it in her hands, struggling to feel the thrill of recognition. A matchbox. Empty.

Abruptly she realizes that little Rebecca is here. She is leaning against Rebecca, resting her head against her shoulder. Rebecca turns to look at her. Little Rebecca is very frightened. Her face is completely white so that her freckles stand out dark across her nose and cheeks. Her eyes are starting from their sockets and she is biting her bottom lip. Rebecca reaches with her left arm and encircles her younger self, pulling her close. She hears the child's soft sigh of relief.

'Well done,' says Titus.

Nestled in the corner of the box is a brown folder, the size of a postcard. Rebecca knows that it doesn't contain a postcard though. She picks up a tiny oval casket made of finely tooled leather. She turns it in her hands and presses the clasp. The lid springs open. It's her childhood jewellery box. There is a mourning brooch, the woven dark hair, encircled with blood-red rubies. She picks up a gold charm bracelet and a string of coral beads and lays them on the quilt beside her.

Next, Rebecca takes the folder in both hands and carefully opens the flap. She sees that it contains a letter from Father Francis.

She reads:

St Benedict's,
Marsham,
Suffolk

My dear Rebecca,

Here I am again, back with the nose to the grindstone and what a grindstone it is! Lovely and full of love but dull is not the word and I fear that the word might be a very wrong kind of word for a priest to use so I will not. Instead, my dear child, I will write about your story that you so kindly enclosed with your last letter.

'Murder most foul, as in the best it is / But this most foul, strange and unnatural!' This is a Shakespearean quotation, which I am quite sure you will come across in your studies when you are older. Shakespeare was awfully good at motive. Could it be that your character

was in some way deluded? Surely she could have found an alternative to violence. I admit that it appears that she may indeed have thought herself in mortal danger but the instinct for flight is often superior to the instinct to fight.

A cornered rat may fight, even when the odds are against it. A wolf or a bear may turn at bay. A wild boar will always charge if cornered, but a child? My dearest one, had she cause? Had she motive? Was there another way? For all that, it was a very thrilling read and I would hate to discourage such creative flair but perhaps we should, in the end, search, in literature as in life, for forgiveness and redemption.

I will say no more, but would urge you to find a quieter end to this particular tale.

Now, to your other news; I am so glad that Alex is taking his guitar playing so seriously and that he is learning to fingerpick as well as playing chords. Neither is superior to the other. Bob Dylan is a great one for chords and Val Doonican a fabulous fingerpicker but I think we both know which is the greater artist.

Martin must be so proud of himself for winning all the swimming races at the end of term gala. I must say I should have liked to have seen that, more than I can express.

Harriet has a new stepfather. I had, of course, heard all about that from dear Miranda but it is interesting to have had your perspective. As you say, there is little chance of him being anything like as bad as Patrick.

*For now, dear one, I must close. Pray for dear
Harriet and for her sweet, silly mother for me, will
you? Sometimes I think that the intercession of a child
may hold more weight than the prayers of a jaded old
man. Pray to Our Lady.*

*Let me just remind you of the words. I know that
it has been difficult for you to get to church recently.
Mummy seems to have become awfully busy lately,
doesn't she?*

Anyway. Here they are:
Hail Mary, full of Grace,
The Lord is with thee.

Rebecca feels her lips shaping the words as she reads.

Blessed art thou among women
And blessed is the fruit of thy womb, Jesus.

'It's all hooey,' says Titus.
'Shush,' says Rebecca.

Holy Mary, Mother of God,
pray for us sinners,
now and at the hour of our death.

'Amen,' says Titus.

Rebecca looks down at the letter lying loosely in her hand.
The sloping copperplate, the huge fuchsia LOVE at the end
and the weight of the paper all bring Father Francis sharply

into focus. Hail Mary, she thinks. Had she motive? Should she have run? Could she have saved Billy Parfitt? In the end, she doesn't think so. No.

She folds the letter and puts it carefully with the others in a shoebox. She has separated his letters from any other papers. Her diaries are in a different box now, too. She still has to sort them into some kind of coherence but decides to leave that particular chore for the moment. She sits back on the bed, resting against the wall, and wonders about Betty. Had she come home with her from the hospital? She can't remember.

She stands up and looks out of the window. The back-to-back gardens below are awash with colour. Wisteria is scrambling over the walls and, along the fences, honeysuckle and clematis romp. Rebecca opens the doors onto the balcony. The air is thick with the scent of lilac and somewhere someone is playing the piano. The few remaining mature sycamore trees are loud with birds and rampaging grey squirrels. Next door, she can see Pomp slumped on the roof of the neighbour's shed. Rebecca draws in a great long breath. She thinks she is fine now.

PIECE 75

Rebecca is watching a spider making a web in a hawthorn bush next to the sapling where she had been sitting just a short time ago. It's one of those round spiders that lives in a woven tunnel. She thinks it's called a labyrinth spider.

'Labyrinth,' she says quietly to herself. It's a lovely word, both soft and sibilant.

This one is weaving at the mouth of its web, moving its abdomen back and forth as it does so. Its shiny red legs arch high above its back. The spider's distended body is covered in tiny hairs. The westering sun, dipping between the trees, catches them now and then as the spider moves. She thinks that it has eggs deep down in the tunnel behind where it is working.

Rebecca moves her head closer so that she can see the spinnerets moving. Behind her she can hear something. She doesn't turn around because she knows what it is. She thinks that the sounds are becoming fainter anyway and when they stop she will be able to pick up her rod and bucket and make her way home. She can smell rain in the air.

Rebecca had hoped to catch quite a lot of fish that afternoon.

She had been going to take them and empty them into the garden pond. Her father says that all she's effectively doing is feeding a very lucky heron. Rebecca knows this is true; she has often seen it standing amongst the bulrushes in the pond's shallows, head cocked, sharp beak, ready to pounce. Now, she has none and the water in her bucket is spilt, all spilt back into the water along with Billy. There's nothing she can do about that now though.

'Bitch,' he'd said. 'Teasing little bitch.' That wasn't very nice. Harriet had said he wasn't very nice.

She hoped he wouldn't tell anyone Betty had pushed him but she didn't think he would. She would tell them what he'd said; then he would be in trouble. She would tell them what he had done.

Rebecca saw that the spider had backed down the tunnel a bit and perched itself with just its front two legs showing. Her spine feels loose like a snake lying up the centre of her back and the blood is swishing in her ears.

'I can't fucking swim,' he'd shouted. That must have been a lie. Everyone, except babies, can swim. Even Giles can swim and he's only five. She had supposed that Billy would get out of the water soon and go away. He would be all wet and he'd know not to come near her again.

The spider is as still as death. It had been an accident that Billy had fallen in but the bank was steep just where the sapling grew and slick with last night's rain and when Betty had pushed him, he had fallen over Rebecca's bucket. Served him right, she thought. Bloody, bloody, bloody. She could still smell the cigarette smoke and something else, sour, on his hot breath. Rebecca closed her eyes. She was going to unsee what she saw; it was making her feel sick.

All was quiet now. He must have got out and gone away. Slowly Rebecca turned around and looked across the dark water. It was quite still. She picked up her rod and her bucket and, without looking back, made for the path at the far side of the pond.

BODY OF MISSING MAN
FOUND NEAR BENHAM

The body of a local man was found in a pond near Benham and police say the death is 'unexplained'. Emergency services were called at 5.15 p.m. yesterday to woods on the outskirts of the village, The man, identified as William Parfitt, 52, is believed to have drowned, but a Suffolk police spokesman said: 'There was no sign of a struggle and there are not thought to be any suspicious circumstances.'

Unemployed Parfitt was reported missing by his sister, Lorraine, on Sunday evening. Local carpenter, Henry Warner, 56, of Marsham, made the tragic discovery on his way home from work.

'I saw what looked like a body floating face down and immediately phoned the police as soon as I got home,' he said. 'I often walk through the woods as a short cut,' he added.

Mr Parfitt was last seen alive, drinking at The Wangfield Arms, where he was a regular. His friend, Patrick 'Pat' Buck told *The Journal*: 'He seemed in good spirits and we were talking about how useless Ipswich have been this season.'

Mr Parfitt had previously worked at a local dairy farm until a bad back forced him to give up his job. He lived with his sister, Lorraine Hicks, who works as a domestic help in the Benham area, and he leaves her, and his two nephews Gary, 20, and Graham, 12.

A file will be prepared for the coroner.

'Did you ever?' said Pen at breakfast the following morning. 'Lorraine is quite beside herself.'

Rebecca started on her third Weetabix. She thought that if she kept on eating then perhaps Lorraine would stop being beside herself and that Billy Parfitt would have learned to swim.

'Probably drunk,' said Rebecca's father, folding the newspaper. 'Rebecca, that's quite enough Weetabix. Alex told me you were sick in that field down by the Cherry Tree the last time you ate three.'

Alex sparkled his eyes at Rebecca across the table. Only Alex could sparkle his eyes without smiling. He said it was a skill but Rebecca thought it was just mean.

'The worms crawl in and the worms crawl out / The ones that go in are lean and thin / And the ones that come out are fat and stout.'

'Be quiet, Martin, that's extremely disrespectful.' Their mother stood up and began to clear the breakfast table, stacking the cereal bowls with quick flashing movements of her arms. She rolled down the tops of the inner part of the cereal packets to stop the contents going stale and picked up the empty toast rack. 'Lorraine said the police told her that his trousers were undone and that he might have slipped.'

'While peeing? It makes sense. It rained a lot on Sunday evening. It must have been slippery.' David scraped back his chair and stood.

'Your eyes fall in and your teeth fall out,' mouthed Martin across the table at Giles, whose bottom lip began to tremble.

'And your brains come tumbling down your snout,' sang Alex.

'Boys, be quiet! Rebecca, come over here and dry up.'

Rebecca slowly got down from the table and followed her mother to the kitchen sink. Martin gathered the cereal boxes and Alex swung Giles down from his seat, jiggling him up and down until his tears turned to laughter.

'I'm going to mow the lawn,' said their father. 'I suppose we'll have to go to the funeral.'

'After the inquest,' said their mother. 'Don't use that cloth, Rebecca, it's filthy.' Rebecca picked up another drying-up cloth from the pile balanced on the cold radiator beside the sink and a large house spider ran across her hand.

She screamed.

'I expect it was the shock,' said Pen to David that evening. They were talking in low voices in the bathroom, which was next to Alex's bedroom. Rebecca had been put to bed in Alex's room with an aspirin and a hot water bottle because it was the nearest to her parents' room. She had stayed in bed all day.

Her father pulled the plug out of the plughole and Rebecca

didn't hear what he said next. The water gurgled from the bath and she heard David heave himself from the water. 'It was a pretty big spider,' he said. 'Pass me a towel.'

'But she nearly passed out. She was ashen. I've never seen her so frightened before, not of a spider. She likes them. Maybe it was the shock of Billy dying like that.'

'She'll forget about it. It'll all blow over soon. Tell Mrs Lightwing not to mention it to her.'

'I doubt she would, not with her history.'

'And keep her away from Graham. Maybe she should go to stay with Harriet for a few days, just until after the inquest.' Rebecca's parents came out of the bathroom and she shut her eyes so that when they put their heads around the door, she appeared to be fast asleep. When she heard them go into their bedroom, she opened her eyes wide and stared into the dark. She could hear Betty skipping on the gravel below her window and then she heard her voice. It'll all blow over soon, she heard.

PIECE 76

'So this man drowned. You saw him drown and you never told anyone until now?'

Rebecca is lying in bed in the dark bedroom. Sam is lying next to her. 'I didn't watch him drown. I watched a spider finish her web. It was an accident. He slipped. I didn't understand what he was doing but I do now. I couldn't have saved him even if I tried. I was too little.'

'Is that why you're terrified of spiders?'

Rebecca shakes her head. 'I don't know. I hadn't made the connection . . . maybe.'

'Did you tell this to Titus?'

'No, I know what happened now. He doesn't need to know.'

Rebecca had sent Titus an email.

Dear Titus, she'd written.

I have decided not to come to see you anymore.

I'm very sorry not to discuss this further with you in person but I am afraid you would persuade me to change my mind. I am well, really I am.

I am also incredibly grateful for all the patience, skill and humour that you have shown me over the past year.

Kind regards, Rebecca Wise

'Titus was just doing his job; I feel much better now.'

Sam props himself up on one elbow. 'You've wielded that man's name like a scythe for the past year and now he's just "doing his job"? I thought I was losing you.'

Rebecca looks up at his shape, a darker black than the room behind him, his big head made bigger by his thick wild hair, his broad shoulders looming over her, and she feels her heart twist with love.

'I don't need him anymore.'

Sam lies down next to her, turning on his side to face her. 'Laura, darling,' he says, 'whatever your dream was, it wasn't a very heppy one, was it?' He is being Fred from *Brief Encounter*.

Rebecca shakes her head, remembering watching the film with her mother and her mother being awash with tears while she and her brothers had collapsed in helpless giggles. 'No,' she says, smiling.

'Is there anything I can do to help?'

'Yes, Fred, you always help.'

'You've been a long way away,' says Sam.

Rebecca laughs. 'Yes,' she says.

'Thenk you for coming beck to me.'

Rebecca takes his face in her hands and kisses him. 'I was always going to,' she says.

PIECE 77

Rebecca writes.

Emily saw Cyrus before he saw her. He is walking towards her down Harley Street, looking at his phone. She is on her way to have Botox injections.

'Why are you doing that?' Sam had asked when she'd told him.

'I want to look inscrutable,' she'd said. Sam had crossed his eyes and said nothing.

Now she says, 'Gosh, shouldn't you warn people?'

Cyrus stops in front of her. 'About?' he says.

'Free-ranging about the place. Shouldn't you send out a text alert or something?'

'It's lovely to see you too,' he says, smiling.

Emily looks him up and down. She trails her eyes from his face down to his feet and up again. He is wearing a baggy dark-green suit with a tiny check woven into the fabric with a bottle-green shirt open at the neck. He has lost weight. His shoes are dusty. He has had a haircut quite recently.

'What are you doing here?' she asks.

'I could ask you the same question,' says Cyrus.

'I'm seeing my doctor,' says Emily.

Cyrus does the thing he does. It's somewhere between a sigh and a tut. 'Of course you are,' he says.

'And you?' says Emily.

'I work here,' says Cyrus.

'As well?' says Emily.

Cyrus nods. 'Have you time for a coffee?' he says.

Emily has.

'Follow me,' says Cyrus. He turns and walks down Harley Street towards Cavendish Square.

Emily follows him.

He swipes a card at an imposing Georgian door. The door swings open.

Cyrus ushers Emily through. He turns left and she follows him into a consulting room. He closes the door behind them. 'Take a seat,' he says, taking one himself.

Emily sits. 'Are you charging me?' she asks.

'No,' says Cyrus.

'Have you read my book?' asks Emily.

'I have,' says Cyrus.

'Did you like it?' asks Emily.

'Not at all,' says Cyrus. 'I had to buy new socks.' He smiles, his sudden white smile. 'You're an absolute nightmare,' he says.

'Thank you,' says Emily.

'The only saving grace I can think of is that Hannah and Magnus managed not to end up in bed together.'

'They couldn't have. Magnus would have lost all his integrity.'

'So instead you decided that he should lose all his dignity?'

401

'Coffee?' says Emily. 'You said something about coffee, didn't you?'

Cyrus stands and leaves the room. Emily looks around.

The room has long Georgian windows. The carpet is grey, as are the walls, but the skirting, the mouldings and the rose around the central light are picked out in white. The desk behind which Cyrus had been sitting is heavy and ornate. It's a bit posher than the hospital, she decides.

Cyrus comes back into the room, carrying two china cups in one hand. He places a cup on the desk in front of her and resumes his seat.

'So,' he says, 'where do we go from here?'

Emily shrugs. 'I don't know,' she says. 'Where do you want to go?'

'I'd like to know why I was so unceremoniously replaced.'

'You weren't. You dumped me.'

'I did not.' Cyrus glares at her and Emily feels her stomach clench. 'I had no choice, as you very well know.'

'I thought you might change your mind. I thought you might ring Sam or do something . . . '

'That would be entirely outside my remit.'

'Are you meant to be this reactive?' she says.

'No, I'm not meant to be anything that I find myself being in relation to you. It is an absolute minefield.'

'Do you prefer ill people?'

Again Cyrus sighs. 'You have been very ill,' he says.

'I'm better now.' Emily picks up her coffee and takes a sip. It is bitter. She makes a face and puts it back down on the desk.

'Sorry, it's all we have,' says Cyrus.

'It doesn't matter,' says Emily.

Cyrus stands up and walks around his desk. He stands in front of her chair. He takes her hand and pulls her to her feet. 'Emily,' he says, 'can we just stop fucking about?'

Emily looks up at him. She has never been so close to Cyrus before. Her breath is becoming short and light. She looks up into his face and their eyes lock. 'Or start?' she says.

PEACE

Rebecca closes her laptop. Dusk had fallen as she wrote and now blue shadows pool in the corners of the bedroom. Outside, a pigeon coos softly in the silver birch tree. Pomp leans against her leg, purring.

She slides her laptop onto the bed, rises and walks over to the window.

Below, a child on a scooter whizzes by on the pavement.

Rebecca breathes in,
listens.
The house is silent.
And hope sings
tiny as a
tuning
fork.

ACKNOWLEDGEMENTS

I would like to thank my editor, Cicely Aspinall, for her brilliant editing skills as well as for her patience – I ask a lot of questions. Thanks too to Seema Mitra for her encouragement and enthusiasm and to the rest of the team at HQ Stories.

Thank you to my parents, Richard and Lisbeth for their unwavering cheerleading, incredibly biased opinions, fantastic PR – everyone in Cornwall knows about Gone to Pieces – and for reading every word several times over.

Thank you to my friends for offering advice and affirmation, especially Penny Rodrigues and Zeljka Pavcovic who have been reading the manuscript for years, it seems, and to Teresa Robertson for her forensic notes and interest in this creative process. Thank you to Simon and Jane Cosyns who have been endlessly supportive and loving. Thank you too to everyone on our Elephant WhatsApp group for their strong opinions, creative input and great sense of humour.

I would also like to thank all the dedicated professionals who work in mental health. They are extraordinary people to whom I will be forever grateful. Thank you Stephen, especially.

And finally, thank you to the late, great Seamus Heaney for inspiring this novel and for the loan of his tuning fork.

ONE PLACE. MANY STORIES

Bold, innovative and
empowering publishing.

FOLLOW US ON:

@HQStories